Looking

For

The Backbeat

Malcolm Hughes

DOMILO

First Published 2008
by
Domilo Publishers
Wirral

ISBN 978-0-9556901-1-2

Copyright © MJH 2008

Malcolm Hughes asserts the moral right to be identified as the author of this work

All rights reserved. No part of this publication may be reproduced, stored in or introduced into a retrieval system, or transmitted, in any form or by any means electronic, mechanical or photocopying, recording or otherwise without the prior written permission of the publisher.

Cover Design © Malcolm Hughes 2008

The secret houses

Which are our souls

Remain uncharted

Except by God

Who made the map ...

        Anon.

'you know, just find the backbeat...'
                      John Lennon
                      Circa 1972

Intro

Fade In On Backbeat

Imagine this set to music.
    Probably in a minor key, like a love song.

Pete Lynwood was my best friend and I looked after him as well as I could. When you love someone, you do your best to make them happy.

Even if it breaks your heart when the final chord fades.

Pete was always looking for the backbeat, the pulse to keep him steady, the rhythm of his life. When you've read this, see if you think he finally found his backbeat in the cellar of the old Camberwell house.

Me? Well…

No, listen to the song. See if you hear the backbeat.

This is what happened. It goes something like this…
One, two…one, two, three four…

First Verse

Running down School Lane, my books held awkwardly in the crook of my right arm, tie blown back over my right shoulder, knees pumping, mouth open, eyes slitted. I could hear with a weird kind of objectivity, my own thoughts. Like a loop of tape being played over and over.

Always the same. After a week of lie-ins, you're on time first day back. Second day, you oversleep and have to leg it!

Over and over and enough to drive you bonkers. And, to make matters worse, I was on homework collection and had to deliver all the books with a note of who had and who hadn't handed the work in. *Before* I went to my first lesson. My first lesson today was, by the by and wouldn't you know it, History with Splutter Barrowclough. There was a man who would never be secretary of my fan club.

I snatched a look at my watch, knowing that late was late was too late. Ten past nine. First lesson began five minutes ago.

I crossed Moss Avenue, not looking for traffic; if I got run over, even Splutter would have to accept that as an excuse. I charged into the schoolyard, not slowing as I rounded the corner of the gym. I was thinking I'd cut through the narrow corridor where the boilers groaned and clanked, saving fifty yards between the gym and the main doors.

Once I was inside the gates, my mind had switched off the tape loop and was trying out some excuses for Splutter instead. I'd more or less decided that whatever I said, I'd get a bollocking so I might as well tell the truth when thoughts of oversleeping, excuses and the cranking boilers were knocked out of me along with my breath.

'Ungff!'

I thought I'd made the noise. I was wrong.

'Wuh...wuh...fuh...why don't you look where you're going you thick prick?'

I looked up from the coconut matting where I'd landed and saw a purple-faced lad with a mop of wavy, black hair. His grey eyes were out on stalks, staring at me. He was on his hands and knees, his legs and backside still inside the doorway.

I hitched in two ragged breaths. 'Suh...sorry pal. I was running cos I'm late for first period with Splutt—'

'I don't give a toss if you're late for the Second Coming!

You could've bloody killed me! You thick prick!'

I was an easy-going lad. It normally took a lot to push me to breaking point. But...I was late. I had History with Splutter. I'd run nearly two miles. My mouth was dry and filled with that horrible, electric-spit taste. My books were all over the floor and this lad had called me a thick prick. Not once but twice. I eased myself slowly to my feet, still taking in great gulps of damp November air and tried to put a name to this lad's face. I couldn't. Strange. He looked about my age and I should've had at least a vague memory but he was a total blank.

'Listen...pal...' I said slowly in as level a voice as I could manage. 'I said I was sorry. I told you I was late. I got winded, too. It's not easy seeing around corners. And what're you doing here, anyway? Taffy Adams is free this period. In which case, you're out of bounds. That means that this,' I swept my arm to take in the two of us and our books, 'Is probably your fault. By the way, I don't like being called a thick prick. Even if it does rhyme.'

He looked at me, his eyes widening, a muscle ticking in his jaw. I could sense he was winding up to throw a punch. You spend over four years in an all-boys school and you learn to sense these things. Looking at him, I sized him up. Which you also learn to do. It might be close but I thought I could take him. The thing to do was push it and see if he was up to it.

'Oh, and by the way...*pal*. Who the hell are you?' I waited. He'd either swing or drop his eyes. I was wrong.

'The name...*pal*...is Pete Lynwood. I'm here because I'm lost. I started today. And it was still your fault.'

At least he didn't go for the Thick Prick Hat-trick. Something told me to give him the benefit of the doubt.

'Okay. Why don't you tell me where you're supposed to be and I'll tell you how to get there?'

'As it happens, I've got History. But with somebody called Barrowclough.'

I nodded. 'That's Splutter,' I said and smiled. Maybe Splutter would be more sympathetic when he heard about Pete Lynwood getting lost in the Funhouse. 'You'll be all right seeing as how you're the new boy. I'll still get a bollocking.'

He followed me through the narrow corridor, past the caretaker's poky little room. The dimly lit passage smelled of mimeo ink and the coarse-sweet smell of the caretaker's hand-rolled fags.

In room 24 where Splutter sprayed his lessons, I apologised for being late and introduced Pete Lynwood. He was granted new-boy privileges and I got an ear-bashing. I forgot all about the way Pete Lynwood bumped into me as Splutter droned on about the Poor Law.

Pete Lynwood, however, hadn't forgotten.

We shared Maths and English after morning break and then he went to Physics and I went to Spanish. I didn't see him in the dinner-hall and assumed he lived close enough to go home. It was in the yard, near the gate that opened onto the path leading to the sports field, when I saw him again.

I was sitting on Phil Jarman's bike, which was padlocked in its usual speck in the sheds. Phil was leaning against the shed supports. Paul Hughes, Pete Forrest and Jeff

Featherstone were all leaning against the fence. We were bemoaning the fact that Lingham Field was covered in mud and we couldn't get a game of football going. It was Paul who spotted Peter Lynwood walking towards us.

'Here's that new lad. He's in our House.'

I looked up from my swinging feet. Lynwood was dodging between some younger lads who were playing touch-rugby with a tennis ball. I had just enough time to think *I know what he's come for* when he arrived.

He put his hands in his pockets and surveyed our little group. Then he looked at me.

'We have some unfinished business, I think,' he said.

The others looked quizzically at each other. *They* might have been puzzled but I wasn't. I was, though, filled with a sort of unbelieving amusement; what did he think this was, *The Three Musketeers*? Jesus!

'You want to settle it now or after school?' he asked and then smiled.

I got off the bike and settled myself on my feet. I half-expected him to produce a gauntlet and fling it at my feet. 'Look, it was an accident. Nobody got hurt so just forget it.'

'You backing down?'

'What the hell's this about?' Paul wanted to know. So I told him what had happened. I didn't take my eyes off Peter-bloody-Lynwood.

'Ah shit,' Phil said. 'Look, just shake his hand and forget it, eh?'

'I asked him a question.' Peter looked at Phil and then back at me. 'Oh, by the way, who the hell *are* you?'

I had to admire his cheek but I was a bit too pissed off to

laugh at it. I didn't know what this soft bugger was after or what he was trying to prove but I wasn't in the mood for one-upmanship.

'The name's Terry,' I told him. 'Barrow. And no craphook, I'm not backing down. I don't know what your problem is but if you really want to be an arsehole over an accident, be my guest. I'm standing right here.'

He looked at me coolly. I was beginning to lose my temper and I didn't like doing that. I think what was really getting to me was that this pillock wanted to fight when I thought all that pecking-order crap was behind me. I'd had enough of schoolyard bullies and fights. I was sixteen, taking my O levels, had a good bunch of mates and was quite content with life. Now, this idiot was acting the outraged gentleman over an accident that had happened over three hours earlier. Life was too bloody short.

'Tell you what, bollocks,' I said. I could feel my voice straining to stay controlled. 'I'll be here, right here, at twenty to four this afternoon. If you still want to be an arsehole, I'll see you then. I'll wait till quarter to. If you don't show up, as far as I'm concerned, it's over. Now, the bell's gone and I've got English Lit.' I walked away.

All through the afternoon, I kept wondering what the soft sod was after. Was it simply a case of wanting to fix his place in school? Two years ago, I might have accepted that but not when we were sixteen. He was obviously intelligent; you didn't get into Moss Grammar without having some brains. So why? The more I tried to figure it out, the more I couldn't make sense of it. By the time the last bell went, I'd decided that whatever it was he wanted to prove, he'd get the chance.

I walked across the yard to the fence, taking in the grey November afternoon. The faint smell of wood smoke evoked memories of days gone by. Days when I didn't have to worry about motivations. Days when I was younger. They seemed a long time ago.

Peter-bloody-Lynwood wasn't there but the others were. I could see confusion in all their eyes. I looked at my watch; two minutes to lift-off.

'Oh Jesus, he's coming,' Jeff groaned.

I'd spotted him already. He walked easily, unhurriedly, books under his arm, breaking the small clouds of his own breath as he came towards us. I sized him up again and still thought I could take him. He was my height, about five ten, around my ten stone weight and he looked as fit as me. It would be the intangible that would make the difference, that something that pushed you past just threats and into fights you wanted to finish. I knew I had it. Did he?

Oxborough is a seaport and seaports are hard places. They're hard to work in and hard to live in. I was born in a two-up two-down terrace in Crayford Road about half a mile from the docks. We moved to a three-bedroomed house a mile further away when I was two. They were then and are now, mean streets. When you're born and live there, you just accept them as normal. I learned early on that fighting was something you were expected to do. I didn't like it but I did it because I was going to get hit whether or not. So I grew up able to look after myself. I didn't consider myself 'hard' the way kids think of that word but I could handle myself. I was about fourteen when I decided that it was stupid to get into a fight at the drop of an insult and stayed away from them as much as I could. Still, those early years instilled in me that extra something that made me want to finish any fight I was in.

Did Peter-bloody-Lynwood have it?

What he did suggested he might.

He walked up to us, handed his books to a startled Paul Hughes and planted his left fist on my right temple. It was the instinct I'd developed in those dockland streets that kept my eye intact. My brain picked up something about the way he moved after handing his books to Paul and I'd moved forwards and ducked slightly. Anyway, that first punch suggested he might have that something. It was what he *didn't* do that told me the truth.

What he should've done was plough into me to take advantage of my initial surprise. He might've ended it there and then with another punch or two. But he didn't and, because he didn't, I suppose I'm writing this.

He just stood there, fists bunched but making no move towards me. There was a split-second when I thought of leaving it at that. He'd had his day in court and I could walk away, knowing the others would see it for what it was. But the truth was, the soft sod had been getting me down ever since that first Thick Prick. Mostly because I found it so hard to work him and his motives out.

I hit him. A straight left to the chin. Not with everything but with enough to rock his head back and bring it forward again. I hit his jaw with a right. I suppose it was the old one-two. Whatever it was, it was enough. Peter-bloody-Lynwood went down like a sack of spuds. Fortunately (for him and me), he crumpled to the grass verge. If he'd fallen onto the concrete of the yard, he might've had a concussion or worse.

He groaned and pushed himself onto this backside, rubbing his jaw and blinking stupidly. His eyes were huge, darting about like flies over the tip. Finally, he focused enough to look at me and grinned. *Grinned* for God's sake!

'Okay, that's it. You got what you wanted. Now it's over. Right?' I said. Part of me wanted to go on hitting him. Part of me wanted to help him off the damp grass, brush him down and see him home. I did neither. I picked up my books and left. I looked back when I reached the gate. He was on his feet, still rubbing his jaw, listening to what the others were telling him. I hoped they could talk some sense into him.

By the time I'd finished my essay on *Macbeth* that night, I'd just about stopped thinking about Peter-bloody-Lynwood. As far as I was concerned, he could vanish in a puff of smoke.

It seemed Peter-bloody-Lynwood and my mates had other ideas.

The next day, I was on time. The weather probably had a lot to do with it. It was the kind of November day I still love; crisp air and blue skies. The kind of day you could easily believe in magic and epic quests. I got to the gates at twenty to nine. Paul Hughes arrived a minute later, his usual grin all over his face.

When Jeff arrived, he sidled up alongside us and said,

'All right Henry?'

'Who?' Paul asked. He was a clever lad but a bit short of nous. You know the sort.

'That was soft lad's idea of a joke,' I explained. 'You know, wit? This Womble's just forgotten that Henry Cooper's been retired a while.' I really didn't want to talk about it but Jeff bludgeoned on regardless.

'When's your next big fight, champ?'

'Oh yeah! I get it!' Paul chuckled.

See what I mean?

'Give it a rest, Jeff. I don't want to think about it. Knock it off, eh?'

Jeff shrugged. 'Okay. Still, it was pretty bloody funny. Is he a barmpot or what?' He looked at Paul since Peter-bloody-Lynwood was in his form.

Paul thought about it for a moment and then, 'His dad's a Civil Servant.' As if that explained everything.

'So?' Jeff demanded.

'Well, they just moved to Oxborough cos his dad got promoted. Must be hard starting a new school in the middle of your O levels.'

Well, yeah but it still didn't seem a good enough reason and I said so.

'Yeah,' Jeff agreed. 'Is he soft or what?'

'Oh no. He's doing nine O levels. Got Maths and English from last year and he's doing Applied Maths and Music this time around. He's got brains all right.'

'But no common sense, obviously. Come on, the bell'll be going.'

We walked across the crowded and noisy yard, not really

noticing either; like the bell and the smell of polish and school dinners, they were constants in our lives. Paul continued giving us an insight into the new boy in school. It seemed I wasn't to be allowed to forget Peter-bloody-Lynwood.

'His dad's the manager of the DHSS office by the Town Hall. The one by the Pier Head. What's it called? Something Place?'

'Canley,' Jeff supplied.

'Right. Anyway, they used to live in the Midlands. Cannock or somewhere like that.'

I was interested in spite of myself. 'Why not get an office near there? Why come all the way up here?'

'When you get that high up,' Jeff explained. 'You have to go where you're sent. My uncle's in the MOD and he told me that if you don't go, you don't get any more promotion.'

'Jesus, what a pain,' Paul said. 'Anyway, that's why he's here. He seemed all right in House Assembly. No airs or graces, like. The lads who do the same stuff as him reckon he's not a suckhole or a poser. He just gets on with it. Rob Jones says Peter's going to university to do computers but Mike Wood, who does Music with him, reckons he's really good and could be something special if he wanted.' Paul sounded impressed. As well he might: Mike was accepted by everybody, including the teachers, as one of life's natural musicians and he didn't hand out compliments that often. If he thought Peter Lynwood was really good, the lad must be bloody-near a genius.

'That makes what the dickhead did yesterday even more stupid,' Jeff said, sounding as frustrated and baffled as I'd been since it all began.

'Yeah,' Paul agreed. 'You sure you just bumped into him?' He held his hands up when I glared at him. 'Okay, okay! Well, I dunno then.'

'Look, Ted,' Jeff said. 'I know you said you wanted to forget it but it's got me curious.' He looked apologetic but I just nodded. Much to my disgust, it had me curious, too. Jeff smiled. 'Okay. Paul, why don't you get a grip of whatsisface and find out just what he's after with all this shite?'

'That's enough foul language, Featherstone.' The deep rumble of Brian Mitchell, one of the language teachers, brought us up sharp, just inside the cloakroom door. He looked at us sternly, his pale blue eyes relentless.

Jeff blushed but even then found it hard to contain his smile. 'Sorry sir. It won't happen again.'

'I'm sure. Especially if you check to see if I'm within earshot first. I suggest you get to class before I think of some suitable imposition. Kemp! Kemp! You disreputable little man! Put Parkinson down! You don't know where he's been!' Mr Mitchell went off to humble some more little men.

'I'll see what I can find out,' Paul said as we climbed the stairs.

I'd just plugged myself into the tape-deck in the language lab' when Paul tapped me on the shoulder. I pressed the PAUSE button and turned to look at him.

'You're not going to believe this,' he said.

For a second, I couldn't think what he was on about.

When he told me, I *didn't* believe it. 'You having me on?'

Paul shook his head but, before he could say anything, Mr Margett's voice boomed out of the class speaker.

'If you two can spare the time, we have a lesson to start. Hughes, get to your seat. Barrow, release your PAUSE button.'

Paul did as he was told, leaving me to deal with Spanish comprehension and the fact that there seemed to be a genuine schizophrenic at Moss Grammar.

Jeff laughed. A short, disbelieving bark that echoed round the cloakroom, which was empty apart from us three 'Come on, Paul. He's pullin your plonker.'

Paul shook his head. 'Don't think so. Looked and sounded deadly serious. He told me his business with Barrow wasn't finished but he'd finish it soon.'

'Well,' I said. 'He's out of luck. I meant what I said yesterday, I—'

A bright bolt of pain shot from my right ear across my face. I thought maybe one of the haversacks had fallen off its peg in the cage-like section of cloakroom we were standing in. It was only when I saw the wide-eyed look of surprise on Paul's and Jeff's face, that I realised it was something more. I turned around and there he was. Grinning.

Peter-bloody-Lynwood.

'That's for yesterday afternoon. I still owe you for yesterday morning.'

There are times when, no matter how much you tell yourself you've had enough of the pecking-order crap and all that he-man garbage, the anger inside, that part of us which is still, after all, the reptilian brain from ages lost in time, gets the better of the higher man. The idea that it should be let's-sit-down-and-talk-about-this-like-adults flies out of the window. The higher man just packs his bags and goes on holiday.

I belted the dipshit in the stomach, grabbed him by his hair, yanked his head up and measured the distance between my right fist and his nose. I wound the punch up from somewhere around my ankles and, it really was this fast, rocketed it at his nose.

A fortnight later, when all the craziness between us was over, I relived that punch and thanked God it missed. Even after all these years, I *know* that if that punch had connected, Peter would probably have died. Either because of the sheer force of it or because his head rocked back against the coat-hooks or down onto the unforgiving composition floor of the corridor, opening his skull to the fluorescent lights.

But God intervened in the shape of Taffy Adams, the gym teacher. He yanked Peter back and my fist flashed past his face, making a whistling noise as it did.

'Fortunately, Barrow, I saw the slap you got. That doesn't excuse your trying to decapitate this one.' He lifted Peter up by the shoulder. 'I don't know what it's all about and I don't want to. If you want to continue this, then I can arrange a boxing match. In the gym, with gloves and me as referee. Is that what you want?' Taff's Welsh accent was lilting but his dark blue eyes were hard and deadly serious.

'Ask him,' I said and nodded at Peter. He was busy trying to get his breath back. 'He started this pantomime. Me? I'd as soon forget everything. Him included. He's a bloody gobshite.'

'Well?' Taffy asked without blinking at the last word I'd used. Probably because he thought it was a good description.

'I...I want to...' Peter began.

I stared at him, convinced the stupid sod was going to ask for the boxing match. If Taffy arranged it, the whole bloody school would probably buy tickets. Right then, I was happy to go along— knocking seven kinds of shite out of him seemed a great idea. Then he fooled me again.

Peter-bloody-Lynwood hitched in another breath. 'I want to forget it, too, sir.' Then he grinned, just like yesterday. Jesus! 'Even with you as referee, he'd probably kill me.'

Taffy let go of his shoulder. 'You're probably right. Now go away. Whoever you are.'

Peter straightened his blazer and walked away. Taffy turned to me. 'I'd like to think, Terry, that you wouldn't go looking for him again. I'd like to think you consider it quits.'

'Don't worry. As far as I'm concerned, he doesn't exist.'

Taffy nodded and walked away. I leaned back against the caging, closed my eyes and let out a long breath. My ear rang and I could feel the shape of Peter's hand beginning to glow red on my cheek.

'Terry,' Jeff said quietly.

'I really don't want to talk about it. So, either shut up or go away.'

We all shut up.

A week later, I was sitting in the hall at a single-seat desk. It was the first day of ten days of mock O levels. I had Chemistry that day. Not my best subject but I thought I had enough to get through. Because of the exams, most of my spare time in and out of school had been spent revising so I'd had little time to think about Peter-bloody-Lynwood. I was grateful for small mercies.

The sun was shining through the skylights in the hall ceiling, throwing rectangles of dust-laden sunlight into the room. The light reflected off the polished surface of the desktops, turning the room into something like a spring-glade in a forest. Which it wasn't. The heating was on and the cumbersome clanking of the radiators was the only sound to interrupt the soft murmuring of the other lads in the hall. That murmuring was regular, soothing, almost soporific. Mr Margetts was the invigilator and he was at the front, sorting through what were probably the actual examination papers from two or three years ago.

I was staring into space, rolling my pen idly between my fingers, trying not to think about atomic numbers and chemical equations, humming Glen Campbell's Rhinestone Cowboy. I was brought back to the hall and the examination by the obviously affected cough of somebody trying to attract my attention. I looked to my right and saw only the silhouette of a lad standing directly in a beam of sunlight. I shaded my eyes and actually groaned. I could feel the anger building up inside me.

'Why don't you emigrate?' I asked through clenched teeth.

He grinned. 'I'm here to apologise for last week,' he said

and turned away. He walked back to his seat on the far side of the hall, near the mural that depicted scenes from the Industrial North. I watched him go, aware my mouth was open but unable to close it again. His course took him in and out of the sun-bars, shading him in light and shadow. And I thought that it seemed to sum up Peter-bloody-Lynwood

And then Mr Margetts laid the pale green paper in front of me. I had an exam to do so I'd have to take the apology for what it was and not paw it around like a cat with a wounded mouse.

It was the Tuesday after my final exam when I learned that Peter Lynwood had spent his time doing more than revising.

It was dinnertime. The weather was grey and drizzly and Lingham Field was again out of bounds. I was in the library reading *I Claudius*. I was one of only three pupils in the room. Mr Gibbons, my English teacher, was the only other person there. All four of us were spread around the library, sitting next to the radiators and enjoying the warmth. The door opened and Paul Hughes came in and walked straight towards me. He reached the table, pulled out the chair and sat opposite me.

'Has he seen you, yet?'
'Who?' I didn't look up.
'Peter. He said he was going to apologise. Did he?'
'Oh aye. First day of the exams.' I still didn't look up.
'Well?'
'Well what?'

'Are you going to accept it?'

Now I looked up. 'I haven't thought about it. Yeah, I suppose so.'

'Good.'

'What the hell does it matter? As long as he stops trying to get me to kill him, I couldn't give a bugger if he apologises or not. Why should you care, anyway?'

'Because he says he wants to get to know you.'

I rolled my eyes. 'Why? Is this some sort of group therapy or what? Let him get to know somebody else. I know enough people. Now, if that's all, I'd really like to get back to all these mad Caesars in Ancient Rome.'

'Hey, Ted. Don't get onto me. I--'

'I just don't understand why it's so important to *you*.'

'I like him. He's okay. But I've known you a long time and I don't want to get stuck in the middle.'

'So don't! You're my mate. Okay? Just because you like him doesn't mean I'm going to stamp my feet and throw a tantrum.'

'Oh. Good.' He took a book from his pocket and began to read.

I settled back into my own book and it was only after he'd repeated himself twice that I realised he was speaking to me again.

'What?'

'I said he's been asking around about you.'

'Oh?'

'Yeah. Me, Jeff and Pete and Mike Wood. Even a couple of teachers.'

This was getting bloody ridiculous. 'Am I his project for

the year or what?' The idea that somebody, possibly a borderline schizo, was going around investigating me bothered the hell out of me.

'I think he's just interested,' Paul told me but in his eyes I could see echoes of my last thought.

'Look Paul, up to when I bumped into him, I was just another lad who enjoyed playing football, liked reading and worked reasonably hard at school. I was a lad with all the normal randy urges when I saw a nice-looking girl pass me. The closest to interesting or strange that I ever was, was *liking* Shakespeare! I would really like to get back to being that lad. Tell him that. Please?'

'Yeah. I don't think he'll listen, though. He really thinks you're interesting. Me? I think you're a prat who plays great football and just *pretends* to like Shakespeare.'

That was Paul's idea of wit. He tried and, they say, God loves a trier. Well, Paul would be okay; I found him very trying sometimes.

'Paul? Piss off.'

That Friday, I found out a lot more about Peter Lynwood. Stuff nobody else knew. Stuff I've spoken of to only one other person since. Stuff that explained nearly everything.

It was in Ruskin's House Room that Peter-bloody-Lynwood became just Pete and my friend.

The room was one of three large science labs on the ground floor of the school. These rooms were housed in an annexe that extended from the side of the building next to the tennis courts. The rooms were set aside for House matters during dinner-break or after school. Ruskin was my house, its colour green and its Housemaster was Mr Margetts who was just wonderful.

I mean wonderful in its true sense. The man was a Welshman of Jewish extraction with a classic Jewish nose and dark brown eyes, magnified by incredibly thick bifocals. From the time he joined the school in the late fifties, those spectacles earned him the nickname of Telstar, after the satellite.

His voice was pure magic. It held all the enunciation of the trained linguist but with the deep resonance and Welshness of Richard Burton. He was short and stocky but nobody ever messed with him. The man throbbed with controlled authority. I'd been in his form in the first year and again in the third and we got along. I respected him because he earned it, not because he was a teacher and I was a pupil. He never failed to remember that kids were people, too. You could disagree with him and he never resorted to his teacher-authority to win the argument. So, we got on and, as result, I often got to sit in the House Room if there was a good enough reason and I didn't abuse the privilege. I never did; I valued his respect too much.

The day Pete told me stuff that nearly curled my hair, I was using the room to make a concerted effort at getting *Ruskin Reaction*, our House magazine, into some sort of shape. I was deputy editor and, since Roy Evans was otherwise engaged (he was busy knocking a slice off the head girl from our sister school in the back room of her house opposite the gate to our playing fields), I was it. I didn't mind. I enjoyed the reading, the cutting, the laying-out. I felt I was helping to produce a genuine magazine and not some tatty, mimeographed folded sheet. Ego, I suppose. Anyway, I was down to sorting space for a fairly well-written argument against school uniform when the door opened.

I didn't look up, assuming it was Bone Dome, Mr Curtis the Physics teacher whose room it was. I heard the door whisper shut and I waited for the teacher's voice to reach me. Instead, the slightly hesitant voice of a teenager came across the room to where I sat by the Van de Graf generator.

'Er...oh, sod it. Terry?'

Coming round after surgery or heard through a mile-long tunnel, I would've recognised that voice.

'*Ooohh Gaaard*! Why can't you just leave me alone, you friggin pain in the arse?'

'You busy?'

'Yes! Yes, I'm busy. Even if I wasn't—'

'*Please!*'

The undercurrent of unease, even anguish, in his voice made me look at him. He was leaning against the door, hands in his pockets, blazer unbuttoned. His face looked pinched and even from a distance of fifteen feet, I could see the pain in his eyes. Something of which I'd only been unconsciously aware in myself rushed through me. I felt, actually *felt* for this lad who'd plagued me for a fortnight, had forced me to fight when I didn't even want to argue. Compassion was a word I'd never used about myself, although I knew I could feel passionately about certain things—injustice, cant, a lack of social conscience—yet what I felt at that moment was compassion. For Peter-bloody-

Lynwood. Jesus!

'You'd better sit down before you fall off those really ridiculous platform soles,' I said and nodded at the backless stool across the sink-table from me. He looked at his shoes, which really were high, especially for school. He grinned and then walked slowly to the table, his grin fading rapidly. He sat down with a deep sigh.

'You got time to listen to a story? A real story. I have to tell it and I want to tell it to you. When I've finished, you can tell me to piss off and I will. I'll never bother you again.'

Now, you have to remember that we were teenagers, not seventeen yet, and we were lads. We were half a school year away from the sixth form and the long, pseudo-intellectual discussions that sixth formers are convinced they have to have. What we should've been talking about was football or girls or how big our doodahs were, maybe telling lies about how we'd finally got our leg over with some girl or how we'd really like to get our leg over the blonde one from Abba or the lead singer with The Three Degrees. We should've been talking about whether kipper ties were better than just wearing the huge flared shirt collars outside our wide-lapelled jackets, whether platform soles and stacked heels were as cool as wedges and if it was true that Rob Shackleton's nineteen year old sister would give you a wank if you got her some wacky-backy (the fact that none of us had any idea where to get cannabis or grass was beside the point; presumably Rob Shackleton's sister did).

But I looked at Peter-bloody-Lynwood and knew that he wasn't about to tell me lies about how he lost his virginity last night on his girlfriend's couch while her parents were out at the pictures watching All The President's Men. No, somehow I knew that Peter-bloody-Lynwood wanted to talk about himself and about things sixteen year old lads didn't talk about to other sixteen year old lads—he wanted to talk about things a lot more important than disco music versus The Bay City Rollers versus Rod Stewart and brief, furtive fumbling almost-sex.

I sensed all this in the time it took Peter to say what he'd said, look at his fingers and then look back at me. And I sensed it would be better to say nothing, just let him talk. I put down my pencil and linked my hands on the tabletop. Peter Lynwood told me his story.

He was born on September 9th, 1960, which meant he was exactly one month older than me. He was an only child who came fairly late into his parents' lives. He spent his first four years in a place called West Derby in Liverpool. His father was an executive officer in a department of the Civil Service called the PSA. When his father was promoted, they moved to Newcastle-under-Lyme where Pete went to school until he was twelve. Then his father was promoted again and they moved to Cannock Chase and from there to Oxborough. Pete's mother didn't work. When he told me this, he looked out of the window, sighed and then looked at his hands.

'She used to be very into things like Oxfam,' he said quietly. 'Then she got very into the vodka bottle. She's an alcoholic.'

You see what I mean? A sixteen-year-old lad talking about stuff like that? To another sixteen year old lad? And not even a lad he'd known for a long time, at that? If Paul Hughes or Jeff Featherstone, lads I'd known for nearly half my life, had told me stuff like that, I'd've squirmed with embarrassment. For them and for me. Yet I didn't squirm when Peter Lynwood told me this stuff and, even as I sat there and listened, I had no idea why.

Carol Lynwood apparently got through a bottle and a half of the stuff every two days, depending on how she felt that week. She'd been to AA and, more recently, to some expensive drying-out clinic. Nothing seemed to work. Carol Lynwood clearly had no great desire to stop drinking. Pete said she drank to forget but she'd never told him what it was she was trying to forget. If Ronald Lynwood knew, he never told Pete.

Ronald was a career civil servant. He'd set his sights on a career in Whitehall but somewhere along his carefully chosen track, his train was derailed or, at least shunted into a siding. He'd only got his Deputy Manager's post by transferring from PSA to DHSS. Although his father never actually came right out and said so, Pete thought he might blame his wife for his failure to reach the corridors of power.

You'd think that would be enough, wouldn't you? Well, no.

His parents didn't seem to have anything in common with Pete and the Generation Gap seemed a very real thing in their house. Pete was a lad with all the normal likes and dislikes, fads and urges of a teenager—food, fashion, girls and pop music—and he went home to a house where he usually found his mother sitting in her chair in front of the telly, drinking from a tall glass of colourless liquid that made her eyes big and her face slack. The food for their evening meal would be laid out in the kitchen and Pete would get it ready so his father would have no complaints when he got home. Tea eaten (in his mother's case, pushed around the plate), Pete would wash up and then, without being asked how school was, what homework he had or what he thought about this piece of news, he would go up to his room and leave his father watching telly while his mother stared out on some landscape only she could see. Pete spent his nights in his room with his homework, his portable telly and his records. And his pain.

Enough you'd think, right? Wrong.

Somewhere in his family tree, there was a quirk. It was a quirk that the doctors who'd bothered to listen, didn't think would be terminal. They called it depression but whatever it was, it sure was a weight to carry. The doctors told him he'd probably grow out of it, like the mild acne that flared on his forehead.

I know more about Pete's condition now but, since this is supposed to be a more or less chronological story, it belongs later. For now, let me tell you how the quirk affected Pete.

The bouts of depression came without warning and seemingly without cause. He'd be feeling 'up' for a long time and everything would be fine; he'd sail through things like exams and his music would really fizz. Then the flipside would come down like a sledgehammer.

'Sometimes, Terry,' he said, still looking at his hands. 'I think that whatever gives me the music, gives me the other thing. I don't know why, maybe it's just superstition. Like saying found money always brings bad luck.' He sighed again.

The reason he felt this was, he said, because neither of his parents were musically inclined; his mother didn't even listen to the stuff and, while Ronald liked what he liked—Sinatra, Bach, Mozart—he couldn't carry a tune in a bucket.

Pete loved his music and was convinced it kept him sane. Even here he was thwarted by that generation gap. At least with his father.

Ronald didn't seem to care what his son was doing in his ordinary day-to-day life but he *did* care that his son excelled at school. Ronald Lynwood had decided, arbitrarily, that his son was going to university and there he would become a computer expert. Ronald had pronounced that computing was the only game in town and that it would soon become the only word in life. He brooked no argument in this and Pete was going to university to do whatever there was to do in computing.

Even at sixteen, I could imagine why those depressions might come.

He explained that the depressions sometimes made him do stupid things. Not always like trying to get me to separate him from his head but similar things that might get him into trouble. He'd done daft things when he was younger and that was the problem. Daft things when you're a kid might even be cute but when you get to those times in life when every day is likely to bring you into contact with some soft bugger out to prove his manhood, daft things might well get you into more hot water than you can swim through.

At this point, I told him he was looking in the wrong place if he wanted a bodyguard. He laughed. It was the only time during that strange half hour when he did laugh but it was genuine. Short but real, you know? He didn't want a bodyguard; he just thought I was the type of person who might stop him doing those daft things. I raised my eyebrows but he told me he couldn't explain it any better other than he saw it in my eyes when I put him on the floor by the bike sheds and I remembered how I'd been torn between ripping the stupid bugger apart and picking him up and taking him home. I told him I still thought he was looking at the wrong bloke. I wasn't the un-genie who could cancel whatever wish he had (he actually used the phrase death-wish but I put it down to teenage hyperbole). Just why did he think I could help?

You live your life under certain conceptions, certain assumptions, possibly even shadows, don't you? You have a view of yourself, even at sixteen, that's gained over the years, formed by circumstances and your reactions to them. You see and mostly understand the strictures society imposes and you condition yourself to act within them. All this combines to create your own idea of who you are.

But there are other things that make up the way you are. Not all of it can be laid at the door of heredity or environment. I think a good part of what we are is the result of something mostly unknowable by ourselves. Or only peripherally.

I think how others see us helps mark the path we walk as

much as anything else. And how many of us get the chance to find out what others think of us? Come to that, how many of us would really want to know? If we don't know, their view of us can't oppose the view we have of ourselves.

Peter Lynwood told me how others saw me, what they thought of me.

At first, I thought it might be quite nice, sort of like going to your own wake and hearing all the nice things people said about you.

I thought of myself as a pretty all-right lad. I got on with nearly everybody. I thought I was reasonably intelligent, quite funny and, well…all-right. Apparently, most of the lads Pete talked to thought much the same. But…I could be arrogant (fair enough); the teachers thought I was brighter than I actually showed in my work (in other words 'could do better'). Being the new boy with a good academic record apparently meant Pete got answers where the rest of us wouldn't even ask questions.

Most of that boosted my ego and I was quite enjoying going to my own wake. I told him I still didn't see how all this could help me help him and that was when he hit me with the stuff that got right down inside me and probably laid a few new yards of tarmac on my path through life. It worried me a bit, too.

During his research on Terence Barrow, Pete came across the thing that he said he'd seen in my eyes when I put him on the floor. He told me he was glad he hadn't imagined it. Virtually everybody, including one or two teachers, especially Telstar, said much the same thing about me. They thought that, not only was I capable of looking after myself physically but that I had an inner strength that could help me look after others, too. Pete asked Telstar what he meant.

Telstar told him that he believed that there was something in me that wanted to take care of people and I'd been given the ability to do just that. Telstar thought I was capable of defusing a situation by exerting some inherent authority. He believed that, as I grew older, this would come to the fore. Perhaps will-power covered it best, he told Pete because, when I made a decision, something made it quite clear that I wouldn't be dissuaded. He said he'd seen it a few times and that, whatever it was, it could be quite frightening.

I wasn't sure I understood all of that but the idea that I could sometimes frighten Telstar frightened *me*. What Pete told me next worried me even more.

'The lads I spoke to,' Pete said, finally looking me in the eye. He paused and I recognised the light in his own eyes. It wasn't just his intelligence that sparkled there; it was his humour and his charm, the things that helped him get answers to those questions the rest of us sixteen-year-old schoolboys wouldn't ask.

'Yeah? All those good mates of mine. What about them?'

He smiled and shook his head once. 'They told me about a couple of fights you've had. I wondered if you remembered them?'

'That's easy. I've only had three since I came here,' I told him. Then I told him about those fights.

The first one, reasonably enough, was in the first year and the two of us got caned for our trouble.

The other two occurred in quick succession during the third year. The first was with a lad called Paul Riley, a fourth year. He thought a really good way to brighten up his dinner-hour was yanking my haversack off my shoulder, ripping the straps and emptying the contents all over a muddy Lingham Field. Basically, the lad was a shit. Even his mates thought so. He was with two of them that day and they stood and watched while I tore into him. They only intervened when Riley was squealing like a pig in an abattoir. They dragged me off and set me on my way into the yard. At the time, I was naive enough to believe that was that and thought no more about it. Two days later, I found out that Riley didn't see it that way.

Riley was a shit but he had a mate in the fifth year who was a *real* shit. Mike Lathom thought that helping Riley recover some of his lost dignity was a fine idea. Lathom was what we called in those long ago days a 'hardknock' and enjoyed his reputation so much he actually went looking for trouble.

It happened in the yard near the toilet block. It was witnessed by virtually the whole third year, most of the fourth and a few Big Wheels in the fifth. At the time, I was more concerned with the situation as it was than with future cause and effect.

There was a lad in our year called Paul (you notice how many lads have the same name when you're at school?) Gillick. He was one of Nature's athletes, quite bright and probably the most devout Catholic I've ever known. His bedroom was a virtual shrine to Mary Mother of God. Honest. Statuettes, candles, the works.

Anyway, the previous summer, he'd been in Italy with his family—Rome, The Vatican, all that. While he was visiting a small village near where they stayed, he saw a group of teenagers playing a game. He brought the idea home and we adapted it for our own use during morning break or dinnertime when the field was out of bounds. Two teams were picked, one team bent down leapfrog fashion but linked together like a rugby scrum in single file. At the head of the queue, one lad stood up to keep a lock on the line. The other team then ran, jumped and landed on the bent-over line and tried to collapse it. Yeah, I know what it sounds like but you know what lads are like.

This day, I was the standing lad, leaning against the wall of the toilet block while my team bent down. The first jumper from the other team landed with a bone-jarring thump on Pete Forrest, the lad whose head was between my legs. We were waiting for the ineluctable six-feet-two and thirteen stone of Paul Lewis to cause his usual havoc when Riley came hurtling over the bent line of our team and knocked the first lad off. It happened to be Gillick and he hit the ground hard. Riley rabbit punched the lad he'd landed on and gripped him between his legs, keeping him in place. There were shouts for Riley to piss off but he stayed put and stared at me.

'Hello shithead,' he said confidently. 'I'm gonna friggin kill you.'

Very loud and very jolly. Then he swung a big, roundhouse right that came up from his hip. I saw it coming and moved to my own right. Not much but enough for his fist to miss me and slam into the wall behind me. The momentum of the punch rolled him off and the lad he'd been sitting on. John Jenkins got up, rubbing his neck and cursing.

Riley hit the ground on his right hip and howled, more from his swelling right hand than any injury to the hip. I looked down at the hand and thought there might be a couple of broken knuckles under the dark, welling blood. His left hand was splayed out as he tried to get up. I had time to think that there was already a crowd gathering and *that* meant that a teacher would be along soon. Then I was simply furious.

I bent and grabbed the splayed left hand, hauled Riley up, twisting his arm as he came. I twisted it up his back, almost to his shoulder blade and rammed him against the wall. I let go of the hand, grabbed his shoulder, turned him to face me and then hit him. Hard. His nose spurted a shower of blood and his teeth broke the skin on my knuckles. He slumped down the wall. That was when Mike Lathom grabbed my hair and yanked me back.

I twisted to get some leverage but he hit me. His right fist exploded stars behind my eyes and the force of it rocked me backwards, out of his grip. I blinked twice, saw a blur I thought might be a face and lashed out. I caught his chin but not hard enough to put him down. He stepped back and we looked at each other.

The stars behind my eyes flared and died remarkably quickly. Then I was looking at a lad who was so close to leaving school that he wore his uniform like the rest of us wore our ordinary clothes. His tie was loose and hung almost down to his belly-button; his top button was undone and he wore the wide flared collar of his pale blue shirt outside his jacket lapels. His platform soles made him a good two inches above six feet. There he stood, almost a man, and so confident in his strength and what he was going to do, he took the time to tell me.

'You're going to need plastic surgery, prickface. And plaster casts on both arms. *Nobody* catches me on the chin.' Very quietly, very slowly. Very sure.

I felt something cold well up inside me then. I opened my mouth and, to the lads watching, extremely stupid words came out of it.

'You can try. But it won't be just one of us at the hospital. They'll have to carry you out in bits.'

He didn't blink. I remember that. He looked at me for about half a minute, drilling his stare into my eyes. Then he spat on the floor between my feet and walked away.

Riley groaned and hobbled off, holding his arm across his chest and snuffling blood back up his broken nose. I waited until both of them reached the gym doors and then leaned back against the rough brick wall, waiting for reaction to set in. I was surprised at how little there was.

I told Pete this and he nodded. Then he told me what I didn't remember. I didn't remember it because I'd never heard about it. I didn't know Paul Lewis' brother, Mathew, was on fairly good terms with Lathom and, like every fifth former there, he wanted to know why Lathom had just walked away. Mathew Lewis asked Lathom. Lathom, far from being furious, told him. Pete had the answer down pat, as quoted in the folklore of the school. Handed down to everybody but me.

"'You wanna know why I backed out Mat?" Pete told me. "Because he meant it. Every single word." When Mat Lewis asked how he knew, Lathom said, so legend had it, "I looked in his eyes. That's how you tell if somebody's all mouth or means it. I looked in his eyes, Mat, and they told me he would friggin batter me. Probably without breaking sweat or breathing hard. When you see that look in somebody's eyes, you walk away or get killed. No mystery, mate.'"

Pete smiled slowly as he finished telling me.

I listened to this dumbfounded. Then I realised that, really, I'd had fewer problems with schoolyard bullies and the inevitable push and shove or fights than I should have done. Sure, most of it was the simple passage of time but now I understood that my non-fight with Lathom had a lot to do with it, too. Still, the overpowering feeling I had as Pete finished telling me all this, was that I didn't like the idea that I could be considered capable of causing somebody, even a Mike Lathom, serious damage. I didn't like that idea at all.

Pete said nothing while I digested this. I struggled with it and then let it go; I didn't go around deliberately putting the fear of God into people. So then I returned to my original question.

Just how did all this make Pete think I could help him if and when he decided to do something daft?

He shrugged and, for the first time seemed to become again the sixteen-year-old lad he was, one like other sixteen-year-old lads, not comfortable with putting his feelings into words. 'I just think you could,' he told me and picked at his fingernails. Without looking up again, he said, 'Anyway, like I said, I wanted to tell you a story and I have. You can tell me to piss off now and you won't be bothered by me again.'

But, before I could say *anything*, he stood up and left the room.

That night, after I'd done my History essay and prepared my Spanish Comp. for the next day, I lay on my bed, put Carol King's 'Tapestry' album on my little stereo and flicked through the mental file I had on Peter Lynwood.

It took me to the end of side one of the record to decide that, though I should tell him to piss off, I wouldn't. It wasn't that I was a sucker for hard luck stories or addicted to waifs and strays. It just felt right not to tell him to piss off.

The next day, I went looking for him but couldn't find him. I found Paul who told me that Pete was off but he didn't know why. At dinnertime, I went to see Mr Hitchins, Pete's form master. He was in his room, his head buried in his tatty briefcase, his ginger hair hanging over his ears, muttering to himself.

'Mr Hitchins, can you spare a minute?'

'Mmmf?'

'I said—'

'Mmff mmff mmff. Mmff!'

I was doing Spanish and French but I didn't think 'mmff' had a Latin root so I said, in English, 'D'you know why Peter Lynwood's off?'

His head emerged from the briefcase. His usually florid

face was now a blazing red, his long ginger hair hanging over his eyes. He pushed his hair up and blinked a few times, as if trying to clear his head and then, 'What? Who? Why?'

I bit back the giggle that was trying to escape. The whole scene was out of Monty Python and I half-expected John Cleese to open the door and stomp around the room doing his silly walk. 'Lynwood. Peter Lynwood. D'you know why he's off?'

'Why?'

Oh shit! 'Er, I lent him a book and er, well...' *Shit!*

'Ah. Well, Barrow, as far as I know, he has a cold or flu or more likely idleitis. I just got the message that he rang to say he wouldn't be in today. Okay? Fine. Now, I have to find my stopwatch in this bloody briefcase so kindly be about your business.'

I watched as he stuck his head back in the case. 'Mr Hitchins?'

'*Mmfff!*'

'It's on your desk.'

His head bobbed up again. He managed to snag the watch with the third sweep of his hand.

'D'you know off-hand where he lives?'

He raised his head and stared at me. 'What exactly is this book? *Fanny Hill*? *The Karma Sutra*? This year's *Shoot! Annual*?' He shook his head. 'Somewhere on Braddock Close. *Don't* ask me what number. Now go. Go, go go!'

'Somewhere on' was close enough. Braddock Close is a road, one of only three, in the posh part of Oxborough. Each road's got maybe six houses, all set in their own grounds. Money, in other words. Peter's father, Ronald, must've done something right sometime. I biked out to see Pete that night.

The three roads that make up Millionaires Row wind their genteel way around the gentle slope of Colley Hill. The most expensive houses perched atop the humped crown of the hill have unrestricted views of the city to the left, the green belt to the right and, from the back, across the river to Seapool and the purple mountains of Wales. If you don't know they're there, you could miss the houses behind their high hedges and evergreen trees at the bottom of their long and winding drives. The area was about three miles from my home. Or three light years.

It was cold and misty and the lights of the city offered little comfort but more than the narrow, single-width road leading to the top of the hill. I doubt if more than six cars passed me on that road and those that did were all that year's model and mostly foreign. Apart from the Rolls that flashed its lights at me as it rolled past, of course.

My plan was simple enough. I'd go to the first house and ask whoever answered if they could tell me where the Lynwoods lived. I didn't realise that the people who live in places like Colley Hill seldom have much to do with their neighbours. At the time, I thought it had to do with the fact that 'next door neighbour' hardly fitted, considering the size of the grounds. Later, when I'd seen more of the world, I realised that it had more to do with their attitudes.

It took me twenty minutes and several stony-eyed faces before I found someone who thought that the people in The Firs might have recently moved in. The woman who told me spoke to me through a gadget like an intercom from the inside of her porch while I stood in the chill mist. I thanked her very much and wheeled my bike down her drive to the road.

The Firs, reasonably enough, takes its name from the four fir trees that stand guard in the gap of hedges running along the road. That evening, they looked like something from a Tolkien story, their Christmas-tree shapes looming in the mist. The drive was gravel, a caramel colour that looked like a chocolate trail in a fairy story. Even today, the sound of my bike wheels on that drive in the still, misty, quiet evening is a part of me. If I hear that sound on the telly or when one of my godchildren rides up on their bike, it evokes memories of Carol Lynwood. It ran straight as a die to the house more than two hundred yards up the hill. On either side of the drive, the grass was mown in stripes, still visible this late in the year. As I stood under those sentient firs, I caught a whiff of the sea; tangy and mysterious. I looked about me and then towards the glimmer of light in the windows of the house. I considered waiting until Monday and then said sod it—I'd biked three miles, been looked at down the noses of the folks on the hill and it had pissed me off a bit.

The house was built in a style I'd only seen in old 50's black and white Ealing comedies about the then Upper Class or on the telly in one of Detective Columbo's convoluted mysteries. Two storeys of red brick, topped with a green tiled roof, double-glazed leaded windows. The house was big. Even from the front, you could tell it went back a long way. From half-way down the left side, a controlled arch of rose trees extended to a point in the distance. On the right, a double garage stood closed. A carriage lamp was fixed to the wall next to the porch. Its imitation candle gave off a bright yellow light that was fractured into shafts by the glass.

I rang the bell and heard faint chimes inside the house. I was expecting Pete to answer and when he did, I was going to tell him I'd decided not to tell him to piss off and then ask him what he was like at making tea.

His mother opened the doors. The front door *and* the porch door.

She said, 'Hello, yes?' but the words signified nothing to me.

I was looking at a beautiful woman. And that was exactly the phrase that went through my mind. Not the normal *'God, she's fit, wouldn't mind some of that'* that I was used to thinking whenever I saw a girl I fancied. She'd obviously been drinking but she was still beautiful. She had high cheekbones, a nose of perfect length and shape and her lips were full, blushed with lipstick. Her forehead was broad and barely lined above eyes of a blue so dark it was almost violet. Her hair was streaked dark brown and silver, swept off her face to fall in gentle waves to her shoulders. The only blemishes on her face were the shadows under those incredible eyes. They weren't bags but, because of the loveliness of the rest, they *were* blemishes.

That she'd had a drink was clear from the way she leaned against the doorjamb and the way her eyes were dilated.

'Hello? Yes?' She repeated and I tried to dislodge the frog that had taken up residence in my throat. I was saved from total idiocy by Peter's arrival behind his mother.

'Terry?' His eyes looked more than surprised, they looked shocked. His mother shifted her weight to look at him.

She smiled at him, a distracted, lop-sided smile. 'Oh, Peter, I think this boy must want you. I'll go in. It's a bit chilly.' She turned to me and offered me the same smile and then made her way carefully back into the house.

'What're you doing here?' Pete asked.

'Getting cold.'

He looked at me for a moment and then smiled. It was very similar to his mother's smile. 'Fancy a coffee?'

'Can't stand the stuff. What's your tea like?'

'Not bad. You're bike'll be okay there.'

'Yeah,' I said. 'People round here probably throw better out.' I followed his laughter into the house

The house was as big as I'd thought. There was an entrance hall, which resembled a foyer in a small hotel, and the stairs ran in a spiral up from the hall. They opened out onto a half-round landing that looked like a balcony. To my right at ground level were four rooms, doors closed. To my left, three rooms, doors ajar. Pete's mother had gone into the middle room and I could hear the low mutter of a television in that room.

'Out here,' Pete said and I followed him into the back kitchen.

Well, that's what it would've been called in our house but the resemblance ended with the name. This one was fitted with everything; cabinets, cooker, fridge-freezer, double-drainer sink. It seemed to have scores of power points and appliances seemed to grow out of most of them. The furniture was polished mahogany, as were the French windows that opened onto the floodlit patio. To the right of the patio was a glass building that looked like a conservatory. The soft, ghostly blue glimmer told you it was a swimming pool.

'How many sugars?'

'What in?'

'You said you wanted tea,' Pete said.

'I mean a cup or mug.' Even as I said it, I was sure there were no mugs in the Lynwood kitchen—china cups and Staffordshire Pottery but no mugs. I was wrong.

'I can put it in a mug.'

'Three then.'

He handed me the mug of steaming tea. 'D'you want to drink it here or go up to my room?'

'I'm easy,' I said and then shook my head. 'No, I'm nosy. Let's go to your room.'

My idea of a bedroom was a room big enough for a single bed, a chest of drawers and a wardrobe. The bloke who designed The Firs had different ideas. Pete's room was about the size of our front and living rooms knocked together. One wall was a fitted wardrobe alongside floor to ceiling shelving. One wall was a window looking down on the swimming pool. He had his own toilet and shower. He also had a piano.

'How the friggin hell did you get that up here?'

'The removal men did it. They used a dolly or something and made it look easy. You going to tell me what you're doing here?'

'I was going to tell you I wasn't going to tell you to piss off.'

He took a deep breath and sat down heavily on his bed. He closed his eyes and a faint but obvious shudder ran through him. He raised his head and looked at me. 'But now you're going to tell me you've changed your mind.' It wasn't a question.

'What? No. Why should I?'

'All this,' he said and waved his hand to take in the house, the pool, the gravel drive, everything. 'And...you've seen my mother.'

I said nothing so he mumbled something else. 'What?' I asked.

'I said it usually does change people's minds. My—'

'If you say 'my mother', you're likely to get this tea all over you.'

He looked up and I saw something in his eyes that might have been some kind of hope. 'But she's a dr—'

'You told me that yesterday. You want to know what I saw when she opened the door? Or, rather, *both* doors?'

'What're you on about?'

'Oh, just that the few people who bothered to answer my knock or ring at the bell barely opened their front door, never mind the porch door. Anyway, that's only part of it. Your mum's beautiful.'

'Eh?'

I frowned at myself and wondered why I'd said that, almost embarrassed to have even thought it about the mother of somebody I was at school with. And then I realised that it was true so why shouldn't I say it. '*Beautiful.*

Besides, I didn't realise that being your mate meant I didn't have anything to do with your mum. Or dad, for that matter. Or will I embarrass you? Being common, like?' The last bit came out more bitter than I intended. Maybe those people looking down their noses at me had got to me more than I'd thought.

'It's not that, Terry. I'm not scared about you meeting my parents.'

'The other way around?'

'No. Yes. Maybe. I don't know. Look, it's just that—'

'Look, Pete, your mum drinks but she didn't come at me with a bread knife when she opened the door. And the house isn't a tip. Maybe you've got a maid or something,' he shook his head and I went on. 'There you go then. She drinks but she's not paralytic and out of it all the time. I haven't met your dad yet, so I don't know about him. Hey, d'you mind if I sit down and take my coat off?'

He nodded. 'I've never...I've never thought about it like that. Mum, I mean. You're right. She looks after this place and it's—'

'Big?'

He laughed. 'Yeah. She couldn't do that if she was passed out all the time, could she? God, I never saw that! Not at all!' He wiped angrily at his cheeks.

I didn't want him to cry; I was only just getting over calling his mum beautiful to his face. Besides, he didn't need an audience if he *did* cry. 'Can I ask you something?' I said. 'Something really cheeky?' He nodded. 'How much did this place cost and where did you get the money?'

'About eighty or ninety thousand, I think.'

'Jesus wept! I thought your dad was a Civil Servant?'

He laughed again and I knew he was over the tears. For now. I thought that, tonight, in bed, he might have to deal with them but for now they were gone.

'He is. There's something else in my family tree.'

'Robber Baron?'

'Nearly. Some of my Mum's family, two or three generations back, went to America and got rich. My auntie Carla died about three years ago. She liked me, thought me being musical was great. She said she always wanted to be but wasn't. Anyway, she used to come over twice a year to see us. When she died, she left Mum and me a lot of money. The house is ours, free and clear. Dad's money is extra.'

'How much did you get?' I was fascinated.

'About fifteen thousand. I get an allowance each month and the rest is in a trust fund for university and after.'

'Magic!'

'You're not jealous?'

'Why should I be? You know, you're going to have to change some of your ideas about people. Especially me.'

'Yeah. Sorry.'

'Never mind. Show me the rest of the house before I go home.'

It didn't take long. Despite my little speech about his mum, I didn't get shown into the room she was in. The front room had what the estate agents call a feature stone fireplace and was clearly for visitors; a place for everything and everything in its place. The other rooms downstairs were much of a muchness except for the smallest. This was a library-cum-study. All those books—I could've spent forever in that room. But, being the age I was and coming from where I did, it was the swimming pool that really grabbed my attention.

The pool was eight yards by twenty-five. There were two sets of changing cubicles, a little bamboo bar in a corner with cane loungers and a couple of rubber plants running amok in another corner. There was a faint smell of chlorine but nothing as overpowering as in our local pool. Behind the changing cubicles was a fully equipped gym. Pete told me the roof could be opened in the summer.

'Friggin stuffy bastard! This is great! Tell you what, Pete, you may never get me away from this place.'

'No sweat, Terry,' Pete said quietly.

It was said simply and honestly and meant more than that typical teenage phrase. He meant that anytime I wanted to come, I'd be welcome and that it wasn't a bribe. I was glad. I wanted to be his friend and would have with or without the money and the pool.

'Thanks, mate,' I said and saw in his eyes that he heard all the things I didn't say. And I think it was then that we became more than just mates. I think it was then that Peter-bloody-Lynwood became my best friend and I became his.

And then it was time to go. We left the pool house and I picked up my coat from the kitchen. I intended to just leave but, as I passed the still-ajar door to the room where his mother sat, I decided that I wanted to say goodbye. I stopped in the hall and started to put on my gloves. It gave Pete the chance to get ahead of me to open the front doors. That was when I pushed the door open on the room where the television muttered quietly.

She was sitting in a high-backed velour chair, facing the television at an angle to the fire. The fire was a 'living flame' that looked almost real. The news was on and I could see a picket line outside some car factory or other. Despite looking at it, Carol Lynwood was obviously not seeing it. On an occasional table next to the chair was a glass tumbler. It was three-quarters full of a colourless liquid. I didn't see a bottle.

'Mrs Lynwood?' I said, expecting her to continue looking at the telly. But she turned immediately and there was no doubt she recognised me. I sensed Pete standing behind me. I could almost read his thoughts. He was torn between introducing me and yanking me back out of the room. 'Mrs Lynwood, I'm Terry Barrow. I'm a friend of Pete's from school.' I crossed the room and offered her my hand. There was something in her eyes that echoed Pete's when I told him I wasn't going to tell him to piss off. It was far back behind the alcoholic haze but it was there. She held out her hand and I shook it, surprised by the unexpected strong grip.

'Hello Terry. I'm pleased to meet you.' She let go of my hand but her eyes didn't wander. 'I... we don't see many of Peter's friends. You must be cold and damp, coming here on your bike. Would you like some soup?'

'Pete's already made me some tea, thanks. I just wanted to say hello and goodbye. I'll probably see you next time I come.'

She smiled and the alcoholic haze lifted a little. 'Really? You'll be coming to see me...us again? That's nice. Really nice. Tell me—'

The sound of a car engine and tyres on gravel caused her to turn and face the leaded windows where the yellow splash of dipped headlights swept the glass.

'That's Dad,' Pete said. 'Come on Terry, it's getting on and you'd best be...' He touched my shoulder.

I eased away from his hand and glared at him. He took a step back. I looked at his mother. She was fiddling with a teardrop pendant that glittered at her throat. She ran her tongue over her lips.

The engine died, the lights went off, a door opened and closed. A dark figure passed the window, wearing a hat. Pete's mother settled back in her chair and took two sips from her glass. The sound of the two front doors opening and closing made her take another one. The tension in the room was palpable. I looked at Pete. He stared back at me, looking lost, almost haunted. The door to the room opened fully and Mr Lynwood stood in the doorway.

He was a tall man. About six feet and built like a rugby player though the muscles were running to fat now. He was bald straight down the middle of his head and the pate gleamed as if it had just been polished. His whole face glowed as if he'd just shaved. His nose was like a blade and the eyes on either side of that straight edge were almost lost beneath bushy brows. They were hard eyes. Pale blue, almost transparent. They looked past me, past his wife and settled on the drink on the table. His mouth made a small moue of disgust and then he turned his hard glance back at me.

He took me in. In that glance, he eyed me up and down and formed his opinion of me. Right or wrong, it was formed and I had the feeling that this was a man who had little time for second thoughts.

'Dad, this is Terry Barrow. He's in my year at school. He came to, er, to...'

'Hello Mr Lynwood. I lent Peter a book. He was off sick today so I came to collect it.' I held out my hand and he shook it. It was a perfunctory shake, a bit like I imagined a politician's handshake would be. Even as he took my hand, he looked at Pete.

'Unwell?' He didn't give Pete a chance to elaborate. Ronald was already looking at his wife. He knew who hadn't been feeling well. His mouth made that moue again and his eyes blazed. 'I see. Well...I'm sorry, what was your name?'

'Terry.'

'Yes. Well, Terry, I'm sure your meal will be ready soon. As ours will be. So...'

I nodded and turned to Carol. 'Goodbye Mrs Lynwood. See you next time.' She looked at me and, despite her husband's hard eyes and his facial expressions, she smiled and her eyes flashed. I thought that flash meant she'd be glad to see me. I hoped so anyway.

I smiled and walked to the door. 'Goodbye Mr Lynwood,' I said as I passed him. He just nodded.

As I turned my bike, Pete said, 'Thanks for coming Terry.'

'No sweat. Listen, why don't you come to the match tomorrow? We're playing at Highfield Park, two o'clock kick off. You can have your tea at ours afterwards.'

'Honest?'

I sighed exaggeratedly and rolled my eyes. 'Honest.'

'Terry? What did you think of my Dad?'

I didn't look back at him when I said, 'He's right about my tea being nearly ready. I'll see you tomorrow, Pete.'

Riding home was mostly downhill and I coasted a lot. And thought. Even now, I find it a bit hard to believe just how grown up those thoughts were. And I know I'm not imagining them because I can remember feeling slightly uncomfortable at how grown-up they were. Probably because it meant I *was* growing up and, at sixteen, that's a bit scary.

What did I think about Pete's dad?

Not much, to tell the truth. Whatever open-mindedness he might've had ran out a long time ago, I thought. No, he was never going to be one of my favourite people. Not because he looked at me like I was something he'd brought in on the sole of his shoe but because I liked Carol. And she needed something from Ronald he was either incapable of giving or wouldn't give. And what was he giving Pete? Pete's attitude to his mum probably said more about Ronald than it did about Pete. And Pete was missing out on her, which was the worst of it.

The fact that I wasn't missing out on my own parents made that seem worse. My Mum was great. Full of fun and life and she always had time to listen if you needed to talk. A lot of the time, that's all you do need. If I needed a couple of bob for football subs, she was there. She always said that, if she had it you could have it, if she didn't, you couldn't. She loved me and my two sisters without qualification.

My Dad was the same and he'd always been my friend.

We talked about everything and, when I was younger, he helped me with my homework. The day I asked him about some trigonometric problem, he looked at the drawing, at the question and then at me. He said that this was where his maths and my homework parted company. We both laughed but both felt sad, too. Him because here was a part of my life he could no longer share and me because I saw the truth of how he'd missed out on further education. My Dad was a clever man. A toolmaker by trade, he left school at fourteen and taught himself everything else by reading everything he could lay his hands on. He could turn his hand to anything and do it well. But the thing he did best was love his family. And he did that every day.

Pete was missing out on all that. The fact that his father was disgusted with his wife and making no attempt to hide it had insidiously formed Pete's attitude. So he was missing out on his mother and she was missing out on her son. Still, despite his father, Pete recognised, if subconsciously, something of what had happened and his attitude towards his father was the result. Pete could see nothing in his father he wanted to emulate. The cold waste between them was made bigger by Ronald Lynwood's apparent antipathy towards the clever, creative son he'd sired.

Pete came to watch me play football the next day (we won) and then to our house for tea. At first, he was a little awkward, a bit boggled by the atmosphere at our place. It took an hour but, really, he had no chance. Not with my Mum's insatiable curiosity, my sisters' endless teasing and my Dad's ability to make it seem like they'd known each other for all of Pete's life. He left at nine that Saturday night and we both knew he'd found a second family.

We spent most of the week before Christmas that year at Pete's during the day and at our house in the evening. Carol Lynwood was always pleased to see me and Pete said he thought she seemed less drunk during the time we were both there. She asked me what I was doing and what I liked. She had a way of asking these questions that reminded me of the way my sisters asked—as if she'd never heard those things before. Which, I supposed, she hadn't. I found her witty and quick and it was obvious she had a brain. The chance to use it made her greedy.

Once Pete realised that his mother could actually make good conversation, he joined in. And that made Carol enjoy it all the more. She didn't follow us around like a lost puppy, though. When we were in his room or in the pool or just farting around in the snow (it came on December 14 that year and gave me my first remembered white Christmas), she only called us when she'd made sandwiches or soup for our dinner. We spent all day on the 18th hanging the decorations and dressing the tree. Pete told me it was the first time she'd done this since he'd been five.

He spent Christmas night with me and mine at our annual gathering of the clan at my Auntie Tessie's house. He was comfortable with my immediate family now but, when he saw my seventy odd cousins, uncles, aunts and close friends who were considered family, his eyes nearly popped out. I left him to it; with my family, there's no way you can sit on the sidelines. I went round saying Happy

Christmas to everybody and oohing and aahing at my younger cousins' Christmas presents—Space Hoppers and Scaletrix and a hand-held electronic game where you had to kill descending Martians—and left Pete to it, He was just another member of the family by the time I caught up with him. Somebody, I found out later it was my Nan, discovered he could play the piano and he was left in no doubt that he would be playing the upright for the sing-song at the end of the party.

He found me in the back room where the ancient upright stood. The lid was closed and the top was covered in buffet but the piano worked fine.

'I can't do it,' he told me simply.

"Course you can.'

'But…'

'But what?'

He coughed and shuffled his feet. 'This is your *family*. I don't want to make an idiot out of you when I get all bollixed up or something.'

There was genuine concern in his voice but I couldn't help laughing. 'Listen, Pete, as far as my family's concerned, nothing will make me a bigger idiot than they already think I am. It's nothing to get worked up about. It's just the way we are. It keeps our feet on the ground. We can say what we like about each other but woe-betide anybody outside the family who slags us off. But you don't get it, do you?' He raised his eyebrows and shook his head. 'You *are* one of the family now. As for the music, it'll be like that old joke. You hum it and I'll play it. By Boxing Day, you'll know more old songs than Max Bygraves. Don't worry about it.'

It took two tunes to work the nervousness from his fingers and two more before he stopped blushing at the comments to 'hurry it up, Pete, you'll have it New Year'. Then he just went with the flow. Being as good as he was, it wasn't long before he began to control some of it. Not much; my family is very strong-willed. As the songs got less recent and the melodies more unknown, he just accompanied them, playing the harmonies and what I've always called the fiddly bits. He did it almost absently because he was *listening*. I could see him hearing a song for the first time and deciding what he did and didn't like. It was the first time I'd seen this and I was made up. *Now* he was alive, running on all four cylinders and fully tuned.

About half three on Boxing Day morning, with all the young kids in bed, the older ones asleep on the floor or the furniture, the record player was turned off for good and cups of tea were being drunk. Pete was sitting on the chair by the piano, his left arm draped protectively around my sister Dawn's shoulder and trying to smoke one of my Uncle Terry's cigars without turning green. I was sitting on the floor at my Nan's feet. She was humming some tune quietly and it was only when she stopped that I realised I was humming, too, because the melody continued.

'Peter, son' my Nan said. 'Why don't you play us one of your own tunes?'

He blinked and looked at me. I shrugged; I had no idea if he had tunes of his own or not.

'I...' he said and paused. Then I saw it. That look which said, *Yes, I've got one and here it won't get me into trouble.*

So he played it and it was perfect for the time and place.

It was quiet and dreamy and very simple. But most of all, it was catchy. That's not very evocative or flattering but it fits. The day after New Year's Day, my Dad was whistling it in his shed while he put the finishing touches to a fireplace he was making for the front room.

When Pete played the final chord, there was a brief pause and in it I saw him look at his hands as if he was unsure just what he had there. Then he looked at my Nan. She smiled and applauded, softly so as not to disturb the sleepers. The rest of the room joined in the applause and I knew he was close to tears and that he was feeling what I already knew; for the time he'd been playing, he had them in the palm of his hand. Oh, he'd go to university and get his degree in computing or whatever it was, but it was his music that really made his soul blaze.

He taught me to play guitar. I wasn't Eric Clapton but Pete taught me well and, in the end, I played it very well, better than Pete. He had a couple of guitars—a full size acoustic and a Fender electric with a practice amp. He played both well but not as well as he played piano. When he sat at that highly-polished instrument in his room, he made it talk.

It was in the afternoon of New Year's Day when he picked up his acoustic and began vamping. I was reading a Michael Moorcock story and the sound of the guitar was just background. I took no notice until I recognised a little of the middle eight; part of the tune he'd played at the party. It was slightly faster between the pauses where he was obviously thinking it through. I dropped back into the story.

'Terry.' His voice was low, occupied with other things.

I looked up and he was at the piano, the guitar on his lap. 'Yeah?'

'Do us a favour and play this for us.' He picked out the slightly faster melody, all the time looking at the piano.

I laughed. 'Yeah, right, Pete. Nah, don't think so mate. I can write essays and take throw-ins but play a guitar? Forget it, mate.'

'Oh come on, it's easy. Anyway, I heard you singing the other night. You've got it.'

'Pete, I was half-shot. Besides, singing doesn't need fingers.'

'Look, I'll show you and you just pick it out at the right tempo. I want to try something on the piano while the melody's playing.'

So he showed me where to put my fingers and la-lahed the tempo. I sat hunched over the guitar, trying to make my fingers do what I wanted, sweating like I was sitting an exam. Awkward and jumpy as my playing was, combined with what he played on the piano, the tune became fuller, richer. And the hell of it was, I found myself fitting words to the tune. At first, they were just words with the right number of syllables to fit but, as we did it again (Pete ignored my protests and told me to 'play it again Sam') the words began to have meaning. Something inside me was capering and clapping but I said nothing to Pete. I wasn't sure of what was going on.

That was the start. He showed me the chords and drove me hard to learn them, ignoring all my whinges and moans, until I could run them together without looking too much at my fingers. Of course, it didn't happen overnight. It was spring before I even had Buddy Holly's early stuff down. I played 'Peggy Sue' all the way through for the first time sitting on the wooden bench in Pete's garden on a Sunday afternoon when the sun hung low in the soft blue sky and the trees at the bottom of the garden were full of chattering birds. There was a faint tang of the sea in the air and you could actually feel the softer, rounder touch of the wind. Summer wasn't far off.

When I'd played the final chord, Pete applauded and then made his Fender emit a long wolf whistle. I stood up and bowed, first to him, then to the birds in the trees and finally turned to face the house. I began my bow but the sight of Ronald Lynwood standing behind the patio glass stopped me half way down. Even from fifteen yards, I could see disapproval in his face. We locked eyes for an instant. It was long enough.

Go ahead and play, his eyes said. *But don't you dare push him off the course I've set.*

He'll do what you want, mine said. *But when he leaves home, you won't be able to run him like you run your office.*

We both knew where we stood.

The school year ran down with the spring and summer, all blues and golds and bright greens. Pete fell in easily with the group I knocked around with. Revision for our O levels went easier than I'd expected. I think it was because when we felt tired of it all, we just picked up the guitars and played. And the more we played, the more I seemed to find words to fit the tunes. Ronald stayed out of our way but

Carol helped us with revision by asking questions. It was when we played the music and she listened, though, that she seemed...well, content I suppose. I began to wonder if she was as unmusical as she was supposed to be.

Then, one Wednesday in May, while Pete was getting a shower and I'd just had a last swim before going home, I came up onto the landing and heard the muted sound of a guitar being strummed. It was so smooth, I assumed it was Pete. When I reached the doorway to his room, I saw Carol sitting on the stool by the piano. She was staring out of the window and swaying gently to her own accompaniment. I just stood in the doorway, astounded. I must've made some sound because she turned and looked at me. In that instant, there was no sign of the alcoholic she was. Her eyes were bright, her colour high and I knew it was down to the fact that she was playing. She looked like Pete.

She leaned the guitar against the piano, still looking at me. She smoothed her oatmeal-coloured slacks and stood up. She stood in front of me and looked at me with steady eyes and a half-smile on her face that made my stomach do a slow cartwheel. I knew my eyes must be out on stalks but I couldn't do anything about it. She placed her right index finger against my lips and raised her eyebrows, her finger still against my lips. I nodded, understanding that she didn't want Pete to know. My mind was full of questions—was this what she was drinking to forget?—but she eased past me and was gone.

I picked up the guitar, the feel of her finger on my lips still there and still making my heart beat fast. When Pete came out of the shower, he assumed it had been me playing all along.

The exams came and went and we enjoyed the carnival atmosphere of the post-exam period. We were allowed to come to school in non-uniform clothes and it was weird seeing all these lads in huge flares and brightly coloured jackets or hooded sweatshirts. And those who could grow them came with sideboards that reached their earlobes and those who couldn't made do with backcombing their hair and parting it in the middle. Barry and Craig Middleton, twins, arrived in the library with matching perms. We really took the piss of out them that afternoon.

Pete's last exam took place two days after my own final exam. I was sitting at home that day, drinking my cup of tea, eating my dinner-time toast, running my fingers over my own thickening sideboards and reading my sister's teenage magazine. At the back of my mind, I was wondering what I was going to do about a job for the summer. The phone rang. I answered it in the hall.

'You busy?' Pete asked and I could hear the excitement in his voice.

'Very. I'm reading about this girl who's fallen in love with her teacher. He's married and she wants this magazine's agony aunt to tell her whether she should wait for him to leave his wife and kids before she tells him she loves him. Oh, by the way, she's nearly fifteen.'

His laughter was more nervous than natural. He obviously had something on his mind. Eventually, he got to it.

'Fancy coming to Spain for the summer?'

'As in the rain stays mainly on the plain, Spain?'

'Right! A friend of my Dad's got a flat or something and he's offered it to Dad for the summer. Dad can't go for the whole summer and Mum doesn't want to go but I think I could persuade her if you say yes. What d'you think?'

I thought it sounded wonderful. I also thought I'd rather not. I thought that Ronald would pull a real lemon-face at the idea of his son and me together on foreign soil. I also doubted Pete could get Carol to act as backstop. The problem was, how did I say all that without getting into an argument? Then inspiration struck.

'Much as I'd love to go to sunny Spain, I can't. For one thing, I don't have the cash. For another, I've got to get some sort of job for the summer.'

He laughed. A real one this time. 'What? Why d'you need a job?'

'The same reason most people do. For money,' I told him, thinking that it would probably end in an argument after all.

'Terry,' he said and his voice had that slow patience people use when they're trying to tell you something so obvious you must've been thick not to see it. I hate that tone of voice; it really gets up my nose. 'Terry, *I've* got all the money we'll need. Enough to get there, to buy food, spend on whatever you like while we're there. Come on, what d'you say?'

Ah well, I supposed it was bound to come to this some time.

'Pete, you might have money. I don't. And the job's not just for money for me. I'm sixteen and my parents have paid my way all those years and it hasn't been easy. I've got two sisters who needed looking after, too. I want a job so they don't have to give me money to keep me off the streets this summer and I want to be able to give *them* some money, too. And if I get a job that pays enough, I'll be able to put some money away for the winter. D'you suppose you can get your head round that? I won't be going to Spain. I'll be working somewhere.' I tried to keep my voice as level as I could but it wasn't easy. Some of the anger must've travelled down the phone because there was a long pause. I thought about hanging up but then he spoke.

'Does this mean we're not mates anymore?' The insecurity in his voice was almost pathetic.

'No, Pete,' I said gently. 'It just means I'm getting a job. That's all.'

'Okay. I'll get one, too.'

This time, I laughed. 'Why?'

'Because you're right. My parents have looked after me, too. It's about time I fended for myself. It'll probably do me good. I might learn something and that's no bad thing. When and where do we start looking?'

We started and finished the next day. We got a job on the Marine Lake across the river in Laketon, the resort area of Seapool. It paid nearly fourteen quid a week, plus fiddles, and we knocked off at seven each night.

We spent that hot, hot summer of '76 getting very tanned if not very rich. I don't think even Spain beat the weather in England that summer. The day we got our O level results, we celebrated passing them all with a drink in

The Eight Bells pub on Seapool Pier. It was the first time I ever saw Pete take a drink.

'I'll have half a lager,' he told me as we went inside. He had the same look in his eyes as he did when he played the piano.

'What's with you? You look like you've found the elixir of youth.'

'Dunno,' he said and smiled. 'Well, maybe it's because the money in my pocket's mine and I earned it and I passed all my exams and my Dad won't nag me and I look fit and feel healthy. Something like that.' He grinned. 'Jesus, I sound like a bloody sixth former already! You getting the ale in or what?'

We sat by the window and looked out across the river, watching the small boats bobbing on the ebbing tide. It was a soothing sight and something in it pulled at me. The sea, I suppose. It's always meant freedom to me. Anyway, we sat and drank and were quiet for a while. Pete got another round in and we talked about all the things teenage lads talk about; girls, sport, music, the telly, even about the strikes at the car factories and the terrorists in Ulster. He still looked as if he'd found the secret of eternal life. I realised I was feeling the same. Maybe it had to do with a sense of being in the right place at the right time with the right people. Even that doesn't cover it all. You probably know what I mean.

We had a couple more halves and then some bloke got up from a chair near the small raised dais in the middle of the room and sat at the piano on the dais. The music up till then had been a tape of that summer's chart hits—Rod Stewart's 'The Killing of Georgie', Dr Hook's 'A little bit more' and 'You to me are everything' by The Real Thing.

This bloke began playing very old tunes, ones I knew only through family parties. He played some sixties stuff but it still seemed a bit odd since most of the people in the bar were not much older than we were, young people out for a good time, dressed in their weekend gear—wide flares and cheesecloth shirts and Adidas T-shirts, pop star haircuts and Farrah Fawcett Majors shaggy cuts, having a drink before hitting the clubs to bop to Abba at the disco and trying to imitate Brotherhood of Man's cheesy dancing. The air in the pub almost reeked of Charlie perfume and Hai Karate aftershave and Ambre Solair suntan lotion. Yet here was this middle-aged bloke in a shiny-elbowed dinner jacket and an elastic dickey-bow banging out tunes from a decade, two decades ago. It just looked and sounded queer. But the thing that really hit me was that Pete could've left the bloke for dead, too. I looked at Pete and saw an odd expression on his face.

'You going to tell me what you just thought of?' I asked.

He looked right round the room before he answered. 'You'll probably want to get a job next summer, too, won't you?'

'Well, it's a long way off but, yeah. Why?'

His small smile got bigger. 'I might have an idea for one. I'm not saying anything yet. I mean it, Terry. So don't ask. Fancy another drink?'

Even in the short time I'd known him, I'd come to realise that, when he said he wouldn't tell me something until he was ready, he meant it. Over the years that didn't change. He always told me eventually and that was good enough. So instead of pushing, I said, 'I'll be carrying you home.'

'Not tonight,' he said lightly and smiled again.

He went to the bar and I watched him, thinking he was right. I'd thought that, his mother being the way she was, he'd be teetotal but that night I realised that Pete must've reckoned that drinking to forget was something he didn't need to do; he hadn't lived long enough to have done or not done anything he might want to forget. I thought that while I sat and listened to the bloke at the piano mangle 'Yesterday' and then I swore at myself for sounding, like Pete had said, a friggin sixth former already.

We left the pub around ten and walked along the promenade to the ferry to catch the last boat to Oxborough. It was one of those nights when you know why God gave you legs. Walking home through summer-warm, summer-quiet nights must be one of life's great pleasures. Sitting on the top deck of a ferryboat crossing a summer-still, dark green river must run it a close second. I could empathise with those people who chose to opt out and live outside of society.

At our house, he got his bike out of the hall and then rode off home. He waved his hand 'tara' and I watched him ride away like he was going home to a house where everything was just fine; where his mother wasn't likely to be drunk, where his father wasn't watching Kung Fu or Kojack or Upstairs and Downstairs repeats, where the conversation would, when Pete arrived home, turn to what happened at work or what did he want for his supper, instead of no conversation at all.

School started again and we began our A levels. I was doing Spanish and French, History and English Lit. Pete was doing Physics and Maths, Music and Biology. We all did the General paper. Pete doing Music caused some problems. Not at home. Ronald realised that his son had passed the stage where he could be moved around like a chess piece. I got the impression that Ronald had hummed and hawed about the Music but Pete put his foot down. No, the problem was the school timetable. Doing Music apparently didn't go with all the other subjects. In other words, the timetable was screwed up.

It also showed me the first of the depressions Pete had warned me about. Sorting the whole thing out took about three weeks. I tried to jolly Pete out of the depression but the more I tried, the deeper it seemed to get. I finally had to go to Telstar since he was the teacher with the onerous task of producing the timetable in the first place.

'D'you know how much work goes into this?' He asked, waving his arm at the huge sheet of paper tacked onto the wall behind his desk. 'I've spent the past two weeks trying to accommodate your friend and the closest I can come is for him to drop Biology. At the minute, he doesn't seem prepared to do that. Maybe you can persuade him?'

Pete hadn't told me about this. He'd apparently decided he was depressed and intended staying that way until he was ready not to be depressed.

I found Pete in the hall, playing the piano. It sounded like a dirge.

'Why the hell didn't you tell me you could give up Biology? You don't have to go moping around like this. What the hell's the matter with you?'

He looked up at me and I suddenly realised that some part of him was enjoying this depression. I wanted to smack his bottom like he was a little kid.

'I'm just indulging in some self-pity. We all do it sometimes. Even you.'

'Yeah but I leave off when the reason for it isn't there anymore. Jesus! You don't even need Biology to do bloody computers!'

'I do!' He slammed his left hand down on the keys and the loud, bass drone made the floor vibrate.

Well, at least it put some life into him.

'Crap! You need three passes. Maths and Physics are the most important and you'll piss both. Music'll be a doddle and you'll pass the General paper. Stop titting about!'

He looked at me and I wondered if this would be the start of the rest of our lives or the end.

'Why don't you piss off and mind your own business?'

Fair enough. Sod him. I went to the library. My last period was a free so I went home early.

He didn't ring me that night and I didn't see him at school the following day. I didn't ring him over the weekend and he didn't ring me.

On the Monday, I was sitting in Telstar's office with the other four lads who were doing Spanish. I was trying to find my place in the set book when Telstar asked me to stay behind at the end. I nodded, wondering what it was about but pretty sure I'd done nothing wrong.

'Your powers of persuasion never fail to amaze me,' Telstar said when the others had left.

'Sorry?'

'Lynwood,' he said. 'Came to see me first thing this morning and said he'd drop Biology. You didn't know?'

The bastard!

'No. I haven't seen him since Thursday. Well, that's okay then.' I left the room fuming. Well, bugger him. He could find his way round the world on his own from now on.

Pete caught up with me at morning break. I was in the toilet and he stood behind me while I washed my hands.

'Telstar tell you?' He asked me, looking at me in the mirror.

I nodded and turned to leave. He put his hand on my shoulder. I shook it off.

'I'm sorry, Terry. I guess I just don't like being told the truth till I'm ready to hear it.'

I thought about just walking out. I was angry he hadn't told me he'd changed his mind, angry that he'd hung onto the self-pity so long. Still, I also knew it was something he was likely to do again and I'd known it was on the cards because he told me that day in the Physics lab.

'You need a smacked bottom. Just like a little kid. Next time, I might just give you one.'

He gave me one of his mother's smiles and that was that. That time.

After that, the autumn went well and easily. Near Christmas, Pete pushed me harder to practise more on the guitar. It was a pain at times because, while I enjoyed playing, I couldn't see the point in banging away at it as if it was going to be my career. Still, I did practise more and, as with most things, the better I became, the more I liked doing it. And I was also finding more words to go with whatever Pete composed on the piano.

It was a Friday night, during the first week of the holidays, when I finally found out why he was so eager for me to practise. It was also the night I found out what it was his mother was drinking to forget.

We'd spent the day in the town centre, shopping, ogling the girls and trying to avoid being blinded by the umbrellas, which were up to ward off the sleet. With the shopping done, we had a cup of tea and a burger in the Burger King over Top Shop and Pete told me he'd see me later at his house. He had to go somewhere. It was sort of a secret but he promised he'd tell me that evening. He also wanted to know if I had the riff from 'Let it Be' down yet. Almost, I told him.

'You're joking!'

It was the only thing I could think of to say. What he'd told me was so ridiculous, so off-the-wall, there just didn't seem anything else to say. Pete just nodded and laughed.

We were sitting in the living room. Outside, the sleet had turned to rain and the wind had picked up. The fire was on and the room was cosily warm. Carol was sitting in her chair, the glass half-full on the table next to her. She hadn't taken so much as a sip since Pete began telling me that he'd arranged for us to be the resident act at The Eight Bells on

Laketon pier. Not just for next summer but for the weekends after New Year and the chance to do more nights during our school holidays. I didn't know about Carol but I could've done with a drink. Or ten.

'It's perfect! We'll get more for two nights than working on the Lake all week. When we're on holiday, we'll get over three times as much. And it'll be good practise!'

I looked at Carol. For help, I suppose, but she just smiled. Ronald was still at work and, as usual, she was more relaxed when he wasn't there. That was another thing; what was Ronald going to say about all this?

So I asked.

A brief flicker of doubt crossed Pete's face but it was gone in an instant. 'What's to say? It won't interfere with school. He'll be okay about it.' He looked at Carol but she turned away. Carol Lynwood knew how likely it was that her husband was going to be okay about this.

'But why?' I asked, not seeing the point. It wasn't as if he needed the money and I wouldn't until the summer and there'd be no problem about getting a job then.

'Because we *can*!' He stared at me and I saw something in his face and heard something in his voice I'd never seen or heard before.

He was telling me that here was something he could do, would enjoy and it would make him feel good. And nothing and nobody was going to get in his way. I was glad to see and hear it but the thought of Ronald kept lurching through my mind like one of those shambling monsters in the films. Then, as if I'd called him with the image, the sound of car wheels on gravel and the sweep of headlights across the window filled the somewhat dark silence that had developed between us.

Oh boy, now it would get good.

'No.'

There was no obvious anger or even emotion in Ronald's voice. The word came out like a dead fish floating to the surface of a lake, somewhere near a nuclear power station perhaps.

'But…' Pete began but Ronald cut him off.

'I will not allow you to hinder your chances at school by this…this pie-in-the-sky idea. Besides, you have to be eighteen to work in pubs. The manager should know better.'

'I won't be serving beer, Dad. I'll be playing piano. The manager sees no problem so—'

'You will not be working in a pub at all. I've said no and I meant it. Now, can we ha—'

Carol interrupted her husband in much the same way he'd interrupted his son. 'Ronald, where's the harm? Peter won't let it interfere with school and it's something he would enjoy.'

Ronald glared at her and I got the impression it was a long, long time since he'd been interrupted by his wife. He didn't like it. Not one bit. I could feel the beginnings of a family row thickening the air in the room. It wasn't a pleasant feeling.

'Enjoy? Enjoyment has nothing to do with what he has to do with his life. You of all people should understand that. I have no intention of discussing this anymore. I want my meal.' He turned to leave the room.

I looked at Pete and saw that same something in his eyes as when he told me about the job. This time, though, it was more defined. It was determination; hard, clear and defiant.

'I'm taking the job,' Pete said in the same tone his father used to say no.

Ronald turned sharply, as if he'd been struck in the back by a pellet. His face clouded over and I imagined it was the same look he'd give to some uppity menial at work. I heard Carol sigh softly. It was the sigh a person makes when they're glad that something has finally reached the 'coming-out' stage. The wind howled and threw a large splatter of rain against the window.

'Peter,' Ronald said, his teeth bared like a dog wondering whether or not to bite. 'I said—'

'I heard what you said. But that's probably because I was listening. You obviously weren't listening to me. I've said it won't interfere with school and it won't. I also said I'm taking the job and I am. I hoped you'd be glad for me but, as usual, I was wrong. It doesn't matter. I'm still taking the job.'

'We'll talk about this later. When…' Ronald glanced at me. It was brief but his wife and son both saw it.

'Don't look at Terry like that. It wasn't his idea and whether he's here or not doesn't make any difference. I'm still taking the job.'

'If you do, you'd better find somewhere else to live,' Ronald said and his face became cloudier. 'If you want to live here, you'll do as you're told.'

'*Ronald!*' Carol's voice was so unlike her usual voice that we all stared at her. She was sitting on the edge of her chair, the glass forgotten on the table. Her eyes flashed. 'Don't you dare say that! Don't you *dare*! This house was bought with my money and Peter is my son as well as yours. If he wants to take this job, he will and you won't threaten him just to get your own way.'

Ronald was furious. It oozed out of him like an oil slick on the Fender. He was almost shaking. For one manic moment, I thought he might start smoking from his ears like a cartoon.

'Wuh...wuh...what right have you to...what right has a *drunk* to tell me how to behave?'

Oh boy.

Pete gasped. So did Carol. A big tear rolled down her cheek and she slapped angrily at it. I just stared at good old Ronald Lynwood. I couldn't believe he'd call his wife that. Not here. Not over something so utterly inconsequential as Pete wanting to play piano in some pub. Not in front of me.

'What did you call her?' Pete asked, looking as if someone had kicked him in the balls.

Good old Ronald laughed. It was hollow, almost maniacal. He looked as if he might have a stroke. With a bit of luck.

'What did you call her?' Pete repeated and took a step forward.

I tensed.

'She's a drunk. An alcoholic. It's not as if you didn't know. Good God, boy, you've had to put her to bed often enough when you've got home!'

'You *bastard*!'

'Peter! Leave it! Please. Just leave it.' Carol was sobbing

now.

'Oh yes! Let's not bring it out into the open. Christ, Carol, you make me sick!'

Pete took the gap between himself and his father in two strides. Ronald was looking at his wife so he didn't see his son coming to take him apart.

I got to Pete in time to link my arm through his cocked elbow as he brought it back to throw the punch. I hauled back on it and he fell against me.

Ronald turned and the disgust drained from his face completely. The part of me that wanted to hit him was pleased to see it replaced by fear.

'You...you'd dare to hit me? Get out of my sight! Get out!'

Pete tensed again and I pulled him back again. 'Take it easy, mate,' I told him. 'Leave it alone. You don't want to hit him. Leave it.'

Carol was hugging herself, sobbing hard, rocking in the chair. Slowly, Pete relaxed and I eased us both out of swinging range. Ronald took a step back and fiddled with his tie. His face was ashen and his eyes were out on stalks. The wind howled again, hard enough to rattle the windows. The gas fire hissed and flared blue.

'I'm going out,' Ronald said and took a deep breath. 'When I get back, I don't want to see you. I don't care where you are but I don't want to see you.'

He left the room and then the house. The sweep of headlights lit the window again as the car roared down the drive.

Pete sat on the couch and put his head in his hands. I

stood between the couch and Carol's chair, wondering if I should go. The cowardly part of me was eager to leave them to it, to go home where my parents would be watching telly or putting up decorations and laughing with my sisters. But the part of me, probably the growing-up part, which felt so bad for Pete and his mother, knew I'd stay until one of them asked me to leave.

'Peter, love,' Carol said between sobs. 'He didn't mean it. He'll've calmed down by the time he gets home. Tomorrow he'll just want to forget it happened.'

Pete raised his head from his hands and looked at her. The anguish on his face was terrible. I moved out of his sightline and sat down on the chair by the window.

'He might but I won't,' he said quietly. 'I won't ever forgive what he said about you.'

'Peter, it's true. I *am* an alcoholic. He was just angry and hit out at me because I sided with you.'

'It doesn't matter. He shouldn't've have used that to get his own back. I hate him. I think I always have.'

'You don't mean that. Peter, say you don't mean that.'

He stood up. 'I'm going for a swim.'

As he left the room, I stood up and made towards the door. Carol hitched in another sobbing breath and called me back. 'Terry, please don't go. Leave him for a while.'

I paused in the doorway and looked at her.

'I'm sorry you were here to hear that. Thank you for stopping him hitting Ronald. That would've been...'

'I know. Anyway, I think I'll go home now.'

'Stay. Please. I want to tell you something. I have to tell it now and I think you're the best person to tell it to.'

I flashed back to Pete in the Physics lab and saw the similarity between mother and son. It was funny; I'd seen the similarity between them before but, now that I thought about it, I'd never seen much similarity between father and son.

'Ronald could've said worse things, you know. Things that would've hurt Peter terribly. And Ronald, too. He chose to use the thing that is most obvious and would cause the least pain. He wanted to hurt somebody and chose to hurt me rather than Peter.' She was looking at me so hard that I found myself blushing. I wasn't sure if it was embarrassment for her or anger against good old Ronald.

'By hurting you, he *did* hurt Pete. You're his mother. He should never've said that.'

She smiled but it was sad. 'Yes, I'm his mother but Ronald isn't his father.'

My mouth dropped open and the strength left my legs so fast that I had to sit on the chair again or I would've fallen on my bum. My head banged and I could feel my pulse loud in my ears.

'Ronald knows of course,' she said and her hand strayed to the glass on the table. Her fingernails clicked on the glass but then a flinty expression crossed her face and she put her hands in her lap. 'I don't mean to embarrass you, Terry but you seem so much more…sensitive than other boys your age. I want to tell you everything. I trust you not to tell Peter. Sometime, in the future, he'll have to know but I think you're wise enough to know when. Can I tell you Terry?'

No! I don't want to know any of this! I'm only seventeen!

Those were the words my mind lined up to say.

So I nodded for her to tell me. She needed to tell somebody and I needed to know. I didn't question that, just knew it was right. She nodded, too, sighed and looked at the fire. I looked out of the window at the rain being blown around in the floodlit driveway. And Carol Lynwood told me her story.

'My father left home when I was fourteen and we never heard from him again. My mother brought me up. We weren't poor but she found it hard to have to work to support us. The divorce affected her badly. It made her very anti-men. She tried to make up for my not having a father by being very strict. She thought a girl needed a strict upbringing. I didn't know any better and, at the time, it was probably true.'

She laughed a little but she still didn't look away from the fire. I looked at her once when she began to speak and was struck by the idea of Carol Lynwood as a teenager not much younger than I was then. It was an odd feeling. Looking at her, it struck me again how beautiful she was. Like Simon and Garfunkel said—how very strange to be seventeen. Jesus, your hormones run riot and the bloody thing between your legs has a life of its own, one that takes absolutely no notice of anything you try to tell it.

'Yes,' she said and nodded. 'It was probably true. The sixties hadn't arrived yet and things were different. Well, she was strict and her bitterness made her instil in me some of that bitterness. How men were the enemy. As I grew older I began to question this. The boys I knew didn't seem to be as bad as she seemed to suggest. I found I *liked* boys. We had rows about it but nothing too serious and she never tried to stop me seeing boys. Besides, I was doing well at school and that pleased her. And music became very important to me.' She looked up at me and smiled.

She went on. 'I really wanted to go to college and study it seriously. My mother seemed happy for me to do that. Then I met Ronald.' She touched her glass again and I thought that she must take a drink but she rejected it again.

'Ronald was charming and very handsome. He bought me flowers and never tried to...you know. I found that nice. He was in the Civil Service. He's three years older than me. He was twenty to my seventeen and seemed very...mature. He met my mother and, although she was cold at first, he charmed her. It wasn't long before she was completely won over. I still wanted to go to college but, when he proposed, I said yes. I explained about my aspirations and, at first, he seemed content for me to go to college. I didn't know till long after that he went to my mother and told her I seemed reluctant to marry him because of what he called 'this music thing'. All I knew was that my mother began to press me about getting married. She seemed to reverse her whole outlook on men. She kept telling me not to look a gift-horse in the mouth, men like Ronald didn't come around every day, I should get him while I could. We had much more serious rows about this and they upset me terribly. They didn't seem to have the same effect on her. It got to the stage where I was turning to Ronald for comfort and he gave it. In the end, I married him. I loved him but I think I married him mostly to escape the rows with my mother. We were married the day after my eighteenth birthday with her blessing.'

She sighed and ran her hand through her hair before she continued.

'The day after our honeymoon in Wales, I started looking through college prospectuses. Ronald asked me what I was doing. He laughed when I told him. He told me not to be silly, I was a married woman now, what did I need with college? I was dumbfounded. I left it for a year, hoping he'd change his mind. You have to remember that this was a good while before Women's Lib started grabbing the headlines. But, by the time the year was over, he was making progress in his job and we had to make our first move. I became the perfect housewife, keeping the house neat and tidy, cooking his meals, supporting his career. I believed we were happy and I suppose we were. The only real problem was my failure to conceive. We both wanted children and took no precautions but I couldn't fall pregnant. I went for tests and I was fertile. Ronald went. He was, too. Still, no children.'

She frowned and I wondered why she'd used two sentences to explain about the fertility tests. Did Ronald go alone? Did he say he went but didn't? After all these years, I supposed there was no point in wondering. Still, I thought Carol must have wondered or else why the frown? And, I was pleased to notice, my hormones had backed off a lot. Hearing how Ronald had stopped her going to college and playing her music had made me angry instead of randy. I was really pleased about that.

'This didn't cause rows since Ronald's career was going

so well. He believed he could become a senior civil servant and children might hold that process back a little. Time went by. I turned twenty-four and Ronald's optimism about his job seemed well-founded. I found, though, that I needed something to occupy my time. He told me to join the local women's groups, the kind that would help his career. And I did. We both joined the Rotary in Liverpool and became quite involved but I still felt I needed more. Finally, I understood I was missing my music. It was so simple, so obvious, I felt stupid. I told Ronald, expecting him to just say 'fine, here's the cheque book.' Instead, he lost his temper. He thought I was 'over all that'. This time, I *did* argue. I put my foot down and it worked. I told him I'd keep house, stay in the right groups, make sure nothing affected his career, but I was getting a piano. I got my piano and things were okay for a while. Then my mother was taken ill. She had a minor heart attack but pneumonia set in. I went to see her and the staff told me that it was only a matter of time. She was still living in Manchester so I had to stay in her house when I wasn't visiting her. I sat beside her bed, waiting for her to die. I spent my twenty fifth birthday in a hospital ward, listening to old women coughing and moaning and my mother talking about the old days with my father.

'I cried, wishing I could do something for her but having no idea what. In the end, when she ran out of breath and memories, I told her, just for something to say, about how well Ronald was doing. She was pleased. I told her I was playing piano again and she was so obviously pleased at this that I told her about the row between Ronald and myself.

Not to gloat, just, oh, maybe so she'd see some humour in it. That was when she told me that she and Ronald had conspired to get me to put away the idea of a musical career and to marry him.'

She ran her hand through her hair again. I was amazed at the calm way she was telling me how her mother and husband had cold-bloodedly plotted to thwart her ambitions. God, what a bastard.

She took a deep breath and continued. 'I was so angry and hurt and...I felt betrayed. I couldn't say anything to her because she was so ill and I could tell by the look in her eyes she was sorry for what she'd done. I just went on to talk about other things. And then it was time to go.

'Ronald rang me every night of the four I was there. When he rang that night, I said nothing of what my mother had told me. I wanted to be very calm when I confronted him. My mother died three days later. I like to think we parted friends. I made all the arrangements and put the house up for sale. She was buried on a Monday. Ronald came up and we went home that night. I faced him with what I knew as soon as we got home.'

She finally took a drink from her glass. Not a big one, just a sip really. There was no trembling in her fingers when she raised the glass to her mouth. She put down the glass and looked at me.

'D'you know what he did? He laughed. He laughed and said that, well it was a long time ago and things had turned out fine. I'd intended to be very cool but the laugh made me go to pieces. I can't remember everything I said but I do remember he told me I should be grateful for everything he'd done for me. The house, the money. And music was such a silly pastime, anyway. Pointless, he called it.

'I left him.

'I couldn't believe how little he understood me after all those years so I left him. I went to America. Peter's told you about my family there, I imagine. In America, I stayed with my aunt, the one whose money paid for this house. She let me work it out of my system without saying anything or offering advice or passing judgement. She had a sixtieth birthday while I was there and I met one of her distant relatives. A second cousin three times removed or something like that. He was kind and considerate and we saw a lot of each other. He was a musician, too but only as a hobby. Still, it gave us another thing in common. I don't need to go into the details, except to say that when he found I was pregnant, he offered to marry me. His family wouldn't hear of it. His family was strict Catholic and I would've been a divorced woman. I left America the week after the pregnancy was confirmed. I returned to Liverpool. I had nowhere else to go.

'Ronald took me back. He nodded when I told him about the pregnancy. That was all. No rows, no outbursts, nothing like that. He just accepted it and, when Peter was born, he treated him as his own. He loved him then and still does. He never used him as a weapon if we argued. I was grateful I suppose but the bitterness never left me. Ronald took to working harder and longer, leaving me alone a lot. I looked after Peter but when he went to school, I took to drinking to fill my time. I gave up the charity groups and stayed home, nursing my bitterness and sadness. I didn't drink a lot but it was regular. And then Peter began showing an interest in music. I was so pleased. I thought that he, at least, would have the opportunity to follow his dream if he had one.

'Ronald was dead-set against it. I still don't understand his dislike of music as something to follow professionally. Still, I'd won one argument over music and I won another over Peter. Ronald backed down but only to the extent of allowing Peter to play piano at home. He refused to allow him to study it at school as much as he might've liked. Peter must've realised how much his father was against it and decided he'd be better served by doing what Ronald wanted as far as school was concerned.

'It was when Peter was very young, very new to his love of music, that I stopped playing piano. A part of me suspected that Ronald would've stopped Peter having *anything* to do with music if I'd continued. Besides, my dream had died a long time ago. Peter had his whole life yet. As far as I know, Peter doesn't remember my playing music at all.'

She stopped talking. I waited a few beats and then stood up and coughed. She looked at me and smiled that smile again.

'Mrs Lynwood—'

'Carol.'

'Carol, I...I think ...'

'Yes, I think a cup of tea would be fine.'

I wasn't thinking about tea. I was thinking about going home but she was clearly not finished yet. I made a cup of tea. In the kitchen, I could see the blurred, blue-tinged silhouette stroking up and down the pool as Pete tried to work off his anguish. I tried not to think about what would happen after I left. I made the tea and took it back into the living room.

Carol was standing in front of the fire. The glass was still on the table by the chair. She'd dabbed her eyes with a tissue and pushed her hair back from her forehead. I gave her the tea and sat down. She began talking again immediately.

'Until tonight I thought it would all turn out. Peter would go to college and do what Ronald wanted. Maybe even enjoy it. And Ronald would let him play his music.'

'Mrs...Carol, Pete will still do that. And he'll still play his music. Don't worry about that. But what about you?'

'What makes you think he'll do what his father wants him to at college? After tonight? He's no real reason to do it now. He stood up to Ronald over this job so why shouldn't he just leave computer studies behind?'

'I just know he won't. The important thing is what will his dad do after tonight? And you?'

I couldn't believe she'd want to stay with Ronald after what had happened. But of course, I was seventeen and cursed like all seventeen-year-olds with the conviction that I knew everything. I didn't know half as much as I thought I did and understood even less.

'Oh, Ronald and I have been together too long now. Peter will probably take a long time to come to terms with what happened but...' She smiled at me in a way that sent the blood rushing to my face. 'You'll help him. You're strong. I'm glad you're his friend. And mine, I hope. I know you won't tell him what I've told you until the time's right and I hope that won't be for a few years yet.'

I just nodded. Something told me she was right.

Pete came in five minutes later and drank a cup of hot chocolate while he dried his hair. I waited for ten minutes, expecting Ronald to return in a screech of gravel and sweep of lights but he didn't. I went home. Even if Ronald came home while Pete was still up, I knew there'd be no repeat of the trouble. I could tell just by how tired Pete looked.

I expected to spend half the night awake, going over and over everything Carol told me. And part of me hoped I would because I didn't want to fall asleep and dream about Carol Lynwood. But I fell asleep almost immediately. When I woke up, I was really grateful that I hadn't dreamed about Carol because one of *those* dreams would've been too much on top of everything else.

I rang Pete in the morning, and had to speak to Ronald. He was very cold, very formal, very short—he'd tell Peter I rang, yes.

Pete didn't ring back, he came down to our house.

I looked at him when I opened the door and he smiled a slow smile and waved his hand in front of his face.

'Can we talk about it later? Like when we're twenty-one? I think it's one of those things, like those embarrassing questions you ask when you're a kid and you're told to wait until you're twenty-one? Okay?'

I grinned and nodded and he came in for soup and a lecture from my Mum about not wearing enough warm clothes in this cold weather. He stayed the night and went home on Sunday morning. I didn't see him till Monday afternoon when we met on Laketon Pier. We gave the manager of The Eight Bells a sample of our wares and made the deal.

We played The Eight Bells each Friday, Saturday and Sunday night from the middle of January and it was great. The first night, though, I was scared to death.

We'd practised every day during the Christmas holiday and I thought I had enough to cope with the two, three-quarter hour sets we'd agreed with Derry, the manager. The tunes didn't bother me because Pete was good enough to carry me if my fingers got sticky. The singing was something else.

The room was big enough to need a mike to reach the corners and would pick up any mistakes I made. And that first night my mouth felt like an outstation of the Sahara. I must've drunk a gallon of lime and lemonade but it didn't seem to make any difference. Pete, the bastard, just laughed at me in the back room behind the bar we used as a dressing room.

'Honest, Terry, you cut me up,' he said as he tuned the two acoustics and two electric guitars. He'd bought me one of each for Christmas. He called them a gift-cum-investment.

'What?' I gulped, squinting at him through watering eyes; gulps of lime and lemonade don't half make your eyes water.

'I've seen you give a dissertation on the rights of schoolkids in front of the whole school. I've seen you play cup finals in front of hundreds of people and you've never batted an eyelid, broke sweat, blushed even. And here you are, panic-stricken at the thought of standing in front of maybe eighty people. Daft!'

'This is different. These people aren't a captive friggin audience, they can stand up and walk out any time they feel like it. It's all right for you, you can play great and this kind of thing gives you a buzz. The thought of singing out there frightens the piss out of me!'

'You'll be fine. Tell you what, we'll start with 'Albatross' to get your fingers working. Then we'll do 'The Boxer'. You do that great.' He patted me on the shoulder and walked out. Fool that I was, I followed him.

While we played 'Albatross' I looked around and got my first lesson in the difference between expectation and reality.

The people there had come mainly to drink and only to listen to us while they waited to be served or when they ran out of conversation.

We went into Simon and Garfunkel's 'The Boxer'. My mouth no longer felt dry and my fingers didn't pack up and by the time we'd finished, I was enjoying it. Pete played piano like a dream and harmonised with me well. I'd never be his equal on the piano but my singing was always going to be better. When I wasn't scared to death, that was. By the end of the night I was looking forward to the next night. It felt good.

By Easter of that year, we were something of a hit. At least in Laketon. The pub was packed every weekend and they were coming to see us rather than just drink. There were a couple of hairy moments when gangs of lads—skinheads in their Doc Martins and punk-rockers with their torn shirts and safety pins in their noses and horrible red-dyed hair—decided to vent their grievances inside the pub instead of out on the pier but the place didn't get smashed up much. Still, Pete and I seemed to get more than our share of attention. Maybe it was because we were stuck up on a little stage in the middle of the room.

Once, the piano took a bit of a beating and Pete got a black eye when some skinhead took a swing at him in passing as he ran across the stage. He took a swing at me but I was just out of reach. I decided to give him a helping hand to the other side by tripping him up. He took off rather gracefully but landed inelegantly on a table and cleared it of glasses. It looked quite funny and tickled Pete so much he had to hold onto the fake pillar in the middle of the stage while he laughed. When he got himself under control, he sat down and played Elton John's 'Saturday night's all right for fighting'. Everybody not involved in the fight thought this was wonderful. The bobbies arrived and sorted it out and the rest of the night went really well. Derry reckoned the takings went up twenty percent and he gave us a fiver bonus each.

That late spring and early summer, I began to write down the words that filled my head whenever Pete played me his latest tune. Mainly because they were driving me round the bend. When they were down on paper, they stopped rolling around my head. Pete's eyes lit up when I showed them to him. He tried them with the tunes and then asked when I was going to start singing them at the pub. I laughed. It was just Pete being Pete.

Except he meant it.

During the summer holidays we worked Tuesdays, Thursdays, Fridays and Sundays and the last three songs of the night were our songs. They went down well. It was the beginning.

That first summer, we both had girlfriends, girls who'd come to the pub for the music and fancied us. Which, after years at a boys-only school was a bit mind-boggling. Pete went out with Kate for the entire summer until she left for a late holiday before going to the LSE. I went out with Christine Samwell for three weeks before she went on holiday and I lost my virginity under the tarpaulin of the number 8 car on the Waltzer one Friday night after we'd finished in the pub. Christine didn't come back to The Eight Bells before the summer ended and she never phoned. And I didn't mind. Not really. Honest.

It was while he was courting Kate and I wasn't courting anybody, that Pete's mum turned up one Friday night to see us play.

The day had been sweltering and Laketon had been packed with day-trippers and holidaymakers and The Eight Bells was jammed with people all day. By the time we went on at half-eight that night, the atmosphere was great and it made us even better than usual. The only problem was that the people in the pub liked us so much, they didn't want to let us offstage at the end. Pete had arranged to meet Kate at the nightclub by the outdoor pool by half-eleven and, for the first time I could remember, he really didn't want to do any encores.

It was also the night that Carol Lynwood decided to come and see what her son and his mate did every weekend.

I spotted Carol sitting by the huge window that looked out on the river just after nine. I told Pete when he left the piano to join me for The Beatles' 'Two of us'.

'What's she doing here?' He craned his neck, trying to see Carol and I could tell by the look on his face—tight lips and slight frown—that he was trying to work out just how drunk she was. Almost to himself, he murmured, 'She'll expect me to go home with her or something, stay around and talk a bit.' He looked at me and I could see in his eyes that what he meant was that she might want to join him when he met Kate and Carol might be a little too drunk for that.

I rolled my eyes. 'Don't get your undies in an uproar, I'll explain to your mum.'

When the crowd finally let us get off stage at twenty to midnight, Pete dashed through the leaving crowd towards Carol, leaving me to get our stuff sorted. I was just unplugging my amp when he came dashing back, holding his jacket over his shoulder. 'I've told her I'm meeting Kate,' he told me. 'And that I'm late and that you'll take her home, okay? Oh, and take the acoustics home, Terry. I've got another tune for you tomorrow afternoon.'

I nodded and raised my eyebrows and he shrugged—he couldn't tell how much Carol had had to drink. Then he was gone. Derry opened up the steel locker in the back room and I put the amps and electric guitars away and declined his usual offer of a pint. I put our acoustics in the soft travelling cases we had and carried one in each hand. I expected Carol to be still sitting by the window, waiting for me but the bar was empty. I wondered if she'd decided to go home after all, possibly disappointed or even hurt that Pete had snubbed her; whatever else Carol was, she wasn't stupid and she'd've known what was on Pete's mind when he'd spoken to her.

'Hello, Terry.'

I turned to my left as I stepped out of the pub and there she was, leaning against the rail of the pier, the blue/white light atop the cupola of The Eight Bells' roof shining down on her, picking out the streaks in her hair and her smile, the folds of her skirt lifting in the soft night breeze. In that light and in that pose, she looked like a younger woman, in her twenties maybe, waiting for her bloke to arrive. My blood seemed to slap gently in my ears like the waves that slapped the pilings supporting the pier.

'Hiya,' I said and wasn't surprised that my voice sounded thick. I told myself it was because I'd been singing for over hour and half and hadn't had my going-home-pint. 'Are you—' I was going to say 'ready' but she cut me off.

'No, I'm not drunk, Terry.'

I shook my head. 'I wasn't going to say that. I—' She cut me off again by the simple expedient of stepping forward and pressing her finger against my lips, the way she'd done when I'd found her playing the guitar.

'It's a lovely night,' she said. 'Come on.'

She walked up the pier, away from the embankment and I followed her. When she reached the telescope that, for a five pence piece, would show you in great detail Oxborough or the crowds on the embankment, Carol paused and touched the barrel and smiled. Then she continued to the end of the pier and leaned against the rail, looking out over the river. I joined her, put the two guitars down on the boardwalk and then I looked at the river, too.

The tide was coming in, slow and heavy, and the lights of the boats moored quarter of a mile offshore bobbed gently, their starboard and port lights flickering with each ripple. The sky had that milky cast that comes after a long, hot summer's day and the stars glowed like pearls. It wasn't silent because the clubs along the promenade behind us had their doors open, trying to coax in some cooler air, and the low thrum of bass could be heard faintly. But it was peaceful and I could feel the adrenaline rush of performing begin to fade and the whole thing—river and stars and lights and the tang of the river—left me feeling almost stoned (Pete and I had shared a joint with Derry one Sunday night so I finally knew what it felt like but it didn't do much for either Pete or me and we'd hadn't bothered since).

'You're a talented man, Terry,' Carol said quietly.

I blinked and turned to face her but she wasn't looking at me, she was still looking at the river. 'No, not really. I'm just a show-off. Anyway, a lot of people can sing.'

She turned head and smiled her lop-sided smile. 'I'm not talking about the singing, Terry. I'm talking about the lyrics.'

'Sorry?' I honestly didn't know what she was talking about and then, as she continued to smile at me, I realised that Carol had never heard the songs we'd written. We practised them in Pete's room but only ever with him on piano and me on acoustic guitar; even the fast-tempo songs.

And we were never that loud in Pete's house in case his dad pulled one of his famous lemon-faces. 'Oh,' I said and shrugged. 'What makes you think I wrote the lyrics?' And this was genuine curiosity.

Something in her smile changed and I was glad the pier's ornamental lights weren't as strong as the pub's roof light because I felt the blood rise in my face. Then she turned back to the river.

'Pete couldn't write those words,' she said. 'Especially the two ballads. Oh, the melodies are lovely but he…' She trailed off, as if looking for the right word. Then she sighed and leaned back from the rail. She leaned down and picked up one of the guitars and then linked her left arm through my right arm. She nodded at the other guitar case and I picked it up. Then she led me to the bench next to the telescope. 'Let's sit down, Terry.'

Her voice was completely different to the one I was used to. There was no hesitancy in it, no hint that this woman ever touched a drop of alcohol. There was a sense of authority in Carol's voice but it wasn't the authority of somebody used to giving orders. It was the voice of a woman who had lived a life, not the voice of a woman who had long ago drowned her life in a bottle. It amazed me, to be honest and not least because I amazed myself that, sixth former or not, I knew I was right in what I was thinking.

And that I was thinking it while her arm was still linked through mine even after we'd sat down and she'd put the guitar she'd carried down on the floor by her feet. I put my guitar down next to it.

'Peter could never write those lyrics,' she said. 'He

doesn't know how to articulate what he feels. It's probably my fault, Ronald's and mine.' She sighed and pulled her arm towards her body, squeezing my arm. 'I'm just glad he can express himself in the music or I think he'd be as unhappy as his mother.'

'Carol…' I paused and then said what had been on my mind since I'd seen her sitting by the window in the pub. 'Where is Ronald?'

'He's away, interviewing people for promotion boards.' She turned to look at me. 'I've wanted to come to see you play since you began but it would've caused too much trouble until now.' She smiled. 'I'm glad I waited.'

I chuckled and it sounded false. 'So am I. If you'd come sooner, you might've been disappointed. Tonight's the best we've been.'

She shook her head slowly, still smiling. 'No, if I'd come sooner, Peter might not have had a date.'

I swallowed and looked away from her, looked at the river, tried to count the number of boats I could see. Waiting out the rush of blood that made my ears thrum and my throat narrow to a pinhole. It didn't help that Carol leaned her head on my shoulder. I was finding it hard to take more than a shallow breath. And, despite counting boats and then pearly stars and finally ripples of incoming tide, I couldn't stop hearing Simon and Garfunkel singing 'Mrs Robinson'.

'I haven't been out at night for so long, I'd forgotten how lovely it is. How lovely it is to just sit and feel the air and smell the river and…talk.' She sighed again. 'Just to talk to somebody who's interested in what I'm saying, what I'm thinking. Somebody who'll tell me what they're thinking.'

Oh Jesus Mary and Joseph.

'Terry, what're you thinking?'

'I...' I had no idea what to say. And then the image of Dustin Hoffman's hand on Anne Bancroft's breast was gone from my mind and I could actually breathe normally and I said, 'If you can stop drinking to...to come here and do this, why can't—'

She pressed her head harder against my shoulder. 'I wish I knew, Terry. I just knew that I wanted to come tonight, to see my son and his friend do what I might've done years ago if...things had been different. It was selfish, I suppose. I wasn't thinking about not making fools of you and Peter, not at the front of my mind anyway. If I'd been my usual self, I'd've been so drunk by now that I wouldn't've been able to make out a note or a word.' She lifted her right hand and wiped at her eyes. Then she snuffled back a sob and lifted her head off my shoulder. I was glad she had but sorry, too.

'So you just...didn't have a drink all day?'

She chuckled and shook her head 'Terry, I'm an alcoholic, I can't *not* have a drink. But I didn't have *as many* drinks. I'm not drunk but I'm a long way from being sober. The thing about my sort of alcoholic is that we can handle it quite well. To a point. It wasn't easy but I managed it. Just.' She turned her head to smile at me again and then reached inside the pocket of the fitted lilac jacket she was wearing. When her hand came out, it was holding an expensive looking hipflask. 'I bought a double vodka and orange in the pub,' she explained. 'And kept my hand on this while I watched you. Even when I applauded, I used one hand and the tabletop instead of both hands. But I didn't open the flask in the pub.' She glanced away from me and looked down at the floor. She nodded once, obviously to herself, then looked at me again. 'But I'm going to open it now, Terry. Okay?'

I nodded. What else could I do?

She took two quick sips from the flask, offered it to me and then, when I shook my head, recapped the flask and put back in her pocket. She put her head back on my shoulder and said, 'Terry, sing me that last ballad, the one about autumn afternoons on the beach.'

'Carol, I—'

She clasped my right hand and squeezed it. 'Please, Terry. I love autumn afternoons and I used to love walking on the beach. Sing it to me.'

I didn't think I could; my heart was beating like a hammer and my throat still felt about the size of a pinhole. But I *wanted* to sing to her. I wanted her to sit next to me while I sang about long walks on the beach while autumn left summer behind and, with it, the bittersweet memory of lost love. I cleared my throat and tried the first word. And sounded like a frog. Carol chuckled again.

'I can't, Carol. Sorry. Perfect pitch isn't in my repertoire.'

She let go of my hand and I felt like the man in my song—alone and wishing for the past, even the very recent past of thirty seconds ago when Carol Lynwood still held my hand.

Carol leaned down and lifted the guitar case up. It was mine and I was obscurely pleased that it wasn't Pete's. She unzipped the case and took the instrument out. 'Okay, Terry, it was in E, wasn't it?'

I swallowed and nodded, stunned at the fact that she'd remembered the song so well. When she strummed the opening chords, it was perfect. I smiled at her and she smiled back and raised her eyebrows. I picked up Pete's case and took out his guitar and rested it on my knee and looked at Carol. She was still smiling. And then I sang her the song and we both played the guitars. Carol played it perfectly, better, really, than her son.

When the song ended, Carol thanked me and then stared out across the river. For five minutes, neither of us spoke and I felt curiously at peace. I could still feel Carol's fingers on my hand and the impression of her head on my shoulder but I didn't have to fight off visions of Dustin Hoffman and his unsatisfactory affair with Mrs Robinson.

'Terry,' Carol finally said. Very softly, almost whispering. 'I miss this.' She waved her free hand to encompass the river, the sky and stars, the night air. 'I miss being some place other than my living room or the garden.' She took a breath through her nose and let it out quickly— a frustrated sound, almost angry. 'And I miss this.' She traced the gold outline of a leaf that ran around the body of my guitar.

I watched her finger on the wood but I felt it on the palm of my hand and I had to close my eyes while I said, 'Why don't you play during the day? When Ronald's at work and we're at school?'

'Because I couldn't stop. Not a second time. It'd be like the drink, Terry,' she told me in that same almost-whisper.

'If I'd had the chance to take drugs, I'd've been a junkie. Instead, I found booze and I'm an alcoholic. If I played at home now, I'd have to play all the time.' She looked at me and I felt my heart break a little at the loss written all over her face and in the shine in her eyes. 'And Peter doesn't need the trouble that would cause.' She smiled sadly and sighed again and then said, 'Listen.'

Carol Lynwood played my guitar then. Just her, her fingers as smooth as silk on the strings, the chords linked like the finest gold chain, the tune she played glittering like that gold. She never once looked at her hands or the guitar or me. She stared out over the pier's rail towards where the river became the bay. She swayed in time with the marvellous music she created and the smile she wore was a heartrending blend of sadness and contentment.

She looked like Pete.

And, just as with her son, I sat there and heard the words to go with the music she created and I wasn't the least surprised to find, when she ran her fingers down the strings to end the music, that I had tears on my cheeks.

'Terry?' She put the guitar down and turned my face towards her. 'What's the matter? Why are you crying?'

I swallowed back some more tears and smiled at her and shook my head. I had to swallow again before I could say, 'Nothing, nothing at all. That was…' I shrugged. 'You know how good that was, Carol. You wrote it after you told me about you and Ronald and about Pete, didn't you?'

She bowed her head and her hair fell in bangs across her forehead. I reached out and lifted her hair and eased it behind her right ear.

'Yes…how did you know? No, never mind. Stupid question. You just did.' She sat up again and said, 'Like I said, Terry, you're a talented man.'

I wanted to tell her that I had words to go with the tune she'd just played but I didn't. Not then. God, there were times later when I wished I hadn't told her at all. Hadn't told her and hadn't sung them to her when I finally did. But life's like that—it's what happens while you're busy making other plans and the path to hell is paved with good intentions, isn't it?

'Time to get me home, Terry,' Carol said and put the guitar back in its case.

'There's a taxi rank at the bottom of Lake Drive,' I told her as I put Pete's guitar back in the case and stood up.

Carol stood up, looked back towards the bay one last time and then turned to me. She leaned forward and kissed me quickly and then began walking down the pier towards the embankment.

I followed her, the brief touch of her lips on mine, barely a peck, hot and soothing, like the salt-bags my Nan used to make for me when I had earache and nothing else worked. When I caught her up, Carol linked her arm in mine again and we walked to the taxi rank without speaking. She thanked me and wished me goodnight when the taxi dropped her off at The Firs and I watched her walk to her front door like a woman who'd never touched a drink in her life, a woman who had just enjoyed a pleasant evening out.

Pete asked me if she got home okay when I saw him the following day. I could only nod because the question set off all sorts of odd feelings in me and one of those was guilt. Carol didn't come to see us play again but it wasn't the last time she and I spent time alone. She phoned me whenever Pete and Kate were going to be out on the Thursday nights when Ronald went to his bridge night at the local Conservative Club in Oxborough. Twice, when Pete and Kate were out during the afternoons, Carol rang me and I went to The Firs.

We talked and I played her the songs Pete and I had written and old rock'n'roll songs from the fifties and early sixties and she barely touched the glass of vodka beside her on the cane table. But she still wouldn't play the guitar in the house or the garden or the pool.

We talked about everything, from Irish politics to whether Leonard Rossiter was better as 'Reggie Perrin' or Rigsby. She talked about what music she liked best and which books she used to like when she used to read. She found out about my family and laughed at the things my sisters said or did and my parents' reaction to them. She told me about her hopes for Peter (she never called him Pete) and how it was those hopes, she believed, that kept her from simply drinking herself into oblivion in as short a time as possible.

'I want to see him happy and…free to choose his own life,' she told me the second afternoon Pete was out with Kate. 'I want to see my grandchildren laughing and, if they want to, playing music.'

We knew so much about each other, it was almost as if we'd known each other all our lives and it filled me with gratitude but guilt, too and I spent long wakeful hours during that summer wondering why. By the time the summer was over, I'd managed to keep that feeling at the back of my mind.

But the trouble with stuff like that at the back of your mind is that it's always there and always eager to come to the front of your mind.

The A-level course seemed to flash by and when we finished our exams, Pete and I got slightly drunk at The Eight Bells. We staggered back to my house, knowing with a kind of certainty I've had only once or twice since, that we'd passed with good grades and we'd both go to Liverpool University.

Ronald had come to terms with the fact that Pete had defied him over the job at The Eight Bells and he was civil enough to me. He expected Pete to still do computer science and Pete was going to do just that. When I asked him why he didn't do music instead, the answer weighed heavily on my mind.

'Because...well, he's my Dad, Terry. I wanted to do it because it seemed so important to him and I found the work easy. The more I did it, the more I liked it. After the row, I thought about telling him to stuff it but I'd gone too far along to pack it in. He told me when I was thirteen and getting really interested in music that if I did computers I could always do music as a hobby or even as my profession but, if it didn't work out, the computers would always be there to fall back on. I know if it was up to him the music would come nowhere but he was right.'

He's my Dad, Terry.

That simple phrase weighed me down at times. Most of the time, I could leave what I knew buried deep in my mind. When he said things like that, though, the knowledge jumped eagerly to the front of my mind and gave me a headache. And, every time that happened, that feeling of guilt I'd buried there jumped to the front of my mind just as eagerly. And, just to round it all off, the tune Carol had played that Friday night on Laketon Pier and the words I'd heard in my head echoed so loudly that, as with Pete's tunes, I had to write them down before they drove me completely round the bloody twist.

Pete's depressions were very few; just one to be honest and I thought that just having a best mate might have solved the problem. But that low made the depression he'd had over the A level timetable seem more like the minor tantrum it probably was.

It was the Sunday before Laketon more or less shut down for the winter, the second weekend in September. On the Friday, Pete had played me seven new tunes that he said he'd written that week. I laughed and told him to try his salesmanship on somebody who didn't know him. But he was serious; he'd written seven tunes in five days. Well, in the early hours of five mornings. And they were all bloody great tunes.

'Need good lyrics, Terry,' he told me around mouthfuls of sausage butty as we sat in his kitchen. 'I just wish I'd finished them on Wednesday instead of this morning. Then you'd've had time to put some words to them and we could've tried them out tonight cos it's the last night we'll have a chance now that we're going to college soon.'

That's how he said it—not in a rush but with hardly a break. And all the time, I could see lumps of masticated sausage moving from one cheek to the other as he ate his butty. It was a combination of what he'd said, how he'd said it and the sight of that chewed sausage that made me laugh.

'Pete, one at a time's plenty you know. I mean, I'll be lucky if I can find some words for two or three anyway.' I shook my head at the look on his face. 'And for God's sake, swallow that bloody sausage!'

He grinned at me, which was worse than watching him chew, and then he finished his butty. He played the tunes to me again and I was a bit stunned to find that I could actually think of decent lyrics for four of the tunes without really trying. I told him this, expecting him to demand I write them down quick so we could practise them for that night. That's the sort of thing Pete did all the time, always expecting me to be as eager as he was. But, this time, Pete nodded and gave me a half-smile and then went back to picking at the strings of his guitar.

I went home to get changed and didn't really think about that half-smile and it only occurred to me later that night, just how quiet Pete had been after I told him I'd come up with four sets of lyrics.

We always got to the pub an hour or so before we went on at half-eight. It gave us a chance to have a natter with Derry and to see what sort of crowd we had in. We had a pretty good repertoire by now and it was versatile enough to suit differing audiences. That Sunday, the people in the bar were mostly mid-twenties, a lot of them couples, maybe not long back from holiday and trying to make the good feeling last a little longer now that they'd had to go back to work. We decided we'd do a lot of Beatles stuff and Neil Diamond and a little Elton John, two Abba songs and then seven of our own after the break.

It was going really well and, every time I glanced at Pete, he seemed as if he were enjoying himself. He certainly played the piano well and even his guitar work came close to mine. And the crowd were really having a good time. We didn't need to talk much onstage because we were that tight with the act so I had no idea just how much off beam I was about Pete.

The day had been one of those England blesses us with sometimes in September. The sun had blazed down all day and the breeze came from the southwest and even after the sun finally dipped beyond the bay, the air felt warm and soft. The fair on the pier usually closed at nine but, because it was the last night of the season and the brilliant weather had brought the crowds onto the pier in force, the Waltzer was still running at twenty past nine, just as we started the last song of our first set. I was halfway through the first verse of 'Crackling Rose', when Pete just unstrapped his guitar, put it on top of the piano and stalked offstage.

There's nothing quite so unintentionally funny as a guitar player and singer carrying on for two bars after it's obvious to everybody else that the song's finished and something else is happening. When I realised that Pete was leaving the bar, I put my guitar down and trotted after him. I glanced at Derry as I got the door and his face was a picture of puzzlement as he lifted the bar top to come with me. I shrugged and pushed open the inner door of the bar. The outer door was open and I could see where Pete had gone.

The Waltzer was slowing down, getting ready to stop but the cars still spun and the occupants still screamed. And the tannoy on its roof was blasting out Boney M's 'Ma Baker' and I suddenly had a terrible feeling that I knew what Pete was up to. Pete really didn't like Boney M. After Sting and The Police, they were probably the group he disliked most of all.

'Terry?' Derry said as he came alongside me. 'What the hell's going on?'

'I hope you and Gordy are on good terms, Derry, cos I think he's going to be really pissed off in a minute.'

Gordy was the foreman on the pier's fair and a pretty decent bloke. But when he saw Pete lean into the little box where the record player was and rip the record off the turntable, I had the feeling that Gordy might not feel too decent for much longer.

But Pete was in a worse state than that.

After yanking the record off the turntable, causing a really horrible feedback whine, Pete threw the switch to send the cars spinning again and then he started to climb up the side of the little kiosk where Gordy sat once the ride had started and all the money was in the little drawer there. Gordy yelled at Pete but Pete was already hanging on to the overhang of the slanted roof of the ride. I was still on the steps leading up to the ride but I knew I'd have to get after Pete because I didn't know what he was going to do next—a sit-down protest or simply jump off the bloody roof? Both seemed entirely possible.

I could walk the Waltzer. That's what the ride-hands called it when you could get on and off the ride while it was moving at top speed. Pete and I had learned how during that summer. It's hard just walking the ride when you're already on the kiosk side of the cars. Getting on from the outside is harder—you have to dodge between the spinning the cars and if you get it wrong, you end up being flipped off the ride like you'd flip a greenfly off your arm. Getting on when the car's are moving at top speed and you're also worried to death that your best mate might just decide to take a header off the roof because he really didn't like Boney M…you can imagine.

It took two complete circuits before I managed to get on between the number 8 and number 9 cars. By then, Pete had clawed his way onto the roof and Gordy was leaning out of his kiosk and screaming at him to get the fuck down. I got to the kiosk and started to climb up to the roof. Gordy grabbed my ankle as reached up for the lip of the brightly painted roof.

'What the bollocks d'you think you're doing, Terry? Bad enough your friggin idiot mate is up there! Get down here!'

I looked down at him. 'Gordy, if I don't get him down, he might just decide to kill himself on your friggin ride! You wanna explain that to Mr Forte?' Then I carried on climbing.

Pete was right in the middle of the roof, where the Tannoy speaker was fixed. He was yanking at the bolt that held it there and his fingers were already bloody. I didn't waste time talking to him. Fortunately, the roof wasn't as canted as the dish of the ride and I got to him without having to worry about falling backwards. I reached past his hand and pulled the cable free from its connection. Then I sat down next to him. He looked at me, frowned, looked at the loose speaker wire, nodded and then sat cross-legged like an American Indian. He stared off into space.

'So,' I said as calmly as my pounding heart would let me. 'You don't like Boney M. I think even Gordy knows that by now. You ready to come down and finish the set?'

Nothing.

I took a deep breath. 'Pete, if it's something specific, tell me, okay? Or is this just another sulk, like with the timetable?'

He turned his head towards me, very slowly. It was like watching a bridge lowering over the docks. When he was looking at me directly, he shook his head once and I knew this wasn't some sulk over Gordy's choice of music. It looked as if his face was about to melt like hot wax, become a running blur. His eyes seemed to be falling back into his skull and, even though I knew he was seeing me, it also looked as if he were looking at something beyond me, too, or looking inside himself at some landscape where he saw nothing good or even normal. His eyes, so far back in his skull, had no life in them, no light, no shimmer where the faint starlight was caught.

And that was it for me. Finishing the set was out of the question. All I had to worry about now was getting Pete down off that friggin roof.

I talked to him and he looked at that interior landscape

and said nothing. I touched his arm and it didn't even make him look at my hand. And, all the time, I could hear Gordy yelling at us and Derry telling him to shut up for Christ's sake, couldn't he see there was something wrong? And Pete stared at me or shifted his head to stare past me. I glanced once down the pier and saw that the last of the customers from the rides were heading down to the embankment. But they were all walking backwards, wanting to get one last look at the two loonies on the roof of the Waltzer, hoping maybe that one or both would bid farewell to the summer by doing swan dives into the fast ebbing river Fender.

'Terry, I'm gonna phone an ambulance, okay?'

I sidled towards the edge of the roof and shook my head at Derry. 'No, mate. I'll get him down. He's…' What was Pete? Depressed didn't seem like a big enough word. 'He's got something on his mind and he's…I'll get him down. Okay?'

Derry shrugged and nodded and went back inside the pub to try to explain to the customers that tonight's entertainment was finished. Unless, of course, they wanted to stand outside and watch the floor show on the roof.

'Pete,' I said and touched his arm again and still got no response. 'Pete, we can't stay here all night, mate. The bobbies'll have us inside quick as blink. What'll I tell your dad?' I smiled at him and thought that something flickered in his eyes, twitched at the corner of his mouth. 'What d'you say, Pete, let's get down and get back to your house?'

Pete blinked and cocked his head to the right. His eyes looked over my shoulder and he ran his tongue round the inside of his left cheek.

'Okay, Pete?'

He looked as if he were giving it serious thought, as if getting down off a fairground ride's roof before the police arrived needed consideration. He sat there, staring over my shoulder and ruminating for a good ten minutes and then he stood up. It was so quick, I nearly fell backwards and rolled off the roof myself. As it was, Pete reached down to me with his left hand and hauled me up as if I weighed little more than a bag of potatoes. It was a bit scary, that strength. Then he walked down the roof as if the roof was the drive leading to The Firs.

I followed him off the roof and watched him walk straight past Gordy, who was telling Pete exactly what an idiot he was. I stopped next to Gordy and apologised.

'He's not well, Gordy. Honest, mate, it's no joke. There's no damage, apart from the speaker wire being pulled from the tannoy.'

Gordy must've seen something in Pete's face or, more probably those distant, lifeless eyes, and he just waved his hand at me. 'Last night, Terry. No problem.' He stopped watching Pete's back and turned to me and smiled. 'Get him well, mate. Derry'll never find another act good as you two.' He winked and clambered back inside the kiosk. I didn't have the heart to tell him we wouldn't be back till the following summer. If then. I followed Pete into the pub.

I packed our gear away while Pete sat in the big bowl cane chair by the window and stared at his hands. I told Derry I'd come back the following night to pick everything up and he said fine. The pub had emptied, more or less, only the die-hards still nursing Skol lager or Watney's draught bitter. Derry phoned a taxi for us and I led Pete down the pier like I used to lead our Erin down it when she was three years old.

It lasted almost a fortnight. Oh, it got better by degrees. *Pete* got better by degrees. But he rarely spoke to me or anybody else during that fortnight and, when he did, it was only to answer simple questions about food. He never touched his piano or guitars. He spent most of his time in the swimming pool and, for the first four days, both Carol and I sat on the cane chairs and watched him to make sure he just didn't go to the bottom and stay there. *That's* how bad it was. Carol said she'd never seen him this bad.

'But,' she said over the rim of her teacup in the kitchen one afternoon while Pete was taking a shower. 'He's never been eighteen before. Has he?'

And I realised that she was right—being a teenager is bad enough but if you're susceptible to depression…well, I only had to look at Pete to see how bad it could get.

The worst thing, though, was that I couldn't stop myself believing part of it was my fault. I'd go home every night and lie in bed and stare at the moon-washed ceiling of my room and tell myself that what had happened with Carol that Friday night on the pier had nothing to do with the way Pete was now. I'd tell myself and tell myself and it didn't friggin work at all. It got to the stage where, by the end of the fortnight, I had to force myself to hum a Boney M tune so I wouldn't hear the tune Carol had played that Friday night, so I'd see Pete sitting on the roof of the Waltzer.

After the two weeks, Pete started to come back a little.

The night before we left for university, Pete rang me just after six and said he wanted to take a walk round Laketon before we left home. I was made up because he sounded a lot more like himself.

We walked round Laketon and I was thinking about all the times I'd crossed the river on the ferry when I was a kid and how simple things had seemed then. It was all changing now. I was technically an adult and that scared me; I was pretty sure I didn't want to be an adult. At least not yet.

It was late September and the sky was cloudless. The sun was going down a dusty yellow over the bay and a light mist was rising off the flat grassland further up the coast. The quality of the light was almost weighty. I liked it. Until Pete asked me the question.

We were sitting on the dunes at the far end of the embankment, where the view is great. You can see Wales, its low coastal hills, purple and green, looking towards Ireland. Makes you feel happy and sad and wistful all at once. Pete sat down on the warm sand and I sat next to him. In that little hollow, with only the sound of the incoming tide to hear, you and your mate could almost think you were the last two people on earth.

Pete broke the quiet with his question.

'D'you think when we die we're just dust? Or do we go on?'

His voice was serious and he wasn't looking at me. He was watching the waves roll in over the wet shore. His forehead was creased. Of course, it's a question that's probably been asked more than any other and I'd always thought the answer had more to do with faith than with proof.

'Heaven, you mean?'

'Or hell. Or something. Just...is there something after? Something else?'

'I don't know. Is this what the last fortnight was about?'

He shrugged. 'I've spent the last five or six years with mathematical theories that can be proven. Even music is a series of logical progressions. That's what science is, I suppose, being able to *prove* something *is*. But life and death or something after isn't. I just wondered if you knew something I didn't?'

'Nope. Not me. I just think if we didn't have at least the hope of something after, everything would seem a bit pointless.'

'*Exactly*! I'd hate to think that when my heart or brain stops, that's it. Trouble is, I've spent so long with provable things I'm finding it hard to have that hope or whatever it is. I'd really prefer to have something more than just hope, though. I don't fancy being alone when I die and not knowing if something comes after.'

I couldn't do anything about the hope he wanted but that little throwaway line about being alone when he died had me worried. He said it so casually, the way you say something you have no doubts about.

'What makes you think you'll be alone when you die? You'll have your family and friends. You'll probably've made some mark in the world, too. All that means you won't be forgotten and I think that might be the point. Leaving a mark in even the little world most of us inhabit should be enough.'

He shook his head. 'There should be more. I *want* there to be more.' He paused and I thought he'd finished. Then he said, very quietly: 'I don't think there'll be family around when I die, anyway.'

He stood up then and walked over the dunes, leaving me sitting on the sand. I wanted to go after him, grab him, shake him until he agreed with me that, yes, he would have people around him at the end, he would have family there. But I didn't. Something about the way he said all those things had frozen any argument I might have had.

He seemed so *sure*.

When I caught him up, I was half-expecting him to have dropped back into the depression, or whatever it was. But he was Pete again, laughing at the fact that he'd found nearly two quid in dropsies, money left behind by the summer's visitors.

And he was more or less back to normal the next day when we left for Liverpool.

Standing up to Ronald about the job in The Eight Bells would never have happened, I don't think, if Pete hadn't worked at the Marine Lake. Working there gave him a sense of his own worth and the money in his pocket was earned by his own sweat. It made him appreciate it more. Going to university taught him other things than just computer science in the same way.

At Liverpool, he learned that he wasn't the only gifted person in the world and neither gifts nor ability were a guarantee of an easy or fair life. The city taught him that there were things over which people didn't always have control and those things could make or break your life in an eye blink.

The initial excitement of being away from home in the big bad world took a fortnight to wear off, during which time we got to know the campus, our timetables and the city. *Then* we found out just how big the difference was between school and college. Nobody was going to stand behind you at college, waggling a big stick, making sure you did the work. If you did it, fine, if you didn't, here's your hat, what's your hurry?

Pete told me one night in a pub near the Adelphi Hotel that he was beginning to wonder if he knew anything about anything. I knew how he felt. I was beginning to wonder if I'd ever spoken French or Spanish in my life. The lecturers all spoke different dialects and they spoke them *fast*.

There were compensations but they were also distractions. There were pubs and clubs and girls and most of the girls seemed more interested in the pubs and clubs than degree courses. As a result, my course was getting away from me at roughly the speed of sound.

I met Judith in the Union bar one wet and windy Tuesday in November. I'd spent the day arguing the merits of a novel by Jesus Santos. All in Spanish. I was tired, dispirited and Pete was stuck in his room, buried under an avalanche of printout paper and loose-leaf binders.

I'd been talking with two lads from the college football team that I'd managed to get a place in and the sense of quiet desperation was gradually lifting. You can't beat talking football with a couple of Scousers. They love their football and know more than most about the game. We spent about fifteen minutes sipping our pints and talking and then they left. They'd been gone about five minutes and I was trying to convince myself I could go to my room and finally sleep when a voice interrupted my reverie.

'Fancy some company?'

The voice was husky and not from Liverpool. At least not exactly from Liverpool. It was almost Scouse but not quite. I turned to see who'd spoken.

She was as tall as me with black hair that glinted almost blue in the muted light of the bar. The eyes were a dark blue and the cheekbones were perfect. It was the type of face that made you wonder why it wasn't adorning some glossy magazine. Even buried under jeans and cableknit pullover, her body looked just as perfect. I'd never seen her in any of my lectures and couldn't understand why she wanted to join me when the place was pretty busy and I must've looked like I was contemplating suicide.

'You're very welcome. Do I know you?'

'Shouldn't think so. Unless you're doing medicine and,' she smiled and her nose wrinkled. 'If it doesn't sound like an insult, you don't look the type.'

I laughed. 'Was it? An insult, I mean? Do I look like they'd bar me if I walked into a hospital in a white coat?'

She laughed this time. It was husky like her voice. I liked it. I liked *her*.

'Oh no! If I'd said you *did* look the type, *that* would've been an insult. I try my best not to look like a medical student. Would you like another drink?'

I shook my head. 'I'd offer to buy you one but I'm that

impoverished student you've read about.'

'Well, I'll buy me one and we can sit and have a long, meaningful conversation about the ridiculously small amount the government thinks is enough for a student grant.'

We sat down but we didn't talk about grants or governments. We talked about ourselves and our courses and it was the most pleasant hour and a half I'd spent, other than playing football, since arriving in the city.

Judith, who preferred to be called Jude, was from a small village called Gayton on the Dee side of the Wirral. She lived with her parents but had taken digs in a house in the Edge Lane area of Liverpool with five other girls. Her father was a solicitor and her mother a QC. Jude told me that, during her rebellious period, she went against family tradition and chose medicine. She smiled while she told me and I got the impression that 'rebellious' had been her parents' light-hearted description of what she'd done.

I told her about me and mine and how my course seemed to be getting away from me. She nodded sagely, telling me the first year was always like that. The same thing had happened to her. She'd spent much of her first year sleeping off the booze she'd drunk. It was during the summer just gone she'd realised how much work she'd missed. She was only here tonight because her roommate Paula was entertaining her latest boyfriend.

'Paula's a lovely girl but her dates should be X-rated. This one will probably go home limping.'

When I'd finished laughing, I said, 'Why don't you live at home?'

'Because I spent the first eighteen years of my life there and I wanted to see what it was like on the wild side.'

There were a lot of questions prompted by that, not least among them was whether her moneyed background was anything like Pete's. But I didn't ask. I asked the other question that puzzled me.

'D'you always ask strange men if they'd like company?'

She gave me a long look I couldn't read and then said, 'Well, I have a confession to make. You aren't really a stranger. Oh God, this is going to sound so juvenile! See, I watch every home game of the college football team. I've watched you all season, trying to work up the nerve to ask you for a drink. I saw you crossing the road by the library tonight as I was leaving. Sorry.'

'For what? I'm more than flattered. D'you want me to walk you home?'

'Yes, but not to the house. When Paula entertains, it tends to be all night. I've a friend in the Halls who puts me up.'

Her friend lived in the same block as Pete and me but she wasn't home yet. I suggested we go to Pete's for a cup of tea while she waited.

When Pete opened his door, he looked like one of those mad scientists. His hair looked like it had been put through a windflow chamber; his jumper was pulled up under his left ear and down to his right shoulder. His face was alive with hectic colour, his eyes sparkling. He just looked at us and then walked back inside.

As always, even when he was up to his eyes in work,

Pete's room looked like the hotel maid had just cleaned it, despite the piles of paper and pencils and pens. Pete couldn't be untidy if he tried.

'This is Jude,' I told him. 'Can we have a cup of tea?'

Since he didn't reply, even to say hello, I made the tea. Jude and I drank ours and waited until he solved whatever problem he had with all that paper. He finally returned to our world as we finished our drinks.

'Right,' he said as that sparkle left his eyes. 'What did you want?'

Jude and I both laughed. 'Tea,' I told him. 'We've had ours. I made you one. It's on the windowsill. Probably cold now.'

He gave us one of his ah-well-you-know-how-it-is-with-me grins and shook Jude's hand.

'This is Jude,' I repeated. 'She's a medical student who watches football so she can chat up strange blokes. Jude, this is Pete Lynwood. He's doing computer science or something equally banal.'

'You didn't actually do that, did you?'

'Yes,' Jude admitted. 'But I had a good reason. I like him.'

The way she said it made me feel warm all over and, for no obvious reason, I began to think I might be able to get a grip of my course after all.

Pete nodded. 'Yeah, that's the trouble. He's so bloody likeable it makes you sick.'

That Friday, neither Pete nor I had any lectures. He came round to my room around half twelve, bundled up in his parka and gloves.

'Come on,' he said cheerfully. 'We're going sightseeing.'

'It's bloody freezing out there. Couldn't we go pub seeing instead? Anyway, what's to see in Liverpool?'

'You're a bloody Philistine, Barrow. This is the birthplace of pop music, for God's sake!'

I knew what he meant, of course. As far as Pete was concerned, The Beatles were the beginning. Anything that came before just paved the way and anything that came later owed everything to them. I didn't agree with that completely but I could understand how he would want to see the places where they'd rocked and rolled all those years ago. When it came to The Beatles and Liverpool, Pete was like an archaeologist and he wanted me to help him dig and dust and make notes.

Oxborough is a big place, a real seaport that suffered like most northern cities from Thatcher's Revolution. Back then, as the seventies were rushing towards the eighties, Liverpool was already suffering.

There was a bloke on my course, Alan Brewer, who had a pet theory. He thought there was oil under the North West coast, from Barrow to Rhyl. He believed the potential for oil was spotted back in '69 and, since then, there'd been a deliberate policy of closing down the area and that his home town of Liverpool had suffered most. His theory was that, if the area was starved of central government aid, the area would fail, the people would move to try to find work, the land would then be cheaper and the population so gobsmacked, they'd have little heart to fight. Then the oil companies could move in and make a killing and the rest of the country (he meant the south) would benefit.

He didn't rant or rave. He told me with that dry humour that's so much part of the people of Merseyside. Alan believed that, sooner or later, probably sooner, the people would realise what was going on and there'd be a backlash.

'Or,' he told me with a terrible kind of patience that made me squirm. 'There'll be another sort of backlash because the ordinary people of this city are getting fed up with being put upon by the authorities.'

This was late '79 and when his prophecy came true two years later, he was only sad for his city.

Pete had lived in Liverpool until he was four and said he couldn't remember much apart from the fact that there had seemed to be less areas which looked like bomb-sites and more ships on the river.

You only had to look around the university campus to see how things were and how sharp the differences were going to be. The area of Toxteth lived cheek by jowl with the Rodney Street. Toxteth was poor, its people hard-pressed but mostly hospitable. Rodney Street was where the private doctors plied their trade. I suppose these dichotomies exist everywhere but it just seemed sharper in Liverpool where life was hard and getting harder.

We spent the afternoon walking round, looking at the places where four ordinary lads played music, drank, farted around. The Cavern was a car park, although another club was built over the cobbled road and its plaque commemorating 'four lads who shook the world', its posters and its signs, never let you forget that this was where it began. I thought the idea of a car park built over the original site might depress Pete but he was philosophical about it.

'I suppose the fact that the rest of the city is falling down or being pulled down makes the fact that a pop group once played here a little inconsequential to the city fathers. The important thing is I've seen it. Can't you feel it?'

'What? The decay, the grit, the smoke?'

'Oh piss off! Cynicism doesn't suit you. The talent, the history, the sense of how they changed everything. God, it's all over the place.'

I looked around the narrow, cobbled street and felt nothing but the same dull regret I felt about the rest of the city. Mathew Street felt more like a graveyard in the cold wind that blew small gritty clouds of dust up from the gutters. A graveyard from where the bodies had been removed but the cold of death still lingered. The thought disturbed me because I wasn't used to such darkly metaphorical thoughts. I looked at Pete but it was obvious he felt nothing like this. His face looked like he was having an epiphany or something. I shivered slightly, just wanting to get away from there, down to the river and gulp some river air. Even if it did smell of diesel and pollution.

'I'll take your word for it. Let's go the river, eh?'

'Okay. Just let me get some writing paper from that shop at the top of the road. You got a pen on you? Got an idea for a tune. I want to get it down before it gets away.'

As he was paying the woman in the shop, he looked down at the glass-topped counter where there was a small display of toys and novelties.

'How much is the harmonica?'

The woman blinked at him, not sure what he meant.

He smiled one of his mother's smiles and pointed. 'The mouth organ?'

'Oh. Er, two quid.'

Pete fished out his money, took the harmonica and we walked down to the Pier Head.

We sat on a bench at the end of the landing stage and Pete blew a run on the instrument to test its fidelity, asked me for my pen and took out the pad he'd bought.

He had that look about him he always got when the music was running inside him so I just sat back on the bench and looked at the Mersey. It was high and grey, under a low and grey sky. I could see a couple of buoys bobbing up and down but only two ships; a ferry crossing to Wallasey and a tanker heading for the Ship Canal. The smell of the river was strong, as it always is in winter and I breathed in deeply, relishing its sharp, tangy smell. Beside me, Pete blew another run of notes and I heard the basic rhythm. He stopped and wrote something on the pad and then played the harmonica again. I found myself tapping my feet. It was a rocker. Pete hadn't written many but this was definitely one. After a few minutes, he turned to me.

'Well?'

'Got a good beat you can dance to. Oi'll give it foive!'

'Yeah yeah, but did you get any words?'

'No. I'd need to hear it on piano or guitar. Preferably piano and you don't have one up here.'

'Yeah,' he agreed with real disappointment and handed my pen back to me. 'Anyway, it's freezing. Let's get back. I want to ring Mum and tell her I won't be home this weekend cos of the dance.'

He stood up and then stood still. He looked out to sea, a strange look on his face.

'What?' I asked.

'Nothing. Come on.'

We played the top of the league that Saturday. It was at home, which made it a bit better—not as far to limp after we finished. Still, I scored two goals and we won and it felt just great, just as it always did. I ached all over but, after a shower, I thought I might manage to shuffle around the dance floor once or twice with Jude.

She called round at half seven and we went to The Grapes first. We called for Pete but he wasn't in. He'd said he was coming so I assumed he'd meet us at the dance. We got to the hall at half eight but there was no sign of him.

'You sure he said he was coming?' Jude asked.

'Yeah. He rang his mum to tell her wouldn't be home. He'll show up. Come on, let's find a table before it fills up.'

We sat to the right of the stage but not so close we'd be deafened by the disco. I'd just got back with our drinks when Pete arrived. He strolled across the floor, looking quite smart for a change. He also looked like a cat that'd got the cream.

'Hiya, Jude,' he said and sat down. 'You getting the ale in or what?' He grinned at me.

'What d'you want? And where've you been? And why d'you look so smug?'

He turned to Jude and winked. 'See what coming here's done to him? He's taking all that thirst for knowledge stuff to heart. I've been busy negotiating and I'll have a pint of mild. All will be revealed.'

Negotiating.

The word reverberated in my mind while I bought the drink. I had a horrible feeling I knew what that look on his face down by the river had been about.

You what?' My voice was strained because I didn't know whether to hit him or laugh like a drain. My mind flashed back to the night he'd told me about The Eight Bells.

'You didn't tell me you were in a band,' Jude said, smiling broadly.

'I'm not,' I told her and waved my hand at her. 'Never mind that. Pete, tell me you're joking.'

'No joke. Straight up. So drink up and let's get our gear.' He grinned at me.

'It didn't occur to you to ask me? You know, just a courtesy since I'm supposed to be joining you on this stage in about three quarters of an hour? Don't you think you should've told me?'

'Why didn't you tell me you played in a band?' Jude wanted to know.

'I don't. Just let me get this sorted out with this idiot. Well? Why didn't you tell me?'

'Because you'd've refused,' he said simply as if it was obvious and thus all the excuse he needed.

The fact that it was true did nothing to help me suppress the anger building inside me. 'Listen, you soft sod, I'm here to do a degree in Modern Languages. Not to play music for the rest of the bloody university. Yes, I'd've said no and I'm saying it now. Forget it. If you want to get up there, fine. I'll watch.'

He just looked at me with his disappointed face and his sad eyes, willing me to change my mind.

Jude touched my hand. 'Terry, why not do it for tonight? It can't hurt. You might even enjoy it. Maybe Pete was wrong to spring it on you but you can't let the bloke who organised it down.'

Pete had told us the bloke who organised it had booked some other band but they'd cried off at dinner time. He'd already agreed with Pete for us to do weekends in exchange for us using the hall's gear (that's what the look on Pete's face had been about down at the river). When he was let down, he got hold of Pete and asked if we could bail him out tonight. Jude was right; the bloke could end up being strung up by his balls.

'Tonight,' I said. 'Forget the rest.'

We went on at half nine. We decided to do what we'd done at The Eight Bells and hoped it would be enough. I barely had time to tune my guitar before it was time to begin. I nodded at Jude as we got on stage. She'd moved one table closer to the stage and smiled at me. The crowd was applauding before we struck the first chord. After that, it just got better.

We finished the first set with 'I saw her standing there' and the reaction we got made me forget how angry I was. I really belted it out and, when it was finished, found I was reluctant to leave the stage. I wasn't sure we could match it in a second set.

I walked off, sweating more than I'd sweated at the game that afternoon and feeling just as good. Pete was talking to some girl at the side of the stage so I went and sat next to Jude.

'Wow,' she said softly as I sat down. 'That was...wow.'

'Panic gets the adrenaline going,' I said and took a sip of the drink she'd bought me.

'But it should've made you jumpy or something. You were almost perfect. Why didn't you tell me you were in a band?'

'Because we're not a band,' Pete said as he sat down. He took a long swallow of his own drink, wiped his mouth with the back of his hand and then said, 'If we were a band, we'd have a drummer. And we need one if this lad is going to rock'n'roll like that. Christ, Terry, where did you get it?'

I shrugged. I didn't know.

'Yeah,' he said as if my shrug explained everything. 'Well, we might have one now.'

'Oh?' I said. There was a set of drums on the stage but I couldn't see anyone near them.

'The girl I was talking to plays. No kidding. She says she's no Ginger Baker but she can keep the beat well enough to keep us tight. What d'you reckon?'

'What the hell, we're busking this anyway.' I grinned. Something inside me was jumping up and down like I'd just scored the winner at Wembley. I wanted to get back up there and play.

After Pete left to talk to the girl, Jude took my hand and smiled at me. It was a knowing smile that made her eyes shine. 'You've found it, haven't you? A passion that makes everything else pale. It's something probably everybody hopes to find but few of us do."

I knew what she meant. I felt it when I was playing football but, even while I was feeling it, part of me knew that it would never last forever because I couldn't play football forever.

'Maybe,' I said. 'I don't know. All I *do* know is that being up there made me feel something I'd only felt after scoring a great goal or winning a cup. It felt good. I don't have any illusions but it's a nice dream to have.'

She smiled again. 'Dreams come true. I think you're wanted.' She pointed to where Pete and the girl were standing near the stage. I kissed Jude lightly on the cheek and went to join them.

The girl was Cheryl Whelan and she could play whatever we wanted.

The songs we had for the second set were mostly oldies from the sixties and wouldn't really last long enough for the whole set. I had an idea what to do to make up the time but decided I wouldn't tell Pete just yet. It was a little of get-my-own-back. Cheryl played a roll and it sounded fine. I looked at her and grinned. Pete sat at the piano and that left me out front. There were three hundred people out there who'd paid good money most of them couldn't afford. I had to say something so I said the first thing that came into my head.

'Hiya you lot!' They shouted 'hiya!' back. 'We've got a new member for the second half. Her name's Cheryl. Say hello Cheryl.' Cheryl leaned towards the little mike above the drums and mumbled hello. The crowd yelled it back. I introduced Pete who stood up and bowed. The crowd yelled 'hiya!' and I felt something surge inside me. It scared me a little but didn't put me off. 'Well, this came as a bit of a shock and we haven't got much of an act but we'll do our best. The songs we've got won't fill the whole hour but Pete wrote some tunes in the break and I found a few words on a beer mat so we'll put them together and see what they sound like. If you've got any requests we're likely to know, just give them to the girl at the table over there.' I pointed at Jude who turned crimson. 'Okay, let's go.'

I turned to Pete to count us in and he looked horrified. I grinned at him; it served him right for working this on me. He'd have to wait till an instrumental break before I told him which of our songs I'd arbitrarily decided on. I felt smug.

We started with 'Band on the run' and after that, it just rolled. Cheryl was brilliant. We found out later she was doing a B.Ed with Music as her major. Our own songs were slower and the crowd seemed glad of the chance to dance a couple of slowies. The requests Jude got ranged from Free to Englebert Humperdink and we played what we could. There were about forty requests for a reprise of 'I saw her standing there' and we did it as the last song. The penultimate one was 'Hey Jude' and, simply because I'd always wanted to dedicate a song, I dedicated it to Jude without pointing her out. It was one of the best nights of my life.

It took us a long time to wind down afterwards and the four of us walked down to the river and sat watching the mist swirl alongside the docks and listened to the lonely hoot of a ship and the dull clang of a buoy bell. We talked in short sentences about how the night had gone. Cheryl didn't seem to feel awkward with us and she told Jude, not me or Pete, that she thought the three original songs we'd done were very special. We went home just as the sun was rising bloody and smoky over the bend in the river down towards the oil terminal.

That night fired more than just the music in me. I found I was actually enjoying the books I was supposed to be reading and the work I had to do. Pete seemed the same, always buried beneath mounds of print-out paper and notes. He tried to explain it to me once and I even understood some of it but most of it went right over my head. When I watched him working, I couldn't help thinking that the sight would have done Ronald's heart good.

Jude and I got know each other as the term drew towards Christmas and we made love on my narrow bed, or the floor or wherever was handy. It was good but I knew she'd set her heart on a career in medicine, preferably research, and that it would take her away for at least a few years. What we had was what we had and we left the future to take care of itself.

Pete and Cheryl had obviously taken a similar shine to each other. I assumed they were doing much the same although every time I went round to Pete's and she was there, they seemed to be trying to outdo each other on the guitars. It was a bit like those duelling banjos in that horrifying film 'Deliverance'.

We practised in the hall every Thursday when we had no lectures. We had a routine we kept to religiously. For an hour, we'd go over the fifteen songs we had down more or less pat and then we'd spend an hour trying more current songs. At the end, Pete would sit at the piano and go through the new tunes he'd composed while Cheryl found the backbeat and I tried to find words to fit them.

Pete seemed to have written an incredible amount of new stuff and they were all rockier than his earlier stuff. I asked him about one day while we were in town eating a Wimpy.

'Muffe a infuss,' he attempted through a mouthful of burger and chips.

'Christ, you're a crude bugger. Didn't anybody tell you not to talk with your mouth full? Finish it and then tell me.'

He did, eating and grinning at the same time which looked just as bad.

'I said the city must be an influence. It's a hard place but the people are great and funny as well as tough. I think it's the irony they find in everything.'

'Oxborough's a seaport but you didn't write like this then.'

'I think I've grown up. It's done something for you, too.'

This confused me; I didn't feel any different than I'd ever done. 'How d'you mean?' I asked.

'Your lyrics are a lot harder.'

'That's cos the tunes are. And faster.'

'But the words must've been in your head to begin with. Walking round this place must've put them there. Anyway, you know I don't like analysing it. I'm just glad it happens.'

And that was the first and only time we ever discussed how what happened with our songs, happened. When we got to Spain and it took off and got silly, we had to try to find some sort of answer for the reporters who wanted to know how we worked but we only told them what amounted to a sketch of who did what, not how it was done.

The only fly in the ointment was that the crowd who came to see us the second week didn't seem to like the stuff we did. We'd spent the whole week before our second gig going over the current top ten—stuff by Elton John and 10CC and The Boomtown Rats—and we couldn't understand why we weren't getting the reaction we got the first time. The three of us trooped off at the end of the first set and sat at the table with Jude. We felt down and dispirited, wondering what we'd done wrong. Jude told us that she'd looked round and seen a lot of the same people who were there the first week so it couldn't be just a change of audience. We were about to go back on stage when a huge bloke with an amazing silver and black beard loomed into sight. He peered down at us from about six and half feet.

'Why d'you change?' This mammoth sounded pained, let down.

I heard Cheryl gulp. I looked at Jude whose eyes were wide. Pete took another swallow of his drink.

'Sorry spud, I'm not with you.' I looked up into eyes of the most startling green I'd ever seen.

'Why aren't yis playin all that good rockin stuff from the goldie oldie days? I brought a load of me mates to hear yis and you play that disco crap.'

'We thought the disco stuff'd be what you listened to on the radio,' I said, wanting to stand up so I wouldn't get a kink in my neck. Then I realised that, even standing up, I'd still be looking up at him.

'Yeah!' He said it with such vehemence that all of us jumped slightly in our seats. 'Right! That's why we wanted the old stuff cos we hear the other crap all day. If we wanted the same stuff we'd go to a club and be deafened by the bloody disco.'

Jude laughed. Pete choked on his drink and I heard Cheryl let out the breath she'd obviously been holding. I just smiled and nodded.

'Tell you what, mate, this half we'll do what we did last week and throw in a couple of our own. Okay?'

'Ace,' said the Jolly-Green-Eyed-Giant and walked away smiling.

'Oldie but goldie days?' Cheryl asked.

'You know,' Pete told her. 'Before John Revolta and Olivia Neutron Bomb.'

'You're never too old, or young apparently, to rock'n'roll,' I said. 'Come on, let's go and give them what they came to hear.'

And that set the pattern for our Saturday nights. We'd play a very few of the current stuff in the first set and then, in the second, we'd do the old stuff and some of our own. The applause we got for them was so good, we were doing ten or more of our own by request. I began to wonder what we might've started.

When we went home at Christmas, we found nothing much had changed. I wasn't sure how I felt about that; it seemed odd that home was the same when I'd been away for three months and so much had happened to me. By the time

I went back, though, I was happy about it. It was nice to know I still had my base, an anchor of sorts.

Pete found the same at home but wished he hadn't. Carol was still drinking, a little more now that he wasn't there. Ronald hadn't changed, still treating his wife with barely-concealed contempt. Pete and his father moved round each other carefully. Pete didn't tell Ronald about us doing the gigs at college and I thought that was right. Peace in the house was more important for the short time they were together.

In May, after my exams, Jude invited me down to her parents' house for her mother's birthday. Seeing her home for the first time was almost *déjà vu*. She'd told me that where she lived was 'rawther posh' and I'd imagined it as something like the lower reaches of Colley Hill at home. I was wrong. Gayton, at least where Jude lived, was even richer than where Pete lived. There were a lot more than just three roads that smelled of money; the whole place reeked of it. Jude's house was at the end of a tree-lined lane and her house was the biggest on that lane. Her house was similar in style to Pete's but bigger and older, more established.

The day we went was one of those May days that seem borrowed from August; very warm and no wind. Walking beneath those trees, I was transported back to my childhood and it took me all my time not to climb the trees in the lane.

After welcoming their daughter with hugs and kisses, Mr and Mrs Mitchell greeted me like a long lost relative and I felt at home immediately. Her father grilled me about what I was doing and what I was going to do. This was a bit difficult since I had no real idea. My own parents thought being an interpreter was the best idea. My Dad reckoned that we were only going to get closer and closer to the rest of Europe as far as the EEC was concerned—'even with Margaret-bloody-Thatcher in charge', he told me—and I was almost convinced but the only thing I was sure about was that I wanted to live in Spain for a while after graduating. Jude's father thought this was a good idea and even offered to give me the names of some people who might be helpful if and when I was ready.

The party went well and I ended up sleeping in one of the numerous guest bedrooms. I woke at half six on the Saturday because the daylight was shining on my face through the window. I got up feeling hungry and light-headed. I had a shower in the en-suite and put on the change of clothes I'd brought. I made the bed and went downstairs, expecting to be the only one up and about and wondering what I could eat without seeming impertinent. Jude and her father were already in the kitchen.

'That's what I like to see,' Mr Mitchell said as I came in. 'Someone who knows that the best time of the day is dawn. Sit down and have something to eat Terry.'

'Yeah,' I said. 'My stomach thinks my throat's been cut.' I said it without thinking and blushed slightly. This was after all, a house big enough to fit my house in its front garden and the Mitchell's were definitely upper-crust. But there was no side to them and Jude's father just laughed. 'I'll just have some tea and toast.'

Jude stood up and offered to do it but I shook my head.

'I suppose you must have some reason to be up this early and I imagine it's got something to do with your dad being up early, too. You carry on and don't mind me. Anybody else want some?'

'I'll have some,' Mr Mitchell said. 'And you're right. I have to be in London later today and Jude is seeing me off. I don't see much of her these days. Perceptive of you to notice.'

'Not really,' I told him. 'I'm very psychic at this time of day.' They both laughed.

When he'd finished his tea and toast, he said goodbye and Jude saw him to the door. When she came back, her eyes were red so I went to the toilet to give her a couple of minutes alone. She was more like herself when I got back.

'What time will your mum be up?'

She smiled. 'She's already left. About half an hour before you got up. She's acting for somebody in Scotland and staying with her sister in Edinburgh while Daddy's away. So,' she said and her smile this time was more knowing. 'Until Monday, we have the place to ourselves. What d'you fancy doing?' The look in her eyes left me in doubt what *she* fancied doing.

Around ten, we came back downstairs and had another cup of tea and drank it out on the patio. The weather was wonderful and the whole situation reminded me of the day I played and sang 'Peggy Sue' for the first time at Pete's. I must've been humming the tune because Jude asked what suggested that song to me. I told her.

'It wasn't that long ago, really but, sometimes, it seems a long, long time.'

'You sound confused. Like you don't know whether to be happy or sad about it.'

I'd been looking at the purple smudges that were the Welsh hills and when she said this I looked at her. Something about the way she was looking at me seemed...well, odd.

'You sound like you want me to lie down on your psychiatrist's couch.' I smiled but, in a way, I hoped she did.

'I can just listen. I don't have to say anything. But I've noticed the way you are with Pete sometimes. Like you're waiting for something to happen. Just once or twice but I noticed.' She smiled at me and touched my fingers. 'Sometimes it's good to talk.'

I realised then that I'd been carrying a load of something round with me for a long time and, while I was prepared to carry it, it felt like the right time to tell somebody. Jude was the right person. She wouldn't go round telling all and sundry anymore than I did. It took about half an hour and the more I told her, the better I felt.

'Doesn't it make you tired?'

'Yes. Yes, it does. Mainly when he's going through one of his down periods. I can't seem to find a way to get him up again. There's really only been a couple of times and he always comes back but I keep expecting him to do something stupid when I'm not there. That and the idea that, as he gets older, the depressions will get deeper and the more likely he'll be to do something really daft. It makes me tired as hell. The worrying thing is that he hasn't had a low for a long time.'

'You think the next one will be a bad one?' I just nodded.

'Well, maybe the doctors are right and he will grow out of it. While he has the band, and Cheryl, he'll have something to occupy his mind. Cheryl's good for him. He'll've told her, won't he?'

I shrugged. 'I don't know. Maybe he doesn't want to put her under pressure. He really likes her and might not want to put that pressure on somebody he likes that much.'

'Except for you?' She looked at me seriously.

'That's different. I chose to be his friend after he told me. Cheryl's already chosen before she knew that part of him. Anyway, I'll be around for a while to help if and when he needs it. Let's have a swim.'

We went back to college on Monday morning.

Pete was fine.

That summer, Pete and I worked at The Eight Bells again so we had our days free. I spent a lot of the time with Jude and Pete spent even more time with Cheryl.

Cheryl. God, she was something special, that girl.

In a rare moment of magnanimity, Ronald had a word with one of his pals on the Rotary or the council or somewhere and fixed Cheryl up as a Playleader with Oxborough Social Services. She spent her days in Lime Park, looking after scores of kids who seemed intent on killing themselves by jumping off those inflatable castles that had suddenly become all the rage. She loved it. Pete helped her most days and I think that's where he finished growing up. Here were kids who, most of them, had little or nothing and not much chance of getting anything. Yet they still played and laughed and hoped. He learned a lot that summer and most of it was taught to him by those kids and by Cheryl.

Cheryl didn't work the pub with us. The room wasn't big enough for a drummer and she was happy to sit with Jude and listen while we worked at getting better. Pete wrote more tunes and, with more time on my hands, I found words to fit most of them.

It was one day while Pete was off at some computer firm doing something for his course and Jude was spending the day with her parents before they jetted off to the Bahamas for three weeks (Jude said she didn't fancy it and I believed it—she's always told me the truth), that Cheryl and I learned just how much we had in common.

She rang me at home from Oxborough station and asked me how I fancied riding the Laketon fair since she had the day off and we'd both been abandoned by our better halves.

We rode every ride on the outdoor and indoor fair, bought candy-floss and toffee apples, giggled at the shapes in the Hall of Mirrors, picked losing numbers on the PickaWin booth. We had the kind of day neither of us had had since we'd been about thirteen.

We had a pint and a Ploughman's lunch in The Eight Bells and listened to the tapes Derry played on his little sound system.

'I suppose you're wondering why I got you here?' Cheryl asked between mouthfuls of food. I looked up and raised my eyebrows. 'Come on, Ted,' she said. Cheryl is the only one who ever called me Ted. 'You may not be a Scouser but I know a sensitive bloke when I meet one. There aren't that many of them.'

'I imagined it must have something to do with Pete.'

She nodded. 'And me. You're his best mate and you should know me as well as I know you.'

'Pardon?'

She smiled. 'For the first five days Pete and I were going together, his main topic of conversation was you. He loves the bones of you. So does his mum and so do I. It's about time you knew about me. Where I'm from, where I want to go, what I want to do. You know, all that serious stuff nobody ever talks about except in their sleep or when they're pissed. What d'you say, Ted, want to find out what weird bugger your mate's tied up with?'

I smiled this time. 'Yeah. If I'm trusting you with the backbeat, I might as well trust you with him.'

Cheryl was six months younger than Pete, born and brought up in Liverpool, the only daughter of an unmarried mother.

'I think my Dad must've been one of the first free-love hippies. He met my Mum, took her out for a drink, took her home, took her virginity and left. Vanished off the face of the earth, apparently. That's what my Mum told me if I asked. I didn't push it because she seemed to have come to terms with it. She said she tried to find him but I wonder. I think she reckoned we were better off without him. Maybe she's right.'

Her mum got a council flat, one flight up in a crescent-shaped block of flats near the centre of town. At first, it wasn't so bad to live there; the neighbours were good and the area not as run down as it became later. Later, it got rougher.

'The only good thing about it,' Cheryl told me that afternoon. 'Is that I grew up in it. It didn't occur to me just how rough it was because I was living it. Mum stayed because they wouldn't move her and, even with the jobs she took, she couldn't afford to move. It was hard, Ted, but it was home.'

Cheryl's mum worked as a barmaid three nights a week round the corner from the flat and five days a week in a factory which made milk bottle holders and those little cardboard drums for pepper and salt and stuff. Her grandmother looked after Cheryl when her mum worked in the pub. During the day, Cheryl's aunts looked after her. All her family was very bright and Cheryl believed that whatever brains she had came from being with them all the time.

'Other kids played with dolls and drew pictures. I learned about history and how to read and write. I'm probably the original hot-house child. You know, like in the States where they use those flash-cards and stuff. I loved it. Still do. I can't stand sitting around and doing bugger all. Give me a book, a Cornflakes packet, the back of a sauce bottle to read. But it was my Auntie May who got me into music.' She laughed fondly and shook her blonde hair out of her eyes. 'Auntie May and her old wind-up gramophone. She had more packets of steel needles than Rushworths, I think. She played records so old, I thought the crackles were part of the arrangement.' Her brown eyes gleamed with the memory.

Auntie May took Cheryl down to the pub where her mother worked and sneaked her in through the side door.

She sat her down in the corner by the fire and, when Cheryl's mum was finished, the landlord would lock the door and Auntie May would teach Cheryl the piano.

'It was okay but it didn't really fire me up. Then, one Easter or Orange Day or something, the landlord booked a trio for the night. There was an accordion and a banjo and this little bloke with a huge moustache playing a tiny set of drums. I was gone. Completely gone. When the pub closed and the trio were having a last pint, I pestered the life out of the poor little bugger to let me have a go. I'm pretty good at that, Ted,' she said and winked. I believed her. 'Anyway, that was it. I had to have a set of drums. Caused a few rows with the rest of the floor but we worked out a compromise. Most of the neighbours were in the same boat as us so it suited everyone if I babysat their kids and the mothers and the few fathers who were there turned a deaf ear to my drumming. I loved it. Not just the drumming but the kids, too. I loved them and they loved me.'

At school, Cheryl breezed through everything. There were ten O levels and four A levels with distinctions in Music and History. She loved school and the teachers loved her.

'What I wanted to be was easy. I wanted to teach kids and to teach them Music. 'Course, you have to get to college to do that but by the time I was in the sixth form, the factory was running down and Mum was only working three days. Money was tight. I just didn't see any way of me getting to university. I began to look around for some office job that would give me some free time to help in a kids' home or somewhere. Sort of a peripatetic music teacher for expenses at a place for handicapped kids. I don't know, anything to keep me in touch. Then something happened which makes me think there might be a God after all.'

The something was what usually passes for a joke in Liverpool. You know that old Cilla Black song about the mucky kid? Well, the verse about Littlewoods providing the cash is what they say when they talk about what they'd like to do or buy or where they'd like to go. It happened to Cheryl's youngest auntie. It wasn't a huge, front-page-of-the-*Mirror* win but it was enough for the auntie to buy a four bedroomed house in Aintree where they all could live and to help Cheryl's mum with the grant, to send Cheryl to college.

'I was lucky. Liverpool offered me a place so I could live at home.'

Luck had nothing to do with it; Cheryl was one of the brightest people I've known and Liverpool was lucky to get her.

'So, that's how come I'm here and how come you and soft lad got your drummer. I'm still going to be a teacher, Ted. I don't want you to run away with the idea that I'll give it all up for music and the free electric band.' She looked at me with the kind of look I recognised immediately. It was the one my Dad used when I or my sisters put a foot over the line he'd drawn.

'You won't get an argument from me, kid.'

'Good,' she said but smiled. 'D'you think you can get it through to that soft mate of yours?'

'I've learned that the best way with Pete is to nod and agree and get on with your own life.'

She laughed. 'Ah, but what if you love him and worry for him? He gets under your skin. You know that, Ted.'

'True. Still, you're a big girl, Cheryl. I'm sure you'll manage.' I took a sip of my drink. 'Why d'you worry for him, love?'

She frowned, a cloud hiding the sun. 'Because I know him like you do.'

'You know about his lows, then? He hasn't had one since we've been at Liverpool.'

'He told me the first night we went out. The same night he told me about how he tried to get you to kill him at school. Did you really wind the punch up from your feet?' She smiled and the sun nearly came out.

'Yeah but I was younger then.'

'Oh aye. You sure you're not a Scouser? Trying to decapitate somebody is very Liverpool.' She smiled and this time the sun came out and stayed out.

We both laughed and finished our drinks. The fact that Pete had told her about himself told me everything, really. The lad was stricken and, just by watching the sun go out of and come back to her face told me Cheryl felt the same. I was glad but a little jealous, too. It's hard to accept that your best mate has found something, or somebody else to turn to, to talk to, to find things in common with. It leaves a little hollow place in your heart where some cold wind can blow. Still, it had to happen and Cheryl was the best.

'How bad does he get? When he's down?' Cheryl asked quietly.

I told her about the night Pete had climbed on top of the Waltzer in Laketon and how long that awful depression had lasted. But I didn't tell her what he'd said to me on the sandunes, about being alone when he died. I didn't tell her because I knew that she loved him and that he loved her and that they were going to spend the rest of their lives together so Pete's quiet but firm assertion meant nothing.

'But,' I said when I'd finished and she didn't say anything. 'Since then, he hasn't been anything but happy.' I smiled at her and she frowned. 'You must know really good jokes, Cheryl. Or something.' I raised my eyebrows at her and she gave me a dig in the arm. 'Anyway, I sometimes wonder if the doctors were right about him growing out of it.'

'Mmm,' she said but looked as doubtful as I felt. 'His home life doesn't help, does it? His mum being the way she is and his dad trying to live his life through him?'

'He told you all that?'

'Not all of it. He told me Carol drank but it was obvious, at least to me, she's an alcoholic. I lived in a place where it's a common virus and easy to catch. As for his dad, well...see, Ronald loves him. You can see it in his eyes whenever he looks at him. *My son.* You know? It's just that they crossgrain each other dead easy. It's a shame.' She looked out of the big window and frowned again. 'I wish Pete could appreciate having a real dad. I never knew mine but I still miss him, sometimes, just the same.'

Oh yes, Cheryl was special. But she didn't know what I knew and I didn't think it mattered. What she'd said about fathers was right. And just how many visits to The Firs did it take her to come to these conclusions? Not many, I bet.

'What d'you think, Ted? Once it's all done and dusted

and he's done what his dad wants him to do, think he'll settle down? Think he'll put away childish things? Settle for being just ordinary weird like the rest of us?' Her smile was there but her eyes were shadowed.

'I suppose that depends on who he's with when it's all done and dusted.'

'Can't fool you, can I, Ted?' She shrugged. 'I don't know. I love him but he…he seems so gung-ho about the music and making his life from it and his enthusiasms are so bloody tiring. I try to tell him I'm going to be a teacher and he just nods and smiles and then starts talking about the band. Why doesn't he see the way I am? I bet he hasn't even talked about the band with you, has he?'

'No but that's par for the course. Like I said, just smile and nod and agree and do what you want to do. It's always worked for me.'

'But it seems so important for him to make it with the music.' She shook her head and shrugged again. 'Ah well, Brian Epstein doesn't live here anymore, does he? And while Pete's waiting for him, he'll do his degree and maybe he'll settle for playing as a way to make pocket money. In the meantime, we can keep his feet on the ground, can't we?'

I don't know is what I thought but what I said was, 'We can try.'

'But I won't kill his dreams, Ted. His father seems intent on that for all he loves him. If we really can't budge him, I'll help him all I can. I'd hate to go wherever we go when we die feeling like I let him down. He's been let down enough. In the meantime, I'll love him the best way I can.'

On a day when the weather was more like winter than summer, one of those days England throws at us in August, when the wind comes out of the east and the rain feels colder than the snow in January, I borrowed my Dad's car and drove up to see if Pete fancied going to Rhyl Suncentre.

I got to The Firs around half ten. I hadn't phoned because it was Thursday and that was the day Cheryl was off work. Thursday was the day she and Pete sat in his room, him at the piano and her at the second hand set of drums they'd bought, and worked out arrangements. I rang the bell and stood under the porch eaves, feeling good despite the weather.

No answer. Strange.

I rang again. Still no answer. Very strange.

I walked round the side in case they were in the pool. The gate to the garden was open as usual but there was no sign of them in the poolhouse. I knocked on the kitchen window and the door and got no answer. I tried the handle and the door opened.

'Anybody home?' I called out, going into the kitchen. I called again and there was still no answer but the kettle was beginning to boil. *Somebody* was at home.

I went into the living room and Carol was sitting in her chair and staring into the fire that was lit against the unseasonable chill. She didn't even turn when I said her name. I began to be worried.

She was drunk but not paralytic. Her glass was only half empty and there was no sign of the bottle. I squatted down in front of her and took her hand in both of mine.

'Carol? What's to do?'

'Hello Terry. To do? Oh, nothing much. My husband finally lost his temper enough to hit me. And he did it in front of Peter and Cheryl. Apart from that, everything's fine. How are you?'

Her voice was flat and her face showed no emotion at all. I didn't think this was the result of the booze, more a case of her finally running out of emotion.

'Tell you what, I'll make some tea and you can tell me what happened.'

When I brought the tea back, she was sitting straighter in the chair and the glass was pushed away from her. It occurred to me that, in moments of real crisis, she didn't do what you might expect an alcoholic to do; she didn't cling to the glass like it was a straw and she was drowning. If she could be strong enough to do that then, why couldn't she do it in the quiet moments? Or perhaps it was because they *were* quiet moments. And what did I know, anyway?

'Peter and Cheryl have gone,' she said as I put the cup on the small table. 'I don't know where.'

I sat on the couch and let her talk.

'Cheryl came down yesterday evening to go to the pictures. Ronald wasn't home and everything was fine when they came back. Right up to the time Ronald told Peter Cheryl should be going home. It was half past eleven. Peter must've sensed what sort of mood Ronald was in and he didn't argue. He just asked to borrow the car to run her home. Ronald refused. He said the car had been acting up and he wanted to make sure it wasn't left half way to Liverpool if it broke down, he needed it. So Peter said Cheryl would have to stay because the last train had gone and a taxi wouldn't take her that far and come back empty. Ronald realised he'd backed himself into a corner. He began to get angry.'

She took a sip of her tea and lit a cigarette. When the first puff of smoke had dissipated into the air, she told me the rest.

'I wasn't drunk. Not really. I asked him not to shout and why couldn't Cheryl stay? We had plenty of room. Cheryl tried to calm things down, saying she'd get a taxi, she'd pay the driver over the odds for the fare. I told her not to be silly, she was staying. Ronald looked at me like I'd just told him I was selling the house to go traipsing round the world. I really don't know what made him so angry. Before Peter came home, we'd even been talking to each other. And it's not as if he doesn't like Cheryl. Once he realised she's serious about her career, he warmed to her. I don't know why he changed so suddenly.'

'Did Pete argue? Did he—'

'No, Terry, he didn't argue or hit out. I must've been drunker than I thought. Or less. *I* did all the arguing, the shouting. Oh, it happened so fast. I can remember Cheryl gasping as if it had been her who'd been slapped. Ronald has never raised his hand to me. Never. I slapped him back.' She looked at me as if expecting me to condemn her. Yeah, right. 'I slapped him back and his eyes blazed and he hit me again. Not as hard but this time I cried. I think because of what I saw in his eyes. He hated me at that moment. I'd seen contempt before but never hate. Peter growled. I think that was worse than seeing Ronald's eyes. It was such an animal sound. I screamed.' She looked at me again and a slow, sad smile crossed her face. 'I think that's why people live in detached houses, you know. They can yell and scream and not worry about the neighbours. My scream made Peter look at me. It gave Cheryl the chance to get between my son and my husband. Ronald glared at me and then left the room. I think he went to bed but I'm not sure. Peter and Cheryl and I stayed here all night. When it got light enough, they left and I've been drinking ever since.' She stubbed the cigarette and lit another.

'Carol,' I began but she went on talking.

'It's all over now, you know. My family, everything. It's all gone. All because I can't stop drinking. I've lost everything. I'll die with nobody to mourn me. All alone with my hands wrapped round a vodka bottle.'

She cried then. Big tears that came in time with deep, wracking sobs. She shook with each sob. I held her hand until she ran out of tears. Outside, the rain had stopped and the sky was lightening. The gas fire hissed softly. It reminded me of the night she told me everything. When she was only making soft sounds in her throat, I started to ease myself back onto the couch but she kept hold of my hand and squeezed and then lowered her cheek onto the back of my hand.

'Carol, none of this is your fault.' I said past the lump in my throat, the lump that had risen up at the closeness of her, the feel of her face on my hand and the almost desperate grip she had on it.

'Yes it is. If I hadn't been drunk. If I—'

'Carol, you probably wouldn't've started drinking if not for the way Ronald treated you. Ronald and your mother conspired against you, betrayed you. When you were married, he treated you like a child who didn't know what was best for her. He acted like this was the Victorian age. None of this is your fault. D'you think Pete isn't going to come home? If for no other reason, he'll be home to make sure his father doesn't hit his mother again. But he'll be home because he loves you. He'll be back today, probably soon. And you won't die for a long time, yet, Carol.'

She gulped one last ragged, deep breath and stubbed out her cigarette but kept one hand wrapped around mine. 'Ronald will make life miserable. I don't mind for myself but Peter shouldn't have to come home to a house that isn't a home anymore.'

'I think you'll find Ronald will steer clear of Pete. He still wants Pete to do too much yet for him to force him out.'

'Computers, you mean?' She laughed, a cynical edge to it. 'Peter will give all that up for music now.'

'If Ronald took the time to find out, he'd know that Pete is as intent on passing the course as Ronald is on having him pass. From what I've learned, he's likely to finish with distinctions. Ronald might've forced him into it but Pete's doing it for himself now. Don't worry about that. And remember that none of this is your fault. D'you want another cup of tea?' I hoped she'd say yes so I could move away from her. Because I was having a terrible time trying to stop myself holding her. *Hugging* her. It wouldn't have been a consoling hug, I knew that.

She lifted her face and gave me one of her best smiles. And I almost gasped as heat just seemed to envelop my entire body, especially my groin. It was hard to breathe properly. Carol squeezed my hand harder and I knew I had to get away from her. I pulled my hand out of her grip and stood up on legs that felt like overstretched elastic bands. I blinked and silver and black fish-shapes danced across my vision and I had to swallow hard.

'Yes,' Carol said.

Her voice seemed to come to me through layers of cotton wool and I looked at her. She was still sitting on the edge of the chair and her hands were linked between her knees, the loose folds of her skirt somehow the most erotic thing I'd ever seen in my life, the front of her cream blouse belled open, the rounded tops of her breasts a slightly darker cream. I blinked again and nodded and stumbled out into the kitchen to make the tea. I stared out of the window while I stirred the tea in the mugs, trying to compose myself, waiting until the heat that had enveloped my body faded, until the hardness between my legs faded. Waiting to see if the Terry Barrow who had come through the kitchen door less than a half an hour ago would come back so he could go and sit in the same room with his best mate's mother and be her friend instead of a bloke who wanted her so much it was almost giving him a stroke.

When I went back into the living room, Carol wasn't there and I was grateful and disappointed in equal parts. I put the tea on the table by her chair and saw that the glass had gone but her packet of Sovereign cigarettes were still there, next to the gold Ronson Ladies lighter. I sat on the couch and stared at the fire and wondered where she'd gone. And what was she doing? And that was when it suddenly hit me that Carol was probably as embarrassed as I was about what had happened. Oh shit, embarrassed nothing, the feeling was guilt and, on top of everything else, could that guilt be enough to send her out of this room and into another room where she could smash the glass and use the wicked edges left behind to do something really silly?

I nearly fell over getting up from the couch and trying to get round it in one movement. I got to the door and was already yelling her name.

'Carol! Carol, where the hell are you?' I stood at the bottom of the stairs, torn between dashing up them and looking in the other downstairs rooms first. And in that pause, I heard the sound of the guitar. It came from upstairs and I recognised the tune immediately. I let out a sigh and leaned against the newel post and closed my eyes. 'Carol, your tea's in the living room.'

'Bring it up, Terry. And my cigarettes. Please.'

Oh no, not on your life, Terry, not on your life.

I was still actually shaking my head when I came out of the living room with both mugs and Carol's cigarettes and lighter in my hands.

She was in the guest bedroom at the back of the house, overlooking the garden. I'd never really been in the room, except to get a blanket when I'd stayed over a few times. I always stayed in the spare room next to Pete's because it had a connecting door to his shower. Now, I could see that this room was almost as big as Pete's room but the bed was a double and the fitted wardrobes had no mirrors. Carol was sitting on the small chair by the window, playing the tune she'd written and swaying gently while she watched the scudding clouds outside. The breaking sun sent long shafts of pale gold onto her hair and arms, almost spotlighting her.

I put her mug of tea on the windowsill, intending to take mine to the other small chair behind the door. But as I turned from the window, the words I'd written to go with Carol's tune filled my mind and, I swear it even now, they came out of my mouth of their own accord. Even as I sang the first two words, I could feel how wide my eyes were and the frown on my forehead.

There was an ugly discord as Carol's fingers stuttered on the strings. 'Terry?' Her voice was hushed, as if we were in church.

I took a huge breath and sucked in my lips as if I could swallow the words, make it so they'd never come out in the first place. I shook my head without looking at her. I kept my eyes on the sky as the clouds broke into tatters and wispy pennants.

'Terry, sing it for me,' Carol said, her voice still hushed. 'No, wait a minute.' She left the guitar on the chair and left the room.

I should've left then. I should've escaped. Even as I stood and stared out of the window, I knew it. But I didn't. Why? Because I wanted to sing the song I'd written for Carol *to* Carol. I'd sung every lyric I'd ever written except for that one and I wanted to hear it set against the sound of Carol playing the guitar. I wanted to sing it because it was part of me, like all my lyrics were. And I was used to setting them free.

She came back with another acoustic guitar and handed it to me. I took it and finally looked at her as she sat down in the chair again. She smiled at me and she looked so young, just as she had that night on Laketon Pier when she'd played me the tune she'd written.

'Please, Terry.'

I nodded and sat on the edge of the bed with the guitar on my knee. I looked at her and counted us in and I sang Carol's song to Carol and she accompanied me on the other guitar and it sounded…ah, God, it was perfect.

The last echo of the final run down the open strings faded and I lifted my eyes from my fingers and looked at Carol. She was smiling at me but her eyes were filled with tears. I wasn't crying but there was a lump in my throat.

Carol was still smiling when she put her guitar down on the thick carpet and stood up. She took a step towards me and leaned down. She placed her hands on my shoulders and kissed me. My head boomed and the lump in my throat suddenly dropped down between my legs. My eyes were open and so were Carol's and she kept her eyes open while her left hand dropped from my shoulder and traced down the inside of my leg, coming to rest against the hardness there. She made a low sound in her throat, one I'd heard so many times in Jude's throat and I made a sound of my own. Carol's hand began to move towards my zip and she leaned into me, pushing me back until I was lying on the bed.

I closed my eyes and put my arm round her and pulled her down on top of me, knowing that we both wanted this, that I wasn't imagining it, that, perhaps, this had been coming since that night she'd told me about her life and Ronald and Pete. Carol's tongue was in my mouth and I could taste the sharpness of the vodka she'd been drinking all night and smell the light, flowery perfume she wore, mixed with the faint smoky smell of the cigarette she'd smoked down in the living room. She had her fingers inside my underpants and my hand was inside her knickers where it had moved from inside her bra and the rigid nipple that I'd been rolling between my thumb and forefinger.

'Oh, Terry,' Carol murmured against my throat and her hand inside my underpants gripped me so hard I gasped and opened my eyes.

And I saw Jude's face hovering just below the ceiling. I saw her face and it was the face I'd seen the first time we'd slept together, the first time we both came together in my narrow bed at college in Liverpool.

And that was enough. Thank God, that was enough.

I slid my fingers, my moist fingers, from between Carol's legs and gripped her waist gently. I used my other hand to pull her hand out of my jeans and pushed her gently off me. I squirmed backwards until I had my back against the headboard and pulled my zip up. I didn't look at her or say anything and she didn't speak. When I looked at her again, she was back in the chair, her head in her hands and crying again.

'Carol…' I didn't know what else to say.

She nodded and snuffled back tears and murmured, 'I'm so sorry…' She took a long breath and, as she let it out, she raised her head and looked at me. 'No, I'm not sorry, Terry.'

And I smiled at her, tears in my own eyes. 'Carol…' I took a breath of my own, struggling for the words. 'Carol, I love you. But…this…what nearly happened wasn't real. Not for you or me.' I looked at her, I think, for help. And I got it.

She smiled at me and nodded. 'We...'

'Don't say we can forget it,' she said, still smiling. 'Because I won't. Because I don't want to. I wanted it, I wanted *you*. If...if it *had* happened, I'd've enjoyed it and I would've wanted it to happen again. But I'm glad you stopped.' She wiped her eyes and picked up the guitar. 'I have the song. If we'd made love, however many times, it wouldn't've lasted forever. But the song will. I will always have the song. Sing it for me again, Terry.'

So I sang her the song again. She didn't play this time, she just sat in the chair and watched me, her eyes fixed on mine. She smiled at me as she committed every word to memory. I loved singing it to her but it broke my heart a little, too, because I knew that I'd never sing it again and never hear it sung again.

Ah, but I was wrong about that.

Pete came home around noon. He looked tired but that was all. He said hello, kissed his mother and then had a shower. We had beans on toast for dinner and I sat at the table in the kitchen and waited for him to confront me about what I'd almost done with his mother. I was sure he must have been able to read my mind, the thoughts there, see the way my mind kept showing me images of Carol on top of me, her hand inside my jeans. They were so vivid, I couldn't believe Pete couldn't just look at my forehead and watch them play, like a film at The Odeon.

But, of course, he sat at the table and ate his beans and never said a word. When he'd finished, he washed the dishes and then went to his room, gesturing with his head for me to follow him. For a second, I thought about shaking my own head and just going home. And, God help, a cowardly part of me thought about never speaking to Pete or seeing him ever again. It was only a second but it was long enough for me to know that I'd think it again in future. Well, even as young as I was then, I knew that there's always a price to pay for the things we do. Or almost do. This would be mine. Just one more weight to carry. As I stood up to follow him upstairs, I was quite proud of the fact that I acknowledged the weight and the reasons for it and the fact that I would carry it gladly. Because Pete Lynwood was my best friend.

'You okay spud?' I asked him when we were in his room.

'Mum told you? Good. I'm a lot better than last night. Cheryl calmed me down. I was all for jacking it in and never coming back. She put me right. I'm not here that much and when I am he's not round much. Whatever bee he's got in his bonnet will fly away soon, I suppose. I can live with that. I could've killed him last night and it wouldn't've bothered me in the least. Isn't that a terrible thing to admit? I think I hate him as much for that as for hitting Mum. You shouldn't hate your Dad, Terry. Shit!'

'How did Cheryl take it?' I asked, already knowing, really.

'She's almost as good as you, you know. But prettier. No, I thought she'd cry a lot but she just kept talking to me until I calmed down. She said she was sorry it had happened but didn't think it had much to do with her, that he wanted to have a row and she was just a handy excuse. She said she thought that, if it was the first time he'd hit Mum, it would probably be the last. The important thing was me being here for Mum. Pretty bloody wonderful, eh? Even if she doesn't take the band seriously.'

'She's a pretty bloody wonderful girl. And she takes the band as seriously as it needs.'

He gave me one of his long looks and nodded. 'Thanks for coming, Terry. I'll tell you one thing, though. Some of my money's coming out of the bank tomorrow.'

'You're going to need it for college.'

'Working the pub'll soon put it back. We're going to buy a car.'

'You're joking! Even if you can afford a car, there's the insurance and as far as the insurance companies are concerned, under twenty five means you're a bloody idiot.'

'I thought maybe your dad could put us on his?' He cocked his head and smiled.

I thought about it and thought he was probably right. To tell the truth, I fancied having a car to get us home and round and about. I nodded and smiled back and the weight of what had nearly happened with Carol didn't seem so heavy.

My Dad agreed readily enough and came round with us to try to find a decent car. As far as I was concerned, if he pulled a face it was better than any RAC inspection. The trouble was, there didn't seem to be any cars we could afford that were worth having. Then my Dad had a brainwave.

My uncle Bob worked for a Ford garage in Seapool but I

hadn't thought of him because it was a main dealership and the cars he usually had were way out of our reach. My Dad called him and then drove us over, not saying anything, just grinning to himself.

Bob had just sold a brand new Granada and taken in an M reg. Cortina in part-ex. Pete got it for £250. It had six months tax and twelve months MOT. By Saturday, we had the car. I say 'we' because Pete made it clear we'd be sharing the car, sharing the petrol costs and the insurance costs.

It made a big difference back at college and kept the peace at The Firs because Cheryl didn't have to worry about missing any buses or trains. As it turned out, it caused problems, too. Mostly for me. Pete was a bloody genius at music and computers but the internal combustion was a mystery to him. I was the one who ended up elbow-deep in the bonnet with oil all over my hands and clothes. I told Pete we'd've been better off buying two bikes. It would've worked out cheaper on phone calls alone. I seemed to spend most of my spare time ringing my Dad up with the latest of a long list of faults. Still, it taught me things, too, not least patience. We sold the Cortina in May '81 and bought a three year old Fiesta which was marginally better but it was a thin margin.

Back in Liverpool, the work got harder but more enjoyable. Jude and I saw less of each because of it but it just made the time we had sweeter. Not least because I found that, when we made love, it was *Jude* I was with and not some shadowy spectre of Carol in that spare bedroom. I realised that I was truly grown-up because, rather than having persistent daydreams about the close call in the spare bedroom (and even more grateful that I didn't have persistent 'wet dreams' about it), I found myself thinking more and more about that night on Laketon Pier when Carol played her tune to me. I understood that it was that night when our relationship changed. What had happened in the spare bedroom had been something else, an aberration or something. No, our relationship was much more than that. It was as close and as deep as the one I had with Pete. And it had something else to it, something Pete and I could never have because I knew things he didn't. The relationship I had with Carol was, despite the spare bedroom, truly platonic and I was immensely grateful for it because it changed my relationship with Jude for the better. It wasn't just a sexual relationship with Jude anymore. When we were together, it was never a case of small talk to pass the brief time between closing the door and making love. If for no other reason, I would always be grateful to Carol for that.

Pete and Cheryl spent more time together and it was obvious to me it was getting really serious between them. We continued doing Fridays at the hall and we got better. My voice was stronger with more range and Pete seemed to bring me a new tune every day. I tried to get him to write some lyrics himself but he just shook his head and then told me why.

'The tunes just bubble up inside me and I take off the ones from the top. I've tried writing the words but they all sound corny. You do the words, Terry. That's what you're good at.'

We went home every other weekend but saw little of each other while we were there. I didn't want to miss the way my sisters were growing up. They were a pain in the arse at times but I loved them just the same. My Mum and Dad were making the house what they wanted and I helped them as best I could and where they'd let me. The few times I went to Pete's house, Carol and I were the same close friends we'd been before and that made the weight of what nearly happened easier to carry. It would have broken my heart if it had spoiled that closeness between us. But her drinking hadn't changed and that worried me so much I asked her about AA. She told me she had no real desire to stop so there wasn't much point. The way she looked and the tone of voice made me go cold. It was as if she'd decided to go to the bitter end the way she wanted and bugger the fact that the drink was hastening that end. I held on to the hope that seeing Pete married (something I was sure would happen not long after he graduated) would make her slow down the race she was running.

Ronald seemed to have mellowed slightly after the row and even talked to us about college and our courses. The fact that Pete was obviously bombing through his probably helped that mellowing.

Jude came to our house occasionally and, as I knew she would, loved my family and they loved her. She loved to visit my Nan and hear her talk about me when I was little. I think she liked the way it embarrassed me as much as anything else. Oh, and she loved my Nan's apple pie and custard. On that, we both agreed.

So, everything was going well. Pete hadn't had a down

since we'd been at Liverpool and I'd half-forgotten about the quirk in his family tree. Then it was December 1980, just before Christmas break, just as the weather turned from damp and misty to cold and blowy, just as we were playing most of the first set of our Friday nights with nearly all our own songs. Just then, it went bad.

John Lennon was shot dead outside his home in the Dakota Building in New York.

I'd made my cup of tea and was filling my bowl with Cornflakes. The transistor radio was on and I was pleasantly surprised to hear a Beatles song playing. Still, it was the local station and it wasn't unusual to hear a Beatles song that early in the morning. It became unusual when the next song was a Beatles song, without any of the normal inane DJ gabble. I began to wonder if it was some anniversary. Then Gerry Marsden came on to talk about what a tragic and criminal waste Lennon's murder was. I stopped eating my Cornflakes.

I was still trying to put it all together when Pete pushed my door open, looking the way I imagined I looked. He put a piece of paper on my bed, turned round and just walked out.

I picked up the piece of paper. It was covered in Pete's neat, stylish handwriting. There were a lot of crossings out at the top. I read it twice, then a third time and then I was crying. I'm not sure if I cried because it was such a bloody tragic, criminal, stupid thing that had happened or because it took such a thing to make Pete commit himself to paper. Whatever, I've put it in this story, not because it's particularly good but to show how it affected him. It was the first really bad thing to happen but not the last. Oh, no.

> *The dream is over, Lennon wrote*
> *But it was ten years later it really died*
> *And with it, a large part of my youth*
> *All those daring years, full of promise and hope*
> *When they really believed it could all be changed*
> *When Life was a path to tread*
> *And not a weapon they used to batter your head*
> *Days when revolution meant flowers and love was free*
> *When people really wanted war to end and said so openly*
> *When music was more than just the backbeat and the melody*
> *What a time it was, ah it was*
> *Sunshine and peace and harmony*
> *With all things possible and to be tried*
> *But the dream died*
> *A little piece of me did, too*
> *So I'll cry now that the dream is over*
> *For him*
> *For me*
> *For you*

No, it's never going to win any awards but I doubt the idea even entered his head. It was just the gut reaction of someone who thought The Beatles hadn't just written songs but History, too. The dream Pete was referring to wasn't the one Lennon had meant when he wrote about the group splitting up, or not *just* that one. The dream he was thinking about was the one where someday, if only for that one day, The Beatles would get together on stage one more time and play. That could never happen now. It broke a piece of Pete's heart. The words were just his way of saying so.

We both had lectures all morning but I expected to see him in the cafe we usually went to at dinner time. I got there about ten past twelve and bought my usual sausage roll and tea and sat next to the old radiator that was wheezing sleepily against the wall. It was bitterly cold outside and the wind was blowing a fine, insinuating rain off the river. I waited for Pete till one and then decided he must've been bogged down with his print-outs. I had one tutorial that afternoon and was back in my room by three but there was still no sign of Pete. I was beginning to be worried.

I went to see Cheryl.

She was doing her teaching practice at a school not far from the campus and I walked over to meet her at quarter to four. She came out, laughing with a gang of kids who looked like they should've been in a documentary about inner-city life. They swarmed around her like she was the Pied Piper, calling for her to sing that song again, Miss. She saw me and waved and sent the kids off to wherever it was they went and walked to meet me.

'Hello, Ted. What're you doing out in this weather? Did you wet the bed or what?'

I took her arm and led her away from the school. The road was busy with traffic and the noise was atrocious. I had to shout to make myself heard.

'Have you seen Pete?'

'I'm seeing him tonight. We're going to the pictures. Why?'

I shook my head and led her to the cafe where I'd waited for Pete that dinner time. I bought two cups of tea and told her what happened that morning. She listened and the frown she wore got deeper and deeper.

'You don't suppose he went home?' She looked at me and I shook my head. 'No, that's the last place he'd go. Ronald would tell him not to be stupid and to pull himself together. Oh, Peter, where are you, you silly bugger?' She ran her hands through her hair.

I looked out of the window. Across the road, near the pedestrianised area of town, a lone girl stood playing a violin and mouth organ; one of the more unusual buskers who frequented the shopping area. I felt like a light had gone on in my brain.

'Bingo!' I shouted and grabbed her arm and dragged her out of the cafe. 'I think I know where he'll be,' I told her outside.

'Ted, why would he come here?' Cheryl asked when we reached St John's Precinct.

'I think he might be paying his idea of homage.'

'What?'

I didn't repeat myself, just led her to the bottom of the escalator and pointed.

'Oh Christ,' she said when she saw him.

He was leaning with one foot against the tiled wall for

support. There was money in his guitar case but I was pretty sure he didn't know. He'd just opened the case so as not to look like a weirdo. Cheryl was all for grabbing him and dragging him back to his room.

'Just listen for a minute, Cher,' I said.

'Why? Shit, Ted, he looks ill. He must be freezing if he's been here all day. Let's just get him home and warm.'

'He's okay. Let him finish. I think he's almost done.'

'Ted,' she said with the quiet patience of somebody about to explode. 'If he's been here all day, why should he finish just because it's nearly five o'clock?'

'What's he playing now?'

She walked a little closer and then came back. "Norwegian Wood'. Why?'

'I bet he'll do 'In My Life' next and then he'll pack up and come home.'

She gave me a doubtful look but it was wiped away when Pete played the opening bars of the song. She did a double-take and then raised her eyebrows at me.

'Just listen. Like them,' I said and pointed at the group of people gathered round him. There must've been a good sixty or seventy. As he sang, they stood silently, some smiling slightly, others shedding a tear or two, dreamy looks on their faces. Pete's voice wasn't strong enough to blast out the rockers but it was good enough to back me and it had a haunting quality that was perfect for this song. This song was also the one he did with the most feeling.

When he ran his fingers down the strings at the end, the crowd applauded and whistled and cheered. Most now had tears in their eyes. Pete looked up and I could tell by the surprise on his face that he'd forgotten where he was.

'Okay,' Cheryl said. 'How did you know?'

I smiled. 'I bet he's been playing Beatles' songs all day. That's his favourite. It's the one he uses to make his point when people slag off McCartney. They use it to prove Lennon could write melodies like McCartney and was the better lyricist and that's why Lennon's just as good on his own but McCartney isn't. The point is, Lennon wrote the words to 'In My Life' for Stuart Sutcliffe but it was Paul who wrote the tune. Pete always says it sums The Beatles up for him. John and Paul writing a great song and then all four doing it exactly right on record. After what happened today, this was Pete's homage.'

We took him home.

It was the following March before Pete was all the way up again. For those three or so months, he seemed to move through his days, his life, as if he were on some sort of small gauge-railway, going where the tracks went. I tried, Cheryl tried, Jude tried but nothing we said managed to put the life back into his eyes. More than once, I noticed how Jude's face, her eyes especially, seemed almost as haunted as Pete's own. Then, early in March, he was back. With a bang.

I was sitting in the bar one Thursday night with Jude, talking about the coming weekend. I was going to her house after the match on Saturday. Pete came over to us, followed by Cheryl. They both looked as if they'd been trekking in Snowdonia. Their hair was all messed up and their faces were red. Pete was holding something in his right hand, tightly, as if it might escape.

'Hello blue,' I said. 'What's up?'

It was Cheryl who answered me. 'Hiya. Can't stop. Listen to this,' she said and Pete put the cassette in my hand. 'Listen to it and put some words to it. See you tomorrow.'

And then they left.

Jude laughed. "What was that all about?'

I stood up. 'Come on, I better listen to this.'

'Bloody hell,' Jude said, almost reverently.

I just nodded. I couldn't talk, not yet. I had too many words rolling round my head. Much too many for any to roll off my tongue. We'd listened to the tape and neither of us had spoken until Jude came out with that almost reverent expletive.

There was ninety minutes worth of music on the tape. Side one was more commercial, quite rocky. Side two was more minorish, thoughtful. It was this side that had crammed my head full of words. And they all had backbeats. Cheryl was on all the tunes. How did that make me feel? I didn't know then and, to be honest, I'm not sure I do now. It was just different.

When the tape finished, Jude stood up and walked across to the window. She crossed her arms across her breasts and took a deep breath, the way you do before you dive into a pool. Something crept up my spine and made it tingle. I tried to think of something to say to stop her saying whatever it was she was going to say. I couldn't think of a thing.

'Has he ever done this amount before? All at once, I

mean?' She kept looking out of the window but there was nothing to see out there. It was March-blowy and twilight dim. Her profile looked tense.

'No,' I said and hated the way my voice struggled to get out. 'Why?' No answer. 'Jude?'

She finally spoke, still looking out of the window. 'I've done a bit of reading about people who have large creative abilities. Not much because there isn't much. Yet. What there is bothers me a bit. Terry, d'you think Pete is more than your average play-by-ear musician?'

'He told me once that he has all these tunes bubbling in his head and just scrapes off the top layer. I got the impression he doesn't like the idea he can't get at the rest.'

She nodded. 'From what I've read, there were a lot of people like that. Thomas Edison, Edgar Alan Poe, Schubert. They all had this huge creative thing and—'

'And what?' I said, cutting her off, not wanting to know the answer but knowing I needed to. God, I hate that!

'They all had it and suffered terrible bouts of depression.' She turned to face me and her own face was pinched, pained, not wanting to say what came next. 'Some of them were suicidal.'

'Thanks Jude. I really needed that. Look, if you've got anything else to tell me, sit down, eh?'

So she did.

'I think Pete might be like that. Everything I've read covers itself by *suggesting* but between the lines, it's pretty obvious they're almost convinced. They think it might be something genetic.'

'Something in the family tree,' I said, mostly to myself, remembering what he'd told me back in the Physics lab.

Jude's laugh was brittle. 'Well, yes. Anyway, the consensus seems to be that the gene that provides the creativity does not have that as its main function. It—'

I held my hands up. 'I'm no scientist. D'you think I could have the *Reader's Digest* version?'

She smiled and it looked better than her laugh had sounded. 'Okay. Well, the coding, the information contained in the DNA. That's...' I nodded. I knew what that was. 'Right. Well, the information built into the different genes makes us what we are. Blue or brown eyes, right or left handed, small, tall. The gene has a function and that's it. Some genes have more than one function but they all have a *main* function. This one, the one they think is coded for creativity, may not have creativity as its main function. The *suggestion* is that its main function might be a tendency to depression or even suicide. The other—'

'You get a little bit of genius to make up for the fact that you might top yourself one day. Bloody magic.'

'Nothing's proven,' she told me again and I could hear her wanting to take it all back.

I shook my head. 'Like you said, they don't think they're far off, though. Besides, it all fits. Even I know about Poe's melancholy and Edison's fugues. Even some of the recent pop stars like Hendrix, Joplin, Keith Moon sound the same. They might not have committed suicide in the classical way but they all apparently had a big enough death wish to push themselves into whatever way they did die. You think Pete might be the same?'

'I don't know. Really. That's why I asked if he'd done this much before. I forget which article I read it in but the word they used was Hypomania. The idea is, where the gene is active, the subject has periods of intense creativity which is either immediately preceded or followed by bouts of severe depression. I just remembered the way he was after Lennon's death and then he comes up with all this stuff. I'm sorry, Terry.'

'It isn't anybody's fault, Jude. I don't suppose any of these articles had any idea what to do about it?'

'If it's a gene, there's nothing you *can* do. It's there. The same way I'm left-handed.' She looked at me helplessly.

I nodded. 'I'll just have to keep him away from sharp instruments or get him to use electric razors and eat only soup.' I said it lightly to break the mood and she smiled again. 'In the meantime, I better find the words for this lot to keep him happy. If I can keep finding the words, maybe he'll be too busy to get depressed enough to want to top himself.'

'Shall I play it again, Sam?'

'Just side one. I've got enough for side two.' I said it absently, telling the simple truth. When I looked up at her, she was no longer smiling. I knew what was on her mind. 'Don't worry. I'm nothing more than your average bloke with a big vocabulary. I'm not the type to get depressed. Words have always come easily to me and I've never had to pay the Piper. I guess I'm just too thick.'

She smiled again. 'D'you fancy getting horny instead?'

*

Nothing much happened in '81 apart from the riots

which hit the country's inner cities. Liverpool seemed to come off worst. Probably because it was the first.

I saw Alan Brewer the day after the first riot in Liverpool 8, soon to be known around the country and possibly the world, as Toxteth. He was sitting on the wall outside the Royal Hospital, waiting for a friend to come out after being treated for injuries received while helping a pensioner out of the firing line. Alan looked like he'd lost his best friend. What he said only confirmed that idea.

'My city's burnin, Terry. It's goin up in flames and nobody'll take the blame for it. They'll all push it onto somebody else. This was a great place once, you know. It still could be if the people in charge would just give it a bleedin chance. The people here are the best in the world. It's not right. They've killed my home town and now they're crematin it. It wouldn't surprise me if some bugger in London is thinking of wallin us up and forgettin all about us.'

There was nothing I could say to that so I just squeezed his shoulder and left him to his mourning.

Oxborough wasn't spared. In fact, an old schoolmate of mine died during the riot that hit the city. Nobody could explain how it happened other than he was in the front line when the police charged. It didn't surprise me; Simon Reynolds was the type who would always join a line if he thought right was on his side.

Pete wrote a tune he called 'Dying to live' but I couldn't or wouldn't find words for it. Each time I heard it, I saw Alan Brewer's sad/angry face and heard his plaintive voice.

The year turned and our finals came with spring. The

idea should've worried me but it didn't; I somehow knew we'd all pass and, after that, what would happen would happen. The world would turn and that was the way God planned it. Jude would go away to continue her training, Pete and Cheryl would be together and, sometime, get married. I would go to Spain and might even come back to get together with Jude again.

Maybe...but, while I hoped it would happen, deep down I was doubtful. Why? Because...well, because Jude knew exactly what she wanted to do and always had. She'd never made any bones about it and, most importantly, had *never*, not even in the hot and steamy throes of passion, come close to saying anything like *I love you*. Oh, neither had I but that was because I knew I wouldn't hear those words from Jude. And it wasn't all about protecting myself, either—I didn't want Jude to think she owed me any sort of reciprocation because that wouldn't've been fair.

Still, maybe over time she'd find out that she did love me after all...stranger things had happened down the years.

Stranger things *did*.

First, a bloke called Pete Leay stopped me as I was leaving the toilets during the break in a dance to celebrate the fact that most of the exams were half-way through—you know students; anything for a piss up. I knew he wasn't a student because he was in his late thirties.

'My name's Pete,' he told me.

I laughed. 'Not another one. You don't want to fight me, do you?'

'Sorry?'

'Never mind. I'm in a funny mood. My last exam's tomorrow. What can I do for you?'

'D'you tape your act?'

Tape? Act? I didn't have the foggiest idea what he was on about.

'I'm not with you, boss.'

'This,' he said and waved his hand to take in the place and the people. 'D'you tape your act. Or have you ever taped it?'

'Oh. I've never thought of it as an act. No. Why?'

'I run an independent record label. I'd like to talk about you making a record.'

'This is a wind-up, right? Andy Much sent you. Or Les Kemp. It's a joke, right?'

He grinned and I liked it straight off. There was no snide lift to it. But I still thought it was a joke.

'Why've you come to me? Why not the bloke on piano or the girl on drums?'

'Because you looked like you were in charge. I can talk to the others.'

'Well, if you're serious, you'll have to.'

'Oh, I'm serious.'

'Why?' Pete said when Pete Leay had explained what he had in mind.

Pete had asked the right question. Why us? There were plenty of other bands who'd jump at the chance.

'Because I like what I've heard and the fact that you write your own stuff's a bonus. Your act is the most energetic I've seen in a long while. I think you could do well and I'd like to do well with you.'

I looked at Cheryl. What would she say? She wanted to be a teacher and had made that clear but she also told me she wouldn't kill Pete's dream. Did Pete want this?

'Well, sunshine,' I said to *our* Pete. 'You got us into this, what d'you think?'

He looked at Cheryl and she looked at him and something passed between them. Then Pete spoke.

'I think,' he said, looking at Pete Leay. 'If you've got a tape recorder and the inclination, you should tape this second set. If you're still interested, we could talk about it when we finish our exams. Now, excuse us while we entertain our public.' He stood up and walked to the stage, never once looking back. Cheryl followed him.

'We'll see you later,' I said. 'Jude here will you give our potted and unremarkable history.'

It was one of those nights. I hit every note and my fingers never let me down once. Pete almost matched his musicianship with his singing and Cheryl played like she'd been born with sticks in her hands. We did mostly our own stuff but finished with a rock-ballad medley. The crowd went wild. I put most of it down to almost-end-of-exam-fever but it still made me feel good.

Twenty minutes after the last song and with the revellers all gone, I was sitting with my arm round Jude, trying to come down a bit. I always felt light-headed after a good night, almost as if I went somewhere else while I was on stage. Pete was talking to Pete Leay and Cheryl was listening. I was brought back to earth by a question from

Pete Leay.

'Sorry, I was miles away.'

'He wants to know if you're ready to listen to what he's got on tape?' Pete told me and rolled his eyes.

'Yeah. If you like.'

'You don't sound very enthusiastic about it,' Pete Leay said.

'Don't worry about him,' Cheryl told him cheerfully. 'The pubs have to send him home before they have Happy Hour. Play the tape.'

It wasn't particularly funny but it made everybody laugh because it was said so dryly and po-faced. Pete Leay played the tape. It seemed to have caught the atmosphere perfectly and our own songs came across well.

'Well, Mr Leay, what d'you think now?' Pete asked.

'That Mister is awful formal. My name's Peter.'

'Yeah but so's mine. It could get confusing. Got another one?'

'Sorry. Not even a nickname.'

'How about Thingie?' Cheryl asked. 'That's what my Mum always says when she can't remember who it is she's talking about.'

'Suits me,' Thingie said over our laughter. 'If it makes you do a record with me you can call me anything you like.'

'Okay, Thingie, still want to record us?'

'More than ever. When can you come to the studio? And have you got more of your own stuff?'

'They've got more stuff than brains,' Cheryl said and that was when I realised that she and Pete had decided, if not to give it all up for music, at least to put things on the back burner. And then she said something that made me feel as if somebody had left the windows open behind me. 'Pete writes them like he's running out of time.'

I looked behind me but there wasn't even a window, never mind an open one.

'And Ted can write lyrics in his sleep,' Cheryl said. 'So, when's good for you, Thingie?'

It turned out that two days after Pete's last exam was good so we settled for that and then Thingie gave us his life story. At least all that pertained to his record label.

The label was called SKYSAW and he'd set it up after being unemployed for two years. He'd always been interested in music and worked for Roxy Music for a time until they'd done the dirty on him over something. He decided to use the contacts he'd made and to take advantage of the Enterprise Scheme and, just, give it a go. He was a nice bloke and I liked him. He didn't try to fill our heads full of custard about how he was going to make us millionaires and bigger than Elton John. If he had, we'd've just walked out.

We left him at Central Station to catch his train back to Wallasey and told him we'd see him on the Saturday at the end of May like we'd agreed.

But we didn't see him that day. I spoke to him at half eight that morning but I didn't see him again.

They say stranger things happen and they do. They also say that worse things happen at sea and that's fair enough. Being asked to record our songs for Thingie's record label was pretty strange but good. What happened next was bad and I'm not sure worse things do happen at sea. Whatever the blokes in the RNA club say.

Carol Lynwood died on Thursday, May 27th 1982. The day before her son's final exam. Ronald Lynwood didn't bother letting his son know until Friday, May 28th at six that night.

I met Pete outside his examination room at three that afternoon and we walked across to meet Cheryl. Jude was meeting us at the dance that night.

The weather was perfect; warm sun, clear skies. I felt the way I did when I was a kid and the holidays started but the feeling went deeper. The sense of freedom was stronger because the future was out there, waiting. And I *knew* I had what it would take to make that future good. Pete walked alongside me, clicking his fingers and whistling and I knew he felt the same.

When we met Cheryl, we walked down to the Pier Head and bought chips. We went up to the roof of the Pier Head building and looked out to where the Mersey became Liverpool Bay, not talking, just drinking stewed tea and eating soggy chips.

'Well,' Pete said and balled up his chip paper. 'That's that.'

I nodded and looked at Cheryl, waiting for her to say something. Her face looked young but still, like she had a secret she'd tell but not just yet. Seeing her like that, it struck me consciously for the first time that I loved the girl. I loved her humour and the way she could prick any pompous balloon you might've inflated quicker than blink. I can still hear her telling me not to be a misery all my life, to take a day off. Then she spoke and I didn't know what she was on about.

'The answer's yes. But not yet.' She didn't look at me or Pete, just kept watching the way the sunlight glinted off the slow waves.

Pete said nothing and I assumed she was talking to me. 'Sorry, love? What was the question to that answer?'

'I'm talking to the queer fellah here. As usual, he's off in wonderland somewhere. Probably thinking up more tunes for us to make our fortune with. Hey, dreamawhile, you with us?'

I looked at Pete. He smiled but continued to look out to sea.

'I heard. Thank you. I'll look after you and we'll do it whenever you say.'

I opened my mouth to ask what the hell they were talking about but Cheryl beat me to it.

'We'll see how this record thing works out since you're dead set on it. But don't get the idea I'll give up wanting to teach. Just so's you know.'

'Fine. I wouldn't want you to give up anything you thought you should do.'

They still weren't looking at each other and I'd had enough.

'Er, listen, you two, d'you think you could tell me what the hell you're talking about? I feel like I'm in the Twilight Zone.'

'I just agreed to marry him, Ted. That's all. But not till we've tried our hand at making a record and just as long as he understands I'm still going to teach.'

'*That's all!* Jesus Mary and Joseph! When did this happen?'

'Just now,' Pete said, finally turning away from the view. 'You were here, Terry. Weren't you listening or what?'

'Buh...buh...buh...'

'Is that Spanish or French?' Cheryl asked.

'How the hell he manages to write lyrics is beyond me,' Pete said and went back to looking at the river.

'You'll be best man, won't you, Ted?' Cheryl asked, smiling at me.

I took a deep breath. 'Yeah. But I always was.'

I was in my room, getting my guitars ready and looking for something fresh to wear when the knock came at my door. I assumed it was Pete and that he'd just walk in. Then the knock came again.

'It's open.'

Frank Simmons stuck his head round the door. 'Phone f'ya, Terry. It's ya dad.'

'Cheers Frank.'

I went into the hallway, wondering what was up. I'd phoned home last night and told them I'd be home Sunday.

'Dad? What's up?'

'Terry?' His voice sounded thick and the line buzzed along the thirty odd miles between us. 'I've got some bad news, son.'

In the split-second before I answered, I saw all my relatives, from my Nan to my youngest cousin. I was positive my legs were going to give way.

'Who is it, Dad? Not Nan?'

'No. Christ, that was stupid of me. It's none of ours. It's...'

'Who is it?' My voice sounded as if it was coming through rusty pipe.

'God, this isn't right. It's Pete's mother. She died. His father rang me about ten minutes ago. Don't ask me why he didn't ring Pete. When I asked, I couldn't get any sense out of him. Is Pete there?'

Carol? It must be a mistake. Pete was coming home to tell her he was engaged. Besides, I hadn't seen her since Christmas and she wouldn't die before I saw her again.

'Terry? You still there?'

'What time did she die?'

'He said about half one yesterday afternoon.'

'*Yesterday*? Why didn't he phone last night?'

'He didn't say. Will you be home tonight?'

'What time is it? I haven't got my watch on. I was getting changed...' I was babbling and my Dad heard it and cut me off.

'Just gone six. Terry, you've got to tell him and then drive him home. Don't let him behind the wheel. You hear me, Terry?'

'Yeah. I'll see you later.'

I put the phone down and walked down the corridor to Pete's room. I was dazed, in shock. Carol Lynwood was my friend, more than a friend, almost a soulmate. Ah Christ, I'd written the lyrics for a tune she'd waited nearly twenty years to write. And now I had to tell her son, my best friend, that she was dead, that he was never going to be able to hug her again, that she wasn't going to kiss him when he told her she was going to be a mother-in-law. She wasn't going to be there anymore when he got home from wherever he'd been and she'd never have the chance to see her grandchildren being happy and

why the hell didn't good old Ronald get in touch when it happened instead of waiting more than twenty four hours?

The sudden incision of the thought brought me up sharp.

Why did it take so long? And why do it through a third party he'd never met?

Oh, I think you can work that out, Terry. And it has nothing to do with shock. It's all in the timing.

Yes, I supposed it was. I didn't want it to be true but I had a terrible feeling that it was.

I knocked on Pete's door and pushed it open.

He was rummaging through a pile of clothes. His guitars were in their cases on the bed.

'That you, Terry?' He asked without turning round. 'Grab the guitars and I'll be with you in a minute.'

How the hell did you tell your best friend that his mother was dead when his girlfriend had just agreed to marry him and he was getting ready to do something as totally unimportant as play music at a dance? I thought of all those films I'd seen where things like this happened, hoping for inspiration but none came. In the end, there's only way to tell it and that's to tell it.

'Pete, I've just had a phone call and...Pete, your mum died. We've got to go home. Tonight. Now.'

When you get information like that, it takes a few

seconds to clear the circuits. You hear it but your brain refuses to accommodate it immediately. Your hands go on doing whatever it is they're doing while your brain processes the information. So Pete carried on rummaging through his clothes for a few moments and then he turned to face me. He looked, somehow, a lot younger and a lot older at the same time.

'Pete, I'm sorry. Sit down, mate.'

'Can't. She's really dead? I have to go home. Best get all this stuff in the car and...Oh God, Terry, she's dead! What am I going to do?'

He fell into my arms and cried. I cried with him. His sobs were hard, as if his tears were bullets and he was firing them. I let him cry and tried to get my mind into gear so I could sort out the logistics of what came next.

As his sobs tapered off, I remembered that our car was out of action. It had a fault I couldn't cure and it was in the garage getting the head sorted out. Shit!

I eased Pete down onto the bed and held him at arm's length. His face was bright red and his eyes were buried in folds of flesh.

'Pete, the friggin car's off the road. Have you got any spare cash? We'll have to hire a car. The train's only run every hour now and no taxi is going to take us to Oxborough on a Friday night.'

He just shook his head. I didn't know if he was telling me he had no cash or if he was denying Carol's death. Sod it.

'You get what you need and I'll see if I can sort something out. I'll be right back.'

I hated leaving him alone but I had to. I phoned my Dad

and got his Barclaycard number. With a bit of luck, I could persuade the hire firm to take it after they'd rung up to confirm everything. I also needed to phone Jude at the hospital so she could let Cheryl know when they got to the dance.

It took ten minutes. When I got back, Pete hadn't moved. He was still crying but silently now. His left hand was pulling at some invisible thread on his jeans. I pulled his case from under the bed and threw in his good shoes and some other stuff and snapped it shut. I forced him into his coat and out into the daylight.

The girl at the hire firm was great. She went through everything in double time and even gave me a box of tissues for Pete. We got onto the motorway at Edge Lane at five to seven. Pete sat in the passenger seat and didn't say a word all the way home. We got into Oxborough just after twenty past seven and arrived outside Pete's house ten minutes later.

As I drove under the fir trees, which should've looked different now that Carol was dead but didn't, Pete sighed and leaned forward and put his head in his hands.

'Just a minute, Terry,' he said and coughed. 'I want to try to look a bit better. For Dad.'

Christ, he was trying to be brave for his father and in about five minutes, he was going to find out what Ronald had done. I put the car in neutral and waited.

'Okay,' he said. 'Let's go.'

The floodlights were on and they lit Pete's face lurid yellow but he walked to the door with a straight back and his head up. He looked like his Mum. As he reached the porch, the hall light came on and Ronald's silhouette came towards the front door. I stayed about five yards behind Pete.

Pete and his father looked at each other for a few moments and then Pete moved towards Ronald and embraced him. Ronald put his arms around his son. Pete broke the embrace and gestured for me to follow him in.

Inside, the house looked the same but felt different, as if some of its warmth had been taken away. I followed Pete and Ronald into the living room.

The fire was on and the telly chattered on unheeded in the corner. The curtains were drawn. I looked at Carol's chair, looking, really, for the table and the glass. They weren't there. I looked away. Ronald sat in the Parker Knoll chair by the fire. Pete and I sat on the couch.

'Thank you for driving Peter down, Terry. I'm sorry you had to be the one to tell him. Will you thank your father for me?'

'Dad, why didn't you ring me?'

I waited.

'Everything was so...confused. I couldn't find the number for your block but I found Terry's home number.'

'Oh. Did she feel...how did it happen...? was she in...?'

'No. Dr Roberts said she had no pain. It was an embolism. Her blood pressure had been elevated for a little while but it was put down to...well, you know.'

Pete nodded and I knew what he was thinking. The drink. The *bloody* drink.

'Last Wednesday, she seemed worse and Roberts wanted

her to go into hospital but she refused. Nothing we said could change her mind. I stayed up all night with her in this room. She talked about you and how well you were doing and how much she liked Cheryl. How she was looking forward to having you home once you'd finished college.' Ronald smiled and, for that moment, I saw the human being in him. I was positive that it hadn't just been Carol who talked about those things. 'On Thursday morning, she seemed better and I went to get the prescription filled. When I got back she was sitting in here. She was...pla...' He paused.

And I knew, somehow, that Carol had been playing guitar. So why did Ronald look wistful? I couldn't imagine Ronald would find anything in Carol playing music that would make him anything but annoyed and angry. But the look on his face when he continued talking *was* wistful.

'She seemed happy and cheerful,' he went on. 'I went out to make her a cup of tea because she said she was thirsty. When I came back she was...she looked asleep. But she had died.' Ronald choked on genuine grief.

I waited for what he'd said to clear Pete's own grief. It finally did.

'Pardon?' Pete's face a picture of confusion. I hated to see that. It shouldn't've been like that. Not when father and son talked about the women in their lives.

'She looked asle—'

'No. When did you say she died? Thursday? Dad, today's *Friday.*'

Ronald tried to look everywhere but at Pete but he always had to come back to those confused eyes. Finally, he stood up and held himself erect.

'You had your final paper today. It seemed...pointless to disturb you. There was nothing you could've done. Peter—'

'Wait. Wait a minute,' Pete said and shook his head. 'You're telling me you left it till this evening because you didn't want to disturb my final paper? Is that what you're telling me, Dad?'

'Peter, there was nothing you could've done. You couldn't've come home yesterday with your paper being today and your concentration—'

'I could've had a dispensation to miss it! I could've taken it another time! It wouldn't've mattered if I never took the bloody thing! You should've told me!' Pete stood up and I stood up, too. This was all too reminiscent of that night Pete had tried to hit Ronald.

'Peter, you worked too hard for three years to have missed out. Your mother wouldn't have wanted you to.'

I held Pete's arm lightly but he shook it off. Still, he made no further move towards Ronald and there was none of the tension of somebody about to lash out.

'She was my *mother*! You should've told me the day she died!' Pete shouted and then sat on the couch and cried.

Ronald put his head in his hands and trembled. I felt almost sorry for him; inside two days, he'd lost the two pillars of his life and deep down inside, he must've realised that they'd been lost through his own carelessness, his refusal to understand either of them.

'I'll...I'll put the kettle on,' Ronald Lynwood said and left the room.

Pete sagged against me and cried those hard, bitter

bullets again. Then the phone rang. Neither Pete nor Ronald was in any state to talk to anybody so I answered it.

'Hello, Lynwood house,' I said. I felt a fool saying it; normally I'd just say the number or make some daft remark about Chinese laundries. But I didn't know this number like I knew my own and this was no time for daft jokes.

'Terry?' It was Jude. 'Terry, I told Cheryl and told her I'd bring her down there in the morning on my way to London but she wanted to come straight away.'

'Jude, listen, I can't talk now. Something's—'

'It's okay. I just wanted to let you know she's on her way down. She got your car from the garage. She's awful hard to hold down.' Jude laughed then and I was glad to hear it. 'She went round to the garage and got the man to finish it while she watched. She left about ten minutes ago. I would've come with her but I've got that interview in London tomorrow. I made her come home with me for something to eat and to get some money. Anyway, she's on her way. How's Pete?'

'Well, you know. Listen, love, can you ring Macca at the hall and tell him? He'll have to make arrangements for the dance. I'll see you when you get back from London. Good luck.'

'Tell Pete I'm sorry.'

'Bye Jude.'

While I was on the phone, Ronald had gone upstairs so I made the tea. I even made one for him. I took them into the living room and told Pete about Cheryl.

'I know exactly how she'll've done it. She'll've buttonholed the bloke, probably under the car lift and threatened him with a spanner. If that didn't work she probably threatened him with the VAT man or her non-existent big brothers. I'll be glad to see her, Terry. I miss her already.'

Ronald came back and sipped at his tea. I counted five times when he began to say something but didn't manage it. The silence and tension in the room was terrible. I broke it because I couldn't go home and leave them to their separate rooms, skirting around each other like two strangers, even if that's what they were.

'Mr Lynwood, that call was to tell Pete that Cheryl's coming down. I know you and Pete have things to sort out but it might be a good idea to wait until after the funeral.' I hoped Pete would agree. Ronald would because he didn't want to lose his son so soon after losing his wife.

Ronald cleared his throat, nodded and then said what I'd hoped he'd say. 'I'll air the guest room and put the electric blanket on.'

Pete stood up. 'That's okay, I'll do it. Terry's right, Dad. We can talk about…things after the funeral.'

When Pete left the room, Ronald turned to me, his face pale and drawn. I nodded, knowing he wanted to say something.

'I thought it was for the best. I…I think he'll understand.'

'Mr Lynwood, I don't think *you* understand,' I said as levelly as I could. 'Whether you thought it was the right thing is beside the point. Pete's twenty one, an adult and he should've been allowed to make his own decisions. You should've told him and let him make his own mind up once he knew. The worst thing is that I think he'd've stayed and sat the paper anyway. Once he knew you were going to manage for a day, he'd've known there was nothing he could do. Now, you've alienated him at a time when you both need each other the most. It's a bloody shame. It's going to take a long time for him to get over this and you'll both be the worse for it.'

He blinked and wiped a tear from his cheek and then nodded. 'I'm sorry,' he sobbed.

'It's not me you have to apologise to. Look, I'll go and say goodnight and then I'll be off home. I'll see you at the funeral. I'm sorry about Carol. I…loved her.'

He looked up from his hands and stared at me. Not an angry stare, more puzzled. Then he blinked and smiled at me. It wasn't a smile I'd ever seen on Ronald's face before. Not that I'd seen many but, even so, it was a smile that held no animosity or cynicism. He smiled at me as if we were good friends.

'Yes,' he said slowly, still smiling. 'And I know she loved you, Terry.' He glanced at his intertwined fingers again and then back at me. No smile this time but, in his eyes, I saw something I never thought I'd see. Ronald Lynwood looked at me with respect. 'In case I never get the chance to say this…for whatever reason…I want to thank you, Terry. For everything you've done for my son, for Peter. And for everything…' He paused, considering, and then finished. 'On behalf of myself and Carol.' He took a deep breath. 'Thank you for everything, Terry. We've all been lucky to have met you.' He stood up and offered his hand.

I shook his hand and nodded, my voice apparently frozen by surprise. I cleared my throat and managed to say,

'Goodnight Mr Lynwood.' Then I left him in the living room while I went to say goodnight to Pete.

Pete was in his room, leafing through a photo album. I wanted to look at those pictures, to see Carol when she was younger, to see her holding her son maybe, when he was a baby. I wanted to but this was Pete's time to look and cry over them and cry for all those things that never get said because you always think there's plenty of time.

'I'll go now, Pete. I'll ring tomorrow. D'you want me to leave the car? I can get a taxi.'

He looked up. His eyes were dry but they were awfully big and his face was as pale and drawn as his father's. His mouth looked like it might never smile again.

'No. Cheryl's coming with ours. We'll probably be down to see you tomorrow.'

I wanted to say something about Ronald but decided to leave it. I nodded instead.

'You take care going home, Terry. Thanks for everything. I'll see you tomorrow.'

But I saw him sooner than that.

I'd just finished the bacon and egg my Mum demanded I eat. I thought I wasn't hungry but, as usual, she seemed to know me better than I knew myself. I wolfed it down. She and my Dad were only waiting for me to finish eating so I could tell them what had happened. My two sisters were upstairs, Erin doing her Spanish homework and Dawn getting ready to go out with her boyfriend. I was told he was shy and I wasn't to take the mickey out of him. I didn't feel much like taking the mickey out of anybody. I told her

Dobbin or Robin or whatever his name was would be safe. It was five to eight.

I explained what had happened while my Dad smoked his pipe. He'd taken it up when the doctor told him all the years working in the leather tanning factory had brought him into contact with the wrong type of asbestos. He didn't have asbestosis but his lungs weren't perfect. The pipe was a compromise. My Mum listened from her chair in front of the fire, not saying anything, just shaking her head sadly from time to time.

When I'd finished, she said, 'I suppose the poor man was in shock. It must be terrible having her die just when Pete was finishing college. She would've been so proud.'

My Mum was the type who always tried to see the best in people. When it wasn't always there, it didn't destroy her faith in people, she just tried harder to find it next time. She wasn't anybody's idea of a soft touch and if anybody tried to take her for a fool, they got a shock. She was nobody's fool.

Our Dawn's boyfriend arrived and we were introduced. He didn't seem too shy to me and the one time I called him Dobbin he laughed like a drain. I liked him. Our Erin gave me her homework to check. It didn't take long; she was a clever sod. Still is. I was settling down to watch the telly at nine o'clock when the phone rang. My Dad answered it and then called me to take it. I assumed it was Pete. Maybe Jude.

It was the police.

'Mr Terence Barrow?' The voice was middle-aged and crisp, used to gathering information and giving orders. I felt my mouth go dry.

'Yes. Who is this?' I said and thought, *Ronald wouldn't*

leave it alone and he and Pete fought.

'This is sergeant Jacks from Wolsey Road Police Station. Mr Barrow, are you the registered keeper of a green Ford Fiesta? Registration number ULV 387 S?'

'Well, I share it with a friend. My name's on the documents because I happened to send it off to Swansea. Why?' My mouth was still dry but I was more curious now that I realised it had nothing to do with Pete.

'This friend? Is it a young woman?'

Now I understood. Cheryl had been racing down the motorway and passed some jam-butty car and been pulled over for something. She didn't have any of the documents and she'd given them my number to confirm she was allowed to drive it because she didn't want Pete bothered.

'No but if the young woman's name is Cheryl Whelan, I know her and she has permission to use the car. It's a long story but she'll explain.'

'Mr Barrow, I'm afraid I've got some bad news...'

Why is it that, whenever a policeman has bad news to impart, he always pauses before he tells you? Maybe it's to give you time to run through all the bad things you can think of and then settle for the least of it. Whatever, I did just that. I went from the car blowing up to Cheryl passing a Police Range Rover and sticking up two fingers as she passed. The possibility of an accident also crossed my mind but I dismissed it because she was a far better driver than either Pete or me. Then that pause was over and Sergeant Jacks was filling it with words.

'Mr Barrow, I'm afraid Miss Whelan has been involved in an accident. She's been taken to Oxborough Infirmary.

Can you go there and speak to the two policemen? We would be grateful.'

I sat down in the telephone seat. I must have sat down hard because it brought my Mum in from the kitchen and my Dad from the living room.

'I...um...is she...' I added a pause of my own but then rushed into it before the man on the other phone could fill it with information I didn't want to hear. 'Yes. I'll drive there right now. Oh, Jesus!'

'Mr Barrow?'

'Can I bring her boyfriend with me? They've just got engaged and his mother died yesterday and...'

'In that case, I think he *should* go with you.'

That *should* gave me all the information I hadn't wanted to hear. I listened while the sergeant told me the names of the policemen I needed to see. I told him who Cheryl's mother was and where she lived and then mumbled something like goodbye. I grabbed my jacket, gave my parents the gist, got the car keys and went to pick up Pete.

When he answered the door, I didn't give him a chance to ask me why I was back. I told him what the police told me.

He stood on the porch, looking over my shoulder. I left him there, went inside, got a coat from the rack under the stairs, told Ronald what was going on and then guided Pete to the car. We didn't talk on the way to the hospital. I parked in the huge car park behind the hospital and then guided him into the brightly-lit Accident and Emergency Department.

The place was Friday-night busy and smelled the way all hospitals smell. I found a nurse who didn't look as run off her feet as the others, found out what I needed to know and then walked Pete up to the room where Cheryl was. The two policemen outside knew who we were because the station had radioed them to tell them we were on the way. I opened the closed door of the room and Pete and I went in.

There was only one bed in the room but it was surrounded by what looked like props from a film about a coma victim. A nurse was making notes on a clipboard while a woman doctor examined the body on the bed. That body was, apparently, Cheryl but I couldn't reconcile it with the funny, vibrant, girl I'd known for almost three years.

Her face was one big bruise, highlighted by streaks of dried blood. One eye was open but it had rolled upward in its socket and stared blindly at the ceiling. Both arms were flat against the mattress, tubes and needles protruding from them. I couldn't see her legs because of the single sheet but the bumps and creases beneath that sheet were mute testimony to the unnatural set of both legs.

I looked at Pete. His face looked calm, almost peaceful. I started to say something but the doctor turned to us and then crossed the floor to stand in front of us.

'Are you family?'

'I...' Pete began and then stopped.

'Her only family in Oxborough,' I said. 'How is she?'

'Let's go outside,' the doctor said and then, seeing the look on Pete's face which told her he didn't want to leave Cheryl, 'It's okay, we won't be long. You can come back in a minute.'

'Miss Whelan is very ill,' she told me as soon as we were in the room next door to Cheryl's. She didn't waste time with niceties. I suppose she didn't have time in her job for small talk. I was glad. 'She's broken both legs as well as her pelvis and one arm. Her face is lacerated. Unfortunately, there are extensive internal injuries.'

She stopped then, letting us take in the enormity of the damage. It wasn't a pause but it served the same purpose and I didn't need to run through the possibilities here. I looked at Pete. The look on his face told me he didn't, either.

'How long will she live?' He asked and his voice was very calm. 'Will she know me or be able to hear me or speak to me?'

'She may live as long as a day but it's more likely to be four or five hours. She may well regain consciousness before the end and, if so, she will probably be able to hear and speak. I'm very sorry. We'll do our best but I'm afraid it won't be enough.'

Cheryl died at seven minutes past three in the morning of May 29th. Her mother was with her. The police had arranged an escort from Liverpool. She spoke with Pete and told him not to blame himself, that Cheryl was the sort who did things her way and nothing would've stopped her trying to be with him tonight. He thanked her and I knew he wouldn't blame himself.

Cheryl did regain consciousness and she spoke to all of us despite the agony she must've been in. I stayed close to the bed long enough to hear her tell me not be a misery all my life and to make sure Pete kept chasing his dream. I moved away then while she spoke to her mother and Pete. She told her mum to find some rich bloke to marry before her looks went and then she smiled at Pete. She licked her lips once and gestured with her head for him to lean forward.

'You say goodbye to your mum for me at the funeral. And don't give up on your dad. Everybody should have a dad, Pete. And make sure Ted writes enough lyrics to make you rich and famous. And don't look so miserable, soft lad, I'll see you again. You're not getting rid of me that easy.'

And then she took one short, coarse breath in and didn't let it out again.

Ronald met us as we left the room. He looked at Pete. Pete looked at him. And then Ronald did something that made me feel as if there might be some hope after all. He held his arms out to his son and didn't try to wipe away the tears from his own cheeks. Pete hitched in a sob and let his father embrace him and take him home.

I got home just after five that morning, too tired to fall asleep. I had a bowl of cornflakes and a cup of tea. I might've dozed off but I was awake again by half six and went for the paper. I read it and did the crossword and then remembered about Thingie and the planned recording session.

I phoned him at half eight, told him why we couldn't make it. He was okay about it, said he was sorry and that we should get in touch whenever we were ready. It all seemed irrelevant. I phoned Jude. I thought about leaving it until after she got back from London but that would've made me no better than Ronald. She cried over the phone and I told her I'd pick her up for Carol's funeral but she told me she'd be in London for an extra two days. She'd be home in time for Cheryl's funeral and she'd see me then.

The police called round for a statement at ten and I finally found out what had happened.

It seemed Cheryl was moving from the inside lane to get into the right lane for Oxborough. There are three junctions close together and the sign gives you good notice. The car ahead had a blow-out. Cheryl saw it and moved into the outside lane. There was a car behind her but not near enough for trouble. The car with the blow-out slewed sideways, clipping the car behind Cheryl, forcing it into the back of our little Fiesta. Cheryl had no chance. The little Ford bounced up onto the central reservation, bounced off and flipped onto its back. Sometimes, it seems that, when God wants you, He makes sure you come. At least He let Cheryl see and speak to the people she loved before He took her.

Carol Lynwood was buried the following Tuesday in Larch Cemetery.

Cheryl Maureen Whelan was buried two days later in Yew Tree Cemetery in Liverpool.

Pete and I collected our stuff from college and we stayed

at Jude's for a weekend in June. We returned to Oxborough for two weeks and, at Pete's suggestion, worked three nights at The Eight Bells for old time's sake.

On Friday, July 30th, Pete and I flew out of Manchester airport on a scheduled flight to Barcelona.

Second Verse

We stayed just over two years in Spain. We lived in an apartment in Barcelona for the first year. The second year, we lived in our own villa on the outskirts of Madrid.

We both graduated, Pete with distinctions. True to his word, Jude's dad fixed me up with an interview with a contact he had at Mobil. They were opening a refinery close to Gibraltar and needed a liaison officer who was fluent in Spanish. I got the job and my wish to live in Spain.

Pete was the problem. He and Ronald had come to a *modus vivendi* after that embrace outside Cheryl's room in the hospital but it was clear that they needed space and time away from each other for things to ever really work out. Oddly, it was Ronald who solved the problem about what Pete should do.

Pete was twenty one, had his university degree and so the conditions of his trust fund were fulfilled. He now had around twenty five thousand pounds in his building society account. Ronald suggested that he move to Spain with me, try to find a job and, if he couldn't, he could just have an extended holiday.

Jude was going to London. It hurt but I never told her because I'd always known she would go away to finish her training and, she hoped, eventually go into research. Besides, we were friends as well as lovers.

'We'll see each other again,' she said before I left.

And we did but that was later.

The grief of Carol's and Cheryl's deaths followed us to Spain, of course. Oh, we both cried at the funerals and I even found myself crying silently one afternoon when I was walking the dog along the shore in Oxborough the afternoon before we flew out. But grief is a process, like life I suppose. It's not like a cold that lasts a few days and then you're over it. And different people grieve in different ways. I expected Pete's grief to bring on a deep depression and, because I did, I probably bit down on my own grief so that I could be strong for him when he needed it.

That low did come; it just took a little longer than I was expecting, that's all.

Pete and I spent the first week in Spain in a hotel close to Las Ramblas. I worked during the day while he looked for a job and somewhere more permanent for us to live. I thought having something to do would stop the depression from becoming too deep and it seemed to work. He was quiet in the evenings. He'd sit in the chair and strum his guitar and occasionally talk to me about what my job was like and, even more occasionally, about his mum and Cheryl, just remembering things they'd said or done. He never gave me any tunes to find words for and I never asked if he was writing again. Sometimes, I'd catch him watching me as I did some paperwork I'd brought back from work. The first couple of times, I put down my pen and turned to face him, thinking he might want to talk about things but he only gave me a half-smile and picked up his guitar. The other times, I'd just catch what I thought was an odd light in his eyes, a strange thoughtful expression on his face.

Pete found the apartment close to the football ground. Mind you, comparing Nou Camp to a normal football ground is like comparing the Isle of Man to the island of Australia. I also found out from my colleagues at work that apartments there were hard to come by. When I asked Pete how he managed this minor miracle he just gave me a Carol-smile and told me what my share of the rent was and I thought back to how he'd found out all that stuff about me at school from the teachers and the other lads. Just Pete and his charm.

A job was harder to find. He spent a fortnight traipsing round the *bureaux de change*, offices of national and multinational companies, asking for a job in the computer departments but there just weren't any. The longer it went on, the more depressed I could see him becoming and I dreaded coming home to him in the depths of a depression so deep there was no way out.

It was, naturally enough, his music that got him off the merry-go-round.

One day, instead of depressing himself in the city, he took the train up the coast, past all the resorts like Calella and Pineda and Blanes. He got off at Blanes and, outside, there was a bus waiting to go to Lloret. Pete got on it. He knew that Lloret was a big resort, a favourite of the English. Our next door neighbour's son, Pepe, worked in a hotel there during the summer and, when he was home on a day off, told Pete all about it.

I got home that night, thinking of nothing more than a long, ice-cold drink of lime and lemonade. It had been one of those days at work. We all get them. When I sat down on the chair by the window and began to sip my drink, Pete got right into it.

'It only takes about an hour to get to Blanes on the train and then about twenty minutes into Lloret on the bus. Not long, that, you know.'

'Good,' I said, watching the sun go down out in the Mediterranean and just feeling relaxation spread through me. 'We can go down one weekend.' There was a long pause and I had the feeling that whatever he'd found in Spain's version of Rhyl was a bit more than an all-night party. I also had the feeling that, whatever it was, I was going to get roped into it.

'I walked round for a bit,' he said eventually. 'And then I went into this huge hotel. Called the Don Juan.' He pronounced it with a hard J, English fashion. I'd tried to teach him some Spanish because it would help get him a job but we'd both given it up as a bad job. He wanted to be fluent yesterday and his impatience got me down. 'It's really massive. Got two outdoor pools and an indoor one and there's a disco in the basement till three in the morning. And there's a big bar-room where they have all the family entertainment and it's only, like—'

'Okay, buggerlugs, what did you get us into this time?'

He grinned that bloody grin and I knew I'd been right.

'Well, the manager told me—'

'How the hell did you get to see him?'

'I asked,' he said and looked at me as if I was stupid to ask. The fact that seeing the managers of those places usually requires a letter from the Holy Ghost was something that never entered his head. 'Anyway, he told me they get a lot of Brits there and they all like English music. He's been getting a bit of a hammering from the local pubs on his doorstep because they all have jukeboxes with English music and they get a couple of acts to do a gig at the weekends. So—'

'So you suggested we do the weekends for him. That's what you did, isn't it? You did another Eight Bells and got us a friggin job singing in some bloody hotel almost two hours away. And I'm supposed to shrug and say fine. Just by the by, have you thought what we're going to do about instruments? We only brought the acoustics.'

'That's okay, Terry. I'll buy the gear tomorrow. I've seen exactly what we need. One good thing, the place has got a great PA. I'll just get a couple of electrics and maybe one of those new Yamaha electric pianos or something.'

'Pete,' I said quietly. I wasn't annoyed like I'd been in Liverpool. I'd been feeling for a while that there was something missing and now I knew it was the music. True, I'd've settled for an electric piano and our acoustics in the apartment if he just wanted to write songs but, also true, you can't beat the buzz you get from performing live. And, most of all, it would help Pete through his grief. Still, there were the practicalities to be sorted out, the stuff Pete hardly ever thought about. I said his name again because he was obviously off somewhere, making more plans. 'Pete? I work in Barcelona. If we do Sundays at this hotel, I don't fancy getting home at dawn because we missed the last train by two minutes. Do the trains run that late anyway?'

'No sweat. We'll buy a car.'

He really was something else. 'Yeah, I knew you'd say that. Christ Lynwood, you get me into some barmy situations. When do we start?'

'I said we'd go down Saturday and show him what we can do. We can buy the gear and car tomorrow. I'll meet you in town.'

Just like that.

We bought the instruments the following dinner time. The bloke in the shop must've thought all his Christmases had come at once. He nearly fell over himself when I picked up a handmade twelve string acoustic. The sound was wonderful, rich, full and resonant. I played a few chords on it and Pete sat at the electric piano, picked out a tune, a new one, while I accompanied him. The people in the shop applauded when we finished and I knew then that I really *had* missed that buzz. The manager agreed to store the stuff we bought till that night and I went back to work.

Pete met me when I finished and we bought a car. Just like that. Mind you, when you're buying brand new and in cash, it's amazing how the red tape seems to thin out. We bought an Escort and drove it to the music shop and loaded our new gear in the hatchback. I drove through the accessible parts of Las Ramblas and Pete tugged at my arm as we stopped at a set of lights.

'Find somewhere to park this and let's get out there. It'll be better than sitting in the apartment.'

Las Ramblas is a boulevard with narrow roads branching off it, close to Catalonia Square. It's one of the city's big attractions. It's a bit like the pedestrianised areas in some English towns and cities but it's got a lot more style. The trees bow over, giving shade, and the flowers and plants imbue it with a smell you just don't get in an English city. It's a great place to just sit and watch the world go by. There's plenty of free entertainment because the buskers and jugglers and magicians roam around doing what they do and they all seem to be smiling.

Pete had seen a group of four lads playing guitars and stomping under the branches of a shiny palm. There wasn't much of a crowd but it didn't seem to bother them. I parked in a side street under a balcony and we grabbed the twelve-string and one of the ordinary acoustics we'd bought and went back into the boulevard.

The lads were playing Free songs and it seemed strange hearing those relics from the early seventies in this foreign country but the people watching and listening were obviously enjoying them. We picked a speck outside a small cafe and began with 'Nowhere Man'. It felt good to be playing again. By the time we'd finished, we had a bigger crowd than anybody else busking there. Even the four lads playing Free songs unplugged their gear and came to listen. The applause got me a little high. It felt like a new beginning.

Lloret really did remind me of Rhyl. There were hundreds of bars and English-style pubs and hotels and discos. I found it difficult to see where the town's natives lived but they obviously lived somewhere because there were so many of them working in all the hotels and bars.

The Don Juan was as big as Pete said, covering about four acres on a small hill not far from where the dry river bed disappeared under the road. The manager saw us, was pleasantly surprised I could speak to him in his own language, took us into the family bar-room, listened while we played and then hired us for the equivalent of thirty five pounds a week. He wanted us to start that night at eight. In the meantime, Pete and I strolled through the town.

That's something you find yourself doing in Spain; strolling. The pace of life is a lot slower and strolling just seems the natural thing to do.

We followed the dry river bed towards the beach but never made it to the actual sand. First we were bushwhacked by the beautiful medieval church and then, through what amounted to a back alley, we found the tree-lined promenade that overlooks the beach.

It's that promenade that is my abiding memory of our time in Spain. It runs the length of the beach, from the point where the river bed meets the Med' up to where the castle stands on its promontory of rock, looking towards Africa. During the day the prom is deceptively sedate in its Catalan elegance and gives no indication of how frenetic it gets at night. Of course, we didn't see it at night so it's the way it was during the day that sticks with me. We'd get to town about two in the afternoon on Saturday and we'd walk the prom, just soaking up the atmosphere or sit and drink a glass of Fundador. It helped relax us before the gig at night.

We worked through the summer until October and we

got better every night. We did a lot of our own stuff in the first set because the room didn't fill up until after half nine when the holidaymakers came back from the trips or the beach. As the summer wore on, we began to get a regular crowd at that first set. In the second set, we did a mixture of old rock'n'roll and that holiday garbage that was going round—'Una Paloma Blanca', 'Viva Espana', and 'The Birdie Song' None of them were our idea of music but the paying customers wanted them and we occasionally took the piss by messing around with the arrangements.

Now that we were performing again, Pete wrote more stuff. I couldn't find lyrics for them all but I found enough. They were lighter tunes, a lot of minor key work but they were just as catchy and more than once we heard somebody down on the prom whistling one we'd played the night before. Pete never seemed to sleep, he was always at the keyboard. I was glad to see him writing again and I hoped that this was his way of grieving, or at least coping with his grief. But now and then, I'd hear Jude talking about Hypomania and I kept watch.

One amusing thing was the way Pete politely but firmly refused the blatant offers he was getting from the girls. Most of them were British on some 18-30 holiday and weren't too bothered; they could always find some other bloke to get them drunk and take them to bed. The Spanish girls thought he was 'lovely'. It was the only word most of them could come up with in English when they used me as interpreter. Pete just smiled and said 'no', leaving them looking slightly puzzled. You could almost read it in their faces—*what happened to all the English promiscuity?*

It was Cheryl, of course, lodged in his mind, in his soul. But he kept his equanimity, just kept on smiling and shaking his head. I wasn't so placid and more than once told them to piss off.

But the grief finally broke the frail barricades Pete had built. It happened the week before we went home for Christmas and I thought that that was the reason for it—realising that he was going home and, for the first time, his mother wouldn't be there when he woke up on Christmas morning. I was partly right but there was more to it and it had a lot to do with me. It came close to ending our friendship but, in the end, actually made it stronger.

I got home one night and found him lying on his bed, in the dark, suicidal. It scared the hell out of me.

I'd spent the day in Madrid trying to sort out work permits for two executives from Mobil who were coming over to finish setting up the refinery. I left early so I could get back; we had tickets to watch Barcelona play Real Madrid at the Nou Camp. When I left that morning, Pete was smiling, playing one of those new computer games that had just come out. He told me he was determined not to let the stuff he'd learned atrophy; if he ever forgot how to write or play music, he could always fall back on it.

'Dad was right about that,' he told me.

So I left him with the game and his keyboard and his manuscript paper and pencils, knowing the game would be forgotten soon and I'd get back to the sound of music.

But when I got home the apartment was silent. All I could hear was the muted tock of the clock and the occasional toot of a car horn in the street. The place was dark, too. The blinds were drawn and no light was on. It was nothing to be worried about, I told myself. I put the light on and called his name.

The place was a shambles.

Pete was the tidiest of people. When he was composing, all the paper would be in stacks, the edges aligned perfectly once he'd finished. Any instrument he'd used would be in its case. The pencils and rubbers would be in one of those deskmate things. His chair would be in its place. I imagined it had something to do with all those logical progressions in computers and music—a place for everything and everything in its place.

That night, his guitar was lying on its strings, half under the keyboard stand. The keyboard was uncovered and paper was strewn all over it and beneath it. The chair was lying on its back, four legs pointing at the window. Pencils littered the floor between cushions that had been scattered everywhere. The grey portable cassette recorder sat on top of the keyboard, the Perspex lid wrenched off one hinge.

Worry began to insinuate itself all down my back. I called his name again and still got no answer.

I picked up a piece of manuscript paper and looked at the dots and squiggles that he translated into such wonderful tunes. The squiggles and dots only went half way down the paper and only half way across it. Below and to the side of them was a long, thick line sloping left to right. The line was scored so deeply that it perforated the paper. I let the paper drop to the floor.

The kitchen made me feel even worse because it *wasn't* a shambles.

Pete had only the vaguest aspirations to culinary expertise but, unlike with the cars we owned, he was convinced he could actually make cooking work. Such was this belief, he tried to cook even when he was on his own. Not sandwiches and coffee for my mate Pete. He'd have every pot and pan in the place out and, once the disaster was consigned to the bin, the pots and pans were left all over the place.

The kitchen that night was immaculate.

T.S. Elliot said he'd show you fear in a handful of dust but for me, *real* fear was coming home and finding the kitchen looking as if it belonged in a glossy magazine photo. It was a bit like finding a spot of blood on the floor outside a locked bathroom, seeing steam coming under the door, hearing the tap running and wondering how many razor blades were left.

Pete, that most gannet-like of people, hadn't eaten all day.

I went to his bedroom and knocked. I called his name again. I pushed the door open when there was no reply and had to wait until my eyes adjusted to the gloom.

'Pete?'

'Hello, Terry.'

Hearing his voice should've made me feel better but it didn't. There was no emotion in it. It sounded hollow, a pale imitation of a human voice.

'You okay, mate?'

'Oh, you know. I'm about through with it all. Used and abused, that's me. Ah well, fuck it, eh?'

I turned the light on and had to blink against the sudden glare. And saw him.

He was stretched out on the bed, arms behind his head, fingers locked, legs crossed at the ankles, dressed in his black Wrangler jeans and a black crew neck T-shirt. His feet were bare. He looked like a hastily-dressed corpse. He was staring at the ceiling with a blank expression on his face that mimicked the tone of his voice. I swept my gaze around the room, looking for that razor blade or its equivalent but saw nothing except a tidy room.

'Turn it off, Terry. Can't concentrate on not thinking with the light on.'

'Sit up. You've put the fear of God into me and I'm not talking to something that looks like an animated corpse.'

'You don't have to talk to me. Nothing to talk about. Just turn the light off.'

'Sit up!' I shouted because I wanted to get angry enough to chase away the cold fear inside me. It didn't work. 'I don't know what happened after I left but you're going to tell me. Sit up, Pete.'

He shuffled up the bed so he was looking at me. He looked terrible. His eyes were horrible. It was like looking at a house where the lights were on but nobody you knew was at home.

'You told me you were going to write,' I said, wanting to look away but forcing myself not to. 'What happened to the music?'

'Ah yes, music. If music be the food of love, we'll all get

indigestion. What has music to do with life? Sweet fuck all. What's the point of it? Come to that, what's the point of life? We're born, we struggle through the bloody obstacle course the philosophers call life, trying to satisfy all the conventions and aspirations of society and our parents. And for what? We get kicked in the teeth, kicked in the balls and shit on from a great height. And if we find a little light with someone, life turns the light out. It happens to everybody and we still carry on. Jesus Christ, it's a friggin joke. Just one big celestial joke played by a God who, if He exists, is probably mentally retarded. So, Terry, my good old friend Terry, what is the fucking point?'

How do you answer that? I could've come out with all the usual platitudes but my heart wouldn't have been in it, you know? He had a point, didn't he? He'd spent the best part of his home life not knowing his mother and then she died just when they might've got to know each other. His father wasn't really his father and the fact Pete didn't know that was really beside the point. He'd found Cheryl and had her taken away just like his mother. All he had left was his music and now he'd decided he didn't want that anymore. And he was so *passionless* about it. He said it all in the tone of voice you use to recite a motorway service station's menu.

I said the only thing I could think of. I'm not sure where it came from but as soon as I said it, I knew it was the right thing.

'The music is the point. As far as both Carol and Cheryl were concerned it was the point.' I waited for him to rage against that and me but he just sighed a cynical sigh and looked at the ceiling. Then the idea came to me to really get his attention. 'I think it's about time you learned the real truth about your mum and about your family history.'

He sat up properly this time and his eyes no longer looked dead but the light there wasn't a pleasant light; whatever was living in that house wasn't necessarily benevolent.

'What? *I* told *you* about that, remember? What the hell're you on about?'

I took a breath and sat on the chair at the dressing table in front of the window. 'Your mum—'

'We can talk about Mum and you later,' he said, cutting me off.

I frowned at him. 'What d'you—'

He cut me off again. 'Later. Tell me about my family history, Terry. Tell me now.'

Oh, the light in his eyes was definitely unfriendly now and, for a second, I thought about shaking my head and telling him to forget it. But I didn't because I couldn't. He was my best mate and he needed help and that's what best mates do where and when they can.

So I told him. That light in his eyes when he told me to tell him about his mum and me later was still there so I told him about Ronald. It was like I could hear Carol telling me that, yes, it was time.

Imagination of course.

That's what I told myself in that bedroom in Spain. Now, after The Camberwell House I'm not sure.

'Did she tell you his name?' Pete asked when I'd finished.

It was the obvious question.

'No, she didn't.'

'And Dad, Ronald, knew all along.' It wasn't a question. 'All these years, I've been living a lie.'

'I don't see it that way,' I told him. 'And I don't think your mum did. Ronald certainly didn't.' I realised, saying this, that I must've felt more for Ronald than I thought. It was a strange feeling but true. 'Think of all the arguments you had. He never threw it in your face. He could've done. Just to spite you or Carol. But the reason I told you is the music. I don't have to remind you what Cheryl said just before she died, do I?'

He narrowed his eyes at me but that light was still visible. 'No,' he said. 'You don't have to remind me, Terry.' He sat up straighter on the bed. 'But you can tell me about this.' He reached under his pillow and pulled out a music cassette and held it up.

The plastic case picked up a glimmer from the bedroom light and my mind's eye showed me the portable cassette player in the living room. The cassette player with its lid half-ripped off its hinges and I knew. Deep down, I knew but, because I'm as human as the next bloke, I played for time.

Yeah, right. As if Pete was going to let me talk my way out of it.

'What about it?' I asked, trying to sound innocent and unaware, hoping maybe he'd think I thought it was a new tune he'd written that he wanted me find some words for.

He bit his bottom lip nodded towards the cassette player on the dressing table behind me. I stood up and took the cassette off him and put it into the player and pressed the button.

And closed my eyes and swallowed hard as Carol's voice bled into the room, singing my words. Her guitar playing was perfect.

Pete waited until the song had finished and then said, 'So, Terry, what about that?'

'It's your mum.'

He nodded and then made a come-on gesture with his right hand.

And still I tried to pretend I had no idea what he was on about.

'What? It's your mum singing a song and playing the guitar.' I shrugged. 'Yeah, I knew she was a musician but she asked me not to tell you.' I took a breath. 'She asked me not to tell you about that or about Ronald until the time was right. Well, tonight was the night.' I shrugged again.

'When did you write the lyrics? Mmm? And,' he pushed his head back against the headboard and stared at me. 'How many times did you and my mother screw each other?'

My whole body tensed up and my head banged once, like a clock striking the hour. 'What?' My voice was tense, too. Angry. My hands clenched into fists on my thighs.

Pete laughed and shook his head. 'You think I don't know one of your lyrics after all this time?'

I shook my head. 'I'm not talking about the lyrics, bollocks. I'm talking about the rest. What the fuck d'you mean about me and your mum?'

'Ah, come on, Terry. The bloody words say it all. Nobody writes stuff like that for his *mate's mother*. Just, for fuck's sake tell me and get it over with.'

I took a deep breath and looked out of the window. The street below was empty of people and moving cars. The glow of streetlamps turned the night into a misty orange that hid the stars and I wished to God that Carol had never played me her tune. Still with my back to him, I said, 'Listen again, Pete. Those words fit the tune. Yeah, they're about love but so what? I loved your mum.' I turned to look at him and he was still staring at me. 'She played me that tune the night you were so worried about her making a fool of herself and you when you met Kate in Laketon.' I raised my eyebrows at him. To make him squirm I suppose. Why? Because I still felt guilty about what nearly happened between me and Carol, why else? 'Remember? Yeah, you do.'

And then I told him what had happened on the pier that night. As I talked, the baleful light in his eyes began to fade. It wasn't replaced by a kinder light but at least it finally went away. By the time I'd finished, Pete was looking at the ceiling with his eyes closed.

But I must've still been feeling a little guilty because I said, 'You know what Pete? I think she might've played the tune to you if you'd…' I stopped because he shook his head and his hands went up to his face. 'No,' I said softly. 'No, she wouldn't have, Pete. I'm sorry…I shouldn't've said that.' He waved his left hand at me—*it's okay, forget it*—and I nodded to myself. 'She was happy, Pete. And sad. Happy that she'd seen you playing music like you always wanted to. And sad because she missed playing music. Playing that tune was something she needed to do. Pete?'

He opened his eyes and looked at me.

'She was good, mate. That's why I wrote the lyrics. I heard the tune and, just like with you, I heard the words. I had to write them down and...' I paused again because I needed to think of a way of explaining how Carol knew about the words without blurting out what had happened at the same time. 'The day after you and your dad rowed about the car...' Pete nodded. 'I called up at your house and your mum was on her own and really upset. She was convinced her family was about to break apart for good. I wanted to cheer her up and I told her she was wrong but...well, she was pretty drunk. So I did the only thing I could think of that might've made her happy. I played her the song. I didn't know she'd recorded herself singing it, Pete. And Carol and I never had sex. I loved her, yeah, but the same way I loved Cheryl and you.' Not quite true but as true as I'd ever get when it came to Carol and that song.

Pete didn't say anything but he looked at me without any narrowing of his eyes or any tension round his mouth. Then he sighed and leaned his head back against the headboard and closed his eyes. I thought about leaving him then, just letting him come to terms with what he now knew but I couldn't. This low, this deep depression wasn't the tantrum he'd thrown in school over the timetable and it wasn't the bad one he'd had in Laketon when he'd sat on the Waltzer's roof. This was the sort of depression that went to his very soul because it was grief, too. And, on top of that, he knew the man he'd called his father wasn't and that his mother had been as good a musician as her son.

Think about it. For years, Pete had played and written music and it went nowhere until I came along. Then he had a sounding board and an outlet and he blossomed. Now he knew that, for all those years when his music just stayed in his head or in his bedroom, he might've been able to share it with his mother. Knowledge like that was perfect food for the depression to feed on. That's the thing with depression; it feeds itself and produces a perfect vicious circle.

'Pete?'

'Mmm?'

'How did you get hold of the cassette?'

Still with his eyes closed, Pete smiled a Carol-smile. 'My Dad gave it to me,' he said. 'Pretty ironic, really.'

Yeah, that was a word you could use. There were several others but instead of saying them, I found myself remembering Ronald's expression the Friday night after Carol had died, that slow smile and the look of respect in his eyes when he thanked me. Good-old-Ronald must've guessed I'd written the words Carol had been singing the afternoon she died. Or had Carol told him? Not that it mattered.

'What, he just gave you the cassette and never told you about your mum?'

Pete nodded. 'He didn't say anything. Just gave it to me along with a load of others he'd dredged up from my bedroom while I was packing to leave for this place. I just bunged it in the Tesco bag with the rest.' He took a long breath. 'And found it today and played it and…

He put his hands to his face and sobbed. I sat there and waited for him to finish and wondered why Ronald would do that, just give Pete the cassette and say nothing.

And, as somebody somewhere said once or twice, answer

came there none. I found out later and I was glad I did. But, like I said, that came later.

It took about ten minutes before Pete's sobs tapered off. By then, he'd slid down so he was lying down again and I realised that he'd cried himself to sleep, the way our Dawn used to when she was little and had thrown one tantrum too many and been sent to bed. I covered Pete up with the quilt and left him asleep. He kept hold of the cassette.

The following morning (I never did get to see Real play Barcelona), Pete was up before me, sitting at the kitchen table eating his Weetabix. The cassette was on the table by his mug of tea. I was almost late and dashed round, grabbing a banana and gulping down some apple juice as I tried to make sure I had all the documents I needed in my briefcase.

'If we ever get to make a record, Terry,' Pete said without looking at me. 'I want this song on it somewhere. B-side or on the album. Somewhere. Okay? You owe me that much.'

I was already nodding, glad he seemed to at least *want* to get through his depression and grief but not really taking the idea of making any sort of record seriously. But those last five words stopped my dash around the kitchen. 'What?'

'You should've told me when you knew, Terry,' Pete explained patiently.

'Your mum didn't want me to,' I told him as evenly as I could but he was shaking his head, the way you do to an errant child who needs to know who the boss is. And, grief and depression be buggered, I wasn't taking that. 'Pete, it's done and I'm *not* sorry. Right? Okay, now I'm going to work. I'll see you later. Just so you got the message, I'm not sorry. Your mum was right.'

I got home that night, half-expecting Pete to be waiting in the hallway, ready for a full-blown row. Instead, he turned round in the chair in front of the keyboard in the living room and handed me a cassette. I just stared at it and then at him.

'It's not my Mum,' he told me. 'Some tunes. With lyrics, I think there's one there that could really do it for us.'

I took the tape into my bedroom and played it straight away on my own little cassette player. There were eight tunes on it and the words came almost immediately. I sat there on the chair in front of the window, words rolling round my head and heard Jude talking about Hypomania again. I prayed to Whoever might have been listening that I'd done the right thing and that I hadn't simply set him up for a big let-down.

Even so, the words were some of the best I ever wrote.

We went back to England for Christmas and I saw Ronald and he said nothing to me about Carol or the cassette but he was friendly, even warm. I thought about asking him straight out but decided against it. Mainly because I didn't want a row with Ronald while Pete was still struggling through the holiday. He was still grieving and still in the depths of the depression and even our family party couldn't help him. He didn't even come into the back room, never mind play the piano at the end of the night. We went back to Spain and he was the same; it seemed that writing those eight tunes had been something of a false dawn. Oh, we played the Don Juan and he was good enough but I knew he was running on automatic, his technical expertise doing the job rather than his heart. And he never once suggested we play any of the new eight tunes he'd written. I wondered if he would ever climb out of the depression and it broke my heart a little more each time I saw him on stage, his eyes far away while his fingers did what they needed to do.

And then it was May '84 and I knew Pete had found enough foot- and hand-holds to haul himself out the hole he'd been in since before Christmas.

We were doing more of our stuff in the first set at the hotel and keeping mostly to the same formula for the second set when the families got back from their days out. The crowd for our first set was getting bigger and most of them were bar staff from the competition.

'You know what it means?' Pete asked me on a Saturday afternoon

I was ogling a gorgeous blonde who was sitting on her own at the bar of the restaurant-cum-bar next to the room where we did our stuff. She was looking at me with what I hoped was a come-on look in her huge black eyes. When Pete asked me the question I just nodded, not really listening. I was trying to think of a way to get her to watch us play.

'Are you listening to me bollocks?' He turned me by the arm so I faced him.

'Yes. No, I don't know what it means but I'm sure you're going to tell me. So why don't you and just leave me with my fantasies?'

'Jesus, Terry,' he said, finally seeing what it was I was

looking at. 'She'd swallow you up and blow you out in bubbles. Why don't you settle for the girl behind the bar in the other room? She thinks you're the best thing since sliced bread and she's just as good looking as that one.'

'What're you on about?' The idea that there was a girl who fancied me and I didn't know about it took the shine off the blonde. I hadn't been a monk since coming to Spain but it hadn't been one a night, either.

'Carla. The one with the big cow-eyes. Anyway, forget about that for now. We're getting more people at our first set and I had a word with Jimmy, the Scots lad behind the bar. He told me the takings were up nearly fifteen percent on last year for that first hour.'

'How did you find about Carla?' I wasn't interested in bar takings. I was interested in Carla saving me all the hassle of tapping off with holiday-makers if I felt like female company. But Pete had said all he was going to say on the subject.

'Oh for God's sake, get you mind above your bloody waist. If the takings are up, we can use it to pressure El Bosso.'

'A rise? He's given us one. He might be Spanish but he's not soft. Anyway, I think what we get is fair.'

He rolled his eyes exaggeratedly. I was obviously missing the point. 'I'm not talking about more cash. I think we get a good screw, too. I'm talking about getting him to let us play more of our own stuff in the second set.'

'Why?' I really didn't understand. What we were doing was enjoyable, why do more of our own stuff?

'Because what we've written is *good*. It's better than the

stuff we did in Liverpool and it's better than some of the current chart stuff. If we do more of our own stuff we might get spotted. We could do that record we never did in England. We can't spend the rest of our lives doing what we're doing. If that's all there is, we might as well jack it in now.'

So that was it. As far as I was concerned, the idea of doing a record had receded a long time ago. To be honest, it had always been Pete's and Cheryl's idea more than mine. I was doing a job I liked, using the education I'd got, using what talent God had given me. Becoming a pop star was nowhere on my list of things to do with my life. But this was Pete and he no longer sounded as if he couldn't give a toss about the world or anything in it. I looked at him and saw his eyes flashing and the way his eyebrows tented above those eyes and I knew he was serious. And, in that couple of seconds, I heard myself telling him that his mum and Cheryl had both thought the music was the point; I heard myself, back in the bedroom that awful night before Christmas, asking him if he remembered what Cheryl had told him just before she died.

'Well?' He demanded.

I smiled at him. 'You really want to try to make a hit record?'

'What else do I have? I can't get a job in computers over here and I don't want to go home on my own. And it's what I'm good at, it's what I do. And I owe it to the two people who meant more than anything to me to try. They made me good at it. You told me that. Playing two nights a week for a bunch of half-drunk holiday-makers is not what I consider worthwhile. But I can't do it on my own, Terry. I can't write lyrics to save my life and you play better guitar than me. I want to make it in music but I want to do it with you.'

My smile broadened. 'Okay. But how? I haven't seen any recording studios in Lloret and we don't know the Spanish equivalent of Pete Leay. I'll do it but I can't go hawking my guitar round the country with you, Pete.'

He smiled at me and I saw Carol. 'I might have a way of short-circuiting all that. The important thing is that you be interpreter with El Bosso when we try to get him to let us do more of our stuff. We'll see him in our break.'

El Bosso was the manager of the hotel, Ricardo Nasciemento Alvarez. He told us to call him Ricki but we couldn't resist El Bosso behind his back. Ricki was twenty eight and started in the hotel business at nineteen, working behind the bar. He was the antithesis of most people's idea of a Spaniard. He was as tall as me, as tanned as a person is likely to be living in that climate but his eyes were pale blue and his hair a dark blonde. He was learning English and German in what little spare time he had and his application was what I admired most about him. I liked the bloke.

It was quarter to ten when we sat in his office behind main reception and Pete, through me, finally persuaded him to let us do more of our stuff in the second set. It took a while but when Pete wanted something, he was hard to hold back.

'The second part,' Ricki said. 'But that's for the families. They like all the tap-tap songs and the silly bump-de-bump tunes. It's why they come to the Don Juan. You know this at the beginning and agreed at the start.'

The fact that his English was failing him told me he wasn't too struck on the idea. I could sense Pete getting fidgety next to me and the last thing we needed was him losing his temper. It would end up with him telling Ricki to shove it and find another act. Which would take all of ten minutes; Ricki could stand on the front steps and whistle and have his choice of half a dozen. Pete held his temper long enough to hit Ricki with the upped takings.

'*Si, verdad, pero*...aah,' Ricki said and shook his head. 'I must speak English! This is true but the takings for the late night are not much changed. This shows the same amount of people still come to the second part. Doing your own songs first is fine but if you do them later, the same number of people might not come. Because they do not hear what they are expecting. Anyway, why suddenly you want to change?'

'Because...' Pete began but I cut him off. This would have to be explained in Spanish or Ricki wouldn't get the emotional side of why Pete wanted to do it.

So I explained how we wanted to make a record and that we thought doing our stuff would help. Ricki took two sips of his brandy when I'd finished and then answered me in English, just to show me he wasn't scared of not getting his meaning across.

'I understand how this might help but I have to think about the hotel, my job. The takings might not stay the same if the people don't hear the songs they expect.'

'Oh come on, Ricki, as long as it's something they can bop to, most wouldn't mind what the hell we played.' The underlying impatience Pete felt made it hard for him to keep his voice level.

'I tell you what,' Ricki said, using a phrase he'd heard us use so often he probably thought it was Oxford English. 'You can play your own songs every Sunday. Not so many families then because of the barbecue in town. Okay? Also, I call a friend of mine in Valencia who has his own record company and see if he will come down to hear you.'

I could sense Pete wanting to argue but I knew it was the best we'd get. 'Okay,' I said to Ricki. 'If that's the best you can do, we'll have to take it. Come on Pete, let's get back on stage.'

The following morning, Pete was gone from the small room the hotel let use overnight. I expected him to be downstairs in the bar-room which served breakfasts in the morning. He wasn't there. I decided to wait until he found me rather than go looking. I spent the time in the indoor pool. It was always quiet in the mornings.

After my family, the thing I missed most was not playing football. I was used to being fit and missed that wonderful feeling of being well-exercised and slightly sore after a hard match. I also missed the camaraderie of the other lads but it was the fitness I missed most. So, every Sunday morning, I swam at least forty lengths of the indoor pool in the Don Juan.

Pete called me as I was half way down my final length that morning. I reached the end and climbed out, listening to him while I towelled myself dry.

'I've just been to La Maisa,' he told me. It was obvious he

was excited.

'They're not going to take us.'

La Maisa was a big hotel on the main drag to the beach, opposite the Hotel Helios. It had a cabaret night but the acts were always billed as international and were laid back, or slick or Spanish folk groups. There was no way they'd want us.

'Yeah,' Pete agreed as I shrugged on my T-shirt and trainers. 'But the act they've got this week is the nearest thing to us. I saw their lead singer. I met him a couple weeks ago at Ruddi's place.'

Ruddi was a smashing lad. He spoke English with a Yorkshire accent because he'd lived with a girl from Leeds for three years. He also spoke Spanish, French, German, Flemish, Italian and a little Japanese. He was just one of those people with a natural ear for language. He worked as a waiter in a bar on the promenade, near where the road led to the Castle.

Pete nodded. 'He introduced me to the singer, Francisco. Anyway, I told Francisco about wanting to get in touch with someone who could help us make a record and he said he'd ask his agent. I didn't tell you in case nothing came from it. Well, today, he gave me the name of a bloke who works for EMI in Madrid.'

I could tell by the look on his face that he was expecting one of my cynical remarks but I just smiled and said, 'Fine. You ring him, ask him to come and see us. If talent and determination count for anything, you'll have this bloke so gobsmacked, we'll be rich by Christmas.'

Pete rang and the bloke, for a wonder, agreed to come

down and see us in two weeks. Ricki's friend agreed to come the same Sunday and we spent the time rehearsing like mad. Pete went over and over the song he'd told me he thought could do it for us and by the time the day arrived, he had me almost convinced.

That Sunday afternoon, we went down to the promenade and sat on the swings at the far end. Pete was a bag of nerves but I felt remarkably calm. It wasn't arrogance or overconfidence, it was just that I had the feeling that Pete was right—this *was* going to be the start.

'Don't worry, spud,' I told him. He was kicking distractedly at the brown dust below the swing. 'It'll be fine.'

He jumped a bit and then said, 'How can you sit there like we're just going to do our normal set? There are *two* of them coming, for Christ's sake!'

'That just means they'll have to outdo each other to sign us. We. Are. Going. To. Be. Great.' And I really was that sure.

Oh boy, were we great. We rocked that little hotel bar till the disco in the cellar emptied its customers into the hotel. People walking outside came in and stood two deep in the foyer because they couldn't get in the bar. We found out later that the street was blocked and traffic couldn't get past. The staff of the hotel that were off-shift and would normally have been long-gone, stayed and watched and cheered and applauded and whistled along with the rest. By the time we finished, the glasses and bottles behind the bar were rattling. It took us ten minutes to get off stage. I had to yell down the mike that we'd be back in fifteen minutes before they let us go.

In Ricki's office, Pete and I downed the pints of lime and lemonade Carla had brought in while the three men in the room waited. But when we did speak, I spoke to Pete.

'Where did they all come from?'

Ricki answered me. 'From the town. They are three-deep in the street. If I had known you could be so...what is the English? Energetic? Yes, I would have let you do your own songs from the beginning. Why did you not tell me?'

'Ricki,' Pete said. 'We never wanted to do *just* our songs. All the great rock'n'roll songs were written a long time ago. The new ones are only copies.'

The big, black-haired man sitting in the corner spoke to Ricki in Spanish. He asked him to ask us if we had a tape of our act. Exactly what Pete Leay said in Liverpool. I was laughing when I answered him.

'No but we've got a cassette recorder and some blank tapes. Why don't you record the second set?' I should've said it in Spanish but I've found that, even when you spend all day speaking a foreign language, when you're emotional or excited, you nearly always revert to your native tongue. Ricki translated and then told us that this was his friend from Valencia. The bloke from EMI introduced himself in perfect English.

'My name is Franco. I would like a copy of that tape. I am very impressed.'

I looked at Pete and we both knew what we were thinking; being taken on by EMI was a bit like being signed by Real Madrid or Liverpool football club before you've played for your current side's first team. And the same sort of risks went with that—you might have to wait a long time before you played for your new club's first team.

'I think the best thing would be for you to take the tape to your bosses in Madrid and let us know when you've made up your minds. Until you've made up *your* minds, we can't. You know?' Pete said and I translated. The bloke from EMI nodded.

The second set went better than the first. The crowd liked our stuff as much as the few standards we played. We did a medley of Beatles' songs and then finished with the song Pete thought would do it for us. Pete played the opening bars and there were a few puzzled frowns but they soon found the backbeat and rocked. When we finished, it got the biggest cheer of the night. That was the moment when I had the vaguest sense of how The Beatles or The Stones must've felt at the height of their fame. I wondered why they felt the need for drugs; whatever hit they got must've been pale in comparison to the soaring high we got from the audience reaction that night.

The following week, Ricki asked us to do what we'd done that Sunday and Pete just winked at me. We didn't hear from either recording companies until the following Wednesday. Pete rang me at work and told me Franco from EMI would be down in Lloret that Sunday.

'Let me get this right,' Pete said, having heard Franco out. 'EMI like what they've heard but they don't think we're ready to be given a contract. But *you* think we should get a single out as soon as possible and follow it up with an album of the songs we do here. So, you want us to sign to a label which a couple of your mates and you've been thinking of setting up for some time?'

'Yes,' Franco agreed.

'Franco,' Pete said quietly. 'I don't want this to sound insulting, but if you want to set up on your own, then maybe you didn't try very hard to sell us to EMI?'

Franco smiled. 'I can see why you might think that. All I can say is that setting up a label is something we have wanted to do for a long time. We want our first single to be a success and we think that with you it will be. EMI would be very good but they will not put a lot of money into you now. If you come with me now, you will be our only group and we can spend lots of time making sure the record is heard. Truly, I think it will be better for you, too.' He held his hands out and shrugged in a typically Latin gesture.

'What's the deal?' Pete asked and Franco looked at Ricki who looked at me. I translated.

'Ah. How is said,' Ricki said. 'Fifty fifty. Any profit will be split down the middle between you and Franco's label. You play music and they deal with …distribution? Yes?'

'EMI would give you money, maybe a lot but then you pay it back when the record starts to sell. After you finish paying this advance, then you have money for yourself,' Franco told us. 'Also, you have to do what they say. Maybe you have to do lots of gigs you don't want to do?'

'I see. Listen, Franco,' I said. 'We'll think it over and let you know before we go on tonight.'

He nodded and smiled.

Pete and I walked down to Ruddi's bar and went in. The

place wasn't that busy since it was up in the high seventies outside and most people were having their drinks on the pavement. Ruddi served a couple of Germans and then sat at our table while we discussed Franco's offer.

'What d'you think,' Pete asked Ruddi when we laid it all out for him.

He took a sip of beer from his bottle before he answered. 'If you do it with this Franco, maybe you don't get so much money straight off but it's all yours. And, like he says, if you're his only act, he's got the time to do it properly. I think you should go with him. What're you gonna do with the money from EMI? Buy instruments you don't need?'

That's the way he was. It was being a barman, I suppose. They say you need to be able to listen and have a degree in psychology to be one. He'd put in a nutshell what we'd been thrashing around for ten minutes.

'What the hell, Terry,' Pete said. 'EMI don't even want to sign us yet.'

I raised my cup of tea. 'Well, we've got nowt to lose. Cheers!'

'All *right*!' Ruddi said and raised his bottle. 'Here's to fame and fortune. What're you gonna call yourselves?'

Pete looked at me and we both burst out laughing; it hadn't occurred to us we'd have to have a name.

'Shit!' Pete said. 'Haven't got a bloody clue. What about you, Ruddi?'

He thought for a moment and clicked his fingers. 'Hey! You like football, don't you, Terry?' I nodded but pulled a face; I didn't fancy being called by the name of some Dutch soccer team. 'And you live in Barcelona. I like their team even with this Englishman, Venables, in charge. I like him because he thinks about football. Like the Dutch. The first time I heard him speak about football, he talked about players with a good first touch. I knew he was a good coach then. So what about First Touch? Or just The Touch?'

We settled on *First Touch* because all I could think of when I heard *The Touch* was that painting by Michelangelo.

*

Franco got everything moving and, on my Mum's birthday, June 13, we went to Madrid and cut the single. We did it in one take and the engineer behind the thick glass, sitting at his mixing desk in the pine-panelled room, played it back and asked if we wanted to change anything. I asked him what he thought. He told us he reckoned that, when you've come within a millimetre of perfection, you best leave it alone in case you cocked it up. He also thought it'd make number one in the Spanish charts. Franco just sat in the mixing room with a big grin on his face. We put down the song Carol and I had written on the B side.

We went to a restaurant and Franco told us how he intended to organise post-production and distribution. We just nodded, happy to let him do whatever he thought was necessary. We went back to the studio and put down what was really the second set from the Don Juan, along with 'Get Back', 'Hollywood Nights' and an old Small Faces hit, 'All or nothing'. We told Santos the engineer to put it together how he liked and he told us it would be a pleasure.

How he managed it I don't know, given the Spanish principle of 'Manana', but Franco had it in the shops within a fortnight and we got the news that it had entered the charts while we were doing our set at the end of June.

That was the night I ended up in hospital.

Pete had just begun to play the opening bars of 'Candle in the wind' when I spotted Franco jumping up and down at the back of the room. He was waving something in one hand and pointing his other hand over his shoulder, letting me know he wanted to see us in the office at the end of the set.

'I have exciting news!' Ricki virtually yelled at us as we walked into his office. He was sitting behind his desk, wearing a huge grin and smoking one of his foul-smelling cigars that coloured the air blue. Franco handed me the glossy magazine that he'd folded at the place he wanted me to look at.

The page was obviously a chart of some sort. Our name jumped out at me the way things do when they're in print and trigger some recognition. I stared at it, making sure I wasn't mistaken and then handed it to Pete without saying anything.

'Ace!' Pete said. 'Is this an Indy chart?'

Franco and Ricki looked at each other, perplexed. I explained that there was a specific chart in England for independent record labels, ones not owned by the biggies like EMI and Decca.

'No,' Franco replied. 'This is the big chart for the whole country. I made sure all the disc-jockeys had the record and I sent a copy of the tape I made here so they know the audience like you. They play the single all the time on the radio. You are stars! Magnifico!'

Pete and I said nothing. What was there to say? Inside three weeks or so, we'd made a record that was now 27 in a national chart. It all seemed a little ridiculous. The annals of pop were littered with stories of bands who'd laboured for years to get a record that high in the charts and most of them were better than I thought we were.

'The album's been pressed,' Franco told us. 'It will be in the shops soon and if it does as well as the single, maybe we'll all be rich soon.' His grin was now as big as Ricki's and he accepted one of those horrible cigars. 'Now,' he continued, full of himself. 'You have more songs so you should make another record and go round the resorts or maybe a big concert or—'

'Hold your horses,' I told him and raised my hand. 'In case you've forgotten, I work for a living. In Barcelona. Five days a week. I can't see my bosses letting me gallivant round the country.'

'Give it up,' Pete said with all the carefree arrogance of someone who doesn't have to worry about working for a living if he doesn't want to.

'On the strength of one minor success in the Spanish chart? We don't have any gigs set up. There's no guarantee that anybody would buy tickets to watch if we did and the record might bomb out as quickly as it bombed in. Forget it. Come and see me when the album's in the charts and Franco's getting earache from all the telephone calls he's getting.'

'If Franco sets up concerts,' Ricki asked softly. 'And tickets sell, will you?'

I thought about it seriously and had the same feeling I'd

had before the night we'd sold ourselves to Franco. Still, I *did* work for a living and Jude's father had helped me get the job and I was reluctant to throw all that away on the caprices of the record-buying public.

'No,' I said finally. 'But I will cut another single and if that does well, then I'll seriously consider doing some kind of tour.' I left the office and Pete followed me. He looked at me just once when we were on stage and then we got into the music.

The room was full and the dancing in full swing. About half-way through the set, a gang of about eight lads came in, three of them with girls in tow. They'd all been drinking but none of them seemed objectionably drunk. I saw them and forgot them until one of them called to me from the floor just as I put my guitar down to get my twelve-string for the next song and Pete was picking up his own guitar.

'Hey mate!' I bent down to face him. His breath would've curdled milk. 'D'you do requests?'

'Depends if we know it. What d'you want?'

'It's that Police song. Er, everything you say or something. Do it now.'

'Every breath you take' was what he wanted but had as much chance of us doing Gilbert and Sullivan. Pete wouldn't do a Police song if he was offered a million quid. He considered their music trite and he hated the lead singer enthusiastically. He thought Sting was a pretentious arsehole.

I smiled. 'Sorry mate, we do old rock'n'roll or our own stuff.'

The lad sucked at the inside of his mouth. It pulled his

cheek in, making him look a little backward. He nodded and went to his seat.

Pete raised his eyebrows as he walked towards me but I just shook my head and we went into a ballad we'd written in Liverpool. We did 'Let it be' and 'The two of us' off the Beatles' 'Let it be' album and then had to change instruments. This time, the lad headed for Pete. I just hoped it wasn't another Police song the lad wanted. I watched Pete shake his head. The lad didn't look too put out when he walked away. It was as we finished the song before our medley that the lad, along with two of his mates, came back to the stage.

It was something about the way they were walking, close together, their eyes fixed straight ahead, mouths working, which made me put my guitar down and walk over to Pete.

'You and that lad have a row?'

'What lad?' I pointed to the three lads who were about ten feet from the stage. 'Oh, him. No. He wanted us to do a Police song and I told him we didn't do any.'

'You didn't also happen to give him your considered opinion of Sting, did you?'

'Well, he *was* getting a bit uppity so I just told him we didn't like The Police much.'

'Oh shit! Bloody wonderful!' I could imagine how Pete told him; with all the diplomacy of a rampaging bull. I could smell trouble.

'Hey you! Bollocks!'

The lad was still a few feet from the stage. I walked to the edge of the stage but didn't bend down this time.

'Look mate, whatever's on your mind, take it off. If you

cut up rough in here they don't mess about. They don't have bouncers like in England. They let you roll around on the floor for a while and wait for the Guardia. And those buggers don't fuck around. They carry guns and aren't afraid to use them. Also, they're not too fond of English drunks.' I said it quietly, hoping he'd hear how sincere I was, knowing I was wasting my breath.

'Piss on that dickhead! We want you to do that song. It's my girl's favourite and you're gonna do it. Me and me mates are *tellin* ya you are!'

I think I might have still handled it but Pete decided he hadn't done anything daft for a while.

'I'm not surprised she likes that crap. The fact that she's going out with you shows how bad her taste is. Just go back to the silly bitch and let her take you home. We don't do it.'

Not only did Pete show bad judgement in insulting the girl (a girl the lad had probably met tonight, would screw later on and then forget what she was called when he woke up), he also bent down to make his point. The lad took one, angry, red-faced breath and butted Pete.

Fortunately, the lad was just drunk enough for his aim to be poor and it only caught Pete a glancing blow to the temple. The lad's two mates moved up alongside him and put their hands on the stage to lift themselves up. I stamped on them. Hard. Their howls gave me no satisfaction. Then the rest of the crew joined in and it turned into one of those saloon bar fights in the films. Except the blood, the pain and broken bones were real. We would've been killed, I think, if it hadn't been for Pablo and Stefan from behind the bar helping us out. And Ruddi who was enjoying his night off.

The stage was invaded by them all.

I managed to put two of the lads away before one of the others kicked me in the balls and then hit me with a bottle. The bottle didn't break but it made my head and ears ring like the bells in the medieval church down by the promenade. Pete got his lip split and his nose bloodied but he fought like it was The Alamo. I think he wanted to hit me because I'd refused to give up work to tour and, because he couldn't, he took it out on the drunks.

The Guardia arrived and hauled the eight lads off in handcuffs. Ricki was all for cancelling the rest of the set but there were only five more songs left so we carried on. It was as we finished the song we had in the charts that I realised I'd been seeing double for the last two songs. I half-collapsed and they took me to the medical centre by the post office. The medico there sent me to hospital in Gerona because of the concussion.

The hospital was big and clean and bright and smelled just like the one in Oxborough. They kept me in overnight. Ricki told me the hotel would pay and Pete stayed long enough to find out the x-rays showed no breaks and to apologise for the fight. I told him to forget it; the lad would've found another excuse to impress his girl.

Being in hospital and on my own, the stranger in a strange land, I began to think about home. I thought about my family and old friends. You know what it's like when you let your mind run free. It jumps from topic to topic with the flimsiest of links. I thought about Jude. We hadn't kept in touch since I moved to Spain. I intended to but things got on top of me and, by the time I realised this, I also realised that Jude hadn't been in touch with me either. For a day or so, it hurt but then I thought that maybe it was for the best. I knew myself well enough to know that, if we'd kept in touch and despite all my good intentions about not pressing her, I'd've probably kept on at her to come out and live with me and that wouldn't have been right. I was pretty sure Jude knew me that well, too.

But, in that hospital bed, my mind stayed with her for a while, wondering what she was doing now, if she still loved medicine as much and what she'd say if she knew the lad she used to go out with was now a singer in a band whose first record was in the Spanish charts. Would she be surprised, maybe a little sad that it had happened without the driving backbeat of her friend Cheryl?

I lay there, my head feeling woolly and my eyes refusing to focus and my mind jumped from thought to thought and then I remembered the smell of the hospital where they brought Cheryl that night when she crashed in our car and out of this world. The smell was so similar in the hospital I was now in that the memories came back in full colour and Dolby sound. I could see the look on the doctor's face when she told us that Cheryl was going to die. Cheryl would love the idea that we looked like we might make it in the music business and she'd've cut through all that crap in Ricki's office with one of her Scouse put-downs.

That was when I cried a little so my double-vision trebled. I missed her. It was that simple. All the other things I missed about home—football, somebody talking in my own accent, the smell of the River Fender—they were still there when I wanted them. Cheryl wasn't. And if I missed her so much, how much more did Pete miss her? The fact that he hadn't taken up with a girl in Spain was only the outward sign. That depression before Christmas showed how it tore him apart inside. He could write and perform and try to fill the void, try to do what she told him he should do but, without her to hear it and see it, to smile when the song ended, it could only be half as good.

I dozed off thinking about Cheryl, which probably explained why I dreamed of her.

It was a good dream. Full of her face, her smile, her dry one-liners, her sparkling eyes as she hammered at the drums. She was as alive in that dream as she had been in life. I woke up with the strange certainty that she was still alive. It was only when the nurse came to check my pulse that the feeling, along with the dream, began to fade. I was left feeling low and depressed. I tried to hold onto the dream but the harder I tried the more tattered it became. Still, like Pete said to me once, dreams are only dreams, no matter how animated or vivid. No matter how long they seem to last, they really only last as long as you sleep and then you have to wake up and get on with reality.

Of course, he hadn't been in the Old Camberwell House when he told me that. *Neither* of us had been down in the cellar beneath that house.

The album was released and it hit the charts and kept climbing. By the end of July, it looked like it might make number one. The single got to number four and stayed there for a month. The radio played tracks from the album what seemed like all day. I didn't tell anybody at work I was half of First Touch but in Lloret, we couldn't really hide it. The crowds got bigger and Franco kept getting more phone calls wanting more information. He was going quietly round the bend and pushing us to go out and promote the album. Ricki had nearly every bar in Lloret asking him to release us from the contract we didn't have to do one-nighters for them. It was all getting silly. Franco urged us to cut another single but Pete told him to let the radio have copies of the live tape and it was that tape which finally pushed us into doing a tour.

I think we did it to stop the Don Juan from being demolished by the crowds who came to see us. By the middle of September, it was obvious to me that I couldn't delay any longer and, to be honest, I didn't really want to. Ricki became our unofficial business manager and arranged dates for us at most of the resorts along the east coast. Pete finally let Franco book us to do another single and we were already being told to move to Madrid. At the end of October, the summer season behind us and the second single at number one, we gave in.

I handed in my notice at Mobil and we left Barcelona to become professional musicians.

Madrid is a totally different city to Barcelona. As cosmopolitan as most world capitals, it has the same aloofness. We moved there because that's where the recording industry is, the publishing companies, the money. Ricki gave up the hotel business and became our full time manager, working all the hours God sent, as if he thought our career might end at the weekend. We played all over the place and had two spots on Spain's equivalent of Top of the Pops, did God-knows how many interviews and, all the time, it snowballed. It got to the stage where we had to take the piss out of it because it felt so absurd.

By Christmas we were almost rich. Actually, compared to the rest of my family, I *was* rich. When I was at school, I'd always thought that happiness would be having enough money from doing something I liked so I wouldn't have to worry about paying the bills. On that basis, I was happy. The way things were going, I would soon be at the stage where I used to dream about winning the pools. It was a strange feeling because I could still remember my Dad working all the hours God sent to keep a roof over our heads and food in our stomachs. And then, back home for Christmas, we found that there always seems to be a price you have to pay.

We got to Oxborough just as the streetlamps were coming on. It was cold and I don't think I've ever driven a car since when the heater was on full and blowing from all the outlets; it was that much of a shock after the Spanish warmth. Still, even the freezing weather was welcoming and I realised it was another thing I missed, like the football.

By the time we arrived at The Firs, the floodlights were on, bringing back all sorts of memories. We'd brought loads of stuff back—duty-free and presents. And our acoustics—my family still held to the tradition of singsongs at the end of the party. It was all in the hired hatchback so I got out to help Pete unload his gear.

Ronald opened the door before Pete could ring the bell.

'Let me help you,' he said and stepped off the porch.

I looked at him. He was backlit by the porch light and front-lit by the car's headlights and I nearly dropped the bag of duty-free I was carrying.

Ronald Lynwood was an old man. It was in his face, which sagged and had no colour. It was in his eyes, which were tinged with yellow. It was in the way he stood and walked. His tall erect, slightly stout body had changed since the last time we were home. He now stooped, almost from the waist, his shoulders rounded, as if his head was too heavy. The stoutness was gone. He was thin. Even his voice sounded thin and old. I glanced at Pete and saw that he'd seen it, too.

'It's okay, Dad. We can manage. Wouldn't mind a cup of tea, though. Not used to all this cold and wind.'

'Oh. Right. Your room's aired and the electric blanket's on. Hello, Terry. How are you?'

Something was not right here.

'I'm fine, Mr Lynwood. You?'

Something crossed his face before he answered. 'Oh, you know, not bad. I've been better, I must admit. And don't you think we've known each other long enough for you to call me Ronald?' He smiled and I nodded, slightly stunned at the lump that had filled my throat when he asked me to call him Ronald. I smiled back, not trusting my voice. 'Good,' Ronald said. 'Now, come in out of the cold.'

The house looked and felt much the same but there was a smell I couldn't quite place. I expected Ronald to listen dutifully but uninterestedly as Pete told him what had happened to us in Spain. But he seemed honestly delighted at our success and even asked Pete if he'd brought a copy of the records. Pete looked at me stupidly and then back at his father.

'Well, we brought copies for Terry's sisters. You could listen to those but I don't think you'll like them, Dad. It's mostly rock'n'roll. There are some ballads but, you know...'

'Peter...' Ronald said and paused, fiddling with the buttons of his cardigan. 'I...well, it's...' He coughed and it sounded unhealthy, raw and rattly. 'Anyway, I *would* like to hear what you've done. You wouldn't mind leaving them for me, would you, Terry?'

'No. You can keep them. One copy in our house will be plenty.' I stood up. 'They're in the car. I'll get them.'

Ronald nodded. 'Thanks. There's a shepherd's pie in the oven. It'll be ready in about twenty minutes. You'll stay, won't you?'

There it was again, that something in his voice that brought a lump to my throat. I glanced at Pete but he was sorting out the duty free bags. It was half past four and I knew there'd be nobody in my house until gone six. 'Smashing,' I said.

'Good,' Ronald said and stood up. 'I've got most of the boxes down from the loft. We can trim the tree when we've eaten.'

This made Pete look up from the bags on the floor. 'What?'

'It's nearly Christmas, Peter,' Ronald said and shook his head slowly, his tone indicating that his son was obviously a moron. But I caught the smile as he turned away and headed for the hall and found myself grinning as I collected the copies of our records from the car. Weird.

With the shepherd's pie eaten and the plates in the dishwasher, we took our mugs of tea into the living room. We draped the decorations around the room and, with each drawing-pin, I kept seeing Carol that first time I'd helped put these decorations up. When the last of them was hung across the chimney breast, Pete brought down the box of fairy lights and bells and tinsel from the loft and the three of us sat and tried to work out why, no matter how careful you are when you pack them away, there's always at least three glass balls that have mysteriously been broken in the intervening twelve months.

'Mmm,' Ronald said when I pointed it out. 'It's probably a metaphor when you think about it.'

Pete was trying to unravel the lights, holding them like they were made of nitro-glycerine and might blow up any minute. He chuckled and asked, 'What?'

Ronald looked up from the tinsel star he was straightening. 'Is that disdain I hear in your voice, Peter?'

I burst out laughing and, at the same time, my eyes filled with something very like unshed tears. Ronald's tone sounded haughty but the look on his face and the twinkle in his eyes told you he was taking the piss. Mostly out of himself. God, why hadn't he been like this years ago? Or maybe he had and I hadn't noticed because I didn't like the way he treated his wife. 'Go on,' I said, probably to stop those unshed tears. 'Tell us why, Ronald.'

He smiled at me and leaned back on the settee and I saw the strain on his face again. 'Actually, I'm not sure I should because…well, I'm thinking mostly about me. And the things I regret.' He looked off to the side, out of the window at the gathering winter night. 'I was so careful about my life. About my career and my earnings and savings and pension and all the rest.' He turned to look at Pete. 'And I was so careful about being careful…'

He paused then and turned to look out of the window again. So many things, so many emotions, seemed to cross his face that it was like watching the clouds cross the sky on a blowy March afternoon. Pete looked at me and raised his eyebrows. I was about to shrug at him and then it hit me and I knew what that smell I hadn't been able to place was and what it meant. It was one of those moments when insight comes so fiercely that it makes your heart miss a beat and then speed up.

'Ronald,' I said and wasn't surprised that my voice sounded thick. 'What's wrong? You're ill, aren't you?'

'What?'

I didn't answer Pete. I was staring at Ronald, willing him to look at me because I knew that if I could get him to look at me, I'd get an honest answer. 'Ronald?'

Ronald sighed and turned his head from the window, slowly as if it took a huge effort and it probably did; I had the feeling that this was why he'd asked me to stay. I thought Ronald wanted me there for Pete. Finally, Ronald was looking at me and that lump in my throat was back.

'I…' Ronald swallowed hard and closed his eyes. Then he straightened his back, nodded once and then opened his eyes and said, 'I've got cancer.'

Three words, spoken on one breath, each word given

equal weight. No anger or bitterness or self-pity. Three words that created a moment of time that rang like a crystal bowl. Three words that made Pete and I stare at him while Ronald stared at his hands.

'Dad…' Pete said and then his voice cracked, and that moment of ringing crystal cracked with it.

'Peter, son…listen. It's in one of the tubes leading to one of my lungs. Just one. I…they gave me a short course of chemotherapy. I didn't even have to stay in hospital. And it shrank it enough for them to be able to…' He winced as if the memory hurt and I thought it probably did. 'Treatment's different now,' he went on. 'They gave me a very powerful but short burst of radiotherapy and…well, the word the oncologist uses is 'optimistic'. What he means is that he believes it's in remission.' Ronald took a deep breath and the strain on his face was clear but there was also something close to a small smile lifting the corners of his mouth. He was glad that was over.

Pete got up off the floor and put his arms round Ronald and I could see the tears on his cheeks. Ronald closed his eyes and hugged his son and then he was looking at me and smiling. I wiped at my own eyes and nodded, letting him know I understood.

'Peter, it's okay. I'm fighting this, believe me.' He eased Pete away from him and pressed his shoulders so that he sat down on the floor again. 'But there's something else I need to tell you.' He glanced at me and then back at Pete. 'There's something you need to know, something you should've known a long time ago. Something…well, something I think is a lot more important than the cancer.'

Pete looked at me and it took me all my time not to blurt out that there was no need, we both knew. But Ronald needed to tell it so I widened my eyes at Pete and he returned the gesture. God, it's amazing how friendship creates that telepathy, don't you think?

And then Ronald told us both what we already knew. He told us everything, just the way Carol had told me all those years ago. He didn't gloss over his actions and attitudes; he was brutally honest about how he'd treated his wife's wishes and passions. He fumbled for the words at times and swore at himself more than once for being unable to tell the story seamlessly, especially when it came to the part where Carol had returned home, pregnant with Pete.

'I was angry, Peter. I was…it was…well, I…shit!' He rubbed both hands down his face and shook his head. 'When she…when your Mother told me, I was sitting in this chair and I wanted to…there was a report I was reading for work. It was in a ring binder and it was heavy and…I picked it up and…Oh for Christ's sake! I really wanted to hit Carol with it, to slam it against her face and…' He banged his arms on the arms of his chair and told himself to get a bloody grip. 'I actually had it in my hand and then I saw your Mum, just sitting there…sitting there and waiting for me to do it.'

He looked at Pete and then at me and his expression asked us if we could understand what that had felt like. And both Pete and I nodded and I knew that we both wanted him to stop now because it was done and Carol wasn't here anymore. But we both knew he needed to do this, to say it because it was eating at him worse than the cancer.

'And I couldn't do it. I think…no, I *know* that part of me, a big part of me, couldn't do it because it was my fault.' He laughed then. No humour, more a bark. 'But I was still arrogant enough to refuse to say I was sorry, to admit my faults. God, we are so bloody good at that, aren't we? So…' And he stopped speaking and leaned back in the chair and stared at his son, the strain written in deep lines again on his face.

'Dad, it's okay,' Pete told him and smiled through his tears. 'I understand, honest. It's okay, you don't have to—'

Ronald leaned forward. 'You're my son, Peter,' he said and his voice cracked and he cried and, through his tears, he said what he'd been trying to say for the last five minutes. 'You were always *my* son, Peter. You have to believe that.'

Pete nodded and hugged his father again. I went to make tea.

When I got back, they were back to checking the Christmas lights and tree decorations. I joined them and, for two minutes, the only sound in the room was of tea being sipped and the soft, sad rattle of broken ornaments. And then Ronald continued his explanation of those broken ornaments being metaphors. As if he hadn't just told his son that he wasn't his biological son. As if he hadn't just told us he had cancer. Only his throaty voice hinted that he was still struggling with emotion.

'I forgot the most important thing of all that we should be careful about.' He swallowed hard and blinked twice. 'I forgot to be careful about making sure the love I felt for my family was…oh, what's the right word?' He looked at me. 'You're the wordsmith, Terry,' he said. 'What would be the word I'm looking for?'

It was something in his eyes. It echoed the humour when he'd taken the mickey out of Pete about the decorations but also hinted at something serious, too. It was my night for clear insights because I knew he knew. I knew Ronald knew I'd had something to do with the song Carol had recorded herself singing. Pete must've seen it, too because he said, 'Dad, don't—'

Ronald turned to him and smiled. 'It's okay, Peter. Don't worry.' He faced me again. 'So, what word, Terry? You know how to express what you feel, even the deepest feelings.' He raised his eyebrows at me but there was nothing malicious in his face, nothing at all. 'It's a gift I wish I had. God, how I wish it.' He shook his head slowly and then raised his eyebrows at me, wanting an answer.

I was holding one of the clear glass balls in my hand. It was shaped like the lantern on the porch wall of The Firs and its edges were sharp. I looked at it as it caught and reflected the glow of the gas fire and the light from the wall lights. I lifted it up and held it towards Ronald and smiled. 'Clear. Or sharp.'

Ronald nodded and smiled. 'Both, I think. Perfect,' he said. 'That's what I regret, son,' he told Pete as he looked at him again. 'Most of all because by not doing so, I broke what I cherished above all else.' He sighed and leaned back against the padded settee again. 'Terry, I want to thank you. For what you did for Carol. I'm not as good with words as you are but…' He chuckled and there was real humour this time, humour that said he was taking the piss out of himself again. 'I've had a while to work on this.'

I sat there with the glass bauble in my hand, speechless. This was so friggin weird. Like the old hippies used to say— too much, man, too much. I couldn't get my head round it at all. Ronald Lynwood, Good-Old-Ronald, was thanking me for helping his wife to play music again. And not just that; the man was laying bare his heart in front of me, as if we'd been on first-name terms since the day I first turned up at his house, as if he'd never looked at me like I was something he'd brought in on the sole of his shoe.

'Peter, I think I did you another disservice when I didn't tell you what the tape was when I gave it you. I think you probably rowed with Terry about it, yes?' Pete could only nod and then glanced at me. 'Well, I'm sure you sorted it out but, in case it still rankles a bit, let me tell you that Terry gave your Mother something she treasured and made her happy at the very end of her life. Which was the least she deserved. Thank you, Terry. For making the last weeks of Carol's life a joy. And they were. She played music and sang every day because of what you did for her, because you wrote the words for her. And because she did…I managed to finally try to explain to her why…'

Ronald closed his eyes and swallowed hard. He took a long breath and, still with his eyes closed, said, 'I finally found the courage to explain why I was so set against music as any sort of profession.' He opened his eyes and looked at Pete. 'My father was a musician. At least that's what he called himself. He played accordion in pubs. And he thought that was enough. He played in pubs four nights a week and drank in pubs the other nights. My mother and I…we struggled. And then my father just didn't come home at all one day. We learned later that he'd been offered a job in London and we never saw him again. I...if I'd've been honest, less arrogant, and told Carol when she...' He shook his head. 'No excuses. I ruined your Mum's life and almost ruined your life, Peter. I can't change that but at least I've had the chance to apologise. I'm sorry, son.' When Pete nodded, Ronald smiled and closed his eyes again and two errant tears rolled down his cheeks. And then he said the thing that finally made my own unshed tears fall. 'I put a line or two of your lyrics on her headstone, Terry. I didn't think you'd mind.'

I looked at Pete and saw he was crying, too but smiling at me.

'Now,' Ronald said, easing himself up from the settee. 'Confession might be good for the soul but it really makes you thirsty. I'm going to make another drink.'

He grinned and, for the first time, I saw Pete in Ronald Lynwood. Pete smiled like Carol but he grinned like Ronald—like his *father*.

Pete and I finished trimming the tree and then Pete went to the toilet. I went into the kitchen to help Ronald make the tea and found him staring out of the window at the garden. The kettle boiled and turned itself off. He must've seen my reflection in the glass.

'Carol told me you wrote the words to the tune she'd written the first time I came home and found her playing the guitar. She was out there, in the garden at the picnic table. It was late evening but warm, the stars just coming out. I...well, I'm sure you know how angry it made me.' He shook his head and let out a long breath. 'But she refused to give in this time. Christ, I wish she'd done it sooner. Years sooner.' He leaned forward and his hands gripped the countertop. Then he turned to face me. 'Anyway, she played every day and I…well, I'm tempted to say I'm proud that I stopped being angry but…' He shrugged and I nodded. 'I loved hearing her play. I fell in love again, Terry. I fell in love with the girl I first met all those years ago. I'd get home and we'd sit and eat the meal Carol had *made* and we'd talk about our days and about how proud we were of Peter and then she'd play and sing.' He wiped at his cheeks but he kept smiling. 'Not just the song you and she wrote but songs from when we were courting. But she always began and ended with that song. And she fell in love with me again. I didn't deserve it but God knows I'm grateful.'

Ronald Lynwood crossed the three yards between us and embraced me the way my Dad did the first time I played in a team that won a cup final. I hugged Ronald Lynwood and thanked Whoever once again that Carol and I had never consummated that frantic fifteen minutes in the spare bedroom upstairs.

'So,' he said as he stepped back. 'Thank you again, Terry. And, when I'm gone, please help my son. Yes?'

I frowned. 'Ronald, if you've lied to Pete about—'

'No, no,' he said. 'I'm in remission and I meant it when I said that I was going to fight this. With everything I've got. But sooner or later, we both know…even Pete knows, I think, that it's going to kill me. You'll help him when I'm not here, won't you?'

I nodded and we made the drinks and took them into the living room where Pete was putting our album on the stereo.

I went home just after nine and got hugged to death by my Mum and sisters and basked in the smile my Dad gave me. Our Dawn put the records on and my family gave me a critique of my work. A merciless critique. Just as well I was used to it, really.

That night, I lay in bed and wondered at the feeling of happiness I felt about Ronald. At first, I was disgusted with myself but, as I fretted at it, I understood why I felt that way. Not everybody has the chance to admit their faults and mistakes before they die. Ronald had done that and more. But, more importantly, he'd done it, not for himself but for Pete. Ronald had stripped himself bare for the man who was his *son*.

I went to sleep almost immediately after I'd understood that.

Pete came round the following evening and we sat in our front room. My Mum and Dad, Erin and her mates and our Dawn and her new bloke were in the living room watching a comedy drama serial. I could tell by the look on his face and his croaky voice that Pete had something on his mind.

'What's to do blue?'

It turned out that Ronald had turned down Pete's offer to take him back to Spain with us when we returned.

'I've told him the money's no problem and the treatment must be the same wherever he gets it,' Pete told me. 'I mean, the weather can only be good for him, can't it? With it being his chest, I mean?'

'Want me to try?'

He smiled a Carol-smile at me and then our Erin poked her head round the door. She wanted us to sing the song on the record.

'You've got the record, you can listen to it any time you like.'

'Sue and Emma and our Dawn's boyfriend want to hear you sing. Please?'

When she said 'please' like that, I couldn't refuse her. I still can't. So Pete and I did an acoustic version and we ended up having an old-fashioned sing-song that went on until the early hours of the morning.

'No.' Ronald said it quietly but very firmly, without a trace of anger.

It was dinnertime and the three of us were sitting in the breakfast room at The Firs, finishing off the last of the cheese sandwiches. Pete had tried again to persuade Ronald to come back to Spain with us. I tried. Ronald refused. So Pete told him that, in that case, he wasn't going back, he was staying at home. *That* was when Ronald hit the roof.

'You will. You have obligations and I won't have you letting people down.'

So, because we were young, we tried again to persuade him to join us when we returned to Spain.

'No,' he repeated. 'I have a job and I don't intend giving it up any more than I intend letting you give up your career. I know how I want to be for however long I have left and I'm going to work as long as I'm able. Now, let's hear no more about it.'

Pete and I went back to Spain, did a twenty-six week tour, finishing at the Bilbao football ground. We cut another single and it got to number one. Ricki informed us we weren't just *nearly* rich now but officially rich. The single got to the joint European chart, too, along with the album. Ricki had an offer for us to do a major European tour and was asked by Capitol to let them release all our stuff under licence in the States, and what about an American tour? Pete and I told him we'd think about it. It was a heady feeling.

Those offers from Capitol came on a Monday. On the Tuesday, I answered the phone in our villa. It was a beautiful day and everything seemed almost perfect. Pete was in Madrid with Franco, booking the studio and Santos, the engineer, so we could record our second album. I left him to it because he liked all that side of things. Me? I just liked doing what I did. So, I answered the phone, thinking about ringing my parents and asking them if they fancied a cruise and what kind of house they wanted because I was now at the point where I *had* won the pools.

'*Si*, Barrow,' I said, thinking it might be Ricki or Franco or some journalist or a Spanish salesman wanting to sell me a swimming pool I already had. I wasn't expecting an English accent.

'Is it possible to speak to Peter Lynwood? This is his aunt Marjorie.'

Ronald was dead. I was convinced of it. All the good feelings I'd had left in a rush. 'I'm sorry, Peter isn't here. I'm Terry, his friend. Has Ronald died?'

'Ah, Ronald has spoken of you often. No, Terry, Ronald

hasn't died but he *is* in hospital. The doctors don't think it will be long. Peter should come home as soon as possible. I hate to ask you to do this but I have a lot to do here. I don't think I'll have time to ring again.'

I flashed back to having to tell Pete about Carol. It was a habit I really wanted to break.

'I'll tell him. We'll be home some time tomorrow. I'll hire a car and drive straight to the hospital. Is it Oxborough Infirmary?'

'Yes. Ward 33. Thank you.'

We got a scheduled flight that put us down in Gatwick at twenty past eleven the following morning. I hired the fastest car Swan Rental had and headed for the motorway. It reminded me so much of the night we heard about Carol. Pete didn't speak till we reached Birmingham and then spoke about everything but his dad.

We got to the hospital with just two hours to spare. Ronald died at nine that night. He went peacefully in the end but I found out later from the doctor that, for the previous three days, he'd been in great pain. He'd refused to allow them to put him on what they called the Traffic Lights; a machine that pumped painkillers into the patient at regulated intervals and looked a little like miniature traffic lights. Ronald told them that, regardless of the pain, he wanted to be fully aware when he spoke to his son for the final time. He was.

He thanked me again for everything I'd done for his family and for everything I'd been to his son. He shook my hand almost formally but there was the slightest squeeze from his emaciated fingers before he let go. I squeezed back gently and smiled through my tears. Even now, I'm slightly amazed at how my feelings for Ronald Lynwood changed. Amazed but eternally grateful that the man found the courage to admit his faults. Not many people are big enough to do that.

For the next hour, he spoke to his son. Pete came out of the room looking strangely content, despite the redness around his eyes.

Ronald was buried in the same plot as Carol and I saw her headstone for the first time. Pete had visited the cemetery with Ronald at Christmas but I hadn't gone with them. I'd never asked Pete what lines Ronald had chosen from my lyrics and Pete never offered.

The day was glorious, not a cloud in sight and the sun was hot but the breeze from the river was soft and cooling. The cemetery was ablaze with colour and the birds twittered in the hedges and trees. I stood next to Pete while the vicar read his benediction over the coffin and I read the words I'd written for Carol. And I cried because I missed her so much but also because Ronald had chosen the lines that he obviously thought said everything *he* wanted to say about the woman he loved.

I thought I'd lost it long ago
Its music, its heartbeat, its rhythm and flow
I found it beneath a summer sky
Still deep and true and it made me cry

It was two days after the funeral that Pete told me he'd made a decision he didn't think I'd like.

'I want to go back to Spain just long enough to cut the new album and sort things out with Franco and Ricki. I don't want to do the tours. Ricki can do what he likes about the Capitol licence thing. I want to come home, Terry. I'm sorry it screws you up but it's how I feel.'

'Okay.'

He looked up from his coffee cup, his eyes big and his mouth slightly open. 'You mean you don't mind giving it all up? Making it big all over Europe?'

'Look, Pete, you're the one who writes the music, the one who made it happen. I enjoy it but I can always play guitar and not becoming a living legend doesn't bother me one bit. You'll still write because it's what you do best and you can't help it. If you want me to put words to some of it, I will. If you want to make a record, fine. It's not the end of the world if we give it up for a while. Besides, I'm about ready to come home for good, too.'

'But you love Spain.'

'But this is where I belong. Coming up the motorway, it hit me. Right by where you can see that place they call The Castle in Seapool. You can see the river where it opens into the bay and I knew that was what I was missing. It must be true when they say the sea's in your blood, saltwater in your veins. I miss it. The salt, the smell of the air, the sight and sound of the ocean. I can remember waking up last Christmas and hearing the foghorns on the Fender. For just a moment, when I wasn't sure where I was, I thought there must be fog in the centre of Madrid. Stupid but I miss it.

'And it's been getting to you, too. The stuff you've written lately has more minor chords in it. It's not as hard, gritty. It's like the stuff you wrote before we went to Liverpool, more straight ballads. I think it's something to do with the air near the sea and the air round the Med' is different. Anyway, that's all by the by. I'll be glad to be home in the cold.'

Ricki and Franco weren't too happy but they knew they wouldn't change our minds. Besides, they had more acts now, their own company was doing well and we assured them that, if we ever decided to go on the road again, we'd use them.

Pete and I set up a company to manage any future royalties and Ricki and Franco would get their share. We realised all our assets and paid the right taxes in Spain and at home. I wasn't a millionaire yet but, with the royalties still to come, it wouldn't be long. Pete already was because of the money Carol left and what Ronald left. And he had The Firs. Neither of us would have to worry about money in the future. We'd just have to worry about what to do with the rest of our lives.

I wondered what Pete would do with his time. I thought he might use it and his money to try to find out about, or even *find* his real father.

'I did,' he told me on the flight home. I just stared at him and he smiled a Carol-smile at me. 'I got in touch with Mum's family after Dad told me everything. I felt I could then, you know? Like I wouldn't be going behind his back because he knew I knew.' He shrugged and grinned a

Ronald-grin. 'Anyway, his name was Connor Flint. He died more than four years ago.' He looked out of the window when he spoke the next words. 'He committed suicide during a bout of depression over some business failure or other. Once I knew that, I knew that was it. I didn't want to know anything about his family and I didn't want them to know anything about me. I told my cousins that and they were happy about it.' Then he looked back at me. 'I don't feel the need. If he'd wanted anything to do with me, he'd've done something about it. I got the impression that he was weak somewhere inside. To let his family run him like that, you know? Besides, Ronald was my Dad. He loved me and, for all his faults, I loved him.'

I nodded and left it there but that one word *suicide* kept echoing in my mind all the way home. The quirk in Pete's family tree seemed to have been strong and it worried me like hell. Especially the idea that it might've been on both sides.

Still, what I'd said about Pete always writing music was true. And having written it, he'd want to perform some time. I'd still be around when that happened and if anything else happened.

I just didn't know how strange that 'anything else' would turn out to be.

Third Verse

For the first six months, I did all the things I'd dreamed of doing and buying all the things I'd dreamed of buying for myself and family. We moved from our tidy terrace by the docks to a five bedroom detached not far from Colley Hill. It had a nice little plot of land, no pool but the garden looked down on the river and that was good enough for us. I used the spare bedroom as a bedsit-cum-study so I had that independence I'd grown used to by living away. I spent my days reading and helping my Dad decorate the house how my Mum wanted. I told them we could get professionals in but my Dad said it was *our* house and *we'd* do it. When he said things like that in that way, you didn't argue, you just took the brush he handed you and got on with it. It was a good time; quiet, easy and peaceful.

In the spring, I finally worked up my courage to ring

Jude at her parents' house. I got lucky because she was off work that week so I went to see her the following day.

'Good to see you, Terry,' she said when we were sitting in her garden. 'How's your Nan and everybody?'

'She feels her arthritis a bit more but you know what she's like. She doesn't let it get her down.' I handed her the bag I'd carried out of the car. 'She baked that when I told her I was coming.' She opened the bag and laughed when she saw the apple pie. 'So, how about you? Not married yet?'

'Not yet,' she said and smiled. 'But not far away. I think you'll like him. He's got the same sort of humour. Can't sing though. Did you bring me copies of your greatest hits?'

This time, I laughed. Three singles and two albums would never be anyone's idea of greatest hits. 'How did you know about all that?'

'I rang your house a few times. Your Erin told me. Full of how her big brother was a star and how she'd known it all along. I told her not to tell you I rang. I don't know why...' She looked almost embarrassed.

I nodded. 'I think I do,' I said. 'I never kept in touch because I'd've kept on at you to come and join me in Spain and that would've been wrong. And, when you didn't make contact, I knew you knew it, too. You know me too well, Jude. I didn't want to make you do something that, deep down, you'd've regretted.'

She blinked a few times and took my hand in both of hers, nodding her head once. 'Yes,' she agreed. 'I'm not going to pretend I didn't miss you, Terry but you're right. What we had was in college and I loved every second but...'

She straightened her shoulders and gave my hand a squeeze. 'We weren't in love the way Pete and Cheryl were. As soon as I met Aiden, I knew the difference. But we can be friends, can't we? I mean, real friends, Terry.'

I smiled and leaned towards her and kissed her softly on the lips. 'We were always friends, Jude. And you'll always be one of my two *best* friends.' And I blinked away the moisture in my eyes as she smiled at me.

She let go of my hand and said, 'Thank you.' She took a breath. 'Anyway, not in love or not, I was still curious so I rang your Erin. I bet Pete loved it. How is he now? I heard about his father.'

I gave her the short version and then she asked me about the thing I'd almost forgotten.

'Does he still get depressed?'

'To tell you the truth, there was only once when he was really down,' I said and told her about the time I'd found him in the dark on his bed, ready to jack it all in. 'Now that I think about it, I'd've expected another bout after Ronald died. Maybe he *has* grown out of it?'

'It's possible,' she said but I read another answer in her eyes. No, she didn't think he'd grown out of it because she didn't think it was anything you *did* grow out of.

'No, you're right and there's another thing.'

I told her about Pete's biological father and her face seemed to close in on itself and she worried the inside of her left cheek with her teeth as I talked. And that was enough for me to drop it—the day was too nice and it was too good to see her and talk over all the things old friends talk about when they haven't seen each other for a while. Anyway, from what she'd said all those years ago, Pete's downswings were only likely before or after a period of intense creativity and he wasn't writing at the moment.

I went home, glad that she was happy but there was no denying that there was a slight pang at the thought we couldn't be what we used to be.

Pete and I didn't see all that much of each other. We spoke on the phone regularly and he helped us move to our new house. Two days later, he turned up on the doorstep with two bottles of champagne. He smashed one on the porch wall to launch The New Barrow Home. Our Erin thought it was hilarious. I thought it was a waste of money buying the stuff in the first place; I've never liked it nor understood what the fuss was about. My Mum thanked him for the thought and then, typically, handed him a brush and shovel and told him to tidy up the mess. My Dad just told him he was a barm-pot. I visited The Firs once a week to use his pool and gym. I'd joined a football team with a few old mates and didn't want to look an idiot by only lasting half the game. Not once while I was there did I hear him playing an instrument. The one time I asked, he gave me an answer that seemed reasonable enough.

'We wrote so much in Liverpool and Spain, I can't seem to get inspired any more. If that's the right word. Sometimes, I sit at the old joanna, thinking I'm in the mood but then it all sounds like something I wrote before. I don't know, Terry, maybe I peaked early and don't know how any more. Anyway, with all these developments in personal computers, I fill my time with them. Maybe when I've had enough of that, I'll be able to write again.'

I looked and listened hard for signs that he was just painting a picture, that he was depressed and trying to hide it from me. But Pete was telling the truth and I was glad because he'd had enough to cope with and he deserved a period when he could just live a day at a time.

And that was it, really. Until January 1987

Pete came to our family party that Christmas. We played for the sing-song at the end. I looked at his face as we played all those old songs he'd learned at that first party all those years ago and I didn't think it'd be too long before he rang me to jam with him up at The Firs for old time's sake.

He did ring but not for that. But first, I got a call from Ricki.

It was a Saturday, near the end of January and I'd just put the kettle on. The weather was freezing and the football match I should've been playing had been called off. When the phone rang, I thought it might be our John, wanting to know if I fancied a pint. It never entered my head that I'd hear Ricki's voice, diluted and crackly, speaking English long-distance.

'Hello Ricki. How's tricks?' I wondered if there was a problem with the royalties.

'Has Pete told you?'

'I've been out. Tell me what? Is everything okay? Nobody sick?'

'No, no. Everything is fine. We are making lots of money and being successful. That's why I'm ringing. It could be better if you and Pete say yes.'

'Ricki, why don't *you* tell me?'

He did. He was so excited, he kept repeating himself and had to rewind and start again more than once. It took about fifteen minutes but I got it all eventually. I could understand why he was excited. In his position, I would've been. If Pete said yes, Ricki and Franco wouldn't just make lots of money, they'd have enough contacts so they could be become a world-wide enterprise.

'You think he'll agree?' Ricki asked.

'I don't know. I better get off the phone in case he rings. I'll be in touch.'

It was quite simple. Capitol in America wanted First Touch to do their next tour in the States. Ricki, to give him credit, told them we were more or less retired but, being American, they wouldn't take no for an answer. They made an offer of really silly money, promised the support and hype normally reserved for their own acts and the distinct possibility that *Fricko Management* could manage any of their acts who toured Europe. The thing was, Pete and I were free agents so it was down to us. To be brutally frank, it was down to Pete. If he said no, I wouldn't do it.

I knew Pete would call eventually but I thought it would be just to say a simple yes or no. He surprised me once again.

'Terry!' Erin called from the hall later that night. 'Pete's on the phone. He's in a phone box. Hurry up!'

'What're you doing in a phone box?' I asked.

'It's not. It's a payphone at a club. Sort of. Can you come

here now? They've got a members meeting or something and we'll have to be gone about half seven. It's down near Seapool Ferry. Fenderview Road. If you come out of the tunnel and, er…'

'I'll find it. Be there in about twenty minutes.' Waiting for directions from Pete was like waiting for the Second Coming. He could get lost going to the toilet at night in The Firs.

He met me at the gate outside the small, neat club. He managed to look excited and sheepish at the same time so I knew he'd been up to something.

'Okay, bollocks, what've you got us into now?'

'Wait till you see inside, Terry. You'll love it.' He opened the heavy door that stood closed against the bitter wind coming off the river.

The club stood on a small rise that ran down to the promenade. It was off the main road, built next to the sports centre. The brick building was surrounded by blue railings that ran up towards the main road and enclosed a neat patch of grass at its rear. It was flat-roofed, bars on all the windows. A sign on the door announced that this was the Seapool Royal Naval Association Club and only open to members and their guests. I followed Pete inside.

On the other side of the doorway was a small hallway. On the left were two doors, one of which was ajar and gave a glimpse of a boiler. The other, presumably an office, was closed. Opposite this door was a wooden plaque listing all the members who'd died. At the top of the plaque was a carved RNA crest and, below that, the words confirming the sentiment of every Cenotaph in the country—LEST WE FORGET. At the end of the hallway, glass double doors stood closed but you could see into the interior of the club. Pete pushed the doors open and we went inside.

It was nice. Really nice. I'd been expecting something like the working men's clubs that proliferate in the north—a long bar and sticky lino on the floor, the smell of stale ale and tobacco. It's a completely false idea, I know but it persists from all those old black and white telly programmes. But this place was plush. And warm.

'Terry, this is Alf Spalding. This is Terry Barrow, Alf.'

He offered his hand and I shook it. 'This is a nice place,' I said. 'Who did it out for you?'

'We did. It used to be the old school dinner hall. When they built the new school on the main road, it had a dinner hall. We got it on a long lease from the council. Your oppo here tells me you're a good duo.'

Alf was in his early sixties and it didn't sound strange hearing that old word to describe two singer-musicians. Actually, it's the right word as far as I'm concerned. 'Band' still has connotations of Glenn Miller and Joe Loss for me.

'So he keeps telling me,' I said. 'What he doesn't tell me is what he's got me into until after he's got me into it. I think you're going to have to tell me, Alf.'

Alf looked nonplussed, his gaze switching from me to Pete. Pete just grinned and shrugged.

'He didn't tell you he wants to use this place as a sort of rehearsal room during the week and then work here on Sunday nights? You really didn't know?'

'Don't worry about it, Alf. I don't anymore. And what

did *you* tell *him*?'

'I told him I'd have to hear you play and think about it.'

I looked at Pete. 'Why didn't you tell me to bring the guitars? He can't hear us if we don't play.'

'We couldn't tonight because of the meeting. I just wanted you to meet Alf and see this place. Look at it, isn't it great? Soon as I saw it, I knew you'd love it. You can almost smell the sea.'

'You'll have to excuse my friend,' I told Alf. 'He gets this way when he knows I'm going to bollock him. But he's right about this room. D'you mind if I look around?'

Alf smiled. 'Help yourself,' he said and went into his office.

I waited until the double doors had closed and then stared at Pete. 'Okay, time to own up, Lynwood.'

'I'll tell you in the pub over the road later. Just take a look around this room, it's amazing.'

I couldn't argue with that. The room was about forty feet wide and about two hundred feet long. The bar was on the right as you came in, small but wonderful. It had a polished top that glowed below the hidden lights. To the left as you came in was a snooker table, obviously well-cared for by the look of the cloth. At the far end of the room was a small stage where, presumably, we'd be working. The floor was carpeted in good quality red/orange Axminster apart from a small space in front of the bar that was shiny lino and a small square of parquet in front of the stage. Bench seats ran around the room and there were wooden chairs by all the round tables. The false ceiling was lit by fluorescent bars. If the members had done all this, they must've been bloody good tradesmen. I'd been in nightclubs abroad that didn't look anything like as good as this place. But it was the stuff on the walls that really caught my eye. Like Pete said, you could almost smell the sea.

There were ship's crests and badges, photographs and drawings of ships going back to Nelson. Most of them had information down the sides of the photos—names, size and weight, number of crew, where and when launched, where and when they fought and won or fought and lost. On the window ledges were ships in bottles and tiny ships in matchboxes, made, I found out later, by one of the members who was almost blind; you'd never know it by those tiny ships. On the stage was an enormous ship's bell mounted on a stand carved out of one piece of wood. The bell gleamed like everything else metal in the club; these blokes had learned the Royal Navy's lessons well. Over by the fire escape were certificates detailing members' service to the RNA organisation. There was history inside this room. Even if Alf didn't want us, I still fancied coming in here for a pint and to talk to the men who'd built the place and who'd served in the Royal Navy through one, possibly two, World Wars.

I was standing in front of a pencil drawing of a tall ship, thinking how hard it must've been to sail on one and wishing I could anyway when Pete broke into my reverie.

'Time to come ashore. You can look some more tomorrow.'

'Told you you'd like it,' Pete said as he put the pint of shandy in front of me.

'It's magic,' I agreed. 'My Dad'd love it. Even if we don't get the gig, I'll ask Alf I can bring him over to see the place.'

We were in the Seapool Arms on Castle Street, just over the main road from the club. The pub was as quiet as a pub was apt to be in this part of the world when unemployment ran above the national average and it wasn't yet eight o'clock. Apart from the two of us, there was the barmaid, an old fellah who looked like he'd come in for a warm as much as a drink, two old women who looked as worn out as the tired wallpaper and a blind man with his labrador. A television burbled from a wall bracket near the jukebox. Nobody was playing darts in the corner.

'Okay,' I said and put my glass down. 'What's the score, Pete?'

He looked up and gave me a Carol-smile. 'I'm sure you know those daft Americans want to give us silly money to tour and they've hinted about...*benefits* for Ricki and Franco. Well, when Franco rang me, my first reaction was to say no but then I got a funny tingling and I realised I'd missed playing. Not writing but playing. I told him I'd think about but, to be honest, I still don't really fancy touring. But that tingle won't go away. Anyway, I came over here yesterday and walked around Laketon. I went into The Eight Bells and had a drink. I sat there and the tingle got stronger. I asked Derry if he wanted us but he's already fixed up. So I walked down the prom, got to the bottom of the hill here, saw a sign pointing the way to the club and here we are.'

He took another sip of his drink and the sparkle in his eyes told me he was really looking forward to playing again.

'What if Alf doesn't like us?' I asked. 'The blokes in there aren't really the age to like rock when all they want is a quiet drink and a talk.'

'That's the beauty of it,' he told me. 'Not many members go on a Sunday night. Alf says they do okay Fridays and Saturdays and even during the week but Sundays aren't too good. It must cost them as much as they take just to open up. If we can increase their take to cover more than their overheads, they'll be made up. Besides, we can play anything they want. Your family taught me all the old stuff years ago. What d'you say, Terry? Fancy it?'

Oh yeah, I fancied it.

'And how much were you thinking of asking?' I was pretty sure what the answer was but it kept him honest to ask.

'I thought we'd tell Alf if he let us use it during the dinner times to rehearse, we'd do Sundays for nothing. We can do the loud stuff at my house. Does that sound okay?'

'Fine. What'll you tell Franco and Ricki?'

'The truth. I don't see us touring but we're rehearsing and, if we change my mind, I'll let them know.'

'Fair enough.'

We had our first sight of the house opposite the club the next day. We arrived at the club at ten past eleven. It was the kind of January day that's more reminiscent of November. The wind was light and off the river but there was a mist that was cold and damp, almost a fine rain, the kind that soaks you without you noticing you've got wet.

I parked my car in the small car park that serves the

council offices on Castle Street and we unloaded the gear. We took the acoustics, a bass and one electric. The club had one of those old, two-keyboard organs and Pete could play that. He said he'd tested the club's PA and there was no problem there.

'Funny place to build a house,' Pete said as he put down the cases by the club gate.

I looked across the road and had to agree with him. There were no other houses in the road and this one stood atop the steep slope running down to the prom. On either side of the house there were just trees and privet hedges. Fender Gap ran down the left side as we looked, blocked to traffic by two shiny, black bollards. You could see the way the house must angle down in the garden so I assumed there was a cellar. It had a bay front looking onto the road with a front door behind a glassed-in porch. Above the front window was a narrow window that looked like it might be a bathroom. The roof stretched to a high point, dominated by a weather vane shaped like an old galleon. The side of the house running down Fender Gap had two more windows downstairs and what looked like an extension built on the end. This extension was only half as high as the house proper, topped with a flat roof. Three brick chimneys perched on the roof but no smoke drifted into the chill air. This wasn't surprising since Seapool had been smokeless for over twenty years. There was obviously a garden at the back but with the planks between it and the Gap, you couldn't see it. The woodwork of the house was painted red, almost maroon and so was the wrought iron gate that opened onto the pavement. It was an ordinary detached house that looked a bit isolated.

'Maybe its neighbours were knocked down or something,' I said and pushed the club gate open. I waited for Pete to follow me but he was still staring at the house, a peculiar expression on his face. 'Pete, if it's all the same to you, I'd like to get inside with this gear. I'm getting soaked.'

He finally followed me inside and we put the gear down. Alf said hello and turned on the PA. I went to get the rest of the gear.

Outside, I glanced at the house and saw the front door open. A man came out. He looked to be in his late forties, wearing a grey jacket zipped up to his chin. His trousers were dark and well-pressed. He stood around six feet and walked erect. As he closed the gate, he looked up and saw me. He raised his hand in silent greeting and walked towards the main road, probably thinking I was somebody from the club he knew. I went to fetch the rest of our gear.

Alf liked the stuff we did. We did mostly Beatles' stuff and a few old songs from my family parties. He agreed to us rehearsing during the week and his eyes lit up when we told him we'd do Sunday nights for nothing. The club was fairly busy. A four-handed game of snooker was going on and more than half the tables were occupied, one the site of a game of dominoes. The barmaid put on a tape of Foster and Allen Irish songs. It was a nice, easy atmosphere and I was enjoying my pint of shandy.

Pete asked about the house over the road. He was obviously interested for some reason.

'The old Camberwell House? Been there as long as I can

remember,' Alf told him. 'Just part of the scenery now. Danny comes in for a drink most days.'

'Is his name Camberwell?' Pete asked.

'No. Camberwell's the name of the bloke who built it. Back in the last century, far as I know. Why are you so interested?' Alf looked amused, the way people do when they've lived somewhere all their lives, know most of the stories and find it hard to understand that somebody could find them interesting.

'It just looked odd, stuck up there at the top of the slope with no other houses round.'

'Never thought of it that way. I suppose it does look a bit funny. If you want to know more, Danny'll be able to tell you. The bloke you really should talk to is old Henry Franklin. He comes in about half one every day. He's probably forgotten more than anybody else ever knew. I'll introduce you. I hope you brought plenty of cash. He's a smashing bloke but he does love his rum. He thinks he's earned the right to have drinks bought for him because he fought in both wars. Maybe he's right. But he tells wonderful stories.'

Alf left us then, his big frame rolling across the floor like he was still at sea. We waited for old Henry, Pete a little more impatiently than me but I was looking forward to meeting him. I've always loved listening to old people tell their tales, ever since I was a kid. I think the tales, the stories they tell, are our real heritage. More so than the land. For me, literature, music, it's all communication. It's somebody saying something he feels should be said and saying it the best way he knows how. And, if we don't communicate, we'll lose our history and that would be the same as forgetting who we are. If we do that, we might as well jack it in and go back to the mud we came from.

*

At exactly half one by the bar clock, I saw Alf talking to a small, neat man at the bar. Alf pointed at us and then came over and introduced us to Henry.

Henry was old but you only knew it by the creases in his face and by the stick he used to help him walk. Nothing else about him was old. His mind was as quick and sharp as anyone's in that club and his eyes blazed with humour and intelligence. He wore his blazer with its RNA badge and a RNA tie set off his white shirt. This was a man proud of his membership.

'Afternoon boys,' Henry said when Alf had gone. His voice was whispery but clear. 'I hear you're going to be the cabaret during the dinner time? I hope you're not going to deafen me any more than I am already. Pleased to meet you.'

I shook his hand. His grip was as firm as I expected.

'Which one of you wants to know about the old Camberwell place?'

'Well, we both do but mostly it's my mate, here.'

Pete nodded and smiled.

'Aye, well, I can tell you all you want to know but it's likely to be thirsty work.'

I laughed. You had to admire a man who made blackmail sound so reasonable. 'We'll pay whatever the going rate is for a history lesson, Henry,' I told him and went to buy him a tot.

'Now, you want the long one or the abridged version,' Henry asked when I got back.

'The long one.' Pete said quickly. His voice was nowhere near as light as mine or Henry's had been. I looked at him but his eyes were fixed on Henry. Almost riveted.

Henry sipped his tot, took out a pipe, lit it with a Ronson lighter and settled into his chair. Then he told us about the house over the road.

I won't give it you the way he told it, with all its pauses while we kept his glass topped up or he marshalled his thoughts and memories but this is the tale he told.

The house was built in the late 19th century by Albert Camberwell, a cotton king who made enough money to have his own fleet of ships, which he berthed in the then bustling port of Oxborough. With the fleet, Albert's fabric traversed the globe and his fortune increased. He decided he wanted a house that overlooked the river where his fast ships came and went. The Oxborough side of the river was mostly docks so he built his house on the Seapool side, almost exactly in the middle of the coastline. He didn't want to be overlooked so he bought the land on either side and planted bushes in and around the trees.

Albert died in 1900 and was succeeded by his youngest son, Edgar, his two elder sons dying in separate wrecks three years earlier. Edgar managed the business well. He diversified, moving into the booming munitions market in the run-up to the First World War. The Camberwell Empire grew and the Camberwells grew richer. Edgar also added to the house on the side you couldn't see from the road. He built a conservatory in which, it was said, he spent his days with his ledgers and his telescope, adding up his fortune and watching the ships sail up the river, bringing him more fortune. When he was twenty one, Edgar married the most beautiful woman in Seapool, Miriam Haverlock. They lived in the house and waited for the next generation of Camberwells to arrive. But there were no children.

As the barren years passed, Edgar and Miriam turned to the town to find a receptacle for their love and generosity. They endowed the town with buildings, parks and libraries. Laketon, where Pete and I first played for a paying audience, was built with Camberwell money. But it was the Camberwell Scholarship that most pleased both the Camberwells and the town. This foundation provided scholarships for children of the town who were gifted but poor. In time, 'A Camberwell Student' became a byword for any boy or girl who did well at school.

The day Chamberlain declared war on Germany, Edgar was sixty and in rude health. Miriam was four years younger but ailing. She died the day of the Dunkirk evacuation.

Henry never elaborated on the deaths in his story, never said they died of the flu or brain fever or smallpox. He just said they died. I noticed it but it didn't strike me as that odd. Later, Pete made a lot more of it. At the time, he asked Henry if there was something strange about a Camberwell Death. I thought maybe he thought there was some mental history Henry wanted to overlook. Henry's answer was blunt and none too helpful.

'They died.' He shrugged but I noticed his eyes lingered on Pete's face for a few seconds before he went on with his story. I saw an expression on his face that I struggled to understand and then it struck me—it was as if Henry was weighing Pete up. I had no idea why or what for but that's definitely what his expression said. But then he was telling his tale again and I forgot about it.

After Miriam's death, Edgar apparently went into a decline, staying in the house more and more, rarely at the office or at the meetings of the Laketon Theatre which he and his wife endowed and both loved. As the man declined, so did the business. It was still making money hand over fist but there were signs of the bad days to come. Fortunately, a Camberwell Student halted the decline. Patrick Sullivan returned from the war and took over as General Manager, using the education he'd received to sort out the company's problems.

Patrick had to slim down the whole mess and, during the three years it took, Edgar's health worsened. While he was still in full control of his faculties, he willed the house and business to Patrick. Then Edgar died.

Patrick Sullivan made a great success of his new-found position and he, too, added to the house by building another wing next to the conservatory. Then, in 1952, he was ill-advised over an oil-drilling venture. It resulted in the almost total collapse of the Camberwell business. He was forced to allow its sale to a huge conglomerate.

Patrick retired and, like Edgar, spent most of the rest of his life in the house on the hill, feeling he'd failed the trust put in him. At first, Kathleen, his wife, and their son, Daniel, made sure his sense of failure didn't destroy him but then Kathleen was knocked down by a lorry carrying freight from what used to be a Camberwell warehouse. When it became clear that she was going to die from her injuries, she and her husband insisted she be allowed to die at home. Once Kathleen was gone, Patrick lost all interest in living and died in 1969.

Daniel, Danny to all who knew him, inherited the house and what was still a large amount of money. He continued to work as a freelance photographer for the local papers. In 1970, he married a gifted musician called Cheryl Connor and they were the classic happily-married couple save for the fact they couldn't have children. It didn't mar their lives and Cheryl made a reputation for herself on the classical music circuit. The marriage lasted ten years until Cheryl died and left Danny to live alone in the house opposite the club.

Henry finished his story and his fourth tot and told us he'd see us the next day

Pete had been enthralled from the start. Right up to when he heard about Danny's musically gifted wife, Cheryl. When he heard that, he jumped in his seat like somebody had pinched his bum. It shook me a little, too. But coincidence covers a lot of things and there must be hundreds of Cheryls who are musically gifted. And everyone dies. Don't they?

Even when Pete tried to make me see more into it, I played it down.

'I think it's Fate, Terry. Look at the way it happened. I could've walked anywhere the other day. Shit, I could've said let's just call Pete Leay and do it that way. And then seeing the house struck a chord in me, made me want to find out about it. And then Henry tells us about a woman called Cheryl who was a musician. There's more to it than coincidence, Terry. I can *feel* it. And what about the way Henry skipped over the deaths? I think there's another story there. How d'you think we could find out?'

'Whoa, Neddy! What's all this 'we' stuff? And why should we try?'

'Because I won't be able to settle,' he said and looked at his hands. Then he sighed and looked at me. 'Never mind,' he said and we left it there.

But in the end, I finally tried to solve what Pete thought was a mystery. I did it not because he wanted me to, more because he *didn't* want me to, was almost intent on stopping me.

Old Henry didn't come in the next day. It was only later we found out he spent that morning having a long conversation with Danny Sullivan. In the meantime, we played our songs for the regulars; slow ones, ones they knew from their youth and we knew from my family. Alf spent the morning spreading the word that we'd be there Sunday night and it wouldn't all be sentimental stuff and they should let their younger relatives know.

It must've worked. That Sunday night the place was packed with mostly 19 to 35 year olds. We did a lot of sixties stuff and Neil Diamond and Elton John. We did a few of our own and then finished with a Beatles' medley. I was expecting polite applause but they cheered and clapped and banged the tables. They shouted so loudly for more that Alf, trying to tell them we'd be there every Sunday, grinned and more or less told us we *had* to give them more. First Touch were back.

Henry came in Monday dinner time. With Danny Sullivan.
When we'd finished running through some Irish sngs, Pete bought a rum and we went across to the table where Henry was sitting.
'Hello, Henry,' Pete said and put the tot in front of hi. 'How're you today?'
'I've been warmer, son. Does that drink mean you wat another history lesson?' He looked at me as he said it and I smiled. Danny Sullivan chuckled and drank some of his pint.
'Well, there were a few things I wondered about. I was thinking you might elaborate?'
'Not today, son. I'm a bit tired. Didn't have a very good night. The cold plays havoc with these old bones. Tell you what, see the old fellah two tables down? That's Jimmy Wilson and he loves to talk. Been around a lot, has Jimmy. I'll introduce you.'
I could see Pete was about to tell him not to bother but Henry was already shouting across to the old man sitting under a picture of a Harrier Jet taking off from a carrier. 'Aye aye, Jimmy! Couple of lads here'd like to buy you a pint!' Henry turned to us and said, 'Jimmy's a bit deaf but he's all there. He drinks bottled Guinness.'
Pete pulled a face but I said, 'Come on, it'll be interesting.

I'll get the bloke a bottle.'

'Thanks for the drink,' Henry said as we stood up. 'By the way, this is Danny Sullivan. I told him how you were interested in his house.'

'Pleased to meet you,' Danny Sullivan said, shaking our hands. 'I like the music you play. I'll be here Sunday. I couldn't make it last night. I had things to do.'

We nodded and went to get Jimmy his bottle. At the bar, I took another look at Danny Sullivan. He was still watching us. He looked...informed and interested. His eyes met mine for a moment and I was sure there was a small smile there but then he picked up his glass and the moment was gone.

Jimmy was 71 and joined the Royal Navy (he called it The Andrew like most of the members) when he was sixteen. He served right through the second war as a gunner. When the war ended, he joined the Merchant Navy and finished when he was fifty five. The bloke was full of stories about his years at sea and he loved to tell them. That first time, he told us about the time he was on a ship docked in the shadow of Mt Etna. The old music hall comedian, Tommy Trinder, was out there giving the troops a show. During the show, the volcano began to rumble and smoke, looking like it might be ready to blow. A reporter fancied getting a photo of the mountain in its volcanic throes and somehow persuaded a spotter plane pilot to take him up. Jimmy told us that everyone who'd been watching the show now watched the plane as it flew over the smoking peak. Then, on its third pass, the plane dropped, presumably so the reporter could get a better shot. The plane was sucked into the boiling mess and never came out the other side.

It was his favourite story and he told it with a relish that made his eyes glint. You could almost see the young man he'd been, watching the smoky sky for a plane that would never be seen again.

At first, Pete was less than attentive and more than once flicked his eyes towards old Henry and Danny Sullivan. As Jimmy warmed to his story, though, Pete became more interested and, by the end, gave the old bloke his full attention. I glanced at Danny once or twice and saw that he was watching Pete closely. I caught that small smile each time.

I bought Jimmy another drink when he'd finished and then we put our gear away. Danny Sullivan and old Henry had already left.

On Saturday, we jammed for an hour at The Firs and then we had something to eat. It was another cold day and the snow that had threatened all week had finally arrived. We watched a robin poking around for something to eat while we finished our soup and bread.

'Remember that day you played 'Peggy Sue'?'

'Yeah. I took a bow to the birds. Seems like a long time ago now.'

He nodded. 'A long, *long* time ago. Did you ever think you'd be a millionaire but still not recognised when you walked down a road in your home town?'

I laughed. 'Never would've happened if you hadn't pushed me into that job at The Eight Bells.'

'Fate, that's what it is. Everything happens because it's meant to happen and no matter what you do, you can't stop it.'

I didn't like the sound of this. His voice had that same tone he'd used in Spain when I told him about his real father. 'No,' I told him. 'I think we always have a choice. We're given the means to get over whatever we're faced with. What brought this on?'

'I was just thinking, that's all. Nothing to get worked up about. Listen, go and give that poor bloody bird some of this bread and then I'll play what I've written.'

'When did you write that?' I asked after listening to the new tune.

'Sunday night, after the gig.'

I smiled. 'About bloody time. The music's so much a part of you, when you leave it alone, you start to change. Your eyes go dull. You're not whole unless you're writing.'

'You're right,' he agreed. 'I don't feel right if I'm not putting something down. It feels like there's a hole inside me. It's a bit like...'

'A bit like what?' I thought I knew, though.

'A bit like how I feel about Cheryl. You know, I keep waking up and thinking that today, it won't hurt so much. But it always does. D'you think I'll ever get over her? D'you think there'll be just memories of the good times to make me smile instead of this hole and waiting to cry?'

I wanted to tell him that time always heals. I wanted to tell him there would be a time when he'd just see Cheryl's smiling face and hear her voice, heavy with irony and that he'd smile. I wanted to tell him there'd be somebody for him in the future. But the truth was, I didn't believe it strongly enough and I wasn't going to lie. For Pete, Cheryl was the one all the poets write about and all the singer-songwriters sing about. I couldn't see anyone coming close to Cheryl as far as Pete was concerned. She'd been the one who fitted all the hollows in him so well that they were almost one person. That's so rare that, if God is good enough to get you together, He only lets it happen once.

I must've had my mouth open, ready to say something, *anything*, as long as it wasn't what I was thinking, because he spoke to me again.

'If you're not going to answer me, Terry, shut your gob. I don't need to see what you had for dinner. I made it. Anyway, you don't need to say anything, it's written all over your face. That's okay, I feel the same. Come on, let's get this tune sorted properly.'

That Sunday, Pete was really buzzing on stage, giving it some stick. I knew it wouldn't be long before he was writing like there was no tomorrow and he'd be expecting me to find the words. That was okay, I'd been feeling less than whole myself. Still, at the back of my mind I could hear Jude telling me that downswings were likely before or after a bout of prolonged creativity. I hoped not. Hadn't he suffered enough? Didn't he deserve some respite, a time to enjoy what he had?

We finished the second set at five past twelve and when we got back from loading our gear into the car, Kenny Phillips, the barman, had set up two pints of orange for us. The only people still left were Kenny, Ron Willis the duty man, and Danny Sullivan. He was standing at the bar, his dark coat wrapped round him, the zip done up to his chin, hands in his pockets. As Pete reached the bar, Danny spoke.

'I enjoyed that. You're very, very good.'

'We do our best,' Pete said coldly, letting Danny know he didn't appreciate being sent to listen to Jimmy's volcano story like a kid being sent out of the room while the grown-ups talked.

'I doubt old Henry would agree,' I said, putting my glass on the bar. 'If we did what we do on Sundays during the dinnertimes, he'd probably resign in disgust.'

'Oh, he's not as black and white as he likes to make out. He has his moments.'

'Yeah,' Pete said. 'I think we caught one the other day. When he decided he didn't need our beer money?'

Danny smiled. 'That's the other reason I'm here tonight. I've known the old fellah a long time and he likes to think of me as a sort of adopted son. He thought he was doing it for me.'

'I'm very happy for you both,' Pete said in that same cold voice. He turned to face the bar.

'Come on, Pete. The man's saying it was old Henry and nothing to do with him.'

'That's right, Peter. I was going to offer you a cup of coffee before you went home. I remember my wife, Cheryl, used to be so full of adrenaline after a performance, she needed a long time to calm down. I thought it might be the same for you?'

Mentioning his wife was probably the only way Danny could've stopped Pete's sarcasm. Now, Pete's mind had moved from cold annoyance to what he'd talked to me about; Fate.

'Well, maybe I was more annoyed at Henry than you. Yeah, we'll have a drink. But make it tea. Terry can't stand coffee.'

The Old Camberwell House looked nice enough from the outside but not that big. Once inside, I began to understand why old Henry made it sound as big as he did.

With the front door open, you got the impression you were in one of those American open-plan houses on the telly. What baffled me was that, from the hallway, I couldn't see the stairs. Danny led us into his living room, the one looking out on the road. It was big but cosy. The furniture was modern but not all that glass and chrome stuff. At the back of the room, an arch led to the kitchen.

'Have a look round,' Danny said. 'I'll make the tea.'

The kitchen was modern and bright and another arch led to another room that looked like a family room. French windows opened out onto a patio. From this room, you could get into the conservatory.

This was really something special. It was all glass and, in the dim light, you couldn't really see where the wooden frame must've supported the glass. It was built in a semi-circle whose full circumference would've been about seventy feet. The floor was polished parquet and fluorescents hung from the domed ceiling. Running all the way round was an upholstered bench-seat. Above this was a counter-like top that acted as a desk. The view of the river was unrestricted and you could see how somebody whose living depended on that river would enjoy that view.

'Where the hell's the stairs,' Pete asked me in a whisper

that I could understand but still found funny. He sounded like he was in church.

'Over here,' Danny said from behind us. Pete jumped and I giggled a little, feeling like a fool.

We turned and watched Danny going to the far wall of the room between the kitchen and the conservatory. The only thing you could see on that wall were bookshelves.

Danny looked over his shoulder and smiled. 'You might appreciate this,' he said and ran his hand up the inside edge of the right hand shelf.

The whole thing split in two and opened out, revealing a staircase running up from the floor.

'Bleedin hell!' Pete said.

'Secret passages,' I said. I think I was amused. 'I thought they were only in books or films. Or old castles. Whose idea was that?'

'Albert Camberwell designed it when he designed the house. He liked the idea of people not finding what they were expecting. He had quite a sense of humour. Come on, I'll show you upstairs.'

There were six rooms upstairs, including the toilet. The toilet was the only room that was not ordinary. It was the biggest bathroom I've ever seen in a house. The other rooms were just ordinary bedrooms. The four at the back looked out on the garden, which was big. It stretched away down the slope towards the railings and the embankment. In the light from the window, it was clear that the garden was well-planned and well-cared for; no bushes ran riot and nothing overgrew the central path.

We went down to have our tea.

The living room fire was lit and the room was warm and cosy. Danny poured us all a cup of tea and then told us why the house was built the way it was, with all the rooms opening into each other, giving the impression the house was circular despite its common angularity outside.

'Albert built the house to reflect his philosophy.'

'How d'you mean?' I asked. For the life of me I couldn't see what philosophy might be reflected in this house.

'He considered a circle the most profound depiction of everything life is about.'

'Sorry, I don't get it,' Pete admitted, putting his empty cup on the table.

I watched Danny as he thought how best to explain. It was there again, that assessing look he'd given Pete that first time in the club. It was the kind of look that usually indicates doubt as to whether something should be told, whether the person is up to hearing it.

'Albert thought that a circle was the perfect symbol of the way things *really* are. That everything comes back if you wait.'

'What goes around comes around,' I said and wondered why I felt cold.

'That's right. It's infinity. No beginning, no end. He believed that and built this house to acknowledge his belief.'

'Why didn't he just build a round house?' Pete asked. 'There's one on the road to Southport. Looks a bit like a miniature Albert Hall. He had the land and money. It would've been a more obvious statement.'

'It wasn't the outside he was concerned about. He believed that it's on the *inside* of things that infinity exists.

No matter how normal, how structured, how geometrically angular things are, the circle is on the inside. Waiting to be found.'

And I understood that look Danny had given Pete; he wanted to see if Pete was the type who could find the circle inside. Something old Henry told Danny hinted to Danny that one of us, Pete, or me would be able to see that circle. Something else occurred to me then.

'This place is built on a steep hill so there must be a cellar. Does that reflect the philosophy, too?'

He shot me a glance; sharp, narrow-eyed, wary. It only lasted a couple of seconds but it hit home. Why would mentioning the cellar produce a glance like that?

'Oh, the cellar's there because it had to be. To stop the floors looking like ski-slopes' Danny said, giving me a small smile as he drank some more of his tea. 'It's just a cellar. It was the house that was important to Albert.'

Plausible enough but...

Why lie about something as ordinary as a cellar?

The thought was so quick and sharp, it closed my mouth before I could say anything. I could see Danny watching me carefully over the rim of his cup, waiting to see if I was going to press the issue. I nodded and the sharpness left his face.

'Well, I hate to push you but I've got to leave for London on the early train.'

As we stepped outside into the still-falling snow, I looked up at the house. It was hard to reconcile the more and less than ninety degree angles of the outside with that circle inside. Albert had done a good job.

'I'll be away till the weekend,' I heard Danny say but, when I looked at him, he was only looking at Pete. 'If you're up this way on Saturday, pop in and I'll show you the garden,' he finished, still looking at Pete.

'Yeah,' Pete said. 'Good.' He looked at me but I was still looking at Danny looking at Pete and I knew the invitation was for Pete alone.

'Fine,' Danny said and closed the door.

Driving home, I wondered why Danny would want to freeze me out but I didn't worry too much about it. You can't be liked by everybody and there'll always be people who like your best mate more than they like you. Still, that thing about the cellar had me obscurely bothered.

Pete didn't say much on the way home. His face told me he was thinking about something. Very hard.

'Terry? It's Jude.'

I smiled at the phone. A stupid thing to do, I know, but you can't help it sometimes, can you? It was good to hear her voice.

'How are you, love?'

'Fine.'

It was Wednesday night and very cold. I'd just got back from The Firs after another hard session with Slavemaster Lynwood. He'd written about fifteen new tunes and wanted the words yesterday.

'Nothing's wrong, is there?'

'No,' Jude told me. 'I'm ringing to ask a favour.'

'As long as you don't want me to be part of some medical experiment.'

She laughed. 'No, nothing like that. I know it's short notice but a week on Friday I'm getting married. I wondered if you and Pete would play at the reception? Daddy can get somebody but I'd really like you to play for me.'

Something warm and soft slipped out of me then. I felt it leave from around the vicinity of my heart. Jude was really getting married and not to me. Ah well.

'I hope this isn't one of those hurry-up jobs?'

She laughed again. 'No, I'm not pregnant. We were planning on a June wedding but Daddy has some work in America and Mummy has always wanted to go to New York. They'll be away most of the summer. D'you think you'll be able to do it?'

'Oh, I think we could manage it.'

'Daddy wants to know how much it will be so he can get the money for you.'

'The Jude I knew didn't insult people.'

'It's what you do for a living, Terry. If I had to hire a band or disco, I'd have to pay the going rate.'

'And you're a friend. A good friend who used to watch us play for fun and pocket money. And *we* used to be a bit more than friends. I'm not taking any money off your dad. Call it a wedding gift.'

'Thank you, Terry,' she said and I could've sworn there was a sob in there somewhere.

'I'll ring Pete now and tell him. We'll have to come down and sort out the sound system and everything. How about Friday?'

'Smashing. You'll be able to meet Aiden.'

Pete was made up at the news when I phoned him, but when I told him about going down on Friday, he left me flat-footed.

There was a pause in which I could only hear his low breathing and those unearthly beeps and boops on the line. I waited, some part of me already knowing what was coming.

'Tell you what, Terry. You go down and sort it out. I've...I've got something to do on Friday. You'll have a chance to talk over old times with Jude.'

'Her fiancée will be there.' I added a pause of my own and, in it, I worried that all those new songs he'd written had been the prelude to a downswing. I was about to ask him if he felt okay and then I had one of those insights again, like the one I'd had about Ronald. I thought I had a good idea why Pete couldn't come with me to see Jude. 'Okay, I'll go down. You going somewhere nice?' There was another pause and I knew I was right and that he wouldn't tell me.

'No, just something I'd forgotten about. Tell Jude I'm really pleased for her. It'll be great to see her again.'

Whatever else he was dissembling about, it wasn't how pleased he was.

Aiden was taller than I expected. Why I thought he'd be short in the first place, though, I have no idea. His hair was blonde and cut short. His eyes were a very dark brown above a nice smile. Jude was right about his humour and we hit it off right away. I was glad. I hadn't been looking forward to meeting him too much but after I met him, I knew he was the right one for her.

The reception was going to be in the house and in a marquee in the garden. With the tent flaps open at the back and some sort of canopy, we could perform out there. Jude told me her dad was hiring large hot-air blowers so nobody would freeze to death. We could fasten the speakers to the two trees at the end of the garden. Just before dinnertime, Aiden and Jude's father went to Chester to sort something out about the catering so it was just the two of us who ate cheese on toast like we used to at college. She asked me about Pete.

'I thought he'd've come, too?'

I shrugged. 'He had something to do. But he wanted you to know how glad he is for you. Just like me.'

'Thanks. I knew you'd like Aiden.' She drank some of her tea and then looked at me seriously. 'How is Pete?'

'He's okay,' I said quietly. I was beginning to wonder by then.

'Still writing? No,' she said before I could answer. 'Like asking if he's still breathing. Does he still miss Cheryl as badly?'

'More each day, I think. The music helps because it's what she and his mum would've wanted.'

'Has he had any more depressions since Spain?' I didn't answer straight away so she must've seen what I was thinking by the look on my face. 'If he's writing more...you know what I mean. Keep an eye on him?'

'I will. I always have.'

Pete never mentioned where he'd been or what he'd

done while I was at Jude's that Friday. Over that weekend, he seemed his normal self. The run up to the wedding, he seemed, not down, but introspective. When I picked him up to go to the wedding, though, he was fine.

It was February but the weather was kind to Jude. No wind or rain and the sun even shone when she came out of the church. The reception went well and so did we.

We did mostly the stuff we used to do in Spain. We took some requests and threw in a few of our own while the guests raided the buffet tables. Jude's dad told us the happy couple would be leaving at five. At ten to, I nodded to Pete and, when we finished that song, I announced their imminent departure.

'But before they do,' I said. 'We'd like to do this next song especially for the bride. I know Aiden won't mind. This goes back a long way and will probably remind her of the first time she heard us sing for an audience. All the best Jude. Be happy.'

'Yeah,' Pete agreed. 'And don't let the sun catch you crying.'

We did 'Hey Jude'. She cried a little. Aiden smiled and then led her out for a last dance. The guests joined in the chorus and then we saw her and Aiden off.

The following Friday afternoon, Pete left the club early, pleading something else to do. I nodded and stayed. I wanted to have a word with some of the younger regulars who, I knew from Alf, all worked for the same contractors.

'Aye aye, Terry, how's things?' This was from Alec, the

youngest of the three. He was a big bloke who always seemed to be smiling. He reminded me a lot of Paul Hughes from Moss Grammar.

'Not bad,' I said. 'Any room at this table? Or are you talking secrets?'

'Not unless you find the amount of sand needed for a good render a secret,' Joey Dicks said. 'Sit yourself down.'

'Sounds top secret to me. I wouldn't know the right amount of sand needed for a sandcastle on Laketon shore.'

They all told me how much they liked the stuff we did on a Sunday night and I listened as modestly as I could. It wasn't that hard because I was trying to find a way of broaching the subject of Danny Sullivan. When Mike Rennie stood up to leave, what he said let me in.

'I'm off now lads. Gotta sort out that stuff for Danny. He wants that path sorted out this weekend. I'll see you tomorrow.'

After he'd left, I turned to Alec. 'Doing some work for Danny Sullivan?'

It was Joey who answered me. 'Yeah. The path in the garden's fallen away again.'

'Again? Happens a lot?' I asked, trying not to sound too eager.

Alec nodded at me over the top of his glass. When he put it down, he said, 'Every couple of years or so. Needs doing properly and we keep telling him but he takes no notice. It's the cellar, really.'

'Yeah,' Joey agreed. 'Needs shoring up or, better still, filling in. We offered him a good deal but he just wants the path fixing when it needs it. Even if he let us reroute the bloody path, it'd be better.'

'Yeah, him and his bloody figure of eight.' Alec managed to sound amused and disgusted at the same time.

'Ah well,' Joey said and drained his glass. 'It's his money. Well, time to go. See you Sunday, Terry.'

They left. I sat and thought.

Figure of eight.

Something about that made my mind itch in a place I couldn't scratch. And why didn't Danny just let them reroute the path if he was only leery of anybody seeing the cellar?

I wondered if Danny had let Pete see his cellar when he'd shown him the garden the other weekend. And if he did, why hadn't Pete mentioned it to me?

'Bloody peculiar,' I said aloud.

'They lock you up for talking to yourself,' Alf said as he passed behind me.

'Only if you tell them and if you do, you'll stop making a profit on Sunday nights.'

'True. In that case, whisper,' he said and walked away laughing.

These things Pete 'had to do'? Was he doing them in the house, with Danny? And was I jealous?

That made me sit up straighter in my chair. Jealousy was something I'd never thought about in all the years I'd known Pete. All the times he'd had girlfriends and I hadn't, the times he wrote like there was no tomorrow and I knew I'd never come close to that kind of talent, I'd never felt even slightly jealous. Could I get jealous over something as minor as this?

Is it minor?

I picked up my glass. It was empty. I looked at the bar clock. Quarter to three. I could go home or I could buy another shandy from Beryl behind the bar and think some more. I bought the shandy.

Should I ask Pete what he'd been doing? Where he'd been? Was it with Danny? More to the point, if I did ask, would he tell me? Somehow, I didn't think so. Ah shit, did it matter?

Well...there was the way Pete went on about Fate, like he'd found the secret of the universe. Now, he seemed to have stopped even thinking about it, definitely stopped talking about it. At least with me. And what about the way he seemed introspective after, what I was sure, spending that Friday with Danny Sullivan. And I'd told Jude I always kept my eye on Pete. And this was just that, wasn't it?

But I stopped thinking about it then. At least at the front of my mind. I continued to think about it, at some level, all the time after that.

When I drove away from the club, I told myself I wouldn't look at the house. So, of course, I did. There was a light burning in the front window, gleaming yellow behind net curtains. I wondered if Pete was over there now, his car parked a couple of streets away, talking to Danny Sullivan about garden paths and figures of eight

(a figure of eight is the symbol of eternity or infinity in some religion or other. Isn't it?)

and cellars and stuff like that.

'Oh do me a favour! You're making it sound like some sort of conspiracy. You're getting paranoid.'

Oh yes. But, sometimes, even paranoids are conspired against and, deep down, I was beginning to believe that there was a conspiracy being hatched in the house Albert Camberwell had built.

'What the hell d'you mean, you're going to London and don't know what time you'll be back tomorrow? We do the club on Sunday and if we're not there people are going to get annoyed. Not to mention Alf. Don't you think it's about time you told me what you're up to?' I tried to keep most of the anger and frustration out of my voice but not very hard; I was pissed off at his cloak and dagger act.

'Oh, I'll be back for the club. I just don't know if I'll be back in time for you to pick me up. I'll probably go straight there. We...I'm going to London in the car. It's nothing to get worked up about. I've just got things—'

'Yeah, I know. You've got things to do. Listen sunshine, me and you are still partners when it comes to the music and if these 'things' have anything to do with that, I'd better bloody find out. Pete,' I said quietly, just so he knew I was finished taking any more crap. 'I know you'll still be able to write and maybe perform but it wouldn't be the same and you know it. I wouldn't enjoy it either but I'm not standing for any more secret service crap. Not even for you.'

There was a long pause. I had the feeling he was waiting for me to try to persuade him more gently but I'd had enough. It'd been a fortnight since I'd found about the path in the Camberwell garden, two weeks when Pete was conspicuous by his absence. We still saw each other at dinner time but the jam sessions at The Firs had stopped.

That was okay, we knew the stuff by heart. I'd simply had enough of being kept in the dark by the bloke who was supposed to be my best mate and I no longer cared if it was jealousy or not.

Finally, Pete filled the pause himself. 'It's no big deal. Danny's got to go to London again and the trains are awkward on a Sunday. I said I'd take him by car. Like I said, no big deal.'

My mind spoke to me then. It was quiet and calm but insistent. I listened.

If he's expecting to be away till late Sunday afternoon and it's now half seven on Saturday morning, nobody's going to be at the house all day today and most of tomorrow. Wouldn't you like to see that path? Maybe even the cellar?

'Okay,' I said to Pete. 'I still think we need to talk but I suppose it'll keep. You going down today?'

'Yeah, in about half an hour. I'm sorry if I got up your nose, Terry.'

'Forget it. You be careful, it's a bit foggy. I don't want to go solo.'

He laughed and put down the phone.

The river Fender is about two miles across at the point where Albert Camberwell built his house. The embankment runs from the ferry at the southern end of Seapool to a place known locally as Smugglers Caves. These are a series of deep holes gouged into the sandstone which turn into shallow caverns that were used by smugglers back in the long-ago. After the caves, the embankment becomes the promenade. The only difference I've ever seen is that the lamps along the embankment are more ornate than the functional sodium lamps on the prom. To get to the embankment at the bottom of Fender Gap you simply walk down the slope alongside the Camberwell house. I could've done that, or gone down the Town Hall steps but I didn't want to take the chance of somebody from the club seeing me. So I drove through the tunnel under the river at five past eight that morning and kept driving along the Dock Road to the Ferry. I parked the car there and walked up the embankment to Fender Gap.

I looked at the grey, swollen river for five minutes before I tried to get into the garden, looking over my shoulder nonchalantly now and then at the bushes and trees that grew behind the high railings of the Camberwell garden.

There was no chance of my pushing through those bushes and I knew I'd have to climb the railings. At twelve, I'd've done it without thinking or breathing hard but I wasn't twelve anymore and the tops of the railings had spiked tips that looked quite capable of disembowelling me. Still, needs must.

I checked that nobody was out for a jog this misty, grey morning, that no brave soul was out walking the dog, and then I chose a likely-looking tree branch that overhung the railings. I was quite pleased I was only breathing a little hard by the time I was on the branch. Still, beneath my padded blouson jacket, I could feel the sweat trickling down my side. I looked once more at the embankment, saw nobody and then heard the low hoot of a tanker on the river. It was a Mobil oil tanker and for an instant, I was struck with a sudden vision of standing by the statue of Christopher

Columbus in Barcelona, watching the sun dapple off the grey-green Mediterranean. Then I turned, looked down at the grass in the garden, eased myself along the branch, refusing to hear its subtle creak and let myself drop.

I was in the garden. I checked the house for moving shadows, just in case Danny had changed his mind. The place looked as closed as a crypt. I shook off that pleasant thought and looked at the garden.

It was about two hundred feet from here to the back door. Its width surprised me a little; it looked a good sixty yards. The trees and bushes on the far side were more tightly packed than here and I was glad I hadn't opted for getting in over there. The path began right outside the back door and ran in a figure of eight, reaching to a point just behind me. The mid-point of the path looked to be exactly in the centre of the garden. It was concrete and, from where I stood, looked in perfect order. I walked towards the house with my eyes down, searching for tell-tale cracks. The first appeared about twenty feet from the back door and there was a slight depression here, too, despite the work Joey and the others had done. Then I was at the door. I tried the handle. The door didn't open. I went back to the depression in the path and looked around me.

The depression didn't stop here, though it was at its deepest. I could see it continued for a good ten yards. In a circle. So, the cellar, too, was a circle. Bigger and better than the one in the house. What was down there? Come to that, how did Danny get into it? I didn't remember seeing any doors or hearing any creaks in the floor that might've been a trap-door. How did you get into the cellar?

I considered a little breaking and entering.

I returned to the back door and looked at the handle. It was nothing special. The handle and casing were brass, worn and shiny after years of turning, tarnished here and there after years of weather. But nothing special. And there were no alarm boxes on the walls and Danny hadn't switched any off when he invited us for the tour and tea. I ran my hand over the brass casing and an idea began to form in my mind. I got out of the garden. I didn't climb any trees, I just peeked out of the back garden gate that opened onto the street, saw nobody around, walked out and closed the door behind me. I drove home.

'This is the receiver, where the tongue goes when the door is closed,' my Dad told me, pointing to the separate parts of the lock.

We were in the shed in our new back garden, in our new house. Since moving here, he called his shed his workshop and grinned when he said it but we both knew he meant it; having a workshop of his own after all these years was something that made him feel good. Right now, he was giving me a crash course on how a lock was made. My Dad never did things by halves. When I asked him if he had saved any of the locks from the old house, he took me right to them and now he was explaining how they worked.

Despite the reason behind the question about locks, I couldn't help but feel good as I sat next to him, smelling the smells that fill sheds and workshops all over the world—paint, turps, oil and the wonderful smell of wood. I felt like I did when I was a kid, watching him make something, marvelling at the way his hands knew where to go and what to do to create the thing he'd seen in his mind.

'How does the tongue move in and out of the casing? What makes it pull back?'

He put the brass casing down on his bench, picked up his pipe and took a puff before he spoke.

'Are you thinking of becoming a locksmith or just thinking about a little breaking and entering?'

I kept my face straight even though we both chuckled. 'Oh, you know, a little of both. No, you know what it's like when you start thinking about something and it won't leave you alone.'

'Aye, well, I can show you on these because I took so many of them apart when we were doing up the old house. The new Chubb and Yale ones are a different matter. Anyway, pass us that screwdriver.'

I handed him the yellow-handled tool and watched him take the four screws from the casing and put them in the glass ashtray he kept for the purpose. With the casing off I could see the workings and how the tongue fitted against what looked like metal leaves, all different shapes and sizes.

'Now then,' he said and put his pipe on the bench. 'The levers here, they'd be called barrels in a safe or another type of lock, open and close the lock. What happens is that the slots, the cuts on the key, fit through the keyhole and slot into the gaps between the different sizes of the levers. The levers are lifted up and that allows the tongue to move back. But the levers have to be lifted at the same time or the key won't work. The main lever, the one at the bottom, is caught by the slot in the key and lifts. As it lifts, the others are lifted by the other slots in the key. When they're all up, the tongue moves back, helped by the tension of the spring here.' He pointed to the thin, tight spring. I nodded. 'Right. The tongue moves back like this.' With the casing off, the levers could be raised without a key. Once the screwdriver had lifted them, the tongue moved back. If it had been on a door, the door would've opened. He looked at me again and I nodded again.

'So it'd be bloody near impossible to pick this kind of lock?'

'I don't suppose any lock is unpickable. I imagine a locksmith would tell you there's hard ones and not so hard ones. With this type, they're old, probably been on a door since the house was built. That'd mean it's worn.' He looked at me and raised just one eyebrow so I knew there was some point I was supposed to pick up on.

'I can see this one's worn but with all the levers needing to be raised at the right time, you'd still need a key.'

'Maybe,' he said and grinned. 'Metal wears and where there's no chance of rust, the way it wears is to get smooth. Look.' He took out his key-ring from his pocket and pushed the four or five keys on it round until a dull, brass-coloured key was left on its own. 'This was the key to your Nan's door. I've had it for, oh, must be fifteen years now. That time she was broken into and I changed the locks, remember?'

I nodded. It happened one Christmas Eve while she and I were in Seapool, taking the pork joint she always bought for her three spinster sisters at Christmas. It was a yearly ritual. I helped her carry the shopping. That year, we got back to find her house a mess. Not much was taken because there wasn't much *to* take but they'd made a right mess. If I could've got hold of them, I'd've killed them, I think. But that was fifteen years ago and right now I was thinking of doing some housebreaking of my own.

'Okay,' My Dad said. 'Look at the way the grooves in the pattern of the key have smoothed down. If we took the lock off your Nan's door now, you'd see that the levers are a lot smoother than when they were new. And the spring would wear too. This one seems pretty tight but it's loose compared to a new one. If you really wanted to pick an old lock like this, you could probably do it with a key that was almost the same as the original. You might need a ward file to nick the slots in it deeper or something, but you'd probably manage.'

I suddenly had a mind's-eye-view of what till then had been technical information. 'Like car door locks? The way you can jiggle the key in a lock, a key not for that car, and a lot of the time get it open?'

He smiled at me through the blue-tinged smoke of his pipe, the way he used to when I was a kid and had finally got whatever it was he was trying to explain. For a moment, I was nine years old again and the rush of nostalgia made me almost light-headed.

'Just like that,' he said and began putting the lock back together again. 'Anything else you want to know while you're here?'

'No. Just trying to find things to stop my brain turning into a cabbage.'

'Well at least I don't have to worry about you turning to

a life of crime. You don't need the money.'

We left his workshop laughing.

By dinnertime, I was alone in the house. My sisters went to the shopping precinct and my parents went out for their dinner. I went back to the workshop.

It didn't take me long to find three of the old-type keys that opened the type of lock I was interested in. I thought that, with luck and my Dad's ward file, I'd be able to make at least one fit the lock on Danny Sullivan's back door.

I left the house at quarter past twelve, still not feeling good about what I intended to do but knowing I'd do it anyway, if I could. The part of me that loved Pete and didn't want him hurt would see to that.

I reached the end of the Gap on the embankment and leaned against the railings as I'd done earlier that morning. The tide was on the turn and there were no ships out there now. The river was still grey and high and the wind had picked up. I checked up and down the embankment for people. The fact that it was dinnertime and the weather looked to be on the change seemed to have kept most people off the promenade and the embankment. I waited until the solitary man with his Alsatian dog had turned the bend and then I got back into the garden of the Camberwell House.

I didn't bother checking the house for lights or people-sized shadows. I just walked to the back door, took out the old key from my pocket along with the ward file and the small of piece of chalk I'd borrowed from our Dawn's desk drawer and pushed the key into the keyhole and turned it. It went almost all the way round so I knew a good few of the leaves had lifted. I took the key out again and smeared chalk over the end. I pushed the key into the lock again, turned it and withdrew it. Where the chalk was smudged, I began to use the file to increase the size of the notches in the worn metal. It didn't take long before the key fitted well enough for some judicious jiggling to open the back door.

I stood on the threshold, my eyes wide, my heart beating wildly in my ears, half expecting somebody to be standing there. But there were only the shadows you always see in a dimly-lit room. I eased the door closed behind me and walked into the kitchen. The light was dim but strong enough so I didn't need to switch on the light.

I went through the house downstairs. Not a sign of any way into the cellar. I pressed every nook and cranny, each side of the bookcase and got nothing apart from springing the door to the stairs. I considered going up and then shook my head; up was up and I wanted to go down. I went round the house again, three times, and ended up staring up those stairs. I was aware that time was getting on. There was no danger of Danny and Pete coming back but I didn't need some friend of Danny's calling, not knowing he was away for the day and night. That friend might decide to try the back door and that same friend might just be on good enough terms to walk in, calling Danny's name.

And still I was standing at the bottom of the stairs.

In that dim light, I peered up those stairs, wondering about lifting the carpets again, looking for a trap-door. And I thought I saw something at the top of the stairs that didn't look like it belonged. I walked up to the top step and peered at what I'd seen from the bottom.

It was close to the newel, looking like a displaced carpet runner. I bent down and saw that it was more like a car gear-lever knob—a wooden bulb on the end of a short shaft that was fixed to the wood of the stairs. The wood was shiny smooth, like the handle of the back door. With the image of a gear knob in my mind, I pushed the wooden bulb into what would've been first gear and it actually moved as if it were dropping into a slot in a gear box.

The first four steps of the stairs dropped down, producing a black oblong in the incline of the stairwell. I sat down on the landing, my breath a struggle in my chest, the apparent inbred fear of the dark and unknown rising in me like a wind building in a field. I stared at the black mouth for what seemed like an age. That black oblong looked like a hole in reality.

But that hole was the way into the cellar and that was why I'd broken into this house. So I stood up, took a deep breath like I would before diving into Pete's pool, and stepped into that black space, holding the banister like it was my personal connection to God.

It was another staircase, going down. I groped for a light switch and found it fixed to the banister. I turned the light on and saw that this staircase was more like a fire-escape; I could see the cellar between the risers. It didn't look so bad with the light on. I walked down those steps and into the cellar of which Danny Sullivan seemed so protective.

At first, it was anticlimactic. It looked like I imagined cellars looked everywhere. The floor was cement and covered in a patina of dust. The walls were boarded but you couldn't see much of them because of the stacks of old boxes, a small armchair that looked as if it had been made for a child and a roll of lino all pushed against them. The light was a bar-fluorescent hanging from two chains.

Oh, it was big, going beneath the garden as it did but that was it, really. I couldn't see anything here to make Danny so protective. I walked around the circular room, wondering if he had all his money stashed in some safe hidden in a corner but there was no sign of anything like that. I turned at the end under the garden and headed back towards the stairs, thinking that I'd probably betrayed Pete's trust for nothing.

Then I saw it.

The reason I hadn't noticed it before was because I'd looked around the room at eye-level. Now, heading back towards the stairs, I was looking at the floor, looking for the first step.

The figure of eight was gouged in the floor and its shape was coloured blue. When it was originally made, that blue was probably dark enough to stand out vividly against what would've been the starkness of the floor. Now, with age, it had dulled so that, against the greying cement, it was almost invisible if you didn't know it was there and weren't looking for it. It wasn't exactly in the middle of the circular cellar but, guessing, I thought it would probably be directly under the figure of eight path in the garden.

In some religion, it means eternity or infinity.

Yes, I was sure it did but what did that mean? Was whatever religion it was Danny's religion? Were Pete's 'things to do' listening to Danny, trying to find something he could believe in? Maybe. And if they were, how did I feel about it?

That was when any sense of anticlimax disappeared. I didn't get a chance to think about religions or whether Pete was trying to work out if he wanted to believe in one that Danny Sullivan might practise.

My imagination has always been vivid and I've always been able to hear colours and see sounds. I know how that sounds but it's true—the first time I heard The Beatles' 'Something', Harrison's guitar lick came out of the speakers as pale pink ovals. Maybe the fact I could do that was the reason I'd never been tempted by drugs; why did I need to expand my perceptions when they were already pretty wide? But all that was beside the point in that cellar.

I was *really* hearing the noise.

It was something like the sound of broom bristles, moving the patina of dust on the floor.

'Or a whisper.'

The sound of my own voice made the hairs on the back of my neck ripple, as if whatever or, worse, *who*ever had made the sound in the cellar was standing behind me. Every nerve in my body tingled and my hands clenched and I had to fight the urge to pivot on my feet and lash out. I didn't want to do that because it would've meant that I was really scared. Which was ridiculous.

'Because I'm alone in this cellar,' I said, trying to sound amused at myself. Instead, I sounded like a kid waking from a nightmare when his mother puts her hands round his face.

And the sound was still there. I wanted to tell myself that it was only because I'd given myself the heebie-jeebies. God,

I wanted to tell myself that but I couldn't because the sound seemed to be moving.

I stood in the middle of Danny Sullivan's cellar and the sound moved. It seemed to move around the cellar. I stood there, still staring at the faded blue outline of the figure of eight, and heard the sound move from behind me to my right and then in front of me and then to my left and behind me again. I didn't feel anything so I knew that it definitely wasn't any sort of breeze, creeping into the cellar through some crack in the ceiling or down the stairs from the house. It was just the sound, that soft susurration—besom twigs on the floor—moving around me.

Okay, whatever it is, it's moving round you. But it's not doing anything else. You can just walk to the stairs and get out of here.

Sounded like a great idea. Trouble was, my feet seemed to have taken root in the old cement floor and I thought of nightmares again, the ones where you know it's a dream and you try to wake up but you're paralysed. Then it got worse because instead of it just being a sound, a noise that seemed to be moving, it became something like a voice. At least, I was sure that I was hearing an attempt at words.

Tell you what, Terry, let's just get the hell out of here and worry about it later. Or never. Okay?

Oh, I wanted to but my feet still felt as if they'd been embedded in the cement when it had first been poured. My fists were still clenched and the hairs on my neck still stood to attention and my whole body felt like an over-strung E string. When the attempt at forming a word got a little closer to its objective, my body finally got the idea that getting away was a really good idea.

'runteeerrrr'

What the word was, I had no idea but it did what my little interior voice couldn't manage. It got me moving. It was still like a nightmare because it felt as if I was walking through molasses but at least as I was walking. I just hoped I was walking fast enough to reach the stairs before the words got any clearer.

I reached the stairs and the voice, moving round the cellar all the time, was still too soft or too far away for the word to be clear. When I put my hand on the rail of the staircase, my body finally did what I wanted it to and I clattered up to the sanity of the main stairs of the old Camberwell house.

I almost broke my neck as I tripped on the last tread but I was out. Breathing hard, dark suns flashing across my vision, but out. I swivelled on my backside and reached for the gear lever that opened the stairs to the cellar and rammed it into neutral and I was past caring if it broke and Danny realised that somebody had been in his house. It didn't break, it dropped into its slot and the stairs closed soundlessly on the dark space. Not quick enough to stop me hearing the voice, though.

It was closer. The word or words—*runteeerrrr*—still made no sense to me as I virtually fell down the stairs to the ground floor. It stayed with me as I hit the panel in the bookshelves and closed the staircase. It stayed with me as I left via the back door, struggling to turn the lock again because my fingers kept trembling. It stayed with me into the garden and as I sidled out into the street. Nobody was there and it wouldn't've bothered me if anybody had been; I'd've thought of something to tell them.

I walked back to where I'd parked the car and the sound of that faraway voice stayed with me, competing with my own internal voice for room to make itself heard.

runteeerrrr

Overdeveloped imagination, mate. You know that, don't you?

I didn't drive straight home. I caught a glimpse of my face in the rear-view mirror as I reversed out of the parking space and I knew I couldn't go home looking like that. My eyes were wide and my mouth was narrow. A muscle ticked in my cheek and I realised I was clenching my jaw. No, going home wasn't a good idea because I looked so unlike my usual self that even my sisters would've known something was wrong. And what would I tell them? That I'd broken into a bloke's house, went into his cellar and heard what my brain kept insisting was an overdeveloped imagination but my ears were convinced had been a voice? No, I didn't think so.

I drove up to Laketon instead and parked at the end of the promenade, not far from where Pete and I had talked about death and what came next the day before we left for Liverpool University, that day when he'd seemed so sure that he'd die alone, with no family around him.

I parked facing the river and stared at it. It was high now and running fast and the boats moored four hundred or so yards off the shore bobbed on the tide, like those old Space Hopper things from the seventies. And I was suddenly reminded of that first family party Pete came to, when he realised that he had a talent that wouldn't always get him into trouble. My young cousins had got those things for Christmas that year.

'Ah God,' I murmured. 'The time goes.'

Yes, but some things don't change. Like Pete wondering if there was anything that came after death, or was it just dust and worms? Doubt that's changed. Unless…?

And that was enough. Enough to stop me fretting at whatever it had been in the cellar.

Not surprising, was it? I mean, it was Pete and he was always going to take priority over something as iffy as a sound in a cellar.

So I thought about Pete and his question about hereafters and, from there, my mind went to what I'd been thinking about just before…whatever it was in the cellar had happened. I thought about whether Pete was looking for solace in a religion that used a figure of eight as a symbol of eternity.

The simple answer was, if Pete felt he needed something to believe in, something to stop him spending his life feeling empty in a place that should have been full of light and happiness, then fine. We all need something to believe in and, given his life so far, perhaps Pete needed it more than most.

I sat in the car and watched the river and the bobbing boats and a gull that was soaring and swooping on the wind and smiled. I smiled as much at how the odd experience in the cellar was already losing its sharpness as much as at the way the thin sunlight breaking through the wind-whipped cloud set the gull's wings aflame with pale gold. It was true, thinking about Pete, *worrying* about Pete had relegated Danny Sullivan's cellar to the very back of my mind. Sitting in the car then, I could even come up with what I thought was a perfect explanation for what had happened.

What I'd heard in the cellar *had* been the wind getting through some crack in the ceiling. The lads in the club had talked about the path in Danny Sullivan's garden starting to fall. Or maybe it had come through the boards on the side of the cellar. Wherever it had come from, the wind, which I'd just realised had increased a lot, had made the sound. After that, it was just my mind playing tricks. Probably because of guilt at the breaking and entering, guilt that I was going behind my best mate's back, poking my nose into something he'd obviously decided he didn't want me involved in.

I leaned forward in the seat, peering at the bobbing boats and the river, watching the gull swoop and dive on the air and waited to see if my internal voice was going to contradict me. The gull swooped twice and then soared high and was lost to my sight and my mind-voice was silent. I let out a sigh and leaned back into the car seat.

Okay, good. All my mind held now was the idea of Pete looking for something to believe in, something that would give him a little light, a little hope that there was something more than just dust and worms when he died. And there was nothing wrong with that, nothing at all. And as for dying alone, well, that wouldn't happen anyway. Not if I was still alive.

'He won't die alone. I'll make sure of that.'

It was a promise I made to myself as well as to Pete.

I drove home smiling, all thoughts of voices in cellars banished, robbed of power by the simple expedient of applying common sense and a little everyday psychology.

It's amazing how well we can fool ourselves, isn't it?

We did the gig the following night but it only took me until the opening bars of our second song for me to understand that Pete was either very close to a downswing or already in one. His playing was mechanical and his singing, while on key, seemed lifeless. The set went well enough because the songs were catchy and the crowd knew us but it wasn't good, just the same.

When the place was closed and we'd put our gear in the car, I sat at the bar and drank the pint of orange the barman had set up for me. Pete stood in front of the game machine, resolutely pushing fifty pence pieces into it like he was feeding the Oracle.

'I'm ready to go, Pete,' I told him and handed the barman my glass.

'One credit left,' Pete said and pressed the button. He stood staring at the flashing lights and then, when no money was paid out, he nodded. It was the kind of nod you give when something you've long expected was true is finally confirmed. Then he headed out of the club.

When I stopped at Pete's front door, I turned off the engine and got out of the car. He looked at me as he pulled his guitar cases from the hatchback—I usually just dropped him off and drove home so his puzzled look was understandable.

'Thought you could make me a cup of tea,' I said and helped him with his cases.

'So,' I said when the tea was made and we were sat in his kitchen. 'You going to tell me what's up?'

For an answer, he picked up his cup and walked into the living room. I followed him. What I saw there transported me back to our Barcelona apartment the night I found him in the dark with suicide on his mind. The room looked like somebody had rifled it looking for an atomic bomb that was timed to go off in exactly one minute.

Pete stood in the middle of the room and waved his arm in a short half circle. 'Now you know,' he said with all the inflection of a six year old reading a piece of Shakespeare.

I nodded and asked, 'Anything specific bring it on?'

'Not really. I just got to thinking that I've got almost everything and I've got exactly nothing and nothing and nobody to do anything for.' He frowned, obviously working out if he'd said what he meant. Then he nodded like he'd done in the club, satisfied. 'I've written, oh, must be nearly forty tunes lately. Good ones, too. Tunes we could probably use as singles. Yeah,' he said and stood in front of the window, his back to me, almost talking to himself. 'They'd probably make us more millions. And that's the thing. What do I need with more money? I don't need anything and I've got nobody to leave it to when I finally shuffle off this mortal coil. So what's the point in writing tunes or making money or saving money?'

This was clearly a conversation he'd had with himself before and was just going over it again. I could feel concern turning to vague worry that would, if I couldn't get him off the conversational roundabout he was on, become real fear that this was the downswing I wouldn't be able to stop.

'Pete...'

He turned to me. 'See, the thing is, Terry, what I have got? You, well, you've got most of what you ever wanted and you've got people to leave it to when you die,' he said and still his voice was dull and flat. 'That's the thing. There's some point to it all for you. I'm nearly thirty, I've done more than most people do in a lifetime but it means nothing because there's nobody to do it *for*. I've got nobody to buy things for, to plan for, to watch growing up, to teach to play the piano, to teach music or teach how to programme a computer.'

And I could still see the apartment in Barcelona and, because I could, I remembered that, then, I'd used the music and his mother and Cheryl as an argument. I couldn't use it now because he was adamant he'd done it all as far as the music was concerned. The writing of it, anyway. So I said the only thing I could think of that might keep the music going in him because it was the music that made him live.

'If you feel there should be somebody to benefit from what you've got or what you've learned, you could always set up some kind of fund, a scholarship maybe for the kids of Oxborough so they can learn music or computing or whatever.'

Oh, I said it so innocently because it felt just right when it formed in my brain. It still sounded right when the words left my mouth. I didn't hear the click of Pete's idea of Fate as those words slotted into the socket he'd made for Fate in his mind. It never even occurred to me how similar my idea was to another idea about scholarships set up for kids from a town not a million miles away from Oxborough.

Pete stared at me for a long, long moment. Then he smiled one of his mother's smiles and I saw a brief flicker of light in his eyes and that light looked a lot like the light I'd always associated with his music. And, because I saw that flicker, I thought I'd got him past the depression again.

Pete didn't say anything, didn't even nod, just that slow smile. I decided that discretion was the better part of valour and told him goodnight.

I didn't see him much during the following week. He had things to do and, for a change, so did I. I spoke to him on the phone on the Wednesday night when he rang to ask me if I knew what my Dad wanted for his birthday but that was all. On the phone, he sounded less depressed but it still wasn't the real Pete. We worked the club as usual over the weekend and he seemed brighter. He sang and played with more feeling. But I still thought he wasn't up all the way. As we left on Sunday night, he asked me to meet him in the club at dinnertime the next day. He didn't want to rehearse or anything, he told me he thought he'd fancy a pint. It wasn't quite the old Pete, telling me something had occurred to him but not to ask because he wasn't going to tell me till he was ready. Not quite but not far off.

I got to the club just after twelve and the only people there were Alf, the treasurer of the club, the duty-man and the barmaid. Monday was the day they did the books so the table by the bar was covered with paper, pens, calculators, rubbers and money. The air was coloured blue by the cigar smoke and expletives so I knew the books weren't balancing today. I bought myself a pint of Tetley's bitter and went to the stage.

The twelve-string acoustic I'd bought in Spain was on its stand by the organ in the corner of the stage. I'd left it there last night and only now realised I had. I amused myself with it while I waited for Pete and found I was singing old sea shanties I'd heard from my Dad and uncles, recalling words I hadn't realised I'd known. After twenty minutes or so, I left the shanties behind and got into some Simon and Garfunkel. That didn't last long because Jimmy arrived. He waved at me from the bar and I suddenly decided I felt like listening to one of his stories. I joined him at his table.

'Aye aye son. On your own?'

'Pete's coming in later,' I told him. He nodded and took a drink of his Guinness. I looked at his hands and there seemed to be more liver spots than the last time I'd looked. His eyes had a jaundiced tinge and his breathing sounded rattly. I didn't know him very well but I liked him and a sudden wave of pity for him washed over me. I couldn't let him know that; he'd done too much and was too proud to allow anybody to pity him. Here was a man who'd lived a life filled with experience who was willing to share them but, soon I thought, he'd be gone and those memories would be gone, too. That would be a shame; kids could learn from a man like this and history from somebody like Jimmy would've been a lot better than the dry stuff they could get in books.

'So, how've you been, Jimmy?'

'Ah, you know, son. Been better. But I've been younger, too.'

'Tell you what,' I said and grinned. 'I'll buy you a rum if you tell me one of your stories?'

'I think I could manage that.'

This one was a funny one from his time in the Merchant Navy. The cook on the ship had been Portuguese and, in Jimmy's words, three sheets to the wind most of the time. When he was drunk, he was a bloody lunatic. The Chief Engineer had been a Scot and he didn't like the cook any more than the cook liked him, mostly because the Chief had a marmoset monkey that he fed on leftovers and had taught to enjoy the rum that the engineer drank. The cook drank rum, too and, when the engineer was in the mess, the monkey would drink the cook's tot as well as the engineer's. Normally, the cook said nothing because the Chief was a higher rank and also built like the brick proverbial. The cook was built like a spoon. Then, one evening, the engineer was called away from the mess. The cook was pissed as a fart. The monkey made the mistake of grabbing the cook's tot. The cook seized his chance. Screaming a diatribe of Portuguese, he grabbed the monkey by its tail and charged up on deck. Jimmy and everybody else in the mess followed him, trying to calm him down. No chance. The cook was pissed, pissed off and he had the monkey in his grasp at last. He hurled the poor monkey over the stern and into the Indian Ocean. When the Chief found out, the cook was sober but in no condition to take the beating he received from the Scot.

'I'll tell you, Terry, the meals we had to put up with on the way home were worse than the ones we had during the war,' Jimmy told me and we both collapsed into helpless laughter.

Pete came in at quarter past one, looking better than the last time I'd seen him. He bought himself a drink and sat at the table with us. He talked with Jimmy for a while till Jimmy went off to join an old shipmate who'd come down from Liverpool.

'I've set up a fund,' Pete said without preamble. 'A scholarship like you said. For kids from Oxborough who want to do music, to study it. You know, to buy instruments, help out with the grants.'

'Sounds good, Pete but a thing like that needs funding for a long time. You've got a lot of money but have you got that much?'

'It's going to be for one lad and one girl and the way the accountant and lawyer set it up, with help from the council and the arts foundations and with gilts and bonds and stuff, it's going to be fine.'

I looked at him and wondered if this was the end of the depression or if the depression went deeper and for more reasons than that he felt there was no end product for what he did. I wanted to ask him but I'd known him a long time and knew that he'd only speak when he was ready to speak. I left it at that.

I didn't see him for the rest of the week. He didn't ring,

either. I had the feeling that he was doing more of those things he'd been doing lately. And how much was he seeing of Danny Sullivan?

I found out soon enough. And I found out Pete's depression hadn't lifted much. Not much at all.

I called up to The Firs that Friday. It was late April now and the weather was more like spring. The sun was shining and the wind was light. It felt good after the wildness of the winter and its cold. It felt good to be out in the fresh air that smelled of flowers. *I* felt good. I thought I might persuade Pete to drive to Wales with me, maybe even go to the Rhyl Suncentre like I'd planned all those years ago but which we'd never managed to do.

And what happened all those years ago happened again. Carol wasn't there and Cheryl was dead but nobody answered my ring at the bell or my call at the back kitchen door. The door was open and the kettle was just coming to the boil and for one manic minute it felt like everything that had happened between the time Pete decided we were going to buy a car and now was just a very vivid dream.

'Pete?' I called out as the kettle switched itself off. Still no answer. I walked into the living room. It was tidy today but there was nobody there. I went upstairs to Pete's room.

The room looked like the living room the last time I'd been here. Pete was sitting on the floor, surrounded by old crisp packets and squashed soft drink cans. The place smelled like a dirty sock. He didn't look up when I walked into the room.

'What?' I asked. He looked up this time but I wished he

hadn't. His eyes had that lifeless sheen to them and his whole face seemed to have been pushed into his skull. 'Pete, tell me what it is. I thought you were over it once you'd set up the fund. I thought that was what this was all about?'

Finally, he spoke. 'The fund,' he said and sighed.

I looked around the room; I'm still not sure for what, maybe that razor blade again. All I could see was the pile of manuscript paper and the way his guitars were laying on top of each other. The piano was covered in more crisp packets. This was bad.

'Enough's enough, Terry. I think...I think it's this house. Too many...'

He seemed to go blank then. He was still facing me but he definitely wasn't seeing me. Whatever made him Peter Lynwood was somewhere else, seeing something else, thinking something else. Then he came back. I watched with mounting horror as his face filled up again with whatever made him Pete.

'...memories. Yes, that's it. And the memories aren't really mine, see? I remember what happened here and who happened here and everything but...but they don't seem to belong to my memory. I think... think...think that I need to find somewhere to make my own memories. My own memories might make it easier to deal with...with the other memories of the other things and other...people...'

And he blanked again. I thought about shaking him. I thought about putting him under the shower. I thought about phoning a doctor. Oh Christ, I thought about all sorts of things that I knew wouldn't work.

So I tidied up.

Pete sat in the middle of the room, moving his legs when I tidied up the stuff beneath them but that was all. He didn't get up or speak. He just kept staring ahead with that blank expression. When the room was more or less the way it usually was, I got him under the arms and struggled him onto his bed. I took off his shoes and pulled the duvet over him and he went to sleep. Just like that. Closed his eyes and went to sleep.

I sat on the piano chair and looked at the manuscript papers I'd tidied up. I counted fourteen new tunes. They were new because Pete had never told me the titles. He always had titles for his tunes even though we rarely used them when they became songs. Fourteen new tunes. Over what period of time? Short, I thought. Oh Christ, I thought they'd been written in next to no time, like maybe one day? God.

I went downstairs and rang Jude's parents' house. Then, with Jude's number written on the scrap of manuscript paper I'd brought down, I rang Jude.

'Terry,' she said after I'd told her everything. 'If it's that bad, he should be in hospital. He needs rest and medication. This...'

I knew what was on her mind. This was the deepest depression and it had come after an intense period of creativity. Depression was the least of it. Suicide was more likely.

'Jude, there's no way he's going to let me get a doctor never mind admitting himself to a hospital. Isn't there anything I can do?'

There was a long pause and I suddenly decided that life was full of too many bloody long pauses, pregnant with bad things. I wanted to slam the phone down, race upstairs and shake the depression out of Pete and knew I wouldn't because it wouldn't work. I waited.

'If you really don't think there's any way he'll accept medical treatment then I think the only thing you can do is what I told you before. What you've always done. You can only be his friend. Try to find some way through to him, some way past the depression. Terry…Terry, I'm sorry. I don't know what else to say. Depression has a habit of feeding on itself. It becomes a spiral. It has to be broken. Terry…'

'I know, Jude,' I said quietly. 'I'll just have to try to break it. Thanks, Jude. I'm sorry I had to ring. It's just that…'

'Terry, we're friends. Friend's don't need reasons. Take care, love.'

Pete slept for twelve hours straight. I rang Alf and pleaded illness and apologised for not being able to work the weekend and waited for Pete to wake up so I could take Jude's advice. When he woke he was no better but at least he ate the food I cooked for him. When he finished the sausage and mash, he washed the dishes. At least he was normal in that way.

'Pete…' I began and he turned from the sink to look at me.

'No, Terry, just leave me alone. I know what you're thinking and what you're trying to do but… see, nothing works anymore. Not even you. But I don't want you to worry. I'm down and I've never been this down before and I don't see a way of coming up soon but I'm still alive. I...I had a dream while I was asleep. I dreamed I was with Cheryl again and she talked to me. She told me it wasn't time yet. Yeah, I know how that sounds but it was really vivid and if it keeps me from trying to get to her too soon, where's the harm? I'll just...I don't know what I'll just but what I *won't* do is anything stupid. Go on home, mate. I'll go for a long drive, I think. Yeah, that's what I'll do. Go on, Terry, go home.'

I couldn't. I couldn't leave him alone no matter what he said about not doing anything stupid. He was still depressed. The fact that he knew he was made no difference. I couldn't just go home and leave him like that.

'Terry, I don't want a row. Not with you. Not now. I'm okay to drive and it's what I want and I want to do it on my own. Just go.'

His voice had some life in it. His eyes had some light in them. He'd washed up. He told me he wasn't going to do anything stupid. If I stayed or argued, that might be enough to lose whatever ground he'd made up during his sleep. Christ, why didn't I do psychology instead of languages? Then again, Jude was a doctor and she admitted that even the doctors weren't sure about this sort of thing. Depression had a way of feeding on itself, becoming a spiral, it needed breaking and Pete said he *wanted* something. Wasn't that a start? Christ, I hoped so.

In the end, I was his friend and did what friends do; I gave him the space he wanted. I went home but only after making him promise to ring me as soon as he got back from wherever he went.

The trouble with a phone is you can't see the person you're talking to so you don't know where it is they are. At least, you couldn't back then. If somebody promises to ring you when he gets back, you assume he's ringing from wherever it was he made the promise. That's the trouble with phones. Also, you can't see a person's face.

Pete didn't ring me that night nor on Sunday morning. He rang me at nine on Sunday night. I spent those endless hours alternating between going to The Firs and camping there till he got home or ringing my own doctor and begging him to do something. But I stayed at home, in my room, listening to records without hearing them and reading books without taking in what I read.

'Terry, I'm ringing like I promised.'

His voice sounded more normal. Tired but not dull, not lifeless.

'How d'you feel now? Did it do any good, the drive?'

'Oh, you know, I'm a bit tired but, yeah, I had time to think or not think and it's helped. I'm not going to try to kid you and say everything's fine. You've known me too long and you know me too well. But I *do* feel better. So, you know, don't worry. Tell you what, I might even go to the club this week and play some soft piano or guitar. Don't know when but...well, I think I might.'

And then he put the phone down. I stared at the phone in my own hand and then replaced it slowly in its cradle.

He sounded more like Pete, I told myself. But I wished I could've seen his face. I was sure I'd've known just how much of the truth he was telling if I could've seen his eyes. But I had to take what he'd said as genuine, didn't I? So, okay, he didn't say what day he'd be in the club but he really sounded like he meant that. Well, I had nothing else to do, no places to go, no people to meet, no promises to keep...well, maybe a promise to myself. I could go to the club each dinnertime and if he turned up, he could play some soft piano and I could play a little guitar and we might even sing some songs.

I went on Monday. Pete didn't show. Or on Tuesday or Wednesday and I decided that I'd waited long enough. Tomorrow, Thursday, I'd just drive up to The Firs and invite him down for a drink and to sing some songs.

But he rang me on Wednesday night and told me he'd meet me in the club the following dinnertime. And he really did sound like he was coming up from the depression. I slept well on Wednesday night.

It was just as I was ready to leave and head up to The Firs to drag Pete out and back to our house, when he showed up at the club.

I'd been there since the place opened, sipping flat Coke and playing my twelve-string, which I kept forgetting to take home, trying not to worry about why Pete was late.

The double doors banged open and Pete came dashing in, his face white, his eyes big, his breath coming in short gasps. He charged over to the stage.

'Terry, Terry, he's dead. I'm sure he is. Come on.'

'What? Who's dead? Pete, what're you on about?'

'Danny. Danny's dead. Terry, he just died. In his chair. I

don't know what to do. Terry, come on!' He stopped gabbling and looked as if something had just occurred to him. 'Maybe he isn't dead! Maybe you can do something. Come on!'

I got up, told Alf to get an ambulance and then followed Pete across the road and into the Camberwell House for the first time since I'd been in its cellar.

'He's dead, Pete. I'm sorry.'

Danny Sullivan was in his chair, looking for all the world like he was fast asleep, having a pleasant dream. There was a small smile on his face. Pete was standing to the left of the chair, his hands in his pockets, his eyes still big.

'What happened? Did he cry out or anything?'

'No. I'd just come down from the toilet and he was sitting there, staring into space. He heard me come in and looked at me. He smiled and then he closed his eyes and sort of sighed. I thought maybe he had indigestion or something but then his left hand curled up and then fell flat on his thigh. I knew he was dead then, I think. I walked over to him and said his name but he didn't answer or move. I put my hand in front of his mouth but couldn't feel any breath. I tried to find a pulse, like they do on the telly, but I couldn't feel anything. That's when I ran over for you. You were always better at this sort of thing. But he's dead.'

'You going to be okay?'

He nodded and sat on the couch. 'Who'll bury him? He's got no family.'

'Somebody'll know what he wanted done. Maybe Henry. He seemed the closest to him.'

'Yeah. He'll be happy now.'

Pete said it as if Danny had just gone somewhere else to live, not died. I looked at my best friend and saw no sign of shock. He looked content with no sign of the deep depression of just a couple of days ago. I made a cup of tea.

The ambulance arrived and a police car arrived just after it. The ambulance took Danny Sullivan to the hospital where a post-mortem would take place. The police asked Pete questions that he answered concisely and with that same look of contentment on his face.

'Come on, kid,' I said when the police had left. 'I'll take you home.'

He was sitting on the couch, his eyes closed. A small smile played at his mouth. 'I am home,' he said.

Shock. The shock's finally hit him.

That's what I thought so I said, 'No, mate. This is the Camberwell House. Come on, let's go home.'

He opened his eyes and looked at me. He still looked content and that small smile still played at the corners of his mouth. 'I am home,' he repeated. 'I bought this place off Danny about a week ago. It's mine now. This is where I'm going to live now. This is the place where I can make my own memories. It's what he wanted and what I wanted. Thanks, Terry but I'm already home.'

I just stood there with my mouth open. What the hell did he mean, a place where he could make his own memories? He had his own memories. All that memories stuff he'd spouted at home had been just part of his disjointed manner in the depression, surely. Besides, what memories could he make here? I'd've wanted memories of my parents if they were no longer around, wouldn't you? And for Pete, those memories were in The Firs.

'Pete. Listen. You're not making any sense. Your home is The Firs. Okay, you've bought this place but you can't be serious about living here. Selling it, fine, but not living here. What's here for you? It's just an old house with its own memories. Come on, mate, let's go home.'

He smiled and for the first time in what seemed like years, it was his mother's smile. 'I am home. Danny and me sorted it all out just the other day,' he told me and I was sure he wasn't talking about the sale of the Camberwell House. That was when I knew he'd rung from here the other night. The long drive he'd taken had lasted all of the twenty minutes it took to get here from The Firs. 'See, Terry, there's things you don't know about this place. I know them and it means I'm going to live here. The best thing is it'll give me a reason to carry on. That's good. Isn't it?'

'Pete...' But I found I had no words. I'd made a fortune from always having the right words but I had none when I needed them the most.

'This is right. This is the way it was meant to be. Fate, like I said. I'll let you know when the funeral is, Terry. I'm home.'

Danny Sullivan was buried in Rake Cemetery on May 5th at ten in the morning. The members of the club gave him a good send-off. They stood to attention, their blazers cleaned, their medals and ribbons and the badges on their pockets a flash of colour in the shadows cast by the blooming trees. Old Henry had all Danny's papers and knew exactly what he'd wanted. The cause of death was a heart attack; Danny had had a bad heart for years. I stood beside a contented Pete as the vicar said the final words over Danny's open grave and we joined the rest back at the club for a final drink to his memory.

And, for five weeks, Pete stayed content and apparently happy. We continued to work at the club at the weekends and he continued to write. He didn't ask me to find words for everything but I didn't mind. I was just happy to see him almost well again.

He sold The Firs. To me. For exactly what we got for our new/old house. I bought it because I'd always loved the place and my memories of it were all good; of Carol and learning to play guitar and even of Ronald, the way he was at the end. My Mum and Dad loved the garden and the big rooms. Our Dawn and Erin loved the pool.

Yeah, for five weeks, I was almost convinced that Pete had turned a corner and that whatever God there was had finally decided he'd suffered enough and it was time for him to live a real life again.

Then it all went downhill. Very, very fast.

'Phone!'

I was half-way down my final length in the pool when our Dawn yelled at me from the door. It was June and the roof to the pool house was open. It was the kind of June day when not even the Bahamas could tempt you away, the kind of day when you think about finishing your daily lengths and maybe calling for your old mate and seeing if he fancies a day out in Wales or somewhere. It was the kind of day when you think the phone call is probably from that old mate who knows you almost as well as you know yourself and knows you'll probably fancy a day out in Wales or somewhere.

It was Alf from the club.
'I think you better get over here, Terry,' he said, his voice low and obviously concerned. 'Pete's drunk. I don't mean tipsy. He's paralytic.'

'He's been here since we opened. Didn't seem too bad then,' Alf told me in his office. It was five past twelve. 'He had two vodkas and three pints of bitter in about quarter of an hour. Ask me, I think he'd been hitting a bottle at home. He needs looking after, Terry. He takes no notice of anybody else but you. Especially today.'
I took Pete home.

The house was a bloody mess, worse than the apartment in Spain or that time at The Firs. I half-walked, half-dragged Pete to the conservatory and put him on the Parker Knoll recliner—the only piece of furniture he'd brought from The Firs. He blacked out.
I spent an hour tidying up, telling myself that tidying up after Pete was something I was getting very good at but very tired of doing. Then I made myself some tea and toast and just sat watching him move from blacked-out to deep sleep.
And then I *listened* to him dream.

He was having a long conversation with somebody. It

wasn't disjointed at all; it was as if he were continuing a conversation he'd been having for a while. At first, it was just yes and no and maybe and I don't know. Then it get very weird, not to say scary.

'I know, love,' he said, his voice normal, not a hint of inebriation or dullness in it. 'But I've tried and it doesn't work.' Pause. Frown. 'I know what Danny said and I paid attention to what he did but I can't make it work. I've been over everything he said and did and all the places he showed me. It's just no good. I'm beginning to think the only way is...that way.' Pause. Half-smile. 'Okay, okay. It's just that, I don't know what else I can...' Pause. Concentrated look on the face. Small smile, not quite a Carol-smile. 'D'you think so? Yes, I know he's always been there for me but...well, I can ask but he's going to want to know...Okay, maybe it's for the best.'

And then he slept. He didn't move and there was no more talking. He just slept like a baby.

For five minutes, I sat in the chair and watched him sleep and then I had to get up and do something because it was too much. Hearing him...dreaming or talking or whatever the hell it had been had sent shivers up my spine but watching him sleep like a baby was, somehow, worse, you know? This was my best mate and he was probably now officially clinically depressed and I just couldn't see any way of getting him back from that depression. To see him sleeping so peacefully, so *normally*, after that weird conversation and knowing that when he woke up he wasn't going to be normal...ah shit, I just had to do something else. I wished to God I hadn't already tidied up.

I left the conservatory and went into the kitchen to make myself a cup of tea and then leant against the sink and stared into space, trying to rationalise what had just happened, what I'd just heard.

All right, Pete was ill, so obviously what I'd heard had been part of that illness. If he'd been awake, he'd probably have been hallucinating. Yeah, okay, so what I'd heard had been that hallucination. In his sleep, dreaming, Pete had seen somebody and talked to him or her.

'Yeah,' I told myself and drank some of the tea.

runterrr

I could see Pete from where I stood and I leaned forward to see if he was about to begin talking in his sleep again. Because that's what I assumed the sound had been, Pete talking in his sleep. Not as clear as before, more a mumble, more like what you'd expect to hear from somebody who was asleep.

Pete was still dead to the world and his mouth was closed.

runnnterrr

I was still looking at Pete when the sound came again and I couldn't tell myself it was Pete mumbling in his sleep because his mouth never moved.

The cup I was holding tipped and it felt like all the bones in my hand had turned to jelly. The tea in the cup slopped out and splashed onto the floor, followed by the cup itself and my mouth went dry and my tongue seemed to want to choke me.

The sound was still more of a mumble but, now that I couldn't tell myself that it was Pete, I realised that it sounded like a mumble because it wasn't in the kitchen, not even on this floor of the house. The sound, whatever it was, was coming from somewhere else in the house. It was the same sound I'd heard down the cellar when I'd broken in. It was the same sound that sounded like an attempt at words and this time, I wasn't alone in the house and I couldn't just open the front door and bugger off. Pete was lying there and I couldn't just leave.

But, God, I wanted to.

The hairs on my body, *all* the hairs, were standing up and my tongue still felt too big for my dry mouth and my legs were tingling with the tension of the adrenaline coursing through my system. Fight or flight. But how could you fight a sound?

Well, you'd have to find out where it was first.

Yeah, right, great idea.

ruunnteeer

I shook my head—no way was I going looking for the source of whatever it was I was hearing, oh no, thank you very much but no.

ruuuunteeer

I bent down to pick up the dropped cup and then paused as movement flickered in the corner of my eye. For a second, I tried to convince myself that it was Pete, stirring on the chair in the conservatory but I knew I was kidding myself. Pete was directly in front of me and the flicker of movement had come from my right, from the direction of the bookcase, the bookcase that opened up to reveal the stairs.

The bookcase was closed, the stairs hidden, the entrance to the *cellar* hidden but that was the direction that the movement had come from. I turned my head to make sure this was still the case and tried to tell myself that the dark line in the middle of the bookcase wasn't there. But, just as I knew I'd been kidding myself about the direction of the movement, I knew I was kidding myself about the line. There was a definite line of darkness down the centre of the bookcase, exactly where they parted when they opened to reveal the stairs.

Still looking at the line, I reached for the cup and picked it up by its handle and stood up. The line didn't widen but it was still there and the sound came again, a little louder this time. I half-turned to put the cup on the drainer and then I was standing in front of that dark line in the middle of the bookcase. I didn't have the cup in my hand so I'd obviously put it on the drainer but, instead of leaving the kitchen and going back into the conservatory, which is what I'd intended doing, I'd walked across to the bookcase. I hadn't done it in a trance or anything like that; some part of me had just decided that, since Pete was asleep and I'd already tidied up, there wasn't any reason *not* to stand in front of the narrow gap. Simple really.

Yeah, right. Simple would've been making sure Pete was comfortable and warm and then getting the hell out of there and going home.

ruuuunteeerr

The sound came from beyond that line of darkness, louder still, and I swallowed hard and then reached for the hidden lever and turned that narrow line into the wide opening it was meant to be. I stood at the bottom of the stairs, waiting for the sound to come again so I could work out where it was coming from, pretty sure I already knew.

I was wrong. When the sound came again, I climbed the stairs. Oh, I did it slowly, still not sure it was a good idea, but I climbed them. And, when I was half-way up them, the sound came again and it was obvious that it was coming from *upstairs* and not through the wood of the risers from the cellar. So I walked past the little gear-lever that opened the stairs and part of me was grateful that the sound wasn't coming from the cellar—it had been bad enough when I'd been there after breaking into this house, to be down there after listening to Pete holding that weird, *sober* but weird conversation in his sleep would have been just a bit too much, you know?

When I reached the landing I waited to see if the sound was going to come again, knowing it would. My heart had speeded up, not a lot but enough so that I could hear it in my ears and feel it in my throat. My hands were clammy and I had those little flutterings in my stomach, not unlike I got before doing a gig but these had nothing like the pleasant edge of those.

ruunnteer

It was very loud now and I could almost tell what the words the sound was trying for but not quite. I walked down the landing towards the bedroom that overlooked the road and the club. I passed the toilet and the sound came again and then I was standing in front of the open door of the large bedroom at the front of the house.

This was where Pete slept. Even from the landing, I could see how tidy it was, how the glass in the dressing table gleamed with reflected light, how the bed was made with its hospital corners and not a crease in sight on the pale blue duvet. The pair of Puma trainers on the rug at the side of the bed was perfectly aligned and the deodorant can and after-shave bottle were positioned exactly in the centre of the dressing table. The sound came again and there was a different quality to it—not as loud and with a different inflection, almost as if whatever was making the sound was relieved. Yeah, I know how that sounds but the whole thing was crazy. Anyway, it was true.

I took a breath, asked myself if I was really going to do this, and stepped into the room before I could answer myself.

The sound was there immediately and back to its previous volume. My heart beat thick and fast in my throat and I thought I was going to throw up but didn't and I tried to turn and leave and couldn't and all the time the sound, *the voice*, was there and something more—I could feel the air in the room beginning to stir and I wanted to run.

No, not run out of there, not run away, just run. Just run round the room, almost as if some deep part of me wanted to run *after* the voice, to catch it maybe, make it tell me what the hell it was trying to say.

Even now, I'm pretty sure that I would've done exactly that if it hadn't been for the change in the shimmer of reflected light in the dressing table mirror.

It wasn't a flicker, more like a subtle change in shape. The reflected light had been just that, a faint blur in the centre of the mirror, a long oval, like a rugby ball on its end. But when I turned my head to look at the mirror directly, the ovoid was smaller and closer to the top of the glass. Below it, the blurred effect had become a narrow oblong. I stared at it for a few seconds, trying to work out if what I thought I was seeing was something I was *actually* seeing. I blinked a few times, tried looking at it from an acute and then an oblique angle until I had to accept that it was true. And then the sound came again and, again, I could almost make out the words it was trying to be and I felt myself wanting to run again. This time, though, that deep part of me that wanted to run knew that, if I did, I'd run on the spot rather than after the voice. Why? Because I'd want to keep my eyes on the mirror, that's why. I'd want to keep my eyes on the new shape in the glass.

And I didn't like that at all. I didn't like it so much that, in the forefront of my mind, I told myself to get out of there. *Right now.* But still I stood and stared at the mirror. Even when the shape in the mirror changed from a blur to something more defined, a shape that began to resemble more and more a figure, a human figure, I stood and watched.

The noise was constant and so was its direction— anticlockwise around the room. The urge to run was becoming almost insurmountable and then I knew what words the sound was trying to make.

Yeah, I know, it should've clicked a lot sooner but, shit, the whole thing was so friggin weird, not to mention scary. But I got it in the end and it scared me even more but the fright wasn't as strong as the urge to run or the urge to keep my eyes on the shape in the mirror.

I actually had my right foot half an inch off the floor, my arms away from my sides, bent at the elbows, ready to begin running on the spot, like warming up before a football training session.

Then Pete called me and I lowered my foot and swallowed and blinked and I had time to hear the almost plaintive tone of the sound, the voice as it urged *ruunnteer* one last time before it stopped. The movement of the air in the room stopped. The figure in the mirror became a long, blurred oval. I let out a long breath and stepped out of the bedroom and called down to Pete.

'Coming, mate.'

I went down the stairs one at a time, hoping my heartbeat would return to something approaching normal before I tried to explain to Pete just exactly what I'd been doing upstairs.

He never asked. I assumed that he'd assumed I was using the toilet. Which should've made me feel better but it didn't because of the way he was now that he was awake. I wouldn't've been able to persuade anybody that he'd even had a drink let alone been paralytic and that he'd blacked out.

'Hello, Ted. My mate, Ted. If I'm in trouble, he's always there. Ever since that day at school when I was a dickhead.' He smiled at me and I saw the sixteen year old boy who had called me a thick prick.

I nodded and smiled back because the lump in my throat wouldn't let me talk. That and a sort of low terror I'd felt when he'd called me Ted. Only Cheryl had ever called me Ted and I heard Pete's dream-conversation and how he'd called whoever he'd been talking to *love*.

I had to work hard to keep that smile on my face, especially as my mind began to change its idea of the words the voice in the bedroom had been trying to say. When my mind showed me how the shape in the mirror on the dressing table could've been the figure of a woman, I actually felt the smile slide away and I sat down on the window seat and told my mind to piss off, it was talking bollocks, it had all been stress related because of the way Pete was. Yeah, right.

'God, it's good to see you, Terry.' He straightened up in the chair and the chair straightened with him.

'Hello, mate. Really had yourself a drink, didn't you? I don't suppose you want to tell me why you felt the need to poison yourself?'

He smiled and it was his mother's smile. 'Certainly will. Just as soon as I've had something to eat and a cup of tea.'

And he did.

'Danny Sullivan told me about this house,' he began and, once he was started, I just let him talk. What he told me was so off-the-wall, I didn't know what to say. 'I mean about what the circles really mean. There's a...well, I suppose power is the only word that fits. That power can be used. Danny told me about it as soon as he realised I was somebody the power was meant for. I know you don't fancy the idea of Fate much but it's true. What I found out just proves it. I told you about wanting to make my own memories and the memories I really want are all tied up with Cheryl. What Danny told me means I can make those memories. The power in this place can help you make really *vivid* memories. That's why I wanted to live here. Danny told me how this house can help somebody, the right somebody, to contact somebody who's...passed on. But that's not all it can do. Oh, it took him a while to convince me. That's what all those things I had to do were. He took me all over the country. I was sceptical at first and he said that was fine. But eventually, I couldn't ignore it.'

He took a long breath and ran his hands through his hair, obviously getting things sorted in his head so he could tell me without going round in circles or backtracking. He nodded once, looking at his interlaced fingers resting in his lap and then continued with his story.

'There's a place, an abandoned church buried in the Cotswolds that's full of voices. When I first heard them, I thought they were a trick of the acoustics. You know, like The Wailing Wall or something. Maybe it was the sound of kids in the schoolyard a mile away, carrying to the church. Danny told me they were the voices of people who'd 'gone on'. He took me to a place in the middle of London, near the river. An old warehouse it is, one the property people haven't turned into Yuppie Heaven yet. Anyway, that was the same. All these voices and then Danny pointed out something else to me. He told me to look hard at the light in the corner of the warehouse and concentrate.' Pete's face filled with the memory and he looked like a delighted kid. 'There was this greenish light that moved in circles and the voices seemed to come from the centre of this light and then race all around the room. There's a hollow tree in the middle of Delamere Forest that's the same. It's a really gorgeous light, Terry. There are places like it all over the country. It doesn't have to be old or abandoned. It just needs to be in a place where the power is.'

He got up to make another pot of tea. I just sat on the bench seat that ran around the conservatory and stared out of the window. He didn't sound mad, didn't look mad but the stuff he was spouting was mad. And when my mind butted in to remind of what I'd seen and heard in the bedroom, I told it to piss off again and thought that it was no wonder Pete was up and down like a fiddler's elbow. Danny Sullivan had really done a job on Pete. If he carried on like this, it wouldn't need me to persuade him to get medical attention. He'd do something crazy in the club or the street and the police would get him sectioned. I sat and stared out at the beautiful June afternoon and watched the light glint and glimmer on the calm, green river and wondered what the hell I was going to do.

Pete came back and got to what was, as far as he was concerned, the real point of this crazy tale.

'Right. So, that time I was away for the weekend, Danny told me that this house was one of the places but it was more than just that. Old Albert knew about the voices and read up on that kind of thing. So, he came up with the circle thing and his idea that nothing's ever lost if you know how to look for it. There's a figure of eight, which is a symbol of eternity and infinity, in the garden and directly beneath it, in the cellar, is another one. The two combined within the circle of the house, increase the natural power that's already here. It means that you can contact somebody who's passed on and, Danny said this but I've never actually seen it, hold proper conversations with them. You can see the person and talk with them.' He sighed then and closed his eyes. He took a deep breath and opened them again and fixed me with one of his pleading, help-me-Terry stares.

'But, the thing is, I can't get it to work properly. I can *almost* get it to but the extra push of energy or whatever, I can't manage. I can talk with Cheryl for a little while but it's very faint. It's better when I'm asleep but I don't want to spend the rest of my life asleep. Anyway, she, Cheryl, thinks you might be able to help. You've always had that incredible strength of mind and she thinks you could help me charge up whatever it is down in the cellar.' He grinned at me. 'You were always there to help me, Terry, always. I know it would work if you tried.'

What the hell d'you say to something like that? I looked at him and saw how much weight he'd lost, how his eyes looked like they were sinking into his skull, how his face was ashen. The lad was so twisted up in this bloody madness, he wasn't even doing the basics like feeding himself or getting enough fresh air. And he wanted me to join him in his...whatever it was. I couldn't.

'Pete, I can't believe you need me to say this but what you've just told me is nuts. Danny obviously had more wrong with him than a bad heart. I understand how much you miss Cheryl but...contacting her? Holding conversations with her in your dreams and taking whatever the dream says as gospel? Come on, Pete. This is all part of the depressions. Deep down you must know that. And deep down you must know I've got nothing to help you. I'm your friend, Pete but I'm not some human battery. Let me get in touch with a doctor and get this sorted once and for all.'

I heard myself saying all that and my voice sounded normal and the expression on my face felt normal. Why not? I was being logical and sensible and, given what Pete had just told me, reasonable.

But, while I was listening to myself and telling myself that I was saying the right thing, something was scratching at my mind, like a cat trying to get in out of the cold and rain.

I knew exactly what it was and I refused to allow it in because the last thing Pete needed was a hint that he could talk me round. So I blocked out what my mind was trying to tell me and I looked at my old mate and willed him to see how completely bonkers the whole idea of power in circles and figures of eight was, willed him to nod at me and shrug at me and tell me to forget it and let's go for a drive out to Wales. If he did that, I wouldn't have to keep telling myself that whatever might've happened in the bedroom hadn't been real, that the words I'd finally made out had been just some odd sound effect, some peculiar harmonic caused by the circular design of the house.

If Pete shrugged and nodded, I could stop feeling scared.

Pete didn't do any of those things.

The grin he'd had faded like dreams do on waking. It was replaced by a light in his eyes. It wasn't the light that always flickered there when Pete was excited by something or by his music. This was a baleful light that flashed in his eyes and was a terrible thing to see. When he spoke, his voice was hard and thin and that was even more terrible than that light. He stood up and balled his fists and the years I'd spent in those mean streets of Oxborough welled up inside me and I stood up too. Because I was angry. Angry with him for letting himself get gulled by Danny Sullivan's queer philosophy and angry with myself for being scared of something that *absolutely, definitely did not happen in the bedroom.*

'It's because I've finally found something that's mine, isn't it? That's why. This is all mine and I don't have to share it with anybody, not even you. I've had to share everything with you for the last fifteen years but this is mine and it really gets to you. You can't stand the thought of me having this house because you feel left out of it. Oh yeah, that's it. I arranged to get this place without consulting you, without asking for your wonderful commonsensical advice and it really kills your pig. You're a dog in a manger about everything to do with me.'

I felt like I'd been kicked in the balls. A part of me, the rational part we all like to keep at the front of our minds, kept telling me this was just another aspect of the depression. The part that lives deeper in us, the part we think of as somehow shameful, the emotional part, hurt. And, I must admit, a lot of it was simple fear at the way he was thinking about the dead and a house with power. Not to mention the small matter of what I was refusing to allow into the forefront of my mind.

Rationality took a tea-break, like it had all those years ago when I almost decapitated him at school.

'Listen bollocks. You might've forgotten but it was *you*

who came to me fifteen years ago. As for sharing everything, it works both ways. I had to almost squash a part of myself to be your friggin safety-valve. I shared my life and family with you but I'm not complaining. Still, you always were a selfish bastard. It didn't matter, I still liked you. Now you tell me it was all a waste of time because you never wanted to share anything with me. As for consultation, I remember spending *hours* consulting with you and discussing the jobs you got me into with the music. Oh, you're real good at consultation.' I kept my voice low but there was no hiding the cold anger. I found I didn't mind; it seemed to banish the fear inside.

'If I'd consulted you about them, we'd never've done what we did!' His mouth was a thin, bloodless line and that awful light was flickering faster in his eyes. 'If it hadn't been for me, you'd still be a bloody translator earning a piddling twelve or fifteen grand a year instead of a friggin millionaire! You'd still be in that poky little terrace by the docks instead of in a mansion with a pool! You never had any talent, I carried you! Well, screw it, I'm through carrying you! Piss off and let me have what's mine on my own!'

I hit him. It caught him on the temple and he went backwards, saved from hitting the floor by banging into the piano he'd moved into the conservatory. A thin ribbon of blood oozed from the nick where I'd caught him with my ring.

'You had that coming,' I said. 'I wanted to help you over this depression but you obviously don't want that. I can't get involved in your delusions, Pete. I'll piss off. See you around.'

I drove home. The car was hot and I had the blower on pushing cold air into the cab, the sun-roof open, the wind *whissshhting* through the crack in the roof. I was pretty sure I'd seen the last of my best friend, Peter Lynwood. Something inside me, deep, deep inside me, died crying. It sounded like the wind inside the car, like a song sadly sung by a whispering wind. It broke my heart and I wiped tears from my cheeks but I was glad for it, you know? It meant I didn't have to think about the bedroom and the mirror and the sound I'd heard in the cellar. The sound I'd now heard in the bedroom. The sound that was a voice trying to say something. Something that I'd finally worked out.

Run Ted.

Like it says on the reprise of 'Sgt. Pepper's,', it's getting very near the end.

For almost three weeks, I heard nothing from Pete and spent that time determined not to let it worry me and trying not to worry about him.

And fighting to keep myself from going round the bend.

Whenever I closed my eyes at night, I saw the reflection in Pete's dressing table change from a blurred oval to a figure. Every time I had nothing to listen to, I heard the voice urging me to *run ted*. I didn't sleep much and I played my records and tapes louder than the rest of the family were used to hearing and I swam a lot and none of it helped much.

Just before the end, I was alone in the house and even playing the records and cassettes wasn't helping and I found myself walking in and out of each room, singing along at the top of my voice without really knowing I was doing it. I found myself upstairs, on the landing between what used to be Pete's room and the bedroom where Carol and I had nearly made love the afternoon I sang her the words I'd written for the tune she'd composed.

The room was now our Dawn's room and what used to be Pete's room was Erin's so I rarely got down to this end of the landing but I was there now and for the first time since moving into the house, that memory jumped right to the front of mind. Its colour and sound and even smell relegated the other things to the back of my mind. I knew those things—the urging voice and the dressing table mirror's image were still there but they didn't matter right now because I was seeing Carol on the bed in what was now our Dawn's room and I was hearing her voice and smelling that intoxicating mixture of tobacco and vodka and the light scent she always wore. I was tempted to walk into the room, to sit down next to my memory of Carol but it was my sister's room now and, even though I knew she was out for the day and I wouldn't be disturbed, I couldn't do it. It was probably something to do with having lived in a house with only three bedrooms and understanding how important privacy is when you're a teenager and tying to grow up as fast as possible.

Anyway, I didn't need to be in the room. Standing on the landing was enough; my memory and my imagination were doing a great job. I didn't even need to look into the room. I could turn and look out of the landing's porthole window to the garden and still see a ghostly image of Carol and hear her voice and smell her. This was good, this was so much better than disembodied voices and mirror reflections.

The track on the cassette ended with a chromatic run of strings, followed by the hiss of a blank tape and then there was no sound but Carol's voice in my head, singing the words I wrote for her tune. And I stood on the landing and stared down at the garden, where the bench I'd sat on all those years ago and made my first decent fist of playing guitar still stood.

And Carol was there on the bench instead of in the glass of the window, a guitar resting on her knee. I sang along with her and I cried.

What the hell, it was about bloody time, wasn't it? About time I cried for *me*, you know? When she died I cried for her son and even for her husband but I didn't cry for me. Not really; like I said, I'd clamped down on my own grief because Pete needed me. Not now, though.

'No,' I told myself on the landing. 'Not now.'

No, he didn't need me now. Not now that our friendship had been torn to shreds by Pete's depression and by Danny Sullivan's belief in a twisted philosophy created by a man long dead. And I knew that a lot of the tears I was crying were also for that lost friendship.

So, when I saw Carol, the Carol I could see through the window, the Carol sitting on the garden bench playing guitar, when I saw that Carol raise her head and shake it, her eyes fixed on the me she could see through the window, I put it down to my vision being blurred through my tears.

When I heard her say *more than ever now, Terry*, I put it down to my ears being confused by the sobs in my throat.

I went into my own room and closed the door and picked up my acoustic guitar and played Carol's tune and sang my words and finished it with the right chord.

And, as the last faint echo of that final chord faded, the phone rang.

He conned me.

If I need a defence, then I'll say it was because he was my best friend; I'd known him half my life and loved him as long.

I heard his voice and almost put the phone down but he must've been expecting that because he yelled at me. Not an angry yell, more amused.

'Don't! Don't hang up, Terry. I'm not after anything. I've just had time to think and you were right. Anyway, the thing is, once I'd got over it, I got writing and it's really good. Some of the best I've done. But it needs words, Terry, and you're the best. I just want you to pick the tunes up. That's all. I'd bring them over but the bloody car's on the blink. I'll leave the front door open. Just come in.'

His voice sounded tired but that was all. I couldn't hear any lies in there and I'd always known how much the music meant to him.

'Twenty minutes,' I told him. 'I'll pick it up but then I'm leaving.'

The front door was open as advertised and I walked in,

closing it behind me. I went straight to the conservatory but he wasn't there. I called him but got no answer. Maybe he'd gone over to the club for something; more booze, a packet of crisps, to pick up my twelve-string which I *still* kept forgetting to bring home.

I walked into the room where the bookshelves hid the stairs. The place reeked of booze and there were clothes everywhere. I looked in the kitchen and it was immaculate, not a dish out, not a pan in sight. No food either. I began to get scared now. It got worse when I noticed what I hadn't noticed before.

The stairs were opened up. Maybe he'd gone to the toilet? I called him again, got no reply and turned to go to the club. Then I heard something, some noise from the stairway.

'Pete?'

'Terr...'

For a second, I thought it was *that* sound, the other voice from the cellar and Pete's bedroom but it was only for a second; I knew it was Pete's voice. It was very faint but there was no doubt it was Pete's voice and it sounded like he was hurt. I stood at the bottom of the stairs and called him again. That same hurt sound came from somewhere up that flight of stairs.

I took the stairs two at a time and saw the black space leading to the cellar. I stopped. The idea that this was some sort of trick crossed my mind but then his feeble voice came again and all the years of being his friend overrode any other thought. I looked down into that black space.

The light in the cellar was off and when I felt for the pull-switch, it felt like it had been ripped out. I called Pete again but there wasn't even his feeble voice this time. I went down the first five stairs. I couldn't even hear him breathing.

'Pete? Where are you?'

Nothing.

I had visions of him lying at the bottom of the staircase, a leg broken, maybe his skull fractured, blood everywhere. Then something crashed behind me and something else disturbed the air in front of me. And I knew I'd been tricked.

'The cellar door's jammed Terry!' Pete yelled and his voice cracked. There was a curious slapping sound, coming closer and fading away.

He's running round the bloody cellar

As soon as I thought it, I knew it was true. In the depth of this depression, fuelled by Danny Sullivan's delusions, Pete thought that by getting me into the cellar and then running round in circles he would somehow magnify the power he believed was inside the house and so be able to contact Cheryl.

I was right but it was even worse than that. He told me as he ran his manic marathon in the dark.

'With you here, and with me running, I'll be able to bring her!' He screeched and his voice was mad. Totally, utterly crazed. 'That's what it needs! I won't just be able to talk to her, Terry, I'll be able to see her! Maybe even touch her!' There was a horrible choked noise as he took in a breath so he could tell me more about how this was going to work, about how all it needed was me in the same space.

And on and on he ran. I got to the bottom of the steps,

determined to grab him next time he passed but I couldn't. I couldn't see him in the dark and he never ran anywhere near the bottom of the steps.

He's running around that figure of eight in the floor.

And I knew that was true, too. I went back up the steps and pushed against the opening to the stairs but, like he'd told me, he'd jammed it somehow. The only thing I could do was sit on the cellar steps and wait till he got tired enough to stop.

And while he ran, he yelled at me, telling me he was sure it was working.

I cried. Softly, to myself, feeling the big tears roll down my cheeks. I sat on the stair and wondered how it had ever come to this while he went on telling me all about the power and figures of eight and green doorways. I just sat there and wished for all the years back, years when the worst that could've happened was that Pete had got us another gig without telling me first.

Then he said something that went through my mind like a cold, cold wind, a wind with ice in it like teeth. What he said dried up all my tears and sent all the hairs on my body tingling, as if I'd had a mild electric shock.

'She knew this would work because of what happened in the bedroom,' Pete shouted, his voice like rusty metal, Rod Stewart with tonsillitis, horrible. And then he laughed and that was an even worse sound. 'She gave me down the banks for waking up when I did and getting you out of there. Cheryl was so close and then I called you and you left the room.'

Oh Christ, how did he know that? He couldn't know

that.

No, not unless…

I didn't want to finish that thought off and I didn't but only because something took its place, other words popped into my mind, words I'd heard very recently.

Now more than ever, Terry.

The words my memory of Carol had said to me from the garden bench. And before I could find some logical way of refuting them, Carol's voice was in my head again.

Trust them, Terry. Both of them. It's what they want and, really what else has he got? Help him this last time, Terry. For him and for her. And for me.

And before I could do or think or say anything to that, Pete's strained, hoarse voice was calling to me again.

'The light's here! God, Terry, it's wonderful isn't it? It's that lovely, soft, dreamy green, like in the places Danny showed me. If you help me, Terry, if you run for me, run *with* me, I'll be able to hear her soon! I'm sure of it!'

And then there was a strange doubling of words—one phrase uttered by Pete's almost shredded voice and almost the same phrase in my mind, uttered by the girl who'd provided the backbeat for us when we played Pete's music and sang my words. Cheryl's voice, in my mind like the harmony in one of our songs.

'Run Terry!'

run ted!

'Run Terry!'

run ted!

For a split second I actually thought of screaming my defiance but then I did what I'd always tried to do—I helped my best mate. Because I loved him. And because I'd loved Cheryl. And because I'd loved Carol.

I stepped off the stairs and ran round the cellar. Slowly and carefully because I still couldn't see much but I ran. I'd only run one circuit of the cellar when I heard Pete gasp and then the sound of his feet slapping on the cement floor stopped.

'Yes! Terry, there's a door! A beautiful, pale green doorway! She'll come through it now! I know it! Thank you, Terry! I knew this would work. It won't be long now!'

I was back at the bottom of the stairs and I sat on the second riser and peered into the gloom, looking for Pete and, God help me, looking for the green doorway he was sure he could see. I couldn't see either one.

'Terry!' His voice was a high-pitched squeak, like a wounded rat. 'The door's open! She's here! Cheryl's here! Oh, Terry, she's even more beautiful! Terry she's smiling! And she's playing drums again! Can't you hear it? And that tune! Terry, I only wrote that tune last night! She's put a beat to it just like she used to! Listen to the backbeat, Terry! Cheryl! I'm…'

The high-pitched squeak stopped. The mad, manic marathon he'd been running was over. There was the sound of one long, terrible sigh and then a crumpling sound followed by a low groan.

I ran into what I thought was the middle of the cellar and squatted. I brushed my hands around in a circle, feeling the grit on the cement floor but not feeling Pete. I shuffled forward, my hands still foraging in the dark. And I touched him. He was lying on his side and I touched his face. It felt bony, terribly thin, horribly hot.

'Pete!'

I pulled him up towards my face. I wanted to feel his gasping breath on my face but all I could feel was the heat baking off him. I laid him down gently and scrabbled round under the stairs. I felt a line of thin cord and followed it. I expected it to lead directly to the bottom of the entrance to the cellar but Pete hadn't wanted to take the chance I'd find it before I'd helped him. The bloody thing went right around the cellar and I had to scrabble on my hands and knees, groping with my fingers to follow it. Pete had fed it behind the junk in the cellar to make sure that it wouldn't've just opened the hatch on a pull. God, he'd been prepared but, shit, it might turn out that he'd bloody well killed himself by being so prepared. It was as I turned back from the far end, heading towards the centre of the cellar that I heard the sound.

I thought it was Pete, *prayed* it was Pete. I looked towards where I'd left him and the sound came again but I knew it wasn't Pete; the sound wasn't made by a voice at all. For all the world, it sounded like sticks on skin—drumsticks and drum skin.

Come on Terry, it's the sound of your heart. You know that, don't you? Follow the cord and get out of here. He needs help!

Yeah, okay, that was a good enough explanation. I began tracing the cord again and found where he'd weighted it down with the corner of the old child's armchair. I pulled it free and shook it and it seemed to be free all the way to its end and I ran towards the stairs, desperate to get some light into the bloody place so I could see if he was still alive.

I barked my shins on the first step and ended up on my knees, swearing at the top of my voice. As I stood up again, the sound

(it's your heartbeat!)

was there and I glanced towards where I'd left Pete and saw that he hadn't moved, that he was still in the recovery position and I…frowned.

How could I see Pete? I hadn't opened the hatch yet so how could I see that he hadn't moved?

Because there was a light. Faint and blurry, more glow really.

That's bollocks, sunshine. You know that just like you know the sound's your heartbeat. You've just got used to the dark, got some night-vision or something.

Yeah, that must've been it. I went up the stairs, but sideways so I could keep my eyes on Pete, and banged the hatch open, letting in honest electric light.

It seemed to *slide* down through the opening, in a band rather than just flooding the cellar with light. Still, I could see Pete properly and he still hadn't moved. I went down the stairs again and as I put my foot on the cement floor, the bulb on the landing went out with a bang that made me yip like a puppy, and I was in darkness again.

But my night-vision hadn't gone completely, probably because of the way the electric light had come into the cellar slowly, in a band; I could still see Pete. I ran to him and tested for a pulse but there wasn't even a thready flicker. He wasn't breathing.

'Shit, Pete!'

I gave him the kiss of life and tried again for a pulse but there was still nothing. At least not from *his* heart. *My* heart was still beating out that rhythm and, with my dark-vision or whatever it was, I could see his face and it looked…shit, there was no denying it, Pete's face looked peaceful. He looked happy. He looked like he was smiling.

It was a Carol-smile and I knew I'd lost him.

And in that moment, when I knew that my best friend was really dead and I'd lost him from my life, my heart gave a double-thump that was so like Cheryl's favourite lick when she hammered out the backbeat to our songs.

And the tears in my eyes somehow made the cellar seem to exist in a faint mist, like the soft, almost dreamy mists that you sometimes see curling along the lanes of Colley Hill at the end of a late-summer's evening.

I carried him back upstairs and into the conservatory. He was so light it was like carrying our Erin when she was four. I laid him on the reclined Parker Knoll chair in the conservatory and phoned for an ambulance. Then I sat on the bench seat and stroked his matted, sweaty hair, still sobbing big, silent tears.

And my mind showed me highlights of the time we'd spent together and let me hear the tunes he'd written and the words he made me find to fit them.

And I was grateful for that because it meant I didn't have to think about the way my heartbeat had sounded so much like Cheryl's favourite backbeat. Or about how my tearful eyes had somehow tinged the air in the cellar that delicate, faded end-of-summer-green.

And I comforted myself as best I could by telling myself that I'd kept the promise I'd made myself—Pete didn't die alone.

That promise, at least, I'd kept.

Final Chord

Pete died from heart failure brought on by emaciation; he hadn't eaten properly for almost three weeks. The alcohol level in his body was high and a contributing factor. His heart simply couldn't take the strain of that last, frantic race he felt he had to run. It went into arrhythmia and finally gave up.

I'm getting old now. Oh, I don't lean on my Zimmer frame in the post office waiting for my pension but what little hair I've got left is mostly grey and my skin looks like it doesn't fit me properly any more. My back and my knees ache in the morning and I have to wear glasses when I read or drive.

Yeah, I'm definitely getting on.

When you get to my age, you start remembering the times when you were young, when your bones weren't always longing for sunshine and warmth.

When you've been to the doctor's, like I did a week ago,

and he's told you the test results showed something that shouldn't've been there, you start remembering those times.

When I got home from the doctor's last week, Bryon, our Dawn's eldest lad, had already let himself in and was sitting on the bench at the far end of the garden.

Normally, he comes with our Erin's eldest, Graeme (they're both fourteen, born sixth months apart) and they've both got their own keys. Graeme comes to use the pool because he's loved swimming since he was a baby.

Bryon comes because he loves music and he wants to play guitar in a band so I give him a lesson as often as he wants. He uses the very first guitar I ever owned. It's the one Pete Lynwood bought me the Christmas before we started gigging at The Eight Bells.

That day a week ago, Bryon was on his own.

I made myself a cup of tea, poured Bryon another glass of lime and lemonade and took them into the garden. I sat next to him on the bench and watched him struggling with F# while I sipped my tea and tried to get my head round what the doctor had told me.

It was only when Bryon tapped me on the knee that I realised he'd been asking me something.

'Sorry, Bry, what?'

'Tell me about you and Pete,' Bryon said. He didn't look up at me; he kept staring at the shape his fingers made on the neck of the guitar.

I frowned—even with his face down and in profile, I could see the expression on his face and it looked just like the expression on his Mum's face when she'd told me she thought she was pregnant a fortnight after getting her A-level results. Dawn hadn't been but she had been worried, really worried.

I wondered why Bryon would be worried about asking about me Pete Lynwood.

'You know all about Pete, Bry. What's up?"

He shook his head and then brushed his dark brown hair out of his eyes exactly the way his mother did. Exactly the way she'd done when she was that worried teenager way back when. Back when she was just turned eighteen and her big brother was a more-or-less retired pop star with about a million quid in the bank.

'No,' Bryon said. 'Not really. I know he was your best mate and he wrote the tunes but that's *all*! Every time I ask Mum or Auntie Erin, they just tell me I already know. But I don't!'

He looked at me then, worry etched deep in his handsome face. What he said next explained that worried look.

'Is there some big secret? Or…a scandal?'

I smiled and sipped the last of my tea. I put the cup on the grass and said, 'No, Bry. No scandal.'

'So why won't they tell me what he was really like then? You know I want to be a musician like you and Pete and I want to know what it was like. I want to know what *Pete* was like and nobody'll tell me!'

He tried another F# but the discord was horrible. He swore and slapped the neck of the guitar. I almost laughed out loud because, instead of looking like his Mum, he looked and sounded like me when I was struggling with bloody F# back in those long ago days.

'I just want to know about you and Pete, Uncle Terry. That's all,' Bryon said and laid the guitar across his knees.

And, God, it was almost like time travel. When my nephew laid my very first guitar across his knees, images from the years when Pete Lynwood was my best mate flashed across my mind like camera shutterclicks.

When one of those shutterclicks showed me Carol Lynwood sitting on this same bench and looking up to the window where I was looking down at her, I closed my eyes and willed those shutterclicks away.

And, for a wonder, it worked.

I let my breath out slowly and then coughed to excuse the way I had to clear my eyes of the unshed tears there. When I opened my eyes again, our Bryon was looking at me and I knew that my cough hadn't fooled him for a minute.

'Uncle Terry?'

'It's okay, Bry. Tell you what, I'll tell you all about Pete. But not now. And I'll write it down for you because it's a long story. I'll even use that sooper-dooper new computer you and our Graeme pestered me into buying. Deal?'

He smiled at me and picked up the guitar again, strumming a perfect F#.

I was glad because it was too much—the way he looked so much like my sister combined with what the doctor had told me earlier was just too much and no amount of phoney coughing would've got me past the tears. And just to make the point, I heard Pete Lynwood telling me how there was something in his family tree that tended to make his life miserable at times.

After Bryon had left, I sat at this new computer with all its bells and whistles that my best mate Pete would've drooled over as he tried to explain to me how it all worked and I began to keep my promise to my eldest nephew.

I honestly thought I was writing it all down for him but it turned out to be mostly for me after all.

I know what happened when our Bryon asked his Mum and Auntie Erin about Pete and I know why he was frustrated by their answers. Bryon's like his Mum—neither of them is stupid and that was why he looked so worried when he asked me about Pete. He didn't want his frustration to upset me. Well, it didn't. In fact, having spent the last few days writing this, I'm grateful.

My two sisters think they're protecting me by not talking about Pete and, tell the truth and shame the devil, I was happy for them to carry on that way.

On her wedding day, our Erin, who could always get me to answer her questions just by looking at me with her huge brown eyes, asked me why I'd never found anybody to share my life with—didn't I get lonely? I smiled at that because she and our Dawn and their husbands and their kids come round to my house every Sunday. They say it's because I'm a better cook than they are but we all know that the real reason is they think I'm lonely.

Erin kept looking at me that morning when she was dressed and waiting for the wedding car, her expression the same as the one she'd used when she was little. She didn't repeat the question, she just looked at me and I answered her.

I told her the truth—I'd had two people in my life; Pete was dead and Jude was married with three kids and if I looked for the rest of my life I'd never find anybody who'd come close to either of them. I suppose if I'd been completely honest, I'd've told her about Carol but your baby sister's wedding day isn't the time to talk about things like that, is it?

Anyway, she'll know when she reads this and I know that both my sisters will understand.

So, yeah, there are times when I'm lonely. But I'm lucky with my memories.

I can remember my Mum and Dad and smile; I can remember my Nan and smile. Oh, sometimes I cry but when that happens, I ring Jude and we talk about my Nan and my parents and her Dad who died two years ago. And we talk about Jude and Aiden's three kids, my godchildren, and I feel better. Sometimes we even talk about Pete and Cheryl but not as often as you'd think.

So that's another reason why I'm grateful to our Bryon— Jude will read this, she'll finally know what happened that day in the cellar of the old Camberwell House, and I think then we'll be able to talk about our two dead friends more.

It's a long time since Pete Lynwood bumped into me that autumn morning and so much has happened since but I can remember it all like it happened *this* morning.

I imagine that's the way it is with the best memories, don't you?

But what about those last few minutes in the cellar under the Camberwell House? Was that misty green light something to do with Pete's magical doorway? Or just the effect of my tears on the faint light coming from upstairs? Was the sound I heard my own heartbeat or was it really the backbeat that Cheryl had, from somewhere beyond, written to accompany the last tune Pete had written?

I've tried very hard not to think about those two questions in the long years between Pete's death and now. And, mostly, I've succeeded in not thinking about them. Now that I've written this, I can honestly say that I still don't know.

No, that's not a cop-out; I really don't know.

When your best mate's just died—actually, not to put too fine a point on it, just committed suicide, I don't think you can trust your senses.

But what about what happened in Pete's bedroom three weeks earlier?

Well, I don't think I can deny that. I mean, I've just written about it and in detail—what I've just typed into this computer is *exactly* what happened. There was no embellishment, no literary licence taken; just the facts ma'am. I heard the voice and finally realised what it was saying. I saw that blurred oval of reflected light change to a figure-shape and I felt the air move.

And what about Carol's voice?

If it had just been that one instance in this house when I saw her on the garden bench, then maybe I could, hand-on-heart say that my emotions got the better of me. If, in the cellar, her voice had only repeated what I'd heard in this house earlier that day, then I could say the same.

But it didn't and what I did hear in the cellar had been true—what else did Pete have? I'd been his best friend for over fifteen years and I knew him inside and out and I knew that it was true—without Cheryl, he had nothing else to live for.

Can the dead speak to us somehow? Well, yeah, *now* I think I can believe that. *Have* to, really

Even so, despite all of that, I still can't find it in me to believe in green doorways or a house where power is tied to figures of eight and circles within circles. That was Danny Sullivan's belief, or delusion. And, I suppose, in the end, Pete's. Still, I hope they were right about one thing—that nothing is lost forever.

If they were right about that, then my parents will already have found each other, Pete and Cheryl will be making music together and Carol and Ronald will be together with the chance of getting it right from the beginning this time. And my Nan will be waiting for me. Maybe she'll have baked an apple pie and there'll be custard in a jug.

I find I can believe in that kind of thing.

I'm on my own now, more or less. When my front door's closed and the lights are on against the gathering dark outside, I am on my own. With just my guitars and my memories.

Lennon and McCartney wrote that the love you take is equal to the love you make.

I believe it; look at Pete and Cheryl

It was The Hollies who sang that he ain't heavy, he's my brother.

I believe that, too; look at me and Pete.

But Lennon and McCartney also wrote that you're gonna carry that weight a long time.

Oh yeah, I can believe that; look at me.

Pete Lynwood was always looking for the backbeat but he was the brother I never had, my best friend, and I loved him.

That's a weight worth carrying.

Fade Out On Backbeat

www.ingramcontent.com/pod-product-compliance
Ingram Content Group UK Ltd.
Pitfield, Milton Keynes, MK11 3LW, UK
UKHW041258180426
11947UKWH00008B/554